Praise for Paige Toon

Lucy in the Sky, 2007

'I loved it – I couldn't put it down!' **Marian Keyes**

'A fab debut and a great summer read' *Elle*

Johnny Be Good, 2008

'Pacy, highly enjoyable insight into life in La-La Land!' *Closer*

'All the warmth and fun that I've grown to expect
from the talented Ms Toon' **Freya North**

Chasing Daisy, 2009

'A fast-paced and funny read... Superior chick-lit
with great jokes and a thoughtful heart' *Daily Express*

'Laugh-out-loud funny and touchingly honest.
This summer's poolside reading sorted!' *Company*

Pictures of Lily, 2010

'An absorbing and emotional narrative – brilliant!' *Heat*

'Another perfect summer page-turner from Paige Toon' *Mirror*

Baby Be Mine, 2011

'Fun, summery, chick-lit with bite; if you want escapism,
this is perfect' *Cosmopolitan*

'Heart-warming and gut-wrenching (yet funny and addictive),
will warm the cockles of your heart' **Giovanna Fletcher**

Also by Paige Toon

Lucy in the Sky
Johnny Be Good
Chasing Daisy
Pictures of Lily
Baby Be Mine
One Perfect Summer
One Perfect Christmas (eBook short story)
Johnny's Girl (eBook short story)
Thirteen Weddings
The Sun in Her Eyes
The One We Fell in Love With
The Last Piece of My Heart

Young Adult

The Accidental Life of Jessie Jefferson
I Knew You Were Trouble
All About the Hype

Paige Toon

the LONGEST HOLIDAY

**SIMON &
SCHUSTER**

London · New York · Sydney · Toronto · New Delhi

A CBS COMPANY

First published in Great Britain by Simon & Schuster UK Ltd, 2013
A CBS COMPANY

This paperback edition, 2017

3 5 7 9 10 8 6 4

Simon & Schuster UK Ltd
1st Floor
222 Gray's Inn Road
London WC1X 8HB

www.simonandschuster.co.uk

Simon & Schuster Australia, Sydney
Simon & Schuster India, New Delhi

A CIP catalogue record for this book
is available from the British Library

Paperback ISBN: 978-1-4711-7107-9
eBook ISBN: 978-1-4711-1340-6
eAudio ISBN: 978-1-4711-6522-1

Typeset by M Rules
Printed and bound by CPI Group (UK) Ltd, Croydon, CR0 4YY

MIX
Paper from
responsible sources
FSC® C020471

Simon & Schuster UK Ltd are committed to sourcing paper that is made from wood
grown in sustainable forests and support the Forest Stewardship Council, the leading
international forest certification organisation. Our books displaying the FSC logo are
printed on FSC certified paper.

For Pete – The Unc – and Gwennie
Hope you enjoy your long holiday . . .
(aka retirement!)

Chapter 1

He's smiling down at me with tears in his eyes as I say my solemn vow:

'I, *Laura Rose Smythson, take thee, Matthew Christopher Perry, to be my lawful wedded husband. To have and to hold, from this day forward . . .*'

I thought I would never feel like this about anyone ever again. Not after Will, my first love . . . Not after the heartbreak and the loss and the trying to pick myself back up again . . . Then I met Matthew, and I know that he has my heart forever: my perfect, gorgeous, adoring Matthew.

And then I wake up. And I remember that he's not perfect. He's so far from perfect that my heart could surely collapse from the pain that engulfs me.

'Sorry for waking you,' my friend Marty apologises from beside me as she vigorously rubs at a damp patch on her jeans with a paper napkin. 'Bridget knocked my effin' drink over with her fat arse,' she mutters. I groggily come to and look across at Bridget. She's fast asleep and partially curled up towards the window, her offending arse anything but fat. Feeling like I'm still in a dream –

1

or, more accurately, a nightmare – I bend down to retrieve my bag from under the seat in front of me. Tissues are the one thing I *did* remember to pack. I would have forgotten my passport if Marty hadn't reminded me.

'Thanks,' Marty says, while I use my Kleenex supply to help mop up the spilt gin and tonic on the tray table. 'How are you feeling?' She gives me a sympathetic look and regards me over the top of her ruby-red horn-rimmed glasses.

'Don't,' I warn, but it's too late. The lump returns to lodge itself firmly in my throat.

'Sorry, sorry!' she says hurriedly before I cry again. 'Here, quick!' I take the gin and tonic that she's proffering – what remains of it, anyway – and throw it down in one gulp. 'Think happy thoughts!' she urges. 'Think of the sun! Think of the sea! Think of the cocktails on the beach and all the hot men!'

Bridget sighs loudly with annoyance at the noise, her back still turned towards us.

Marty purses her lips at me and I mirror her expression, tears kept at bay. For now.

'Laura? Do you want another one?' my friend asks in a loud whisper, pressing the call button on her armrest before I can reply.

'Sure, why not?' I nod.

'I'm going to,' she says, as I knew she would. 'May as well, seeing as they're free and all.'

'Is everything okay, ladies?'

We look up at the air stewardess hovering in the aisle.

'Could we get another couple of these, please?' Marty asks.

'Gin and tonic?' the air stewardess asks frostily.

'Them's the ones,' Marty replies jauntily, adding, 'snooty cow,' under her breath as soon as the woman turns her back. 'So I

2

reckon, when we arrive, we'll just get the car and drive straight up to Key West.'

'Down,' I correct. Her geographical knowledge is probably on a par with a seven-year-old's, which is funny, considering her job as a travel agent.

'Whatever. You don't want to see Miami this afternoon, do you? I know Bridge is desperate to go, but we can always do a day trip.'

'It's six hours there and back,' I remind her.

'So we'll check it out on the return journey, like we'd planned. What do you think?'

'Sure,' I reply. 'It will be good to get to our hotel and—'

'—and get into our swimming costumes and head to the beach-slash-bar,' she finishes my sentence for me, although that wasn't what I was going to say.

'We could unpack first,' I suggest.

'No. No,' she says firmly. 'You are not unpacking. Not this time. On this holiday you are going to throw caution to the wind. There will be no unpacking, no trawling through the tourist brochures, no writing of shopping lists, or anything like that. I'm not having it.'

I roll my eyes at her and say thank you to the air stewardess as she returns with our drinks.

Bridget shifts in her seat on the other side of Marty and sweeps her wavy, medium-length brown hair over her shoulder as she tries in vain to get comfortable. It's been a long flight and we had an early start.

'Have you managed to get any kip?' I ask Marty quietly.

'No. I'll sleep on the beach. Cheers.'

We chink glasses. Matthew's face appears in the forefront of my mind and I wince. I take a gulp of my drink.

'Stop thinking about him,' Marty snaps.

'I wish I could,' I reply, not taking offence at her tone. Anything but sympathy.

She changes the subject. 'How long until we land?'

I check my watch. 'Two hours.'

'Just enough time to watch a movie.'

'Good plan,' I agree.

She reaches into the seat pocket in front of her for the entertainment guide and then presses the call button once more.

'You haven't finished your last one!' I exclaim.

She sniggers like a naughty schoolgirl. 'I know. I thought I'd ask the snooty cow if she has any popcorn . . .'

For all her bravado, Marty doesn't last long before she falls fast asleep in the front passenger seat of our hired red Chevy Equinox. Bridget is driving and I'm relieved because we'd barely turned out of the airport car park before we'd had two near misses – the drivers here all seem a bit nuts.

We're on a long, wide, straight road heading away from Miami and towards the Florida Keys. I stare out of the window at the fat palm trees planted in the central reservation. It's a bright, sunny afternoon and in a rare uplifting moment, I think to put on my sunglasses, but then I remember that I packed them in my suitcase and I can't even be bothered to feel irritated. It's hard to care about anything much these days.

Jessie J comes on the radio and Bridget turns up the sound. We haven't said more than two words to each other since Marty crashed out. We're not friends.

That sounds wrong. What I mean is, she's Marty's friend, not mine. It's not to say that I don't like her. I do. Sort of. But Marty and I have been best friends since childhood. Bridget only dates back to Marty's early twenties, when they shared a flat together in London. They're great friends, but not old friends. When it comes to longevity, I win. And yes, it does feel like a competition.

I wasn't supposed to come on this holiday. Bridget is a travel writer and Marty, as I've already mentioned, is a travel *agent*, and between the two of them they had this holiday sewn up long before I came along and ruined it.

That's not strictly true. Marty invited me. And Bridget couldn't exactly say no, considering 20.10.12.

20.10.12. The date of my hen night, the date of Matthew's stag do, the date that popped up on one of his Facebook messages just two weeks ago:

> Are you the Matthew Perry who was at Elation on 20.10.12?

'There it is!' Bridget interrupts my dark thoughts with a gleeful cry.

Before she fell asleep, Marty challenged us to be the first one to spot the ocean. Bridget thinks she's the victor.

'That's not the ocean, is it?' I say doubtfully from the back seat, although I think I can smell salt water, even through closed windows. 'It's a lagoon.'

'A lagoon . . .' From her side profile I can tell Bridget is looking thoughtful. 'Do you know, I have never said that word out loud.'

'Neither have I, come to think of it.'

'Don't suppose there are many lagoons in London.' That's where we live. 'Or England, for that matter,' she adds. 'Probably the whole of Europe. Mangroves!' she exclaims, her blue eyes

5

widening as they look at me in the rear-view mirror. 'Don't they grow in swamps?'

I laugh. 'I have no idea. But swamp or lagoon, it's still not the ocean.'

'I'll beat you yet,' she says in what I *think* is a joke serious voice. Perhaps she's more competitive than I thought.

We pass a palm tree farm on our left, followed on our right by a tangled sprawl of multicoloured bungalows with boats in their back yards.

I'm struggling to keep my eyes open, but I feel bad about abandoning Bridget. She may have nabbed the driving just so she could sit in the front seat with Marty, but I won't hold that against her. Don't want her to fall asleep at the wheel and kill us all – much as it's hard to imagine how I'll ever live with the humiliation of what my husband is putting me through.

'There!' she shouts as we pass a huge expanse of water.

'Nope.' I shake my head. 'Still a lagoon. Look, you can see land over there.'

'Shit,' she mutters.

I smile to myself. The sunlight on the water is blinding, but I force myself to look at it. I need some light in my life. The last two weeks have been *dark*.

'Hang on,' Bridget snaps. 'We're in Key bloody Largo! You can't tell me that's not the ocean.'

'Okay, you win,' I concede. I told you, it's hard to care about much these days.

Four white sails project out of the mangrove swamps as they make their way towards open water. We pass a bank of houses on stilts and I can see the water glinting beyond them. The houses and shop fronts are painted in colours of blue, green, aqua, yellow and cream, and in front of some flies the American flag on a gentle breeze. Polystyrene buoys hang like garlands on strings over fences and outside bars, and there are a lot of scuba-diving and bait and tackle shops. I keep catching flashes of the ocean through the lush, tropical vegetation. And all the time, the long straight road goes on. How strange that it will come to a permanent stop in Key West, the southernmost point of the USA. Then all that will be left in two weeks' time is for us to get back on this same road and come home again. The thought depresses me. Maybe I'll hitch a boat ride to Cuba instead.

Marty lets out a loud – and I mean LOUD – snore, and Bridget and I crack up laughing.

'What? *What?*' Marty jerks awake.

'You were snoring,' Bridget says.

'No, I wasn't,' Marty scoffs.

'Yes, you damn well were! You sounded like a whale. Didn't she, Laura?'

'Whales don't snore,' Marty retorts, before I can answer.

'A pig, then,' Bridget says.

'I'd rather be a friggin' whale!' Marty exclaims.

We all crack up and then Bridget lets out a huge snort at the end of one guffaw, which only makes us laugh more.

'God, I'm tired,' she says when we've all calmed down.

'Do you want me to drive for a bit?' I offer.

'No, it's okay.' She brushes me off. 'I slept on the plane, so I'm alright.' She yawns loudly. What a martyr.

'What have I missed?' Marty demands to know, wriggling in her seat.

'Bridget spotted the ocean first,' I tell her as we drive onto a massive bridge with ocean all around us.

7

'Wow, exciting stuff,' she replies sardonically.

I guess this is why they call it the Overseas Highway, I think to myself as I look out of the window. The Atlantic on our left is choppy and sparkling, while the Gulf of Mexico on our right is glassily still. Two pelicans glide over the road ahead, huge and grey with an enormous wingspan, and then we're back on land again.

We pass a dolphin rescue centre with a sign out at the front saying: 'Have you hugged a dolphin today?'

'I want to hug a dolphin!' Marty shouts at the top of her voice, making Bridget jump out of her skin. Marty and I giggle. And then I see another sign on someone's front gate, saying: 'Wish you were here', and for a brief moment I imagine Matthew sitting on the empty seat beside me and I miss him so much it hurts.

The urge to get out of the car overcomes me.

'Can we stop for a moment?' I ask, trying to keep the desperation out of my voice.

'What's wrong?' Marty whips her head around to look at me.

'Sure,' Bridget replies, nonplussed, indicating left. She pulls off the road into a small car park next to a white sandy beach. A middle-aged couple sits at one of the picnic tables, but other than that it's deserted.

'Don't know if there's a loo here, though,' she adds, misunderstanding my needs.

'I just want some air,' I explain, opening the car door and climbing out. I hear the sound of Bridget's car door opening, too, but Marty says something to her in a quiet voice, so they stay in the car. My oldest and dearest friend knows me well.

Head and heart pounding in unison, I walk to the water's edge and kick off my shoes, stepping into cool, clear, turquoise-coloured water. Then I take a deep breath and momentarily close my eyes before opening them again and staring out at the nothingness of the vast ocean.

On his stag do, my husband-to-be got wasted beyond recognition and ended up kissing a random girl at a club. He didn't tell me this before marrying me a week later. Nor did he think it would be wise to confess to it during our first seven months of marriage. He probably wouldn't have confessed to it at all except that, two weeks ago, I saw a message on his Facebook page from a pretty girl called Tessa Blight. It soon transpired that she'd been messaging every Matthew Perry she could find – trying to track down *my* Matthew Perry. My Matthew Perry, whose kiss with a random girl at a club called Elation had somehow developed into dirty sex in the club's toilets. And now that random girl is having Matthew Perry's – *my* Matthew Perry's – baby in less than two months.

My husband is going to be a father to another woman's child for the rest of his life. There's no getting away from that. No getting away from the crippling humiliation of all of our friends and family knowing that he had sex with another woman a week before marrying me, the so-called love of his life. He's sorry, of course he's sorry. He's not a terrible person, but it was a terrible, terrible mistake. He didn't mean to hurt me, he didn't mean to do it at all – he was so drunk, it just happened. And he will do anything he can possibly do to make it up to me.

But he will never be able to make it up to me. I'll never forget. How could I when this baby will be a constant, lifelong reminder?

I feel like he has ripped my heart out from my chest and thrown it to the sharks. And in this moment I want to hurl myself into the water to join it.

Chapter 2

I hear the car door slam behind me and, moments later, Marty is standing in the water at my side.

'You okay?' she asks warily.

I nod, not meeting her eyes.

'You're doing the right thing,' she says, but I still have my doubts. 'Two weeks away will give you space to clear your head, decide what you're going to do.'

She used this argument on me in England, but it seemed to make more sense then. Now I just wonder what I'm doing. Running away is only prolonging the inevitable. I don't even know what the inevitable is yet, but shouldn't I be back at home, trying to work that out?

'Has he contacted you?' she asks.

'I don't know. I haven't switched on my phone.'

'Oh. Probably for the best.'

'Mmm.'

Pause.

'If a tidal wave came along right now, we'd be well screwed,' she muses.

'Thank you for that comforting thought, Marty,' I say with as much sarcasm as I can muster.

'EEEEEEEEEEE!'

We turn with a start to see Bridget, in a lime-green bikini, running into the ocean. We squeal as water splashes in our direction.

'Come on!' she shouts, sinking to her knees on the sandy bed, so the water comes up to her neck, soaking half of her hair.

Marty grabs my arm. 'Come on.'

I hesitate, but she's made up my mind for me. She drags me back to the car to hunt for our swimming costumes.

She's right. This is what I need. And even if it turns out I'm wrong, I'm not going to get back on a plane today. We'll see what tomorrow brings.

I heave my suitcase out of the car and unzip it. Where's my bikini?

Marty is already dragging her T-shirt over her head, keeping an eye out to make sure the middle-aged man at the picnic table isn't perving.

'Don't tell me you didn't pack one,' she says as I rummage through my belongings at an increasingly frenetic speed.

My heart sinks. It's bright bloody yellow. If it were here, I would have found it by now. I can see it so clearly sitting in my drawer at home – a purchase for my honeymoon, taunting me ...

'For fuck's sake!' I erupt, furious all of a sudden. I said it was hard to care about anything, but right now I DO care. I care immensely.

'Have mine,' Marty insists, shoving it into my hands before I can protest. And the next thing I know, she's flinging herself into the water in her mismatched red bra and stripy knickers. If the man hadn't noticed us before, he has now.

'Hurry up!' she shouts back at me. She's a little shorter and curvier than me, but her costume stretches to fit. I'm not about to let her immodesty go to waste, so I hurry up and join her, this time with a smile on my face.

An hour later, our hair still damp, tangled and salty from the seawater, we drive into Key West. The final Florida key is only about four miles long and two miles wide, so it takes us next to no time to pass through the characterless part of the new town before we reach the old town, where beautiful historic houses, hotels and B&Bs line the tiny lanes and streets. Tropical trees and plants are crammed into the small front gardens, casting welcome shade over colonial balconies and front porches. The weatherboarded houses and their wooden shutters are painted with contrasting hues: pink and lilac, grey and green, yellow and white, and everywhere the blossom on the trees is bursting with vibrant colour.

'I think this is it, here,' Bridget says, turning into a small car park.

Our hotel is situated a few blocks east of Duval Street, where most of the nightlife is, and as we get out of the car and pull our suitcases around to the front entrance, I feel a small flutter of anticipation. The hotel, set within a lush landscape, is white with green shutters and has an overhanging porch. Mike, the friendly, gay, front-desk clerk takes us on a short tour of the property, and I can't help but smile at Marty as we round a corner to see the cool blue pool. The sunloungers are still full of people chilling out with drinks in the late afternoon sunshine, and my eyes inadvertently fall on three well-rounded middle-aged men in skimpy, brightly coloured briefs. There's also a hot tub, a hammock area set under palm trees, and swinging chairs hanging from the porches. Mike informs us that happy hour begins poolside at four p.m. daily and lasts for an hour, when we can help ourselves to as many free drinks as we'd like. It's already in full swing, but he gives us three complimentary beers to take up to our room in case we don't make it down in time. He doesn't know Marty very well.

We're staying in a loft apartment on the first floor at the front of the house. We have our own secluded balcony with a swinging chair, plus two more white, wrought-iron chairs and a small table. Inside the apartment there is a double bed situated at the top of a spiral staircase, which Marty had agreed Bridget could have because her travel feature is scoring them a good discount on this place. The sofa converts into a second double bed for Marty, and underneath the staircase is a blow-up single mattress: my sleeping quarters.

'I don't mind going there,' Marty says graciously as I put my bag next to my bed, which is half a metre high and pretty impressive for an inflatable.

'No, it's okay,' I reply, sitting down and almost sliding off. It looks sturdier than it actually is. Bridget snorts.

'I'll crash upstairs with you, if you're not careful,' Marty warns her. 'Laura can have the sofa bed.'

'Yeah, yeah, you're always trying to cop a feel,' Bridget jokes, trying to drag her enormous suitcase up the spiral staircase, noisily bumping it up one step at a time. 'Give me a hand, would you?' she finally snaps. I quickly get up and crack my head on the underside of the staircase.

'Shit, are you alright?' Marty exclaims.

'Ow,' I reply, pressing my hand to my head. That really hurt.

'Quick!' Bridget gasps, snapping us to action. Marty runs to her aid, before the suitcase can come crashing down on me, too. I carefully step out from under the staircase and my head continues to throb as I straighten up. At the foot of my bed is a bathroom with a shower; there's a flat-screen TV in front of the sofa and a small kitchen area behind it, with a tiny fridge, microwave and coffee machine. Finally, after much effing and blinding, Marty and Bridget deposit Bridget's suitcase and return downstairs. I'm not surprised they struggled. Almost half of our luggage allowance was used up by Bridget's bag alone. Just as well I packed light, otherwise we could have been paying excess. I remember my forgotten bikini and sigh. I'll have to buy a new one before I can take a dip in that glorious-looking pool.

'Happy hour?' Marty suggests.

'I might jump in the shower first,' I say.

'Oh, no, you don't.' She grabs my hand and pulls me across the room towards the door.

'Can't I wash my hair?' I beg, dragging my feet.

'Your golden locks look stunning, as usual,' she says wryly, not paying any heed to me. I give Bridget a pleading look over my shoulder, but she just purses her lips and follows us out of the apartment.

'Have you brought us to the gayest place on the planet?' Marty snipes under her breath at Bridget ten minutes later, as we gawp at the second set of skimpily clad, rotund middle-aged men who have just climbed into the hot tub. 'Don't think I didn't see all the rainbow flags on our drive in here.'

'Oh, shush,' she snaps.

'Good one,' Marty adds with a deadpan expression. 'Just what we wanted for an all-girls holiday.'

I try not to giggle as Bridget defends herself. 'This is a top destination for hot guys—'

'Gays,' Marty annoyingly interjects.

'STRAIGHT guys on stag weekends and . . . and . . .'

Marty shoots her a warning look and Bridget's voice fizzles out as she realises what she's said.

They know of course that the last thing I want to see on this holiday is a bunch of wasted stags chatting up girls while their girlfriends and future wives are stuck at home in blissful ignorance. I feel ill as I picture, not for the first time, how Matthew must have looked on his stag do.

'Sorry,' Bridget apologises.

'Don't be silly.' I brush her off, and violently shake my head to rid myself of the images that are still dwelling there. 'I'm going to get another one,' I say, standing up. 'Same again?'

'That's the spirit,' Marty says approvingly. 'Yes, please.'

I wander over to the trolley on the other side of the pool, where a few people are gathered, helping themselves to drinks and savoury snack thingies. I extract three large plastic cups from the stack, pouring at least two shots of vodka into each. I reach for the jug of cranberry juice, but freeze mid-move as another hand gets there first.

'Let me get that for you . . .'

I look up to see a bare-chested guy in sunglasses and a baseball hat grinning at me, jug aloft.

'Thanks.' I hold up the three glasses.

'Say when,' he murmurs as he starts to pour.

'That'll do,' I tell him as he fills the first to about two-thirds of its capacity. I inadvertently glance at his chest as he starts pouring the second. He's toned and tanned, an All-American kind of guy, and I can tell he's good-looking, even with his face partially obscured.

'You like it strong,' he comments as he moves onto the third glass .

'May as well.'

'British?' he asks.

'Yes.'

'What's your name?'

'Laura.'

'I'm Rick.'

'Nice to meet you.'

'You here for long?' he asks.

'Two weeks.'

'Cool.'

'What about you?' I feel obliged to ask.

'A few days. My buddies and I are here for a jet-skiing tournament.'

'Wow. That sounds like fun.' I nod at the drinks and make to move off. 'See you around, no doubt.'

'No doubt.' He flashes me a pearly-toothed grin and I wander back over to our sunloungers.

It's when I'm only a few feet away that I look up to see Bridget and Marty staring at me, agog.

'What?' I ask a little defensively.

'Check out you, chatting up the hot guy!' Bridget cries with glee and a touch of envy.

'Shh!' I frown. 'He helped me with the drinks.'

'I bet he did.'

'Who are his friends?' Marty asks in a low voice. We look over to see two similarly shirtless, tanned and toned guys in baseball caps and sunglasses jog down the steps from the sundeck.

'They're here for a jet-skiing tournament,' I say with a shrug as they join Rick at the trolley and crack open a couple of cans of beer. 'Probably gay.'

'No way.' Marty takes a very large gulp of her drink.

'You mean there are some straight guys in Key West?' Bridget asks pointedly. 'Are you quite sure, Marty?'

'Happy to prove it to you,' Marty replies, glugging down a few more mouthfuls.

'Whoa, slow down!' Bridget exclaims, but Marty raises her eyebrows cheekily as she downs the rest of it. 'Oh . . .' Bridget says knowingly, knocking back half of hers, too.

Marty gets up with a look of steely determination on her face as she eyes the boys at the trolley.

'Wait a sec,' Bridget gasps, taking another gulp and getting to her feet.

'I'm going to go and take a shower,' I call after them.

Marty glances back at me, her brow momentarily furrowed, before she concedes. 'Sure. Bridge and I will be up soon, then we'll go and grab a bite to eat. Okay?'

'Okay.' I nod, trying to ignore her warily sympathetic smile before I head in the opposite direction.

Chapter 3

I wake up with a start in the middle of the night and it takes a moment for me to get my bearings. Then I realise where I am and what I'm doing and an unwelcome feeling of foreboding settles over me. I wonder what the time is. I peer around in the darkness, but there isn't a digital clock to be seen. I'll have to switch my phone on, I think with a sigh, trying to psyche myself up before digging around blindly in my bag beside the bed. Ah, there it is. I start to roll off onto the floor and quickly right myself, my arm pressing against some paper on my bed as I do so. I snatch it up. It's a note, but even as my eyes adjust, I can't read it in this light. I switch on my phone and wait for it to come back to life, then turn the glowing screen towards the piece of paper.

Gone for dinner at the restaurant next door. Might head into town afterwards for a couple of bevvies. You were snoring – like a Whalepig – didn't want to wake you. Call me if you get this and want to join us.
M xxxxxxxxx

I check the clock on the screen. It's two o'clock in the morning, US time. Marty is on the sofa bed, her chest gently rising and falling with slow, rhythmic breaths. I'm confused. What time did they go out and when did they get back? Did they go out with those jet-skiers? What happened? I came up here to have a shower, and then collapsed on the bed, waiting for them ... And obviously fell asleep. I feel half relieved and half annoyed that they didn't wake me.

My phone suddenly buzzes and I jolt.

Please let me know you've landed safely. I love you and miss you so much, LL xxx

LL. That's Matthew's nickname for me: Lovely Laura.

My nose starts to prickle and I sit up in bed as an unbearable urge to call him comes over me. No. Don't. He doesn't deserve it. I get to my feet, remembering at the last moment to duck my head as I emerge from underneath the stairs, and throw my phone onto the bed. I go to the bathroom and close the door before switching on the light to face myself in the mirror.

I look terrible. My light-blonde hair is crimped and mussed after I went to sleep on it while it was still damp from the shower, and my blue eyes are tinged red and underlined with puffy bags. I splash water on my face and stare at my reflection dolefully. I'm wide awake. There's no way I'll fall back asleep after crashing out at, what time was it? Five thirty? I've had – I calculate the time in my head – eight and a half hours. No way. That's the best night's sleep I've had in weeks. Shame it wasn't a *whole* night's sleep. What on earth am I going to do with myself now? I remember the swinging seat out on the balcony and decide that's as good a place as any to pass the time. I sneak out of the front door, resisting the urge to take my phone with me.

Latin music wafts towards me from a distant bar as I climb onto the swinging seat and fold one leg up, using the other to propel me back and forth. I can hear water trickling down rocks from the nearby water feature, and wind chimes chinking together while ceiling fans whir overhead. I take a deep breath and slowly exhale.

I should text Matthew back to let him know I've landed safely. No. Let him stew.

But a text won't hurt. It's the decent thing to do. I start to get up, and then force myself back into my seat. No.

I hear laughter coming towards me on a breeze and the strains of Latin music grow stronger. It sounds like it's nearby.

Clutching this welcome distraction, I climb down from my seat and wander to the end of the balcony. Peering right I can see the sundeck, and beyond it a slightly unkempt-looking garden. From this distance I can see spirals of smoke trailing up into the sky. Predominantly male laughter rings out again. I feel a vicarious thrill as, on an impulse and for want of something better to do, I creep stealthily in my bare feet down the stairs and around the corner to the pool area. The tropical plants near the swimming pool and reception areas are underlit with pretty green and white lights and I can hear the hum of traffic from the road.

I climb the steps to the sundeck, eyes and ears alert, but it's deserted. I can hear the low murmur of voices as I push my way through the leaves of the palm trees shading the deck – they're rougher and scratchier than they look, but I feel like I'm Lara Croft, so I suck it up.

The garden – or back yard, as I should call it – of the adjoining ramshackle house is overrun with weeds and the odd piece of rubbish. I spot a rusty bicycle lying in some long grass, and a couple of broken stone statues of female torsos. Lanterns hang from oversized tree leaves and a rope light has been coiled up the trunk of one of the palms. Two guys sit on a beaten-up sofa underneath this tree, opposite a man and a woman in a couple of mismatched armchairs. One of the guys has a cigar and I watch transfixed as the smoke drifts through his fingers. Then he turns to stub it out and I glimpse his face.

I inhale quickly. He has dark eyes and dark eyebrows, olive skin and shortish, black, slicked-back hair. A shadow of stubble graces his chiselled jaw. He's dressed casually in board shorts and a T-shirt, but he looks like he could be a film star. He's one of the most beautiful men I've ever seen. A feeling of déjà vu strikes me, but I don't know why. I realise I'm holding my breath, and I have to concentrate to exhale.

He turns back to his friends and says something. They all laugh and the girl leans forward to slap him on his thigh. He good-naturedly bats her away and reaches for a bottle of beer to take a swig. I tear my eyes away from him to scrutinise her. She's attractive: olive-skinned like him, with medium-length, dark-brown hair. She's wearing a short, patterned summer dress and flip-flops. I wonder if she's his girlfriend and I feel strangely piqued. The man on the armchair next to her has a shaved head and a goatie and looks a bit shifty, but the second man on the sofa is quite cute, with short, dark, curly hair and a big smile. Marty would like him, I think, before returning my attention to Mr Beautiful.

He's stunning. He looks nothing like Matthew, who has blond hair, blue eyes and is unanimously acknowledged by practically everyone I know as freakishly good-looking.

'*He's the most beautiful man I've ever seen . . .*'

I feel flat as I recall the reason for my déjà vu. Those were the same words my friend Susan used on my hen night to describe my future husband.

Out of the blue I feel overwhelmingly sad, a feeling which is swiftly followed by foolishness. What am I doing here, spying like a silly little girl? I back out of the scratchy palm leaves, which, to add insult to injury, are now forking at my hair, and make my way back to the apartment, where my blow-up mattress – and my mobile phone – await.

I gingerly climb onto the bed and open my text messages, staring at the one from Matthew . . .

For goodness' sake, I think crossly as I pound the space button before finally accepting that my laptop has well and truly died. Matthew's MacBook Pro is jubilantly plugged into the charger. I hate it when he does this. His is set up in the bedroom, but he likes checking his emails at the kitchen table, where there's more light. As do I; that's why I keep my laptop charger here. Fat lot of good it's doing me at the moment. I pull the plug out of Matthew's machine, the sudden movement bringing his screen to life. My laptop always takes forever to start up, and as I connect the plug I glance at Matthew's glowing screen to see his Facebook page is open. With idle curiosity, I click on his messages to see who's been in touch recently. He won't mind; he's not touchy about stuff like that. Wait. Who's she? The profile picture at the top of the list is of a pretty, smiling brunette called Tessa Blight. Frowning, I open the message:

Are you the Matthew Perry who was at Elation on 20.10.12?

What's this about? I recognise the date because it's exactly a week before our wedding; he had his stag do in London and I know he went to a club called Elation. Who the hell is this girl? Matthew's working late, so I can't ask him. I study the picture more carefully. It's small, but I think she has blue eyes – they look clear and bright, not dark as though they could be brown. Her hair is shiny and straight, and she has a blunt fringe which is cut right above her eyebrows. On the spur of the moment I reply to the message with a simple 'Yes'.

My laptop has whirred to life so I try to turn my attention to my own Facebook messages, but it's difficult. I keep checking Matthew's page, just in case she replies. I feel oddly nervous and on edge. I trust him, but something about this feels wrong. Suddenly, another message pops up from her:

Oh, thank God it's you!!! I need to talk to you urgently! Can we meet up in London this week? Tomorrow, even?

What the . . .?

I stare at the message in confusion. 'Oh, thank God it's you'? What's that supposed to mean? And what's with the urgency?

I hesitate for a moment before replying:

What's this about?

She writes back instantly:

I'd rather tell you face to face.

Tell me? What's there to tell? I quickly type:

23

Paige Toon

No, I think you should tell me now.

And then I add for good measure, feeling a bit sick now:

Do you know that I'm married?

It's a good few minutes before she replies, and the suspense almost kills me. But finally it comes:

No, I didn't. I'm sorry. But I'm afraid that doesn't
change anything. I didn't want to do this by
messaging, but I can see that it's going to be
complicated. As if it's not complicated enough! Sorry.
I'm pregnant. You're the father. I'm due in two months.
I thought you should know. For the baby's sake, not
mine. So as you can see, we need to meet up. When's
a good time???

*I feel like I'm falling, or spinning . . . And then I hear a key in the lock.
I turn to see my husband walk through the door.*

*'Hey,' he says, dropping his bag on the floor and kicking off his
shoes. Then he notices my face. 'What's wrong?' he asks with alarm.
I can't speak. He crosses the room and I turn the laptop in his direction. He leans over me, and my head throbs with adrenalin as I study
his face. The blood drains from his honey-tanned features, his eyes
widen in shock and his mouth drops open – all simultaneously – then
he tears his gaze away from the screen to look at me.*

*'What is going on?' My voice is barely a whisper and I feel like I'm
going to throw up.*

He shakes his head, lost for words.

24

'Did you have sex with her on your stag do?' I ask in a tiny, scared voice as I put two and two together.

The look on his face: anxiety, remorse, guilt. All these emotions cross his features, but I just need one answer. And he closes his eyes in despair before giving it to me:

'Yes.' He slumps down on the chair beside me, and I'm so tense I feel like my limbs could snap. 'I didn't mean to.'

'And you got her pregnant?' I whisper.

He shakes his head again and glances at the laptop screen. 'I . . . I don't know,' he replies with difficulty.

'It sounds like you did,' I point out, feeling oddly detached from my body. 'What happened?'

Suddenly he has the nerve to look exasperated. 'Oh God, Laura, I don't know. I was really pissed. Really fucking pissed. I . . . I . . .'

'You fucked her,' I say in a strangely calm voice. 'Do your mates know?'

This thought momentarily hurts me more than anything else.

'No!' he exclaims, and I feel an odd sense of relief. Then he adds embarrassment to his motley catalogue of emotions. 'I . . . We . . . It was in the club's toilets.'

'You had sex with this girl in the club toilets?' I ask, still in that abnormally detached manner.

'I was really bloody drunk,' he says again.

And then it hits me. The enormity of this. Matthew, who I married only seven months ago – is going to be a dad. Not to our child – my child – the child we were planning on having in couple of years, but to this girl's baby. This bitch's baby. This . . . slag's baby.

I lose it. I thump him hard in his chest and he cries out in shock as I thump him again and again, hitting his chest and then his face. He reaches out to grab my wrists, but he can't stop my wails, my screams,

25

my hysteria. Somewhere, blindly, deep inside, I wonder what the neighbours will think.

The neighbours were the least of our problems, I remind myself as I come out of my daze and refocus on the message from Matthew, asking me to text him when I land. I angrily punch out a reply:

I'm here and I shouldn't have to remind you that I need some space. So don't text me again.

Chapter 4

'Good morning, sleepyhead!'

Those are Marty's words to me when I finally open my eyes to see the sunlight streaming between the slats in the venetian blinds.

'What time is it?' I ask her. I played Sudoku on my phone until the early hours and finally dropped off at around six a.m. after devouring the whole packet of Oreos which we'd picked up at the airport. It was a long night.

'Eight thirty,' she replies.

'Is that all?' I thought I'd sleep for at least another couple of hours.

'Is that all?' she squeakily echoes me. 'You fell asleep at about five yesterday afternoon!'

'And woke up raring to go at two this morning,' I say wryly.

'Oh. Did you?' she asks with confusion.

'Yep. You were fast asleep. I was up half the night.'

'Bummer.'

I join her on the sofa bed and tell her about Matthew's text message and my response.

'Did he text you back?' she asks.

'Yeah. He wrote back immediately to apologise again, remind me that he loves me, and to promise to give me some space.' I shake my head. 'I didn't reply.'

Bridget hangs over the railings, dressed jubilantly in her green bikini. 'Who's ready to hit the pool?'

I didn't even realise she was awake.

'Me!' Marty replies, jumping up.

'Um, I can't,' I say. 'I need to go and buy a swimming costume first.'

'Borrow one of mine,' Bridget says, disappearing for a moment.

'Really?' I ask hopefully as she reappears. We're pretty much the same size, but her generosity takes me by surprise.

She throws a fifties-style, navy-blue-and-white polka-dot costume down to me. She shrugs. 'I brought three.'

I remember the weight of her suitcase. Of course she did. 'Thanks,' I say with a smile.

'Come on, then.' Marty snaps us to it.

We barely move from our poolside positions all day. Marty goes off to source pastries from a local bakery for breakfast, we order lunch from the restaurant next door, delivered directly to the pool, and we're still here, hogging our three sunloungers at happy hour. The Germans have nothing on us. It's so unlike me to do this; usually I have to be out there sightseeing and filling up my day with activities, but today ... Sigh. It's been all about the sunshine.

I'm feeling surprisingly okay. This may be because I'm trying not to think about Matthew. I came away to clear my head, and while this might imply that I plan to do some serious thinking, what I really want to do is take that sentence literally: clear my head of everything involving my husband. I don't want to think about him *at all*. Or rather, no more than I can help it.

It's my turn to get the drinks, so I tie my canary-yellow sarong around my waist – I did remember to bring that, at least – and wander over to the happy hour trolley. I'm just shaking some savoury snacks into a plastic cup, when I see Rick and his two mates approaching.

'Hello again,' Rick says with a smile as he grabs three beers out of the bucket and hands two to his mates. 'We must stop meeting like this.' He cracks his can open and I laugh nervously, trying to pick up the drinks I've just prepared. But four cups are a struggle, when you include the snacks. 'Let me help.' His hand swoops in and picks up one of the drinks. 'Where are you sitting?'

I nod towards Marty and Bridget, who are lying on their backs with their sunglasses on, oblivious to everything.

'Aah, Marty and Bridget,' he says as he follows me over there. 'We met them last night.' Which I know, of course. Marty told me earlier that they had a few drinks by the pool. 'Your name's Laura, right?'

'That's me.'

'Carl and Tom,' he says, jabbing his thumb at his buddies, and we exchange a hi, even though I already know their names, because Marty told me earlier. She's been wondering all day where they are – Tom in particular. Now, as we arrive back at the sunloungers, she bolts upright.

'Oh, hi!' she exclaims. Bridget swiftly follows suit.

'How's it going?' Rick asks, passing Marty her drink and set-tling down on my empty sunlounger. Carl and Tom make themselves comfortable next to my friends, so I have no choice but to sit alongside Rick.

'You girls had a good day?' Tom asks Marty.

'It's been suitably unproductive,' she jokes, indicating her surroundings. 'What have you been up to?'

'Jet-skiing.'

'All day, every day?' Marty asks with a grin, as the image of them bronzed, wet and glistening probably pops into her mind.

'Just today. We're taking tomorrow off to go scuba-diving.'

'I'd love to be able to scuba-dive,' Bridget enthuses.

Actually, so would I. I've often thought about learning.

'Come with us?' Carl suggests, turning to look at her.

'Don't you have to do a PADI course or something?' Bridget asks.

'Yeah, but you could ask about it. They do snorkelling day trips, too.'

'Snorkelling would be good,' Marty chips in. 'You up for that, Laura?'

'Sure.' I take a sip of my drink. This is okay. They're just people; we're only talking; I am perfectly capable of holding an ordinary conversation . . .

'Where did you disappear to last night, then?' Rick asks me, taking a swig of his beer before putting it on the ground.

'I went upstairs to take a shower and ended up falling asleep.'

'Lightweight,' he teases, removing his cap and sunnies and running his hand through his sandy-blond hair before leaning forward and turning to look at me. Whoa. I almost reel backwards. His eyes are a piercing blue, even bluer than Matthew's. I instantly decide that I don't like blue eyes and inadvertently shiver.

'You're not cold, are you?' he asks, his eyes dropping to my cleavage. I don't have much of one normally, but Bridget's swimming costume cinches me in.

'No, I'm fine,' I reply, turning my attention to the other two boys – much safer. 'When's your jet-skiing tournament?' I ask.

'Wednesday,' Carl tells me. That's the day after tomorrow.

'We'll have to come and watch you,' Bridget says with a tipsy giggle, patting him on his muscled thigh.

'You like to watch, do you?' Carl asks with a grin and a raised eyebrow.

Bridget giggles and a red spot forms on each of her cheeks.

'Are you all hitting Duval Street later?' I ask.

'Hell, yeah,' Tom replies, resting his elbows on his knees. 'Thought we'd check out Sloppy Joe's,' he says of the infamous bar, once frequented by Key West's most prominent former resident, Ernest Hemingway.

'So what are you chicks doing down here in the keys, anyway?' Carl leans back on his elbows. They are all ridiculously tanned and fit.

'Just a little girls' holiday,' Marty replies, tucking her hair behind one ear. 'Bridge is a travel writer so she's doing a piece and we're making the most of her discount,' she adds with a smile.

'Nice job. Wasn't your boyfriend pissed that you brought your friends instead of him?' Carl asks Bridget with a sideways glance – *definitely* fancies her.

'I'm single,' she replies with a shrug.

'No boyfriends for us, thank you very much,' Marty adds flippantly.

I open my mouth to speak, but she silences me with a look.

'Girls just wanna have fun, hey?' Rick says.

'Absolutely!' Marty says. I raise my eyebrows, but keep my mouth shut. I down the rest of my drink.

'You want another one of those?' Rick asks.

'No, I'm going to get ready. You coming?' I ask Marty meaningfully.

She hesitates before nodding. She knows she's in for it.

'I'll be up in a bit!' Bridget calls after us.

'See you at Sloppy's,' Rick adds and I glance back to meet his eyes, wishing a split second later that I hadn't.

'What are you doing, telling him I'm single?' I hiss at Marty when we're out of earshot.

'I didn't say you were single,' she replies glibly. 'I said we didn't have boyfriends. Technically it's true.' We reach the apartment and she rummages around in her beach bag for the key.

'You're misleading him,' I say when we're inside. 'I'm married.'

Her face softens. 'I know. I'm sorry. Let's just follow Cyndi's mantra and have some fun, eh? They're only here until Friday.'

I sigh. 'Okay.'

'You jump in the shower first. I'm going to raid my suitcase for an outfit to knock Tom's socks off.'

'Just his socks?' I ask wryly. She sniggers and I head into the bathroom determined to put Rick out of my mind, along with every other blue-eyed boy I've ever fallen in love with.

Chapter 5

'You should have your palms read!' Bridget cries gleefully. We're on our way to Duval Street after dinner. There's a palm-reading stall set up on the pavement with a wiry-looking, deeply tanned man of indeterminate age sitting at a table.

'Definitely not.' I shake my head with drunken determination as I try not to look the palm reader in the eye.

'You should!' Bridget persists loudly.

'You will *never* get Laura to do that,' Marty butts in, slurring slightly. 'She once had her palms read when we were in Ibiza – she *totally* freaked out.'

'Really?' Bridget asks with curiosity as she zigzags on the pavement. 'What did they say?'

'Nothing.' I wave her away. 'It's a load of tosh.'

'That's not what you thought at the time,' Marty says with a smirk.

'Anyway, what are they going to say now?' I move on quickly. 'That my life is crap and my husband is a bastard?'

'Maybe they'll tell you that you're about to find love – or at least lust – with a mysterious jet-skier.' Bridget punches me playfully. 'Oh, his face when you went upstairs!' she exclaims for about the fifth time. 'He was heartbroken!'

'Cut it out,' I snap. 'I'm not interested.'

'That's not possible,' Bridget says, brushing me off.

'Oh, it definitely is,' I try to say firmly, but it's difficult considering all the alcohol I've already consumed this evening.

'We'll see how you feel after a couple of shots of tequila,' Marty says.

'I am not doing tequila shots,' I reiterate, and then suddenly a giant cockerel hops onto the pavement in front of us and lets out the loudest cock-a-doodle-doo I've ever heard.

'What the *hell*?' Marty splutters.

'Where did he come from?' Bridget cries, taking my arm and giving him a wide berth. He cock-a-doodle-doos again as we pass and we all jolt in shock before cracking up laughing.

'Hey!' a male voice shouts from ahead of us. Through blurry vision brought on from tears of laughter I recognise Rick, Tom and Carl approaching.

'That rooster just scared the shit out of us!' Marty exclaims, pointing back at it. 'What on earth is a rooster doing wandering the streets?'

I wipe away my tears to see Rick smiling down at me. He's wearing cream-coloured chinos and a pale green polo shirt. No cap tonight. 'You haven't noticed the chickens before?' he says.

'What chickens?'

'They're everywhere.'

'Are they?' I ask with disbelief.

'Look.' He points up at a tree and, sure enough, there are a few hens roosting on a branch. 'They're all over the place in the daytime with their chicks. Hell knows what a rooster is doing up at this hour, though.'

'That's taking "free-range" a step too far,' Marty says. She is not a fan of birds.

Tom and Carl have also forgone their caps and sunnies tonight, revealing short brown hair and blue eyes (Tom), and even shorter brown hair and ... what colour are Carl's eyes? Green. Whoops. He just caught me staring at him.

'You heading to Sloppy's?' Rick asks.

'Guess so,' I reply. 'I don't think I need to drink anymore though.'

Suddenly a man dressed as a giant baby swerves onto the pavement in front of us from a side street. He's quickly followed by seven mates, chanting and laughing and carrying plastic glasses with beer sloshing over the sides.

Stags. I freeze on the pavement.

Marty appears at my side. 'Tequila?'

Bugger it. 'Go on, then.'

Bad idea. Bad, bad idea. Naughty Marty.

'WOOOOOOOOOOO! I *LOVE* this song!'

Yep, that was me screaming. And now I appear to be dancing on a table. How did that happen?

I have a flashback to my hen night, when my friend Natalie tried to teach me how to tango. I wonder if I can tango on this table. I could also really do with one of those penis whistles Cheryl gave me that night. I need to make some NOISE!

'Laura, come down!' two Bridgets shout up at me. Yay! Now I'm seeing double. 'You're going to kill yourself!'

I crack up laughing and stumble. Straight into Rick's arms.

'You okay?' he asks with amusement as he puts me down.

'You are definitely not pissed enough,' I berate him.

'Pissed?'

'Drunk,' I explain, forgetting pissed means angry, here.

'Oh.' He shrugs. 'I don't drink much. Anyway, we've got a dive tomorrow.'

Whoops. The snorkelling. Forgot about that.

'Take Your Mama' by Scissor Sisters starts to play and another memory of my hen night comes back to me: Shona and Sharon doing karaoke! That was a fun evening. I should do it again sometime. *Do it again?* Another hen do? Suddenly I find this thought absolutely hilarious. I burst into uncontrollable laughter.

'I think you've had one too many tequilas,' Marty says, swiftly replacing Rick at my side.

'Correction!' I say in a comedy American accent. 'I haven't had enough! More tequila!' I shout. 'Bloody hell, I loved my hen do. We should do it again sometime!' I squeal out loud to Marty. By now I'm in hysterics.

'I think we need to get you something else to eat,' Marty says firmly.

'Peanut M&Ms!' I erupt. 'Do you remember how Amy and Susan had those on tap on my hen night? Where are they now? They should be here! On THIS hen do! And where're Allison and Andrea? Where *are* they? Why didn't you invite *them*?' Out of the blue I feel angry with her.

'Time to get you to bed.' Marty marches me out of the bar, grabbing a resigned Bridget as we pass. 'See you in the morning, boys!' she calls in their general direction.

'You are no fun at all,' I say as we spill out onto the pavement, right into the path of an oncoming hen, wearing a veil and

L-plates. She's followed by a gaggle of girls all laughing and dressed up to the nines.

'Hey! You!' I shout as they start to pass us. The bride-to-be gives me a look of surprise over her shoulder. 'Don't do it!' I yell at her, before loudly lamenting: 'Where are all the GAYS?'

'Shhhhh!' Marty warns, pulling me away. 'Ignore her, she's drunk!' she tells the stunned girls, who warily move on.

Without warning, my anger turns to despair. 'She's having my baby! MY baby, Marty! It's not fair.'

'I know it's not, shush, shush,' Marty murmurs as she pulls me into her warm embrace.

'Why did he do it?' Tears start streaming down my face. 'How could he do this to me? Wasn't I enough?'

'Of course you're enough!' Marty tells me fervently, shaking me at the same time. 'He's an idiot! He made a mistake!'

I start to sob. I'm vaguely aware of Bridget flagging down a cab, and after that: nothing.

Chapter 6

I can't believe we're going through with this. I've already thrown up twice in the night, and now Marty seems to think it's a bright idea to put me on a moving boat.

'Have some more Nurofen,' she says.

'What are you, my dealer?' I reply sarcastically, but take the tablets from her and down them with a drink of water from my bottle.

I feel like shit. I wanted to stay in bed, but Marty was having none of it.

'You are not allowed to dwell in your own misery. You need something to take your mind off things.' Blah blah blah.

And so here we are at a dive centre a few keys away, getting kitted out for masks and fins – or goggles and flippers, as Marty insists on calling them. Marty and Bridget are talking in low voices – no doubt recounting the events of last night – but I'm happy to ignore them. I really don't want to talk.

Under instruction, we head outside and walk around the corner to where the dive boat is moored. Up ahead, Rick, Tom and Carl are barefoot and bare-chested, wearing black wetsuits peeled down to their waists.

'*Hello, boys*,' Marty murmurs appreciatively under her breath. I don't even have the energy to roll my eyes.

'How's your head?' Rick asks me with a grin as we approach.

'It's seen better days,' I reply, and my voice is gravelly, thanks to the alcohol – and retching. Urgh.

'The fresh air will help,' he says as he guides me aboard.

The boat is wide, flat and low to the water. Bench seats line each side, with air tanks secured behind them. A canopy hangs over half of the boat, but the rest of the seating is in full sunshine. There are a couple of other groups of people with us, about half of whom seem to be diving, so the boat is almost full. I sit down next to Marty and rest my elbows on my knees. Rick, Carl and Tom settle down opposite us. I'm wearing white shorts and a cream-coloured vest over Bridget's polka-dot swimming costume. I really must buy my own.

I take a deep breath and exhale slowly as we make our way out through the canal, past boats moored up at jetties outside residences mostly obscured by thick vegetation. I stare out of the back of the boat at the minimal wake we're leaving. Rick is right: the fresh air is helping. I glance across at him to find him watching me, before turning back to stare at the diminishing shoreline.

As soon as we reach the reef, the boat becomes a hive of activity with the scuba-divers attaching weird hoses to their air tanks, adjusting weights on their belts and making various checks on their equipment. It all looks very complicated to me. We'd already be in the water, but we forgot to apply sunscreen. I turn so Marty can slap some on my back, then I return the favour and, while applying cream to her shoulders, I notice a man in shorts and a T-shirt on the other side of the boat. An olive-skinned, black-haired ... No way, it's *him*! The guy from the other night!

'What are you doing?' Marty asks me with annoyance. I come to with surprise, realising that my hands have stopped moving. I apply the rest of her sunscreen, trying not to stare too much.

He's talking to the other guy: the cute one, the one I thought Marty might like. That guy is dressed in a black wetsuit and is obviously about to go diving. I wonder why Mr Beautiful isn't diving. He turns and ducks down into the cabin. Hmm. It looks like he works here. He reappears and makes his way down the gangway towards us. I can't take my eyes off him, and as he passes he brushes my arm with his, making my hairs stand on end. He's tall – about six foot three or four, compared to my five foot eight, and he has broad shoulders and a slim waist.

'Get a move on,' Marty urges me, and I turn in a daze to see that she has already stripped off and is struggling to pull on one of her fins. I quickly lift my vest over my head and wriggle out of my shorts.

'You snorkellers ready?' He speaks! He has an American accent.

'Yep,' Marty replies, giving me a nudge.

I pull on my fins, intensely aware that I look like a complete idiot as I take a giant step in my enormous footwear towards the back of the boat. Please don't let me fall over ...

'Have a good one,' Rick calls after us.

'You, too,' I call back, wobbling slightly as I step down to the platform. Then Mr Beautiful's hand is on my arm, steadying me. I freeze for a moment and look down at it with shock, before coming back to life. My cheeks blush a deep red, but thankfully he's looking behind me at my friends.

'It's better to walk backwards,' he tells them.

The water is a brilliant blue and there are dark shapes moving beneath the surface. I feel a flurry of nerves.

'Okay, in you go,' he says to me.

'What are *they*?' I ask him with worry.

'Fish.' He says the word as though I'm an idiot.

'As long as they're not sharks . . .'

'Reef sharks won't bite you.'

'You mean, there *are* sharks?' I ask with apprehension.

'Of course. But it's the barracuda you should be worried about.' He turns to Marty behind me and I'm effectively dismissed.

'Why would I be worried about the barracuda?' I'm sorry, but, with my apprehension mounting, I'm not ready to get into the water yet, mister. I don't care how gorgeous you are.

'They bite if provoked,' he snaps over his shoulder.

'Get a move on!' Marty hisses, and I glance behind her to see that some of the divers are ready and have started to form a queue behind us.

'Big step.' The man flashes me a look with his dark-almost-black eyes. 'And don't stand on the reef, because you'll break the coral,' he warns, assuming that I'm an amateur.

'I know,' I snap back, because I have been snorkelling before, even if it was years ago.

I bite on the snorkel and take a large stride out into the ocean, gasping as the cool water engulfs me. We turned down wetsuits, but maybe that was a bad idea. I'm a good swimmer, but I feel exposed in my swimming costume. I place my masked face under the surface and blow hard to expel water from my snorkel, before taking long, slow breaths. A rush of adrenalin pulses through me, and everyone and everything else in my life is instantly forgotten.

The water is crystal clear and I'm amongst a shoal of silver and yellow fish. The sand below is pure white, and the nearby rocks are covered in pretty, intricately shaped coral. Tiny electric-blue fish dart amongst plants swaying in the current as I swim away from the boat. It's a dazzling sight and I start to relax and enjoy myself. The salt water makes me incredibly buoyant so I barely have to kick. I look around to see Marty and Bridget snorkelling a few metres away. We give each other the thumbs up and try not to smile, otherwise we'll get mouthfuls of salt water. Several steady streams of large bubbles rising from the sandy ocean floor reveal the whereabouts of the scuba-divers. I spot a starfish on some rocks and, taking a deep breath and blocking the end of the snorkel with my tongue so I don't take in water, I duck beneath the surface and swim down to take a closer look. It's breath-taking here. I feel so weightless and . . . free. It's the happiest I've felt in a long time.

Later, we return to the boat and everyone is full of stories about the fish that they've seen. I hear several excited divers discussing a shoal of barracuda, and gather that there were also a couple of black-tipped reef sharks nearby, which I feel oddly disappointed about not seeing. I don't know what's got into me, but I'm even more certain I want to learn to dive. I look around for Mr Beautiful and find him at the front of the boat, where his friend is talking animatedly to him. I notice later that he's the one to drive us back to the dive centre.

Back on dry land, Bridget, Marty and the boys head to the nearby Tiki Bar for a drink, and I go to the dive centre to enquire about diving courses. A redheaded girl comes out of the office to talk to me.

'Did ya see any good fish?' she asks with a funny accent as she scrolls down the screen of the computer in front of her, looking up potential scuba courses for me.

'Yeah, it was amazing,' I tell her.

'Cool.'

'Where are you from?' I ask, trying to make polite conversation.

'Auckland,' she replies. 'New Zealand.'

'Have you been here long?'

'Three months,' she says, not looking at me as she studies the screen. 'Gotta go home in a couple of weeks cos my visa runs out.'

'Oh. That's a shame.'

'So there's a PADI open-water diver course starting next week on Thursday through Saturday—'

'It's three days long?' I interrupt with surprise.

'Yep. The first day is in the classroom and the pool, and Days Two and Three are in the open water.'

'Okay . . . But is there nothing available earlier?' We fly home a week on Sunday and had planned to have a few days in Miami before we leave. 'There are three of us wanting to learn,' I add, hoping she can squeeze us in.

'Hang on a minute,' she says, calling back through to the office. 'Jorge?'

'Yep,' comes the reply, and a moment later Jorge appears and I feel a vicarious thrill when I realise he's the gorgeous guy's friend from the boat. He's now wearing a white T-shirt with graphics on the front and beige-coloured shorts. His short curly hair and his eyes are dark brown, and he's cute, with very white teeth.

The redhead explains our situation.

'I was wondering about Monday?' she says. 'You've only got two.'

'Hmm.' He frowns. 'I wouldn't normally take five in a class.'

'Leo could help out?' she suggests.

An inexplicable flurry of nerves passes through me. Leo? Is that *his* name?

'I'll ask.'

Jorge starts to walk out of the dive centre, but he turns back and motions for me to join him. He crosses over the road to the Tiki Bar, where my friends are currently ensconced. Its roof is thatched with palm leaves, and the walls are non-existent, the wooden interior open to the elements. I spot Marty and Bridget on the far side with Tom, Carl and Rick, but Jorge leads me straight to the bar, to a man sitting on a stool with his back to us, reading a newspaper. His toned, muscled back is visible through his pale orange T-shirt, and his black hair is slicked-back and glossy. Of course it's him.

'Leo,' Jorge says. Leo looks over his shoulder and adrenalin pulses through me for the second time today.

'This lady and her friends want to learn how to dive. I've already got two on the course on Monday. Can you pitch in?'

Leo's eyes graze over my body and back to my face. I can't read his expression, but he doesn't look very happy. As I feel my face heat up, he casually turns back to his paper.

'Sure.' He shrugs.

'Really?' Jorge checks, a little surprised, it seems.

'Yeah, why not?' he replies absent-mindedly.

Jorge flashes me a grin.

'Come in Monday morning at eight thirty and we'll sort out payment and paperwork then. Bring your passports.'

'Thanks.' I return his smile.

'Laura!' I hear Marty call. She's spotted me from across the bar.

'See you then,' I say to Jorge, taking one last look at Leo's broad back before I make my way over to my friends.

'What took you so long?' Marty snaps. 'Your Piña Colada has thawed.'

'Looks drinkable enough to me,' I say with a goofy grin, my mood now vastly improved. I sit down and glance over my shoulder at Leo. We make eye contact momentarily, his dark eyes boring into mine for a millisecond before his attention is returned to his paper.

But he *was* looking at me. He was definitely looking at me. And my hammering heart is proof.

Chapter 7

The six of us go out again that night, and I'm on a surprising high. Marty and Bridget have stepped up their flirtations with Tom and Carl to another level, and although I've relaxed considerably, I'm trying not to encourage Rick. It's not always easy, and a sad little part of me accepts that it's nice to feel desirable, after everything I've been through. So I dance the night away and try not to drink too much.

The next day it's the jet-skiing tournament, so we go to watch, and I have to admit it's impressive stuff, the way they fly through the air and manoeuvre their machines with speed and control. Carl comes third, but Rick and Tom don't fare as well, coming eighth and tenth respectively. Regardless of results, Marty and Bridget are practically salivating as they get ready that night. I feel slightly anxious, because I don't want to feel left out, but I'm trying to stay strong.

'How about here?' Marty asks later after dinner with the boys. She has to raise her voice over the sound of live music as we approach

46

a busy bar, one with dollar notes stapled to the ceiling. There's a guitar-wielding girl sitting on a stool and singing into a microphone with a deep, sultry voice. She's wearing jeans and has long, dark, curly hair tied back into a ponytail, kept in order by a bandana.

'Sure,' Rick says, taking my hand and leading me into the bar. My eyes widen at his touch and it takes a moment before I think to extract my hand. By then we've already reached the bar and he needs his hand to retrieve his wallet, anyway.

'My round. What are you having?' He turns his piercing blue eyes on me.

'Um . . . Maybe just a mineral water.'

'Really?' he asks with surprise.

'I don't want to get too drunk tonight.'

'Why not? You're on holiday. And it's our last night . . .' he says with a significant look.

'I think I'll stick to water, anyway,' I reiterate, looking around for the toilet. The barman points me in the right direction.

'You want some company?' Marty calls after me.

'No, I'm good,' I reply. I'm actually craving some space. Matthew has started to plague my mind again. I don't want to be here, watching my friends flirt outrageously. And I don't want to lead Rick on.

As the night wears on, Rick becomes more and more tactile. Maybe if I were drinking, I wouldn't mind so much. But I feel very different to last night, when I was on such a high after snorkelling. He keeps squeezing my shoulder, his arm draped over the back of my chair, and he doesn't seem to notice how I tense up every time he does this.

Finally, I'm ready to call time on the evening. I lean in and pull

Marty away from whatever she's giggling about into Tom's ear, and tell her that I'm going to go back to the hotel.

She looks momentarily disappointed, then replies, 'We'll come with you.'

'No, no!' I argue, but she's already turned to the rest of the table. 'Wanna come back for a drink on our balcony?'

'Hell, yeah!' come the enthusiastic replies as they knock back their drinks and stand up. Argh! I just want to go to bed.

'Slow down, Laura, my heels are killing me!' Marty shouts a short while later.

I reluctantly drag my feet.

'You in some kind of rush?' Rick asks, keeping step with me.

'I'm just tired,' I reply a touch grumpily as the others erupt into drunken laughter about who knows what. 'I want my bed. I've never wanted to sleep on a horrible single blow-up mattress so much in my life,' I add, making sure I'm not implying that I'd like him to join me.

'You can't go to bed yet.' He brushes me off. 'It's not even midnight.'

'Yes, I can. I'm shattered and still feeling jet-lagged.'

He doesn't get it. He's never travelled outside America, so he won't understand the effect time, distance and travel can have on your body clock. I've used small talk as my defence tactic all evening, so I know quite a bit about him: he's only twenty-five – four years younger than me – and he's from Connecticut. He went to university in Chicago and learned to jet-ski on the Great Lakes. He's lived and played there ever since. He doesn't seem like the type to have had to work hard for a living. But maybe I'm misjudging him.

'Tom and I are just going to go and grab a few beers from his room!' Marty calls when we reach the hotel. They hurry off, and I can hear Marty trying to stifle her laughter. I doubt she'll be back anytime soon.

'Come and see inside our apartment,' Bridget suggests with a raised eyebrow, pulling Carl through the door.

A moment later I hear the muffled sound of them snogging the faces off each other, only to be replaced by their feet on the spiral staircase.

I could actually cry. I just want to go to sleep. I turn with dismay to see Rick staring at me in the darkness, a smile playing around his lips.

Oh, fuck off.

I stomp to the swinging chair and climb into it, crossing my legs – and my arms. Back off, buster.

'Is there room for a little one?' He nods at the small space next to me.

'You're not little,' I say.

'No, I'm not,' he murmurs in what he thinks is a sexy voice as he ambles closer.

'I'm sorry, but I'm really tired,' I say and stretch out before he gets any ideas. I've been polite to him all evening, but even a slug would have flirted more. How can he not have got the message?

His face falls slightly, then he laughs and tries to budge me over. 'You're funny,' he says.

'I'm serious,' I reply, stiffening up and holding my own. 'Sit on one of those chairs.' I point at the two by the coffee table.

He falters. He still doesn't know if I'm joking. I hear Bridget gasp from inside and he grins at me. Oh, his confidence. It really is something. Suddenly he scoops me up and collapses down on the swinging chair, pulling me onto his lap.

'That's better,' he says laughingly as I feel his erection pressing into my backside. When the hell did he get that? I scramble off him in shock.

'For God's sake!' I squawk, my voice going up an octave. 'I told you, I just want to go to bed!'

He'll probably take that the wrong way, too, I think hotly as I storm off towards the steps. I jog down them and hurry around to the pool, which is dimly lit by lights under the palm trees. There's a gate at the far end and I push through it, finding myself in the car park. I hurry across it and out onto the road. I turn right and walk past a restaurant, which is dark inside, the lights turned off, and then I lean up against the wall and take a deep breath.

I'll go back and rest on a sunlounger in a while, but I want to make sure he's buggered off, first. Why didn't I simply tell him I wasn't interested in so many words instead of saying 'I just want to go to bed'? I may have drunk water for the last couple of hours, but I'm still not thinking straight.

A dog barks near the fence and I jump. I hear a man call, 'MAX!' and whistle to the dog. Out of the blue I realise where I am. Peering through the leaves of a tree, I see the unkempt garden. The sofa and armchairs are empty. The dog continues to bark and I decide to walk on before I'm spotted, but when I turn I bash straight into someone.

I gasp as two hands steady me, and then I'm looking up into Leo's dark eyes, my heart pounding wildly.

'What are you doing here?' he asks accusingly, and I think he recognises me, but I can't be sure.

'I ... I ... I'm staying at the hotel.'

More barking. I hear the man again shout: 'Max!'

'It's okay!' Leo shouts back. 'It's just me!'

I glance through the leaves to see Jorge on the other side of the garden, near the house. He whistles once more and this time I see the sleek brown figure of a dog run towards him. He bends down and pats the dog. 'Where are you?' he calls to Leo.

'Out here,' he calls back, and then he looks down at me and I realise that his hands are still on my arms. He lets go abruptly, leaving a searing heat behind.

'Go back to your hotel,' he says firmly. 'You shouldn't be out here alone.'

He turns to walk away, but I find myself blurting out: 'I can't!'

His brow is furrowed with annoyance. 'Why not?'

'I can't go back there,' I mutter with embarrassment.

'Why not?' he repeats, more insistently this time. I have a feeling he doesn't suffer fools lightly.

'My friends are . . .' My voice trails off.

'Where's your boyfriend?' he asks bluntly.

I shake my head. 'I don't . . . He's not my boyfriend,' I tell him.

He holds my stare, his body partly turned towards the gate, half staying, half going.

'I . . . I'm trying to avoid him.'

Now he looks interested. 'Why?'

'He wants . . .' Again I let my words trail off. 'But I don't want to.'

'Aah.' The way he says it, so knowing. He turns his body back to face me, crossing his arms. 'So you're hiding from him.'

I don't reply, but he knows.

'Leo! Where are you, man?'

Jorge.

'I'm coming!' he snaps back sharply. 'This way,' he says to me, jerking his head in the direction of the garden.

My foot instinctively lifts to step towards him. What the hell am I doing? 'Where?' I ask, faltering slightly on the pavement.

'You can't hide out here,' he calls over his shoulder, reaching down for the gate. He holds it open for me, and, taken aback by my own willingness to follow him, I find myself stepping through. Marty would kill me if she knew where I was right now. She'd think I'd lost my mind. Maybe I have. But I don't care. She has other things on *her* mind, after all.

I pause by the gate as Leo closes it, and then I follow him into the garden. It looks even more of a mess from down here, with its broken statues and rubbish claimed by overgrown grass.

'There you are!' Jorge exclaims from the porch, and then his mouth falls open when I step out from behind Leo. His brow furrows as he scrutinises me, trying to place me.

'Take a seat.' Leo directs me to the beaten-up sofa. 'You want a beer?' he asks, heading towards the house.

'Sure,' I reply uncertainly. So much for not drinking tonight. I sit down on the sofa, trying not to pay attention to Jorge's confused look as he mouths, 'What the . . .?' to his friend. Out of the corner of my eye I see Leo shrug and bend down to flick on a switch. I'm instantly bathed in a glow of light as the lanterns and rope lights come on.

Leo soon returns, cracking open a bottle of beer and handing it to me. He slumps in the armchair opposite and lights up a cigar. Jorge appears a moment later.

'So . . .' Jorge says. 'You're hiding from your boyfriend?'

'He's not my boyfriend,' I reiterate.

He grins and collapses onto the other armchair, leaving me alone on the sofa. I wonder where the girl and the other man are tonight.

'It *was* you snorkelling yesterday, wasn't it?' he checks.

'Yes, that was me,' I reply.

'You're doing the course on Monday, right?'

'Yes,' I confirm with a nod. I'm wearing a tight black top and skinny white jeans. I applied quite heavy make-up tonight, and I hope my eyes are still looking smoky and not smudged to hell. I certainly look different to the hungover, bare-faced girl who went snorkelling. No wonder he couldn't place me at first. 'I wouldn't have come in here if I didn't know who you were,' I add pointedly, but I'm not actually convinced. I'd follow Mr Beautiful anywhere, I think with a smirk to myself, knowing I'm being ridiculous.

'So what happened with your guy?' Jorge asks with amusement, settling back into his chair and crossing one knee over the other. Leo watches me through the trail of his cigar smoke and I have to focus on concentrating.

'He was getting a little too amorous for my liking,' I reply, and Jorge chuckles and flashes his mate a look. Leo raises his eyebrows, but doesn't take his eyes from mine. I feel myself flushing. I really need to learn to control my reactions to this man before I start my scuba-diving course next week.

'I'm Laura,' I find myself telling them.

'Jorge,' Jorge replies. 'And Leo,' he adds, pointing at his friend.

'I know.' I take a sip of my beer and glance at Leo's legs. They're long and tanned, the hairs on them dark. He's wearing shorts again, navy blue this time, with a white T-shirt.

I hear the clunk of the gate latch and Leo lazily turns around. I follow the line of his sight to see the girl from the other night, followed by the third man, wander into the garden.

'Who's she?' Those are her first words. And she doesn't sound pleased. All my hackles rise.

'Laura,' Leo tells her calmly, puffing on his cigar before unhurriedly stubbing it out in an ashtray.

'Laura, this is Carmen,' Jorge says more affably. 'Carmen's my sister,' he explains to me.

'Hi,' I say warily, because her expression is far from friendly.

'And that's Eric,' Jorge adds, nodding at the shaved-headed man behind her. He nods at me, but doesn't say anything. He's lighter-skinned than the others, not of Latin or Hispanic heritage, at a guess.

'Laura is staying at the hotel next door,' Jorge explains.

'What's she doing here?' the girl bites back. She looks older than she did from the sundeck, in her late thirties perhaps. She's wearing a white vest and a colourful flowing skirt, and her long dark hair comes to halfway down her back. Up close, she's not as beautiful, her face more lined and weather-burned, but you can tell she was a stunner once.

'Chill, Carmen,' Jorge says calmly. 'She's doing a PADI course on Monday.'

'That still hasn't answered my question.'

'I should probably get going, anyway,' I say edgily, standing up and ignoring Leo's eyes on me.

'Are you sure?' Jorge asks. 'You don't have to.'

'No, it's okay. I think the coast will be clear. Thanks for hiding me,' I add, Carmen's angry stance making my smile waver.

'Nice to meet you,' I mutter as I walk past her. She doesn't step aside for me, so I have to squeeze past yet another scratchy palm tree.

'Rude.' I hear Jorge berating her with this single word as I exit

54

the gate. I don't hear her reply – maybe she doesn't even bother to give him one.

I'm back within the hotel grounds before I remember Rick. I haven't been gone long and he might still be lingering. I don't want to risk bumping into him again. I despondently eye the sun-loungers, wondering which one will do for my bed tonight.

Chapter 8

By the time Monday rolls around, Marty and Bridget are back to their normal perky selves. Friday and Saturday were a washout — they were feeling so flat about Tom and Carl leaving that they didn't even notice that I was annoyed with them for failing to consider me while they got their rocks off. Last night we went to a movie, and now we're feeling refreshed and ready to learn how to dive. I'm so excited I can barely breathe.

Matthew has tried to call me, but I diverted his call. I'm becoming quite efficient at putting him out of my mind. My head is still full of a certain someone, and for now I intend to embrace that distraction, thank you very much.

Leo ... Where's he from? He has an American accent, but is olive-skinned like Jorge. Is he Spanish? Mexican? Cuban? I remember his dark eyes regarding me through the trail of his cigar smoke and I sigh and look out of the window.

We pass a church with a billboard out in front. The message reads:

**God says, don't wait for
the storm to pass;
learn to dance in the rain.**

I'm not overly religious, but I like the sentiment. I'm not learning to dance, but I wonder if scuba-diving counts.

Three hours later, I'm feeling substantially less enthusiastic. We've been sitting in a muggy classroom, and Leo is nowhere to be seen. I daren't ask Jorge about him, and I'm certainly not going to ask Tegan, the redhead in the office, who seems to be helping out. The promise of a dive in the swimming pool after lunch has been dangled in front of us all morning, but even Marty and Bridget seem a bit fed up.

We head to the Tiki Bar for lunch, and my heart sinks when there's still no sign of Leo. I feel pathetic as I repeatedly scan the joint.

Afterwards, we go into the dive centre to try on wetsuits. Tegan has a good eye, and manages to choose each of us a perfectly fitting wetsuit, first time. We carry our equipment out to the swimming pool and sit on the edge, with our feet dangling in the water to keep cool. Thankfully, the wetsuits are short-sleeved, because full-length wetsuits would be pretty unbearable in this heat. Jorge appears after a little while and instructs us to put on all our equipment. He gave me a knowing wink when we arrived this morning, but hasn't mentioned the other night. I still haven't told Marty and Bridget about it. I was sure they'd give me hell for going into some strangers' garden, and I didn't have the energy to deal with it, even though I knew I could give it back tenfold.

Jorge watches me connect my air tank to my jacket, to make

sure I'm doing it right, but he seems pre-occupied, looking over his shoulder.

I can stand the suspense no longer. 'Is Leo still coming?'

'He'd better be,' he mutters, and steps away from me, his shoulders slumping.

Just then a battered-up old white hatchback pulls off the road into the car park.

'Right on cue,' he says under his breath, as Leo climbs out of the car. 'No rush!' Jorge shouts with sarcasm. Leo gives him a dark look, but doesn't reply as he gets a black bag out of the boot and heads into the dive centre. Jorge moves on to help Bridget with her equipment, and I try to look busy for when Leo comes back. My mind is racing and I inwardly berate myself. Get a grip. I know I need a distraction, but this is silly.

I shrug on my jacket – otherwise known as my BCD: Buoyance Control Device. The air tank is attached to it. I thought my weight belt was heavy . . .

'Check your buddy's equipment,' Jorge instructs us.

Marty, Bridget and I turn to each other.

Scuba-diving operates under a buddy system, which means ideally a pair of divers – sometimes three – of similar experience diving together, looking out for each other, and staying close by underwater so they can offer assistance if someone's air runs out or anything else goes wrong. There's another couple on the course with us – a guy and a girl in their early twenties called Ted and Monica – so naturally they're buddying each other, which leaves the three of us. Bridget, Marty and I take turns to check that each other's scuba tank is securely fitted to their BCD, and then we scrutinise the air gauges to make sure our tanks are full. Jorge barks out instructions so we don't forget anything.

'When you're ready, you can get in the water,' Jorge says, moving past us to the steps. 'I hope you've remembered to inflate your BCDs!'

I press the button to inflate my jacket, then pull my mask down over my eyes and breathe through my mouthpiece. At that moment I see Leo sauntering out of the dive centre in a black half-body wetsuit, carrying his BCD and fins.

One thing's for sure: he looks a darn sight better than I do. I force myself to stop gawking and try to concentrate on the steps.

'Laura, you're using up your air. Breathe through your snorkel until you're ready to go under,' Jorge commands.

By now I'm in the water, and my BCD is acting like a life jacket. The cool water of the pool seeps into my wetsuit and it's a welcome relief, although I know the trapped water will soon warm up.

I swap my snorkel again for my mouthpiece and tentatively deflate my BCD. My breathing quickens as I sink underwater. It's such a weird sensation being able to breathe like this. We're given time to practise and get used to our equipment. I attempt to go into deeper water, but sink too quickly and forget to pinch my nose to expel the air from my ears. The sharp pain takes me by surprise. I panic slightly, trying to find the button to re-inflate my jacket, and then Leo appears in front of me. He re-inflates my jacket and the pain disappears.

'Okay?' he asks as I resurface.

'Yes,' I reply with embarrassment. 'I forgot to equalise my ears.'

'Try again.'

This time I go more slowly, pinching my nose and blowing to force the air out of my ear canal as I sink to the depths of the pool. I kneel on the bottom and Leo kneels opposite, giving me the okay sign. It's the sign scuba-divers use most often as part of the buddy system. I return it and try not to smile. This is so cool, resting here on the bottom of the pool. I look around and see my friends experimenting with their buoyancy. Leo makes the sign with his hands to encourage me to level out. Jorge has told us we need to find the point where we're not sinking to the bottom, but rather hovering above it. We don't want to be damaging the coral when we're out in open water. I push the button to inflate my air, but start to rise too quickly. I deflate again and sink back down. Leo pinches his nose to remind me to equalise. I keep leaning slightly to my left, my weights pulling me that way, and it's awkward. He notices and points towards the shallow end. We swim side by side before resurfacing.

'Your weights are unbalanced,' he says, putting his mask on top of his head and revealing his very dark brown eyes. Sigh . . . 'Take off your belt,' he commands.

I reach under my BCD to release the strap, then hand it to him. He begins to feed the weights off the belt until they're more evenly weighted.

'Did you manage to avoid him?'

He's talking about Rick, of course. Bridget and Marty are still underwater, thankfully, so they're oblivious to his question and my reply.

'Yeah. I slept on a sunlounger and I have the mozzie bites to prove it,' I say jauntily as I show him the red bumps on my arm. He doesn't look amused.

I stayed on the sunlounger that night until Carl's heavy footsteps on the stairs over my head alerted me to the fact that he had vacated our apartment. 'He wasn't too happy to see me the next morning,' I add, remembering the cold-shoulder treatment I received when I bumped into the boys in the lobby. They were checking out and I was on my way to Duval Street to buy a swimming costume at last: black, for a change. A nice, safe, colour choice. 'But he's gone home now, so that's a relief.'

His eyebrows rise ever so slightly, but he says nothing as he hands me back my belt. I try to put it on underneath my bulky BCD, but it's a struggle. He waits patiently.

'Was that your girlfriend the other night at the house?' I try to sound casual, but I'm nervous.

He laughs sharply. 'No,' he says quite firmly, and I can't be sure if he means he never *would* or he never *has*. There's a very big difference in my mind, but the relief is still apparent.

Nearby, Bridget, Marty and Jorge resurface and give each other the okay sign. Jorge pops his mask on top of his head.

'Yes, good,' he says to Leo with an approving nod as he notices us together. 'You buddy Laura.'

Thank you, God!

Marty looks at me and then I see her eyes narrow as she scrutinises Leo. There's no way I can keep the smirk from my face.

'Who the hell was *that*?' she asks later when we're changing out of our wetsuits into our normal clothes.

'Who are you talking about?' I ask innocently.

'You know *exactly* who I'm talking about. Your new *buddy*.' She says the word ominously.

'Leo?' I reply, keeping up the act for as long as humanly possible.

'Yes! Where did he come from?'

'Yeah, he was a bit *phwoar*,' Bridget chips in, entering the

61

conversation. 'If you want me to take him off your hands, I'd be happy to oblige.'

My stomach clenches.

'Thanks very much!' Marty exclaims with mock outrage. 'Are you trying to get rid of me?'

Bridget just laughs. 'You can buddy Laura instead.'

'No, it's okay.' I try to keep my voice calm, but I'm buggered if I'm letting her swap with me.

Bridget grins and nudges me knowingly. 'I don't know, poor Rick.'

'What do you mean, poor Rick?' I snap.

'Well, he never got anywhere, did he?' she says with amusement.

'How does that make him poor Rick?' I ask, unable to keep the edge from my voice. 'Why should he *expect* to get anywhere with me?'

'Chill out, Laura, she's only teasing you,' Marty chides.

I feel my face heating up at my overreaction. 'Are we going for this drink or what?' I say.

'Seems like you need one,' Marty replies. I choose to ignore her.

To my barely controlled delight, Leo and Jorge are at the bar when we walk into 'Ye Olde Thatched Tiki Hut', as Marty has taken to calling it.

'How did you enjoy today?' Jorge asks us.

'Brilliant,' I enthuse.

Bridget and Marty agree.

'Wait until tomorrow when we head out into open water,' he says. The thought makes me feel excited *and* anxious.

Leo's hair is still wet and there's a damp patch where the water has dripped onto the back of his T-shirt. I have an intense urge to get out my towel and dry his hair. It's even sexier when dishevelled like this.

'Laura!'

I come to with a start and realise that Marty is speaking to me.

'Sorry, what?' I ask.

'You're in another world,' she berates. 'What are you having?' She nods towards the bartender.

'Oh, um . . .' I notice Leo is drinking beer. 'A beer, please.' He puts the bottle to his lips and swigs from it. Butterflies fill my stomach.

'Pull up a stool,' Jorge says. 'So where are your boyfriends?' he asks Marty and Bridget with a grin, and I purse my lips at him because he knows full well that that's the wrong description.

'Oh, they're not our boyfriends.' Marty brushes him off.

'We met them last week,' Bridget adds. 'But they've gone back to Chicago now.'

Jorge seems amused as he flashes me a look. I shift uncomfortably.

Marty pays for our drinks and hands them over, settling herself on another stool.

'Do you both live here?' she asks, not fazed in the slightest by the most beautiful man in the world. I envy her nonchalance.

'Nope, just here for the summer,' Jorge replies. 'We live in Miami most of the year.'

'Are you a dive instructor, too?' Bridget asks Leo.

'No,' he replies resolutely, barely looking at her.

'Leo drives the boat,' Jorge explains. 'He's a dive master, so he helps me out sometimes.'

Leo takes a swig from his bottle.

'He's a helpful guy,' Jorge adds in a singsong voice, giving me a knowing look. I blush furiously. I think he's guessed I haven't told my friends about them.

'How long are you here?' I'm startled as Leo's voice breaks the silence. I realise his question is directed straight at me.

'We leave on Sunday,' I reply, and suddenly my mind is flooded with images of Matthew and I can't help but flinch.

'Well,' Marty interrupts uncertainly. 'Maybe Thursday or Friday. We were thinking about going to Miami for a couple of days.'

'You have to do at least one dive as fully qualified divers,' Jorge says with disappointment.

'So maybe we'll go on Friday,' Marty says.

'Or Saturday?' I add weakly.

'Friday,' Bridget concurs with Marty. 'I want to have at least a couple of nights in Miami.'

I tune out. I feel horrible. What is going on back home? Has Matthew seen her? That *slag*? I can't bear the thought of it, can't bear the thought of returning to him, to pick up the pieces . . .

'Why don't you want to go home?' Leo asks in a low voice, and I'm surprised to find him watching me.

I shake my head, my nose starting to prickle. Oh hell, don't cry.

I hear Marty's voice falter as she notices this exchange.

'Who *does* want to go home after a holiday?' she interjects jollily. She thinks she's coming to my rescue, but her interruption feels brash and wrong. I force a smile onto my face and glug down my beer, intensely aware of the warmth of the man sitting beside me.

Chapter 9

'What on earth was *that* about?' Marty asks accusingly as soon as we're in the car.

I shake my head and steadfastly ignore her. I knew this was coming.

'What?' Bridget asks with confusion. She's back in the driver's seat, Marty beside her.

'Laura,' Marty explains to her. 'And Leo.' She swivels in her seat again to look at me. 'You fancy the pants off him, don't you?'

'I do not!' I object as my face burns.

'Who wouldn't?' Bridget casually says. 'He's sex on legs.'

'Yeah, but he's not Laura's type,' Marty tells her flippantly.

'What?' I snap, my humiliation being swiftly replaced with annoyance. 'How would you know?'

'Well, he's nothing like Matthew, and definitely nothing like Will.' Will was my first and only love before Matthew.

'I think that's probably the point,' Bridget interrupts.

'Eh?' Marty asks her with a furrowed brow.

'She hasn't exactly had much luck with either of those two, has she?'

My eyebrows pop up in surprise and, as Bridget eyes me in the rear-view mirror, I silently thank her for understanding.

We're on the boat heading out to the reef. It's Day Two of our course and, after another morning in the swimming pool, we're about to have our first Open Water dive. Leo is driving the boat and Tegan is up at the front with him. I keep staring to see if I can sense any chemistry between them, but it's not clear. I take it she's staying on the boat while we do the dive.

We arrive at the reef and Jorge tells us to get our equipment ready. There's still so much to remember and it blows my mind. Leo appears by my side and my pulse quickens.

BWRAF – Begin With Review And Friend – that's the acronym PADI uses to make sure we remember the five buddy checks we need to make.

B is for BCD. We inflate and deflate our jackets to check the mechanism is working, then inflate enough so that we'll float when we get into the water.

W is for Weights. The weight belt must always be worn in the same way, with a right-hand release. Leo might have to be the one to release my weight belt should we ever need to make an emergency ascent. I suck in a sharp breath as I feel his hands on my waist, making sure I've buckled up my belt properly. Feeling like I'm all thumbs, I do the same to him. I glance up to see him regarding me with those dark eyes of his and my heart threatens to beat out of my chest. Can he feel it too?

R is for Release. Our BCDs – jackets – should be fitted securely and snugly.

A is for Air. We check that the regulator is functioning properly, that the tank valve is open and that the air tank is full by checking the pressure gauge and breathing through the regulator. Leo hands me his alternate second stage – his spare air source – in case I need it in an emergency. I take it and breathe from it a few times, avoiding eye contact, then hand him mine so he can do the same. I feel like these checks are going on forever, but, thankfully, that's pretty much it. Apart from the Final Okay, we're done.

'Leo! Laura! You go first,' Jorge instructs loudly, making me jump. I remember to walk backwards to the dive platform at the rear of the boat. Leo, I notice, puts his fins on with ease once we reach it.

'Follow the rope all the way down and wait at the bottom,' Jorge tells me as Leo checks over my mask and flashes me the okay sign. I do the same to him – making an 'O' shape with my forefinger and thumb.

'Big step,' Leo says, and I smile and raise my eyebrows at him because his voice is for once laced with amusement. He must remember the last time I stood on this boat, when I was worried about reef sharks. I'm not worried about them anymore. Not when I'm with him.

I pull my mask on, breathe through my snorkel, and comply. He joins me in the water and we slowly descend.

Nothing prepares me for what it is like this time. The visibility is far better than last time, and the crystal-clear water must span for over twenty metres. I reach the bottom and kneel. Leo gives me the okay sign and I give him double thumbs up in return. He shakes his head slowly and takes my hand, fashioning it into the okay sign. Even underwater, his touch makes my skin tingle. I grin and water seeps into my mouth. I expel it quickly and try to stifle my giggles as the rest of my course-mates appear around us. We form a circle on the sand and our lesson begins.

*

'That was good,' Leo says approvingly when we're back on the boat. 'You've picked it up quickly.'

'Thanks,' I reply, his compliment warming me from the inside out.

I was able to adjust my buoyancy much more easily this time. Bridget and Marty seemed to struggle, and I could tell Marty absolutely hated the bit where we had to remove our masks and put them back on again underwater. I didn't like that much, either. I liked the buddy sharing, though – the bit where Leo and I had to practise using each other's air, passing the mouthpiece between us. Bloody hell, I fancy him.

I'm crushed when Bridget and Marty want to go straight back to the hotel to get cleaned up before dinner.

'Just one drink,' I plead.

'Oh, Laura, the salt water is making my skin feel all tight and disgusting,' Marty moans. 'I need a shower,' she adds annoyingly and I could kick her.

'We'll be quick!' I know I'm sounding desperate, but I don't really care.

'Come on, just the one,' Bridget chips in, and I could *kiss* her.

Marty sighs. 'Go on, then.'

Jorge and Leo are already there. Tegan is with them.

'Forecast not looking good for tomorrow,' she comments as she turns around from her position at the bar and hands beers to Jorge and Leo. To my dismay, she pulls up a stool next to Leo. 'Storm coming.'

'What does that mean for us?' I ask, halting in front of them instead of going straight to the bar. It's my round.

'Call the office in the morning,' Jorge replies. 'We might have to postpone the dive.'

'Postpone it to when?' Bridget asks worriedly.

'Depends on the storm,' Jorge says.

'It will probably last only a day,' Tegan chips in. 'You should be able to continue on Thursday.'

'Good,' Bridget replies. 'We're going to Miami on Friday,' she reminds us.

I don't want to go to Miami. I want to stay here.

'Are you getting the drinks, or what?' Marty nudges me.

'Yeah, yeah. Beer?'

Bridget and Marty nod as I go to stand at the bar, to the left of Tegan.

'We're going to Miami this weekend too, actually,' I hear Jorge say. I glance over my shoulder to see him asking Leo: 'You are coming, aren't you?'

Leo shrugs. 'Haven't decided yet.'

Leo in Miami while I'm in Miami? Maybe Friday won't be the last time I see him. My heart is on its own emotional roller coaster: up and down, up and down.

'What can I get you?'

I look up to see the barman speaking to me.

'Three beers, please.'

'My sister's son is coming back from his travels,' I hear Jorge telling Marty and Bridget. 'We're collecting him from the airport. At least, *I* am. I'll check on my apartment and pick up my post while I'm there.'

'Where has he been?' I ask Jorge, paying the bartender and taking the drinks back to my friends.

'South America. Cuba, too, but don't tell the authorities.'

I read somewhere recently that since the Cold War, US citizens have been forbidden to travel to Cuba without a special licence.

'Cuba?' I ask with interest, my eyes flitting between Jorge and Leo. 'Do you have any family there?'

'Going *way* back,' Jorge replies with a grin. 'My grandparents were Cuban. Leo's father was, too.' He glances at Leo, but Leo doesn't react.

'What shall we do in Miami, then?' Marty asks. 'Any good recommendations?'

Jorge said Leo's father *was* Cuban. Past tense. Does that mean he's dead? It's not a question I feel comfortable asking.

Later, Marty, Bridget and I find ourselves on our balcony with a bottle of vodka and a couple of cartons of cranberry which we picked up from a nearby off-licence after dinner. We decided to head back here rather than hit another bar. The wind has picked up and we can definitely sense a storm is coming. To my disappointment, it looks like Tegan was right about the dive being postponed.

'That is so rubbish about tomorrow's dive,' I say. I'm squeezed next to Bridget on the swinging seat. Marty is on one of the two wrought-iron chairs, with her bare feet resting on the other.

'I think your disappointment is greater than ours,' Marty replies with a knowing look.

Bridget jovially nudges me.

'Okay, I fancy him. So what?' I snap, buoyed by the alcohol.

Bridget bursts out laughing. 'Too right!' She chinks my glass. 'And why shouldn't you?'

Marty's face softens. 'That's hilarious.'

'What is?' I ask, feeling relief more than anything. It's nice to be able to come clean and not have the piss taken out of me.

'I love that you just admitted it,' Marty says warmly.

I scoff and take another gulp of my vodka cranberry. 'It's not like I'm going to do anything about it.'

'You should just shag him and be done with it,' Bridget says.

I splutter and almost spit out my drink. 'I don't think so!'

'I would,' Bridget confesses between giggles.

'Yeah, I know *you* would.' I nod emphatically in the direction of her bedroom inside the apartment. 'You already did,' I add.

'Aw,' she says fondly, thinking of Carl, before asking Marty, 'Did you really not shag Tom?'

'Nope,' Marty replies casually and I can't help liking her more for her response. Marty has never slept around. Neither have I. It's one thing we absolutely have in common.

'How many men have you slept with?' I ask Bridget curiously, unable to stop myself.

'Oh, blimey, I don't know,' she replies.

'You don't know?' My voice sounds a little squeaky.

'She's lost count,' Marty says wryly.

Bridget kicks Marty's foot good-naturedly. 'I haven't lost count. I just haven't counted.' She glances at me. 'I don't know, twenty? Twenty-five? What about you?' she asks before I can react.

'Three,' I reply.

'*Three?*' She giggles. 'You definitely need to shag Leo, then.'

'Stop it!' I slap her thigh.

'So who were the three?' she asks.

'Will, Guy and Matthew,' Marty butts in on my behalf.

'Who's Guy?' Bridget asks. She knows about Will and Matthew.

I sigh. Guy was a mistake. My one mistake. The only reason I know I may be able to find it in my heart to forgive Matthew. Because I've cheated, too. Not on him. On Will. My first love.

71

I confess this to Bridget.

'*Really?*' she asks. I know she wouldn't have pegged me to be the cheating type. 'But you didn't split up over it?' She shakes her head, almost confirming what she already thinks she knows: that we were still together when Will died.

Only she's wrong, of course.

'No. No, this happened years before the accident,' I tell her. 'Guy was someone I worked with. I let my crush get out of control, and Will was away racing a lot at the time.'

'Jeez, you've had a shitty time with men,' she blurts out.

'Oh, stop it.' I wave her away. I'm no angel; I've just divulged that.

'Seriously,' she says, and I hear the anguish in her voice. 'How the hell did you get over his death?'

Marty stays silent, her expression serious as she watches our exchange.

'Matthew,' I reply, my own throat closing up with that one word.

My first boyfriend, Will, was my childhood sweetheart. I was literally the girl next door. We were neighbours in a tiny village in Cambridgeshire and I still remember how his grandfather used to take him go-karting every weekend as a boy. Years later he secured a drive in a Formula One car. But while it was impossible not to be proud of him for his incredible achievements, I could never be happy. The racing scared the hell out of me, and in the end, my fears were justified. I loved him to death. I still loved him when he died, when he was killed in a car racing accident. But he no longer loved me. At least, not like he used to. He called it off with me weeks before the race, told me it was over. It was no great surprise – we had been growing apart for some time. I suspect he was interested in someone else. I'd seen the way he'd looked at this girl who worked for the racing team. Of course I'll never know for sure. And I don't want to know. The thought of one man being unfaithful to me is quite enough, thank you.

In a way, the hardest thing following his death was the fact that no one knew we had split up. We hadn't made that fact public. To my everlasting shame, I had asked Will to keep up appearances until after the race. I worked for a charity at the time, and we'd organised a ball to take place at the British Grand Prix, Will's last ever race. His presence there was paramount to the charity's success, so he did that one last thing for me. And then he died.

I still remember the press plastering images of us together all over the tabloids, how dishonourable I'd felt not telling them the truth as they went on about our love, the fact that we had grown up together and were destined to marry.

We weren't going to get married. It was over. We'd split up. But oh, how they went on. I didn't think they'd ever let it lie.

'What were his last words to you?' they'd ask me. 'Did he tell you he loved you, like in the song?'

That damn song. 'Tell Laura I Love Her'. It may have hit the charts decades ago, but it haunted me. The song relays the story of a racing driver who tells his girlfriend – named Laura – that he loves her before he dies in a car racing accident. Uncanny, huh? Yep, the press thought so, too.

I probably added some fuel to their fire when I set up a charity in Will's name: Trust for Children. I still head it up. Guilt pricks me now as I think of my assistant, Becky, having to handle things on her own. But she'll be okay. She's a great assistant. She was shocked when I revealed my current situation.

Luckily the tabloids pretty much leave me alone these days, otherwise I'd have the humiliation of most of Britain knowing about Matthew.

Okay, so yes, I've had a shit time with men.

I swallow the lump in my throat. 'Matthew helped me get over Will,' I tell Bridget, who has remained silent and contemplative for a change. Then I confide in her the truth: that Will and I had split up before he died.

'No way?' She's stunned. 'Why?'

I tell her about how we'd grown apart, and about the girl, the one who worked in hospitality for the team.

'Do you know for sure that he cheated on you?' she asks with a furrowed brow.

'No, and I don't want to. If he did, he did. But it's done now.'

'Did you ever want to ask her?'

'No. I had my chance, once. I bumped into her after Will's death. But I couldn't. I couldn't bring myself to ask her. Anyway, she moved on and so did I. She's seeing another racing driver now. Will's ex-teammate. At least I think they're still together. Are they?' I ask Marty. She watches Formula One.

'Yes,' she replies a touch edgily. 'I think they've just got engaged, actually.'

'Good for her,' I say to Marty's everlasting surprise. She can't understand my 'generosity of spirit', as she calls it. I liked the girl the few times I met her, despite my concerns about Will's feelings. And if she did love Will, then she lost him, too. I guess she found someone to help her heal, like I did.

74

The Longest Holiday

I met Matthew only months after Will's death. He's a journalist, but I never felt as though I couldn't trust him. He was writing a story about my charity work and my attraction to him was immediate. I could tell the feeling was mutual, but oh, the guilt. Even though Will had possibly cheated on me before ending our relationship, I couldn't bring myself to start over with anyone else. But Matthew and I became friends, and when our friendship developed I fell head over heels. I couldn't stop myself. His proposal came quickly. And even though my parents thought I'd lost my head, I said yes. Why not? I deserved a second chance at love.

I let out a bitter laugh. 'What a fuckwit.'

'Who?' Bridget asks, taken aback by the acrimonious tone that has crept into my voice.

'Matthew. But Will was a bastard, too, in the end.' I sigh. 'Can we change the subject? What were we talking about before we got onto my disastrous love life?'

'We were talking about Leo,' Marty reminds me with a twinkle in her eye.

'Move on!' I practically shout. 'No, how many people have we slept with, that was it.'

'Aah, yes,' Bridget says, remembering. 'What about you, Marty?'

'Jack, Ben, Keith, Simon and ... Pablo.' I crack up laughing as I say this last name.

'Who's Pablo?' Bridget asks with confusion. I only laugh more.

'Piss off,' Marty says with a grin, kicking my foot this time.

'Pablo was her one true love,' I tell Bridget as I try to stifle my giggles. Marty mutters and shakes her head, but I know she doesn't mind me taking the mickey.

'She met him in Ibiza, when we were eighteen. At the end of the holiday she didn't want to come home again.' I grin. 'We've all been there, right? Except Marty *didn't* come home.'

'Really?' Bridget looks surprised.

'I still remember your dad's face!' I say, hooting loudly. I've definitely had a few too many vodkas. My hysteria is infectious.

It wasn't funny at the time, me turning up at the airport, *sans* Marty. He went absolutely ballistic. It took me *months* to forgive her for sending me home alone, even though she followed only a few weeks after me, in the end. With her tail between her legs. Turns out Pablo wasn't The One, after all.

'Oh, I wish I'd been there,' Bridget manages to spit out, as tears trail down her cheeks.

The memory comes back to me of Marty's dad's stunned face as he stands next to my dad at the airport. Then, in my mind, he transforms into Matthew. Imagine how Matthew would feel if *I* didn't come home? The thought is tremendously appealing.

Chapter 10

Today the flags look like they're trying to get away from their masts, like overeager puppies on leashes being restrained by their masters. The rain has stopped pelting down for a moment, so we decide to brave the weather and go out for breakfast.

At the weekend we discovered a place called Blue Heaven, a restaurant with two indoor spaces and a large outdoor area and bar. We didn't bother with food because the queue was enormous, but we sat and had a few cocktails, trying to avoid the deposits from the cockerel perching precariously on a branch over our heads.

We're hoping it will be less busy today, with the bad weather and it being a Wednesday, but it's still full to capacity, so we wait by the outdoor bar for our names to be called.

This place is the very definition of eclectic. I look around at the murals and battered blue, yellow and grey weatherboarding. A man on a small stage plays a leopard-print guitar and his harmonica, while surrounded by statues of angels and mermaids. Vines hang down from the big old trees shading the tables – not that we need shade today – and the sandy ground is dotted with broken-up bits of tiles and bricks. A family of chickens wanders freely around the yard. Despite the weather, practically everyone here is wearing beach dresses or Bermuda shorts. I notice a skinny, leathery brown woman in a short fluorescent-pink dress with a palm tree tattooed on her ankle. Anything goes. I smile to myself and glance past her to see Leo sitting at a table on his own, drinking a coffee and reading a newspaper.

'It's Leo!' I gasp in Marty and Bridget's general direction as they stand by the bar. 'I'm going to go and say hi.' I don't wait for them to answer.

Wet sand seeps into my flip-flops and I try to kick it out as I make my way between the stone tables and wrought-iron chairs to talk to him. I'm almost at his table before he looks up.

'Hello!' I exclaim, barely able to contain my delight. Not very cool of me.

His eyes widen briefly with surprise. 'Hello,' he replies.

'What are you doing here?' *So* not cool. He's drinking a coffee – dur!

He lifts up his cup in response.

'But of course I can see that. Silly me.' Without thinking, I pull up a chair and sit down. 'Bummer about the dive today.' I lean forward and put my arms on the table. He's slouched right back in his chair, his elbow resting on the armrest. The saying, 'He's so laid back he could be in a coma,' comes to me.

'Yes.'

'Have you got the day off?'

'Yeah.'

A man of so few words. But I'm not giving up.

'What have you got planned?'

He shrugs. 'Nothing.'

'We were thinking about going on one of those little conch train tours.'

Out of the blue, he throws his head back and laughs loudly.

'What's so funny?' I pretend to be offended, but I'm grinning, too.

'The thought of you three jiggling around Key West on one of those things . . .' The corners of his eyes crinkle up very attractively when he smiles.

'Bridget and Marty would rather visit Ernest Hemingway's house,' I confide with a shrug.

'Don't you want to do that? He has a lot of cats,' he adds with a trace of irony.

'Not fond of cats.'

'Really?'

'No. Prefer dogs.'

'Me, too.'

Aw. 'Anyway, I'd rather learn some of the history about this place.'

'I can tell you that.'

The mini gymnasts living inside my stomach start to cartwheel. 'Can you?'

'Yeah, sure.' He brushes me off. 'Send them off to Hemingway's. Are you having breakfast?'

I was planning on it, but I won't if it means him leaving without me . . .

'Um, depends.'

'Laura! Table's ready!' Marty calls.

'Do you want to join us?' I ask him quickly.

'No, you go ahead. I'll wait for you.'

'Are you sure?'

'Absolutely.' He grins and looks away from me as he takes a sip of his coffee. I get up and walk towards a smirking Marty with a great big smile on my face.

'You are NOT!' she cries under her breath when I tell her about the change of plan.

'So we're not doing the conch tour?' Bridget asks, to be sure.

'No, you guys can go to Hemingway's,' I say flippantly.

'Maybe we'll join you on *your* tour,' Marty teases.

'No, he wants me all to himself,' I joke, but, actually, he did say to send Bridget and Marty off to Hemingway's, so maybe it's not so far from the truth.

I can barely concentrate during breakfast. Marty orders the Lobster Benedict, Bridget chooses pancakes with maple syrup, and I opt for a fruit platter with banana bread, but I pick at it.

'Go on, then,' Marty says finally when she's had enough of me fidgeting. 'We'll settle the bill.'

'Are you sure?' I ask hopefully.

'Absolutely.'

'Have fun,' Bridget says with a wink as I scrape my chair out from the table in my hurry to leave.

'Thank you!'

I hear them discussing me before I'm even out of the room. I hurry outside and back around the corner, hoping Leo is still there. He is!

'That was quick,' he says, downing the last of his coffee. He stands up.

'I wasn't that hungry,' I tell him.

'You should eat more.' He nods towards the exit so I lead the way out. What does he mean by that? Am I too skinny for him?

'I've lost a bit of weight recently,' I feel compelled to confess as we step out onto the street.

'Why?' His brow furrows as his hand waves me in the right direction.

'Oh, you don't want to know about all that.'

He says nothing, tucking his newspaper under his arm and shoving his hands into the pockets of his shorts.

'So how long are you in Key West?' I ask, trying not to feel hurt about his disinterest as we set off. Yes, I know I asked him *not* to show any interest, but *still* . . .

'For the next couple of months. Until the summer season is over.'

'What do you do in Miami?'

'This and that.'

'What sort of this and that?' I probe.

'Working in bars, cigar factories . . . Nothing very interesting.'

'It must be interesting working in a cigar factory?'

'No. It isn't.'

Matthew is a journalist, working for a respectable newspaper. Just as with Will, I've always felt proud of his drive and achievements, although at least with Matthew I never have to fear for his life.

'Have you noticed the houses here pretty much all have tin roofs?' Leo breaks into my thoughts.

'Oh, er . . .' I look around, but of course he's right. 'Yes?'

'Fire prevention. Key West has been almost razed to the ground in the past, the wind carrying the fire from rooftop to rooftop. Now tin roofs are mandatory because they don't catch alight.'

'Cool,' I comment.

'See the woodwork?'

He points up at the porch belonging to a colonial house. The wooden decoration hanging from the eaves is intricately carved like lace. It's very pretty.

'It's called gingerbread,' Leo explains. 'There's a lot of it here in Key West. Hand-carved by master carpenters and ship-builders. I've seen some in the shape of geckos, flowers, violins, palm leaves ... One house even has it in the shape of gingerbread.'

I smile at him with delight and he smiles back at me. 'I'll have to keep my eyes open for that one.' We keep walking. 'How do you know so much about the history here?'

'I used to work on the conch trains when I was a teenager.'

'You didn't!'

'I did.'

'And there's you taking the mickey about us going on the tour!' I whack him on his arm.

'Ouch.' He shakes his arm.

'That didn't hurt,' I chide, as a man dressed like Elvis rides past us on a scooter. 'He looked like he was taking himself seriously,' I say and Leo smirks. 'So where are you taking me?' I ask.

'Southernmost Point. Have you been there yet?' he replies.

'No. Keep meaning to go.'

'Did you know we're closer to Havana than mainland Florida?'

'Is that right? Nuts.' I want to ask him about his parents, but I settle on a more comfortable subject. 'Do you think you will go to Miami this weekend?' I ask hopefully as we continue to stroll.

'Nah. It doesn't take two people to collect my nephew.'

I'm despondent, but then I realise what he's said. 'Your nephew? I thought it was Jorge's nephew?'

'It is. He's both.'

'You and Jorge are brothers?' Eh?

'No.' He chuckles. 'Jorge's sister Carmen was married to my brother.'

'Oh! Where's your brother, then?' The man's name comes back to me from the other night: 'Eric?'

'No.' His response is sharp. But of course Eric and Leo look nothing alike. 'No. Eric is Carmen's boyfriend. Alejandro is dead.'

I falter in my steps and look up at him in shock.

'Oh God. I'm sorry.'

I realise he's also come to a stop on the pavement. I turn to look at the enormous tree he's staring at.

'Have you seen a banyan tree before?' he asks me.

'No,' I admit, feeling slightly out of kilter at his revelation.

The tree in front of me is strange; its roots look like they're dripping from the tree, like candle wax. I notice other, thick, vine-like trunks coming down from the branches, so that the whole front of the tree appears to span three front yards.

'This one is a hundred years old. Every time a root touches the ground, it forms a new trunk.'

'That's amazing.' It is genuinely remarkable.

Suddenly the heavens open.

'I forgot my umbrella!' I cry, as Leo tugs me further under the tree for shelter. The touch of his hand on my arm ... It actually takes my breath away. It's the oddest sensation – I've never had that before with a man.

A mother hen with a dozen chicks scuttles across the road and into the undergrowth.

'Seriously, what's with all the chickens?' I blurt out.

'They were brought here in the mid-nineteenth century for cock fighting and food.'

'Is that right?'

'Now they keep the scorpions in check.'

'Scorpions?' I inadvertently look at the ground, while scrunching up my toes in my flip-flops.

He smiles and looks down at me as another shiver goes through me. I don't think I've ever been this attracted to another human being before. It really is a first-class distraction.

A drop of rain makes its way through the leaves of the banyan tree and lands on my head, making me flinch.

'You never answered my question, by the way,' Leo says casually. 'Why don't you want to go home?'

'Oh.' My heart sinks. 'It's complicated.'

He regards me for a moment as I stand there, quietly contemplating whether or not to tell him, and then his gaze drops to where the fingers of my right hand are unwittingly fidgeting with the ring finger of my left hand. I left my rings at home, as a bitter reminder to Matthew about what he'd done. My finger feels vacant without them.

'Married,' Leo says in low voice, which doesn't belie his surprise. His eyes dart up to meet mine. I don't deny it. He sucks the air in through his teeth.

'Like I said, it's complicated.'

'Why isn't he here with you?' Pause. 'Have you left him?'

'I don't know. Maybe,' I reply. I'm vaguely aware of more raindrops falling through the leaves and running down Leo's slick black hair. My T-shirt is feeling damp. He seems oblivious.

'What did he do?'

'How do you know it wasn't me?'

'It wasn't you,' he says firmly, with odd insight.

My reply comes out in a rush. 'He had sex with another woman a week before he married me. She's seven months pregnant.'

He breathes in sharply. 'Whoa.'

It's the most animated I've seen him.

'Fuck,' he adds.

His response makes me laugh. 'Yeah, you could say that.'

But he doesn't mirror my expression. His eyes have clouded over. He looks away from me, staring into the distance. An uneasy feeling settles over me. 'When did you find out?'

'Two weeks before I came here. Marty persuaded me I needed to get away, have some space, clear my head.'

He nods shrewdly. 'Did he tell you himself?' he asks.

I roll my eyes. 'No. I saw a message on his Facebook page, asking if he was the Matthew Perry who was at a club called Elation on the night of his stag do. She was just some random girl he shagged in the club's toilets.'

My face burns with humiliation as I relay this. He doesn't seem to notice as he ponders what I've said. 'How did she know his surname if she was so random?'

I tut. 'I asked that question, too. They met while dancing to "I'll Be There for You", the theme tune from *Friends*. You know Matthew Perry is also the name of one of the actors? My Matthew joked his nickname was Chandler.' I shake my head, hating the thought of him flirting with the slapper.

He snorts in disgust. 'What are you going to do?' he asks finally.

'I don't know. I don't know if I can ever forgive him. I haven't had enough time to think about all this. At the moment, I never want to see his face again.'

Anger overcomes me, but it's swiftly followed by a deep and aching sadness. To my horror, a lump forms in my throat and out of the blue I want to cry, but there's nowhere to run in this downpour.

He holds my gaze for a long time, and miraculously my tears abate. Right then, I want nothing more than for him to hold me, for him to take me in his arms, for me to press my face into his chest. It's not about the sex, it's about the intimacy, and suddenly I crave that with this man. But his hands stay firmly wedged in his pockets. He looks away from me and I take a shaky breath as I notice that the rain has all but stopped.

'Let's go,' he says, but neither of us speaks for a while as we walk. It takes some time before it even occurs to me to wonder why we're walking back in the direction we've just come.

'Where are we going?' I ask with confusion.

'Hemingway's house is up here.' His pace seems to quicken.

'But I . . .' I didn't want to go to Hemingway's house!

'You should be with your friends,' he mutters. 'And I've got some things I need to do.'

My stomach falls flat and my throat closes up. So that's it. I've scared him away. I can't speak. I'm too shocked and disappointed to utter a single word.

We come to a stop outside a white house with a brick wall around it. It shouldn't be too hard to find Bridget and Marty inside, should I choose to go in. It's more tempting to go back to the hotel and sob my heart out, instead.

'See you tomorrow, yes?' he asks bluntly.

I'm almost too hurt to reply, but I force myself to act blasé.

'If the storm has passed by then.'

'It should do. Storms never last long in Key West.'

I nod curtly. 'Thanks for the tour.'

'You're welcome.' I see something in his expression, but I turn away before I can think any more about it.

Chapter 11

That day I feel like my heart has broken all over again. I don't go to Hemingway's house. I feel too sad to put on a brave face in front of Marty and Bridget. I also feel too humiliated. So I jump in a passing cab and head back to our hotel. All the tears from the last week and a half flood me in one go, and I sit on the sofa and make my way through half a roll of toilet paper.

I can no longer use Leo as a means of taking my mind away from what my husband has done to me. But I'm shocked to realise that I feel more pain when I think about Leo than I do when I think about Matthew. I know this pain isn't real, though. It's just more immediate. I think I'm mourning the loss of my distraction.

I'll be leaving Key West the day after tomorrow. Tomorrow I will have one last dive with Leo. I have a funny feeling that he won't even turn up, and I know it will hit me badly if he doesn't. I don't feel in any way excited about the prospect of a couple of days in Miami, but maybe it's what I need. One last . . . *distraction*.

How am I going to go home again? That slag is having his baby in . . . Her due date is only five and a half weeks away! I start to cry again. Matthew will go to see it. The baby. After the paternity test, of course. I've been clinging onto that one last little bit of hope, that maybe the baby won't be his, after all. Maybe I would be able to forgive him, then. Maybe.

My phone starts to vibrate on the table, making me jump. I pick it up, expecting to see Marty's caller ID, but it's Matthew. My finger hovers across 'divert', but on impulse I answer the call.

'Hello?' I ask in a shaky voice, still heavy with emotion.

'Laura?' The delight in his voice is apparent.

'Hello.'

'How are you?' His words come out in a rush. He clearly didn't expect me to answer.

'Not good,' I say in a small voice.

'Oh, baby, I'm so sorry.' Pause. 'I wish I could hold you.'

I say nothing.

'Laura?' he asks gently.

I take a deep breath. 'What do you want?'

'I want *you*, Laura. I miss you. I'll be there to pick you up from the airport on Monday morning. Is that okay?'

I don't agree, or disagree, but the thought of him now, comforting me in his embrace . . . I want nothing more. What the hell have I been thinking? I'm not going to run from one bastard's arms into another's. I sigh. Matthew's not really a bastard. And neither is Leo. Probably. I guess I'll never know.

'Have you seen her?' I ask him.

'No!' he exclaims. 'Of course I haven't!' He sounds horrified and relief floods me. 'I won't ever see her again if it means you'll forgive me.'

'You can't do that,' I say dismissively. He's being unrealistic. 'What about the baby?'

'I don't know,' he says quietly.

'Well, you can't just not see your child,' I say.

He doesn't comment, but I'm done with this conversation. He's just telling me what I want to hear, but I don't want to hear that. I'm not a complete bitch. It's not the baby's fault, what's happened.

'I've got to go,' I say darkly.

'Please don't!'

'I'll see you on Monday.' My voice is firm and I can hear him breathe a sigh of relief.

'Okay. Okay.'

I hang up without saying goodbye.

Argh! Men!

Still, anger is a much easier emotion to handle than grief, and I feel a whole lot better by the time Marty and Bridget walk through the door.

'How was it?' Marty asks, her eyes lit up with anticipation.

'Oh, it was alright.' I brush her off.

'What happened?' She's confused.

'Nothing,' I reply. 'Saw a few bits and pieces and came back here.' I feel too stung to tell her the whole truth.

'Oh.' She shoots a look at Bridget, which I choose to ignore.

'Is it happy hour yet?' I ask.

'Not even close.'

'In that case, I might go for a swim.'

'In this weather?' Bridget asks with surprise.

'May as well.'

If I have the pool to myself, all the better.

I try not to let my nerves get to me the next day, when we wake up to blue skies and calm winds. Day Three of our course is upon us, and we're going for our final Open Water dives.

I'm resolute as I get ready. I will not let him see that he's got to me. He hasn't. He's just some bloke, and I'm married. I'm going back to work things out with my husband in three days, and I'm going to enjoy the last bit of time that I have away from everything going on at home. I pause in my actions for a moment, realising that I just said I'm going back to work things out ... Am I? Maybe. Anything's possible. I'll see how I feel when I get home, but it's certainly becoming clearer that that's where I need to be, away from all this nonsense.

He's not here. His battered white hatchback is not in the car park when we arrive. I still have that funny feeling that he's not going to come, and the disappointment is hitting me so hard it's painful. Stop it, Laura!

I'm furious with myself, but I can't stop feeling nervous as we get kitted out for the dive.

I see Tegan on the boat as Jorge leads the way. And then Leo steps out from the cabin and my heart flips over and over and over, and I wish I could stop it but I can't. I could kick myself for being so happy to see him. What is *wrong* with me?

His dark eyes bore into mine and he nods brusquely. I quickly avert my gaze and step onto the boat.

I sit at the back, near the platform. Marty and Bridget chat amiably to Jorge and the others, but I watch the receding shoreline without talking to anyone. When we finally moor up, I set about quickly getting ready, keeping my back to the front of the boat so I can't see him approaching. I sense him behind me before he speaks.

'BCD?' he asks, and we set about making our buddy checks, but I don't meet his eyes.

Leo's fingers seem to linger on my waist when he checks my weight belt, and it makes my pulse quicken, but I make the same checks on him succinctly and perfunctorily, feeling his gaze on me as I continue to avoid eye contact.

'All set,' he says eventually.

'Yep,' I reply bluntly. I take my fins to the platform and slip them on there. I'm buggered if I'm going to walk backwards like a dickhead when he doesn't. I pull on my mask and he does one final check, flashing me the okay sign. I don't return it.

'Big step,' he says, and I raise one eyebrow at him, seeing the amusement in his eyes, before doing just that.

Once again, the life underwater takes my breath away. Tiny yellow fish dart around coral, swaying in the current. A shoal of black and white stripy fish passes by as we sink to the bottom. I kneel on the sand next to Leo, but don't look at him. Then his hand is on mine. I look as sharply as I can under the circumstances, but he's flashing me the okay sign. I feel anything but, although I return the gesture, and then Marty and Bridget have joined us.

Jorge leads us in a group across the coral, and once more I find it quite easy to adjust my buoyancy. Down here I feel weightless – literally and metaphorically. I feel better with every kick of my fins as we glide through the brilliant blue water.

Leo and I are behind the others when I see the reef shark. I know it's highly unlikely to hurt me if unprovoked, but I still tense with fright and grapple for Leo's arm. He looks around quickly and follows my gaze, before taking my hand in his. It instantly calms me, but that feeling is swiftly followed by jitteriness. He doesn't let go of my hand as we watch the shark dart around the nearby coral before swimming off into the blue. He's still holding my hand and by now my heart is beating so loudly

I'm surprised the fish aren't frightened by it. He lets go only when the others come to a stop up ahead. I'm glad he can't see my blush underwater.

Back on board, I can barely look at him, and for all the wrong reasons.

'Good dive,' he says quietly as he strips off beside me.

'Yeah.'

Tegan calls him away to help her with something and I slump onto the bench as the weight slowly but steadily returns to my shoulders.

We go for a quick drink at the Tiki Bar. Marty and Bridget are in high spirits at completing their course. Now we can go diving anywhere in the world, and I should be happy like them, but I just feel dead inside. They sit at a table with Ted and Monica and I go to the bar to order our drinks.

'What time do you leave tomorrow?' I freeze as I realise Leo has joined me at the bar.

'Eleven-ish,' I reply with a sideways glance at him. He nods and looks up as the bartender materialises in front of us. I give him my order, then turn to Leo. 'What are you and Jorge having?'

'I'll get these,' he says.

'Don't be silly, it's the least I can do . . . for my buddy,' I add in a slightly silly voice.

He smirks and glances at the bartender. 'Two beers.'

'Could have guessed that.' I smile at him and suddenly feel awkward.

'Are you feeling any better about going home?' I realise he looks as uncomfortable as I must do.

'No,' I say with a half-hearted shrug. I can't think of anything better to say and then the bartender returns with our drinks, so that's the extent of our conversation.

'Come on, then.' Marty slaps my knee half an hour later.

That means we're going. I've barely spoken since sitting down. It's like Leo and I have been in a competition to see who can say the least.

'Good luck, girls! Have a great time in Miami,' Jorge says warmly.

'You, too,' Marty responds. 'Maybe see you there!'

'I doubt it. It's a big city,' he replies cheerfully.

'Thanks so much for everything. You're a great instructor,' Bridget says to him.

'You're welcome.' He grins. 'Keep diving!'

'Yeah, thanks,' Marty adds.

If I could feel any less alive I would surely turn into a zombie.

'Bye,' I say to Leo.

'Bye.' He offers me a brusque smile, but it doesn't meet his eyes.

'See ya later!' Bridget calls as she and Marty start to wander away to the car, but I can't tear myself away yet.

'Thanks again for all your help,' I tell Leo.

'You didn't need it,' he says.

'Leo!' We turn to see Tegan beckoning to him from the office.

He stands up, so we walk together across the road towards the office and the car park. But I can't think of anything at all to say, and neither, it seems, can he.

'See you, then,' I say when I reach the point where I have to tail off.

'Bye,' he responds, heading into the office with his head down.

I feel so flat. That felt wrong. Surely that won't be the last time I see him? Maybe I can pop by in the morning. I hold onto this thought to try to ease my pain.

We go out for one last night in Duval Street before returning to the balcony for a nightcap. Bridget and Marty call it a night, but I tell them I'll stay here for a little longer. I've got too much on my mind, and I'm not ready to say goodnight to Key West yet. I can hear the low hum of traffic passing by on the street below, and the leaves on the Spanish laurel tree in front of the balcony are rustling in the breeze. Latin music makes its way to my ears. On autopilot I get up and walk to the far end of the balcony. Leo's garden is lit with fairy lights, and I don't care if it's a bad idea or not but I'm going to say goodbye.

I hurry down the steps before I can change my mind.

My spirits deflate when I peer through the palm tree near the street to see Carmen and Eric sitting on the sofa, but thankfully Jorge and Leo are in the armchairs. I'm damned if I'm going to let Carmen put me off what I set out to do.

Four sets of eyes stare at me as they hear the gate latch.

'It's just me,' I say, lifting my hand in a half wave as I close the gate behind me. Leo and Jorge seem surprised, thankfully not unpleasantly so. I try not to look at Carmen or Eric.

I halt in my steps as the dog starts to run towards me, barking. Damn. Forgot about him. I hope he doesn't bite me.

'Max, enough!' Eric shouts, but Leo is on his feet and jogging over to me. I freeze as Max crouches and growls at my feet. Leo tugs him away with a few sharp words. The dog runs off with his tail between his legs.

I glance up to see Leo giving me a guarded look. He's wondering what I'm doing here.

'Sorry, I couldn't sleep. I didn't really get to say goodbye before,' I tell him quickly.

He nods his head towards the house and I follow him.

'Hey, Laura,' Jorge says as we pass the chairs. He looks relaxed, like he's been drinking for a while.

'Hi,' I respond, adding, 'Hello,' out of politeness to Carmen and Eric. He replies with a lazy, 'Hey,' but she just gives me a hard stare.

'Laura.' Leo's voice sounds from behind me. He motions for me to follow him into the house. I would so rather be inside with him than out here with her, so it's a relief to go with him.

'Ignore Carmen,' he tells me roughly as he leads me into the kitchen. 'You want a beer?'

I look up at him. I think he's had a few, like Jorge. 'Sure.'

He grabs two bottles from the fridge, cracking them open and passing over one.

'Thanks.'

He takes a swig, leaning back against the counter and staring at me. He's wearing a navy-blue T-shirt and well-worn denim jeans, and looks sexy as hell. I tear my eyes away to study the kitchen. It doesn't look like it's been touched since the seventies: yellow and grey lino on the floor, pale orange cupboards with melamine peeling off them. Dishes are stacked in the sink, and the counters are covered, too. It's a mess. I meet Leo's eyes and I think something akin to embarrassment passes through them before he puts his guard back up.

'Come through.' He leads me into the living room. It's still a mess, with old battered sofas and armchairs, and a huge box-shaped

TV that looks like it left a factory in the eighties and surely can't still be functioning. I take in a few more details, like the picture frames hanging on the browned walls and the antique chests of drawers and matching wardrobe. The odd thought comes to me that someone used to love this place, but it's been unloved for far too long.

'Whose house is this?' I find myself asking.

Leo glances at me sharply. For a moment he seems a little bit lost. He collapses onto one of the armchairs.

'It's complicated.' I'm familiar with this answer – I used it on him only yesterday – but it's not one I was expecting.

I sit down on the sofa and tuck my knees up. He shifts awkwardly and looks out through the door. I follow his gaze, but there's no one there and I can hear the others outside on the chairs.

'This was my mother's house,' he says quietly. 'I grew up here.'

'Where is . . .'

'She passed away a long time ago.' He glances down at his hands, then takes a swig of his beer. He runs his hand through his black hair and rests his elbow on one of the armrests.

I try to prompt him. 'But now Carmen and Eric live here?'

He half rolls his eyes and leans forward to plonk his beer down on the stain-spotted coffee table. 'Yes, they do.'

Bloody hell, he wasn't joking when he said it was complicated. 'Spit it out.'

He laughs. 'Oh, Laura. I hate talking about this.'

Warmth floods me at the familiarity of the way he just addressed me. 'I didn't want to tell you about my crap, either,' I shrewdly remind him. 'But I did.'

He holds my stare. 'Yes, you did.' He sighs. 'When my mother died, she left this house to me. My brother Alejandro was very angry.' He says Alejandro with a Spanish accent, and it's sexy as hell. 'He was my older brother.'

'Sorry, how old are you?' I interrupt.

'Thirty-three,' he replies. Four years older than me. I nod for him to continue. 'In the end, I went to Miami, and Alejandro, Carmen and Javier came to live here. Javier is my nephew.' He gives me a knowing look, and I gather he's speaking about the same nephew Jorge is collecting from the airport this weekend. 'Alejandro died eight years ago.'

'I'm so sorry.' I regard him with compassion, knowing as I do now that his parents are also dead. 'Was he your only sibling?'

'Yes. But Jorge is like a brother to me.'

We smile at each other. 'I can see that.' The two uncles . . . 'So if Alejandro is no longer around, and Carmen has moved on with Eric, why don't you ask for your house back?'

'Like I say, it's complicated.' He stares at me directly and it makes me feel shivery again.

I try not to stutter when I speak. 'Javier . . . You let them stay because of Javier?'

He hesitates and then nods. He still hasn't taken his eyes away from mine.

'But how old is he now?'

'Eighteen, almost nineteen.'

'And he's just been travelling. He's flown the nest.' He shrugs. 'I see what you mean when you say it's complicated.' He finally breaks eye contact when he reaches for his beer. 'Would you like to live here?' I ask him.

He thinks for a moment. 'I don't know. When I come back for the summer, like this, I can see myself living here. But Miami has its draws, too.'

'I'm not sure I'm going to like Miami.'

He raises one eyebrow. 'Really? Why not?'

'It all looks a bit big and scary to me.'

'It's big, but not scary. Not when you get used to it.'

'We've only got two days,' I point out with a smile.

'Just enough time to ride around Miami Beach on a Segway and do the boat tour past the celebrities' houses.' He throws his head back and laughs loudly.

'Bugger off,' I joke, because obviously he's taking the piss. Again.

'Well, well, well, looks like we're missing out on the party.'

I look up to see a clearly unamused Carmen standing at the door. Eric appears behind her, and I can hear Jorge in the kitchen. I think this might be my cue to leave, unfortunately. But she steps past the coffee table and slumps down onto the sofa next to me.

'Laura, right?'

'Yes,' I reply warily, because I don't like the look in her eyes.

'Jorge says you're married.' She says this with a pointed stare at Leo. A bad feeling settles over me.

'Carmen!' I hear Jorge saying sharply from the kitchen.

'I'm going to bed. Night, night,' Eric says dozily from the doorway. No one pays him any attention.

'You should get some sleep, too, Carmen,' Leo says in a low, warning tone. 'You look like you need it.'

'Fuck off, Leonardo,' she snaps, taking me by surprise when she says what is obviously his full name. 'If anyone needs sleep, it's you.' Then her glare turns into a fake smile. 'But I guess you don't plan on getting any tonight,' she says silkily, looking at me. 'Sleep, that is.'

Okay, time to go.

'She's drunk. Ignore her,' Jorge says angrily as he comes into the room and over to her. 'Come on, off to bed, sis.' He grabs her arm and hauls her off the sofa, but I'm on my feet by then, too.

'I should be going anyway,' I say to Leo.

He nods abruptly and slowly gets to his feet. I hear Carmen laughing as Jorge leads her down the corridor. I walk into the kitchen and put my beer on the countertop.

'Thanks for this,' I say, turning around to walk to the door, but coming to an abrupt stop when I discover he's right in front of me. I look up at him with surprise, but he leans past me and puts his own bottle down on the counter. My heart skips a beat as I breathe in his warmth. His neck is so close to me . . .

'I'll walk you back,' he says calmly, seemingly unaware of the butterfly-inducing effect he has on me.

Neither of us says anything as we wander through the unkempt garden to the gate, or on the way around the corner towards the hotel's back entrance. Finally we find ourselves in the uplit garden by the swimming pool. There are goosebumps on my arms, but they're not there from the cold.

I turn around to face him. 'Our apartment is just up the stairs.'

'I hope everything works out for you,' he says quietly, seriously.

'You really won't come to Miami? Show us around?' I plead in a small voice. I don't want this to be the last time I see him.

'I can't.' He shakes his head slightly in the relative darkness.

Can't or won't?

'Where are you staying?' he asks.

'South Beach,' I reply. 'Where do you live?'

'In the Wynwood district,' he tells me. 'Check out the Wynwood Walls if you get the chance. A few of my friends are graffiti artists and they work there.'

99

'Graffiti artists?' I ask with confusion. Isn't graffiti illegal?

'*Professional* graffiti artists,' he explains with a smile. 'The exteriors of the buildings in Wynwood are like one big accessible art gallery. It's pretty cool.'

'Okay, thanks. I'll definitely do what I can to check it out.'

He touches my upper arm lightly, then his fingers trail down my arm and fall into my hand. He gives me a quick squeeze.

'Good luck,' he says, stepping away from me. I grip the tip of his fingers with my own fingertips as his hand slips away from me, trying to hold onto him for a few seconds more. My chest constricts as he walks out of the gate.

Chapter 12

Will Smith blares out of the stereo: '*I'm going to Miami . . .*' and practically everyone on the boat starts to bop along to the music; next to me, Bridget and Marty sing along, too. I see the female tour guide yawn. She looks bored as hell, and I know how she feels. I wonder how many times she's had to listen to this song.

I don't *care* how much Rosie O'Donnell's house sold for. I don't want to know about Gloria Estefan's club-slash-restaurant. I'm *embarrassed* to be sitting here on this boat, passing by the properties of celebrities and millionaires as a tour guide informs us over a loudspeaker how much their homes are worth. I can't believe anyone in their right mind would choose to live in this goldfish bowl. If Leo could see me now, on this frigging boat . . .

I miss him so much.

Oh. My. God. We have just passed a yacht full of bikini-clad girls dancing to music played by the on-board DJ. It's the middle of the day! I can't believe what a cliché this place is.

I've been here only twenty-four hours, but as you can probably tell I'm not much of a fan. I want to like Miami. Bridget and Marty seem to. And it is sort of fascinating.

Everything is so shiny here. Glittery and shiny. Yesterday we drove into the city past mirrored skyscrapers that glowed blindingly white in the sun, before taking the bridge that would lead us to Miami Beach. This is a city built on water, like a giant sky-scraper-ed Venice. Millionaires' yachts populate the harbours and you're never far from the ocean. Even the people are shiny. This morning at breakfast there was a big girl sitting at the table next to us dressed in a sequinned top and a short skirt, as though she was going out clubbing, not eating a plate of pancakes. Another woman was wearing glittery gold moisturising lotion. Most of the handbags and sunglasses I see are designer, glinting gold in the sunlight. I went into a shop and the walls of the changing rooms were covered with tiny spheres of glass, glittering like droplets of water, frozen in time.

I do like the art deco buildings in South Beach. It's impossible not to like them. This morning we hired bright red bicycles and rode along the sidewalk adjacent to the beach. That was sort of fun, even if I did feel like I was riding a shiny tomato. And I couldn't help but smile at the sight of people on the Segways, standing upright like wallies as they whizzed around everywhere on two wheels. No wonder Leo laughed at the thought of me on one.

I can't stop thinking about him. And Key West. I wish I were back there ...

That night we go to the Delano, a white, four-winged art deco tower which, when it was built in the late 1940s, was the tallest building in Miami. Philip Stark designed the recent renovations, and it's stunning. The long back garden runs all the way down to the beach and houses a cool swimming pool and a bar crammed with white sofas. Bridget called ahead earlier and told the concierge that she's writing a travel feature, so we're being well looked after in a roped-off VIP area. The sun is just starting to go down behind the building and the light, if you look at it, is blinding. It's the most relaxed I've been in Miami. This has got to be my favourite place of all. A wily brown bird hops onto the table in front of us.

'Do you want to go to see the Wynwood Walls tomorrow morning?' I ask Bridget and Marty.

'What's that?' Marty asks.

'It's like an outdoor art gallery, apparently – graffiti artists have painted the walls of all the buildings. It sounds amazing. Leo told me about it.'

Marty looks sceptical.

'Well, I really want to do some shopping,' Bridget replies.

Marty looks torn. 'I still haven't checked out Banana Republic.'

'There's a Banana Republic in London!' I exclaim. 'And a Gap, Mac, Guess and everything else.'

She glances at Bridget.

'Make up your mind in the morning,' I say sullenly. I suppose I could go on my own, but I really don't want to.

Later we go clubbing in South Beach. The street comes to life at night: rope lights wind around banisters, plants glitter with fairy lights, candles flicker on tables under interesting designer lampshades, beers come in glasses the size and shape of jugs, colourful cocktails in cups the size of bowls, and neon signs light up the art deco buildings.

We enter a club where a DJ plays music loudly enough to

pierce eardrums and order three mojitos from a bartender with a Spanish accent. The majority of people in Miami speak Spanish. I try to remember what I learned from a module I took at university, but feel ashamed when I come up with nothing.

We polish off our drinks and head onto the dance floor. Music pounds in my head and fills up my chest, consuming me like a giant heartbeat. Imagine if Jorge were here. He's in Miami, but where? Imagine if Leo changed his mind and came with him? Imagine if I saw him here, now? I've had too much to drink, but I allow my imagination to carry me from the dance floor all the way to his bedroom, and I feel hot and shivery. And then I imagine going through life without ever seeing Leo again. The pain is intense! I can't do that. There's no way I can live with that. Maybe I could ring the dive resort and ask for his contact details. We could keep in touch – and if things don't work out for Matthew and me . . .

Stop! I may as well cheat on him while I'm at it! That would make me just as bad as Matthew. No, I know I have to let Leo go.

A lump swells in my throat and I fight the freakishly strong urge to burst into tears. I flash Marty a look and head off the dance floor. She quickly follows me, with Bridget in close pursuit.

'Are you okay?' she asks.

'What's wrong?' Bridget looks concerned as she reaches us.

'What do you think Matthew would do if I didn't go home?' I blurt out.

Marty gives me a sharp look. 'We are talking theoretically, aren't we?'

'I . . . I . . . Yes,' I reply warily.

'He'd be absolutely devastated,' Marty barks.

'He'd deserve it,' Bridget adds flippantly and Marty gives her a warning look. 'What? It's true,' she says defensively. 'I wouldn't go back to any man who did that to me.'

'Bridget!' Marty exclaims.

'I wouldn't!' she exclaims back. 'Fuck him! And on that note, fuck Leo! Literally.'

'What?' I misunderstand her. Leo hasn't done anything awful to me.

'You should have shagged him,' she says, shaking her head at me with regret, and my face heats up.

'Bridget!' Marty exclaims once again, with outrage.

'What? She should have! She would have felt a whole lot better about what Matthew did, if she had.'

'That is just not true,' Marty says firmly. 'She would have felt just as shit about Matthew and then would have had to add guilt to the mixture. You don't know what the hell you're talking about.'

Bridget looks at me. 'You wish you'd shagged him, don't you?'

Marty regards me with shocked horror.

'I think I've had too much to drink,' I say, trying to brush them off. 'I'm feeling all emotional.'

Marty's expression changes to one of dismay. 'Have I messed up, asking you to come on this holiday with us?'

'No!' I cry.

'It's just that . . . I don't know, you seem even more confused now than when we left.'

'I just don't feel like I've had enough time, to be honest.'

'She still wants to shag Leo,' Bridget chips in.

'Shut up!' Marty snaps at her. Bridget shrugs, unfazed. 'I don't know, Laura,' Marty says. 'Maybe you can come back—'

'Maybe I just shouldn't go home,' I interrupt.

'We're not eighteen anymore,' Marty says.

Bridget laughs sardonically and Marty glares at her.

'I'm sorry, but I'm with Laura on this,' Bridget says, and I like her more in that moment than I ever have.

'I'm with Laura, too,' Marty says in a tone that is bordering on angry. 'I want the best for her, I always have.'

'I know,' I say, putting my hand on her arm. 'Look, I think I should go back to the hotel and get some sleep. Do you mind?'

'Of course not,' Marty mutters. She turns to lead the way out, but I freeze when I see a curly-haired man near the bar. Bridget bumps into me.

'Sorry!' she says, then follows my gaze as I stare at the man. 'It's not Jorge,' she says gently in my ear. A moment later the man turns to the side and I can see that she was right. And then her arm is around my shoulders and she hugs me tightly. 'Whatever you do, you have my support,' she says fervently. 'But I wouldn't go back to that bastard if he was the last man on earth.'

Chapter 13

As we drive away from the glittering city of Miami towards the airport, the roads become wider and the cars faster. We pass one McDonald's after another, zoom past vast soulless-looking shopping centres, and multiple 7-Eleven grocery stores and Walmarts. I feel like I'm living in an American TV show – everything is different, yet familiar. Overhead, planes fly through the blue, blue sky and I pray that ours will be delayed so I don't have to face going home yet.

I'm in a daze as we check in our luggage. There's a knot of anxiety in my stomach and the feeling of freedom I've had periodically in the last couple of weeks has well and truly vanished.

'It's going to be okay,' Marty tells me as we step into the queue to go through security, but I can't respond to her. Bridget squeezes my arm and gives me a sympathetic look. I feel half dead as we shuffle forward.

My mobile phone starts to buzz from inside my bag and I pull it out. It's Matthew calling me, I see with a frown. I press answer.

'Hello?'

'Laura, it's me.' He sounds breathless, worried. 'Can you talk?'

'I'm about to go through security.'

'It's—' I hear him take a deep breath.

'Hang on,' I interrupt him, turning to Bridget and Marty. 'I'm going to take this call,' I tell them, nodding back towards the airport terminal. 'I'll see you through there.'

'We'll wait for you,' Marty says, pausing in the queue.

'No, no, it's okay.' I brush her off. 'Go and get us a seat at the bar or something.'

'Okay.' She nods, but looks concerned.

I excuse myself as I duck back through the people in the queue and come out into the open space of the terminal.

'Tell me what's wrong,' I say to Matthew as the knot inside my stomach tightens.

'Tessa . . .' He's obviously finding it difficult to spit it out, but I hate hearing him say her name. My footsteps freeze at the sound of his next words. 'She's had the baby.'

'What?'

'She's had the baby,' he repeats.

But she's, what? Five weeks early?

'Is it okay?' I ask in a small voice, and although I'm ashamed to admit it, part of me hopes the answer is no.

'He's in an incubator, but he should be fine.'

He? 'It's a boy?' I ask as my throat starts to close up.

Another deep breath. 'Yes.'

I don't recognise this man on the other end of the line. What did I just hear in his tone? Was it pride? Love? I cannot cope with this.

'And Laura,' he says, his voice on the verge of breaking. 'He's had the paternity test.'

I hold my breath.

'He's mine.'

My world shatters around me. What tiny piece of hope I had left is gone. My knees threaten to buckle under me and it takes enormous effort to keep standing.

'Baby, please,' Matthew says.

White-hot fury rushes through me at his words.

'I'm. NOT. Your. Baby.'

There's so much venom in my voice as I spit these words out. No, I am not his baby. He has a baby of his very own and I hate his guts for it.

'Fuck you, Matthew. Fuck you.'

I hang up on him, and as I stare at my mobile my hands are shaking. This is real. This is really happening to me. I hate him. I hate my husband. I don't want to ever see his face again. Why am I stepping onto a plane? I don't actually have to do this.

I say this sentence again inside my head: I don't actually have to do this.

I could stay. I don't have to go home. I think of Becky, my assistant, and feel guilty, but I quash the thought. She'll be okay. She can handle things for a bit longer. A weird calm begins to settle over me.

I look out of the huge windows at the blue sky beyond. What would I do?

Come on, I know exactly what I'd do. I'd go back to Key West.

I think of Leo's surprise at seeing me again. Then his surprise changes to alarm. Would he consider me delusional if I appeared on his doorstep? I shake my head vigorously at this unwelcome image before thinking: forget Leo! Even if he thinks I'm a

nutcase, the fact still remains that I don't want to go home. I'm
not ready to face everything. The feeling of calm grows stronger.

Acting on impulse, I turn and walk out of the airport, and the
blissful feeling that hits me as I step into the warm sunshine
almost takes my breath away. I think I might be losing my head,
but I don't care. I'm not going home. I am NOT going home. I
look around for car hire signs.

'*Laura?*'

The smile is on my face before I even turn around. This must
be fate. I spin on my heels and come face to face with Jorge. He's
standing alongside a younger man – Javier, at a guess.

'Is everything alright?' he asks me with a perplexed expression.

'I'm not going home, Jorge,' I tell him in a slightly breathless
voice, my grin stretching my face.

'What do you mean?'

'I'm not going home. I'm going back to Key West.'

His expression turns wary. Yep, he thinks I've lost it, and he's
probably right. I don't care!

'Are you okay?'

'No, I'm not okay!' I say in an oddly jubilant voice. 'The
woman my husband had a one-night stand with has just given
birth to a baby boy! Hurray for them!'

Jorge's expression becomes dark, and I try to ignore the
freaked-out stare coming from Javier.

'Hi, I'm Laura,' I say to him brightly, offering my hand. He
takes it hesitantly.

'Sorry, did you know about any of this?' I ask Jorge apologetically, feeling even more detached from my body as I continue to
warble on.

'Leo mentioned it,' he tells me.

The sound of his name – the confirmation that he is real and actually exists beyond my imagination ... It does something strange to me. I take a deep, shaky breath and try not to cry.

'Come on,' Jorge says quietly, putting his hand on my arm. I do as I'm told. 'This is Javier,' he says as we walk. The boy continues to regard me with bewilderment.

'I've heard a bit about you,' I say.

'Laura and Leo are friends,' he tells Javier, and his words make my insides melt. Leo ... Leo ... Leo ... The thought of him consumes me.

A moment later I think to ask where we're going.

'To my car,' Jorge replies. 'You want a ride back to Key West?'

Panic momentarily engulfs me. Am I really, really doing this?

'Are you okay?' he asks with concern.

'Yes, yes,' I reply fervently. 'Where's your car?'

'Over here.'

We reach the car, a blue hatchback, and Javier puts his suitcase in the boot.

More panic hits me. I don't even have my bag! I see Jorge realise this at the same time.

'They'll courier it to you,' he assures me. 'They won't leave it on the plane if you're not on it.'

Javier returns to the car and hesitates, as though he's not sure whether to get into the front or back.

'I'll go in the back,' I tell him, my heart pounding as I climb in.

Jorge reverses out of the space. 'How were Marty and Bridget about you staying?'

I barely hear the second half of his sentence, because the moment he says Marty I jolt out of my seat. Oh my God, Marty! My heart starts to pound more violently.

111

'They don't know you're not going home?' Jorge asks incredulously over his shoulder as he stops in the middle of the car park.

'I'll call Marty in a minute,' I try to assure him. A car beeps from behind us, so he drives forward, but I can tell he's uncomfortable. I pull out my phone and vaguely realise that my hands are still shaking. I have three missed calls from Marty. I dial her number.

'Laura! Where the hell are you? They're calling our flight!' she practically shouts down the phone.

'I'm not going home,' I tell her.

'What?' she screeches.

'I'm not going home.'

'Where are you?' she demands to know. 'I'm coming to get you!'

'I'm in the car with Jorge. He's taking me back to Key West.' I hold my breath in preparation for her onslaught.

'*Are you out of your mind?*'

I screw up my eyes tightly.

'*What the hell are you doing?*'

It keeps coming.

'*Jesus Christ, Laura!*'

And coming . . .

'*Get your arse back here, RIGHT NOW!*'

'No,' I say firmly. 'No. I'm not coming back.'

'We're going to miss our flight!' she continues to screech.

'You're not going to miss your flight,' I tell her in a surprisingly calm voice. 'You're going to get on it, with Bridget. But I am NOT coming home, Marty. I am not coming back to that bastard of a husband. She's had the baby, Marty. She's had a baby boy. And it's Matthew's. So that's it. I am not ready to come back. Not yet. No way.'

I barely even paused for breath while saying that, and now the silence on the other end of the line is deafening.

'Jesus Christ, Laura,' she says again. But at least she's stopped shouting. Now she just sounds stunned. 'I don't know what to do,' she adds in a small voice.

'You don't have to do anything!' I tell her vehemently. 'Get on that plane, go back to your job.' She's due back at work on Tuesday. 'I'm going to be okay.'

'You're in the car with Jorge?' she asks again.

'Yes.'

'Jeez.' This time her words are more of an exhalation. In the background I can hear an announcement over the tannoy. Last call for our flight.

'Go,' I say gently. 'Call me when you're home.'

She sighs loudly.

'We'd better go,' I hear Bridget urge in the background.

'Okay,' she says to me down the line. 'I guess you know what you're doing.'

But it's a lie. That's clear to us both.

Chapter 14

'You can stay with us,' Jorge tells me as we drive into Key West.

I've been asleep for most of the journey. I think my emotional exhaustion has properly kicked in.

'What do you mean?' I ask him with confusion. 'I'll just go back to the hotel. See if they've got a room.'

'You can do that, of course,' he says. 'If you can afford it.'

I haven't really thought about the cost of things. I don't earn mega-bucks.

'But my sister lives in a seven-bedroomed house,' he continues. 'There's more than enough room if you don't mind sharing.'

His sister. Carmen. I shudder.

'She'll be okay,' Jorge says kindly, as he reads my mind. He glances at his nephew and I remember that Carmen is his mother. 'Javier agrees,' Jorge tells me. 'Don't you?'

'Sure. She won't mind,' Javier says.

So naïve!

'Well, okay, thanks,' I say genuinely. 'Just until I get myself sorted and work out what I'm doing.'

114

'You can stay as long as you like,' Jorge tells me, even though I know that it's not really his choice.

I recognise the roads as we enter Old Town, and a flurry of nerves passes through me. I wonder if Leo is at the house. What will he say when he sees me? Once more I imagine alarm on his face and I actually cringe.

Jorge parks the car on the street outside the house and I wait with trepidation as he gets Javier's case out of the boot. I follow them through the gate.

'*Mi vida!*' I hear Carmen shout with joy, completely oblivious to me as she rushes over and throws her arms around her son. Javier looks slightly uncomfortable as he lets himself be swallowed up by her hug, but he's nowhere near as uncomfortable as me. I look around warily for Leo, but he's not in the garden.

'*What the . . .*'

Carmen has noticed me.

'Sis, you remember Laura,' Jorge says calmly.

'What's she doing here?' she asks with angry confusion.

'I'll tell you all about it later,' Jorge says. 'Where's Leo?'

'Out.' Her reply is curt.

'Laura needs to stay with us for a little while.'

Carmen starts to lay into him in Spanish, and I don't know what she's saying, but I certainly understand the underlying meaning and I wish the ground would swallow me up. Leo's name seems to come up quite a lot. Jorge, it seems, gives as good as he gets, and it's only when Javier interrupts them with a loud, 'Shut up!' that they actually stop arguing.

Carmen grabs her son's arm and storms off, and Jorge offers me a small smile and nods towards the house.

'That went better than I thought,' he says.

'You're being sarcastic, right?' I mutter.

'Actually, no,' he says with surprise. 'You can stay in Leo's mother's room.'

Leo's mother's room? Jorge leads me up the stairs. Even though it's run-down, even though it's been unloved for a long time, I can see that this old colonial house was once truly beautiful. The old floorboards were once painted white or cream, but now there are worn tread-marks underneath our feet. The walls are dirty from years of handprints, but the old-fashioned coving over my head hints at its beauty. I run my hand up the intricately carved banister and imagine what it would look like with a fresh coat of paint. Jorge pushes open a door to a bedroom at the far end of the corridor, near a second, smaller, steeper staircase. Dust motes whizz through the air as I survey my surroundings. A double bed rests in the centre of the room on dark wooden bedposts, and there are two chests of drawers, one on either side of it. A silver photo frame perches on the dresser, in front of a mirror tarnished with age. A vase of dried flowers sits on the windowsill. The petals look fragile, as though, if you touched them, they would dissolve into dust in your fingertips.

'It could do with a good clean,' Jorge says apologetically.

'It's perfect,' I say.

'I'll get you some sheets.'

The bed has a dusky-pink bedspread on it. Perhaps it's already made underneath, but he's gone before I can check. I wander into the room and study the picture on the dresser. In it a beautiful young woman with long dark hair cuddles two young boys as they sit on her lap.

'Leo's mother,' Jorge tells me as he re-enters the room.

'Are these Leo and Alejandro?' I point at the boys.

'Yes. Leo told you about Alejandro?' Jorge asks with surprise.

'Not much. Only that he was his brother and that he died eight years ago.'

'Aah, okay.'

What else is there to tell? I have a feeling quite a lot. 'What happened?' I ask Jorge.

'Drug overdose,' he replies and I inhale quickly. 'Leo doesn't often talk about his family,' he advises me. 'There's a bathroom two doors down. Use anything you need, make yourself at home, and come down for a bite to eat when you're ready.'

'Thank you!' I call after him.

I don't know what to do once he's left. I settle for making up the bed with fresh sheets, and fold the bedspread and put it on a chair. I have a look in the wardrobe and drawers; they're empty, but a pleasantly musty smell wafts out, as though, over the years, perfume has ingrained itself into the wood. I wonder what Leo's mother was like.

Finally I pluck up the courage to go downstairs. I hear the clatter of knives and forks coming from a room off the living room. I follow the sound and pause nervously at the doorway. Jorge, Carmen, Eric and Javier are seated around a large eight-seat dining table. There is still no sign of Leo, and I'm strangely relieved not to have to face him yet, even though I won't relax until his reaction is out of the way.

Carmen is asking Javier about his travels. She's more animated and happy than I've ever seen her, but she tenses when she becomes aware of my presence and I sense that she doesn't have many female friends.

'Come in, sit down!' Jorge gestures to me. Javier gives me a

117

small smile, Eric nods his acknowledgement, and Carmen pretends I don't exist.

'Thank you,' I murmur, pulling up a chair next to Jorge.

In the middle of the table is a large platter of rice with chicken pieces. My stomach twinges with hunger.

'*Arroz con pollo?*' Jorge asks me, taking my plate in one hand and a large serving spoon in the other.

'Yes, please. It smells delicious.'

'It's Carmen's speciality,' he tells me as he fills my plate and places it in front of me. I notice Carmen still at this revelation, but she pretends not to be paying attention.

I load up my fork with the colourful rice and a small chunk of chicken and pop it into my mouth. It tastes divine – I can identify spices like cumin and oregano, plus red pepper, garlic and something tangy.

'Mmm,' I say, looking up to see Carmen watching me. She shifts in her seat and looks away, but I smile to myself when I realise she was waiting for my response. 'This is amazing. What's in it?' I ask her directly.

She reels off a list of ingredients, including, to my surprise, beer.

'Beer?' I ask.

'I can give you the recipe if you like,' she says offhandedly.

'I would love that.'

Out of the corner of my eye I see Jorge trying to suppress a smile. Eric dives in for seconds.

'Save some for Leo,' Carmen snaps at him. He begrudgingly spoons some rice from his plate back onto the platter.

I try to act casual. 'When do you think Leo will be back?'

'Who knows with Leonardo?' Carmen replies shirtily. 'He hasn't been around much at all this weekend.'

'Oh?'

'He always goes AWOL on the anniversary of his mother's death,' Jorge explains quietly, and Carmen's sharp look in his direction doesn't go unnoticed.

Jorge's revelation makes me feel uneasy. He goes AWOL? Where? Doing what?

'But he always comes back,' Jorge adds, for my benefit, I think. He can probably see my mind ticking over. 'Shame he refused to come to Miami this weekend. It would have taken his mind off things.'

'Eat before it gets cold,' Carmen interjects. That's enough of the family history for now.

After dinner, I help Carmen clear the table. The kitchen is in even more of a state than it was the other night, the pots and pans she'd used for cooking adding to the mess. I falter in my steps, hardly knowing where to start.

'I've been very busy at work,' she informs me, stopping short of saying 'sorry about the mess'.

'What do you do?' I ask tentatively as I try to clear some space on the countertop.

'Mostly waiting on tables, but I also work in a gift shop during the holiday season.' She piles her plates on top of an already precariously stacked pile. 'What about you?'

'I head up a children's charity in London.'

'Oh.' Even she has the grace to look marginally impressed.

'My colleague is handling things right now,' I add with embarrassment, unable to use the word 'assistant', which is technically correct. God bless Becky. I'll call her tomorrow. What's the time? I look at my wrist, forgetting that I haven't worn a watch for the last two weeks. Well, it's Sunday night,

119

which means it must be Monday morning by now in the UK. My flight is due to land in a couple of hours. My mood turns dark as I remember Matthew will be waiting at the airport to collect me. I go to the sink with the intention of filling it with hot water and starting the washing-up, but it's full of dishes and there's nowhere to put them.

'Leave it,' Carmen snaps, and I already know she's not someone to be trifled with. 'I'll do it tomorrow,' she adds more complacently.

I make a silent plan to beat her to it. I have nothing else to do tomorrow and I have to make myself useful somehow.

I try to stifle a yawn, but it's impossible. I don't know why I'm so tired, considering I slept in the car.

'Would anyone be offended if I called it a night?' I ask.

'No,' she replies.

'I'm so tired,' I add for good measure.

'I hope we don't keep you up,' she says, but I'm not sure she means it. I still don't get any indication that she cares about my feelings one iota. But maybe that will change with time. I *want* it to change. I hate animosity.

'You won't. I'll be out like a light.'

I pop my head around the door to say goodnight to Jorge, Javier and Eric, and then climb the stairs to 'my' bedroom. I wonder where Leo sleeps. I feel on edge as I think about him, but soon I'm not thinking of anything as I fall into a deep, deep sleep.

Sometime in the middle of the night, I come to, feeling strangely disorientated. Something has woken me up, but what? I lift my head sleepily. There, in the doorway, is a dark figure.

120

He's breathing heavily – I can see his chest rising and falling from here – but I can't tell if he's angry, freaked-out or something else.

I find my voice. 'Leo?'

'Go back to sleep,' he mutters in a low voice, pulling the door shut and stomping down the corridor and up the stairs.

Easier said than done, my friend. Easier said than done.

Chapter 15

Miraculously, I do manage to doze off again, but the house is silent when I wake. I sit up in bed and survey my surroundings. Dawn spills beneath the blinds – it must be early morning and I'm relieved to have some time to get my head together before I have to face anyone. I had to go to sleep wearing nothing but a T-shirt last night. I must call the airport today and ask about my suitcase. I remember Leo appearing at my doorway during the night and it makes me feel uneasy. He went upstairs. I guess that's where his room is. I wonder if I should go and talk to him. No. He'll probably be out cold; anyway, I still feel nervous about the idea of facing him, let alone going into his room.

I climb out of bed and pull on my clothes. I'll go shopping this morning for a couple of things to get me by. Thank goodness for hand luggage – at least I have my purse and passport. I can manage without everything else.

I study my reflection in the mirror and wipe the sleep from my eyes. I run my hands through my light-blonde hair and, when that doesn't work, try to muss it up a bit. If it's going to look just-slept-in, it may as well look *stylishly* just-slept-in. I sigh and go out of the door and tread quietly down the stairs. To my surprise, Jorge is sitting at the dining-room table, drinking a coffee and reading the newspaper.

'Hi!' he exclaims with a bright smile. 'Sleep well?'

'Yes, thanks.' I don't mention Leo's appearance in my doorway. 'Is it early?' I ask him with confusion. Are there no clocks in this house?

'Seven thirty,' he tells me. 'I'm working today.'

Oh yeah, he's a dive instructor. They start early.

'Another course?' I ask, pulling up a chair.

'Fresh recruits,' he replies jovially. 'What about you? Have you got any plans?'

I take a deep breath. 'I probably just need to focus on switching my phone back on.'

He offers me a compassionate smile.

'I'll also call the airport and try to sort out my bags.' I hesitate. 'Do you think Carmen would kill me if I tidied up a bit?'

'Are you kidding? She hates housework more than anything.'

'Oh, good,' I say with relief.

Jorge folds up his paper and downs the last of his drink before standing up. 'Help yourself to coffee,' he tells me. 'I've got to get off.'

'Okay.' Pause. 'Is . . . Leo working with you today?'

'No.' He gives a curt shake of his head. 'Not until tomorrow. Today we're in the pool.'

'Oh, yes, of course.'

He tuts. 'You forget so quickly.'

'I don't want to forget. I might have to go for another dive sometime.'

'Absolutely,' he agrees wholeheartedly. 'You've come to the right place.'

'Thanks,' I say, and mean it more than he can ever know.

'You're welcome.' He makes to leave.

'I really mean it,' I blurt out, making him turn around. He notices my eyes welling up and his face falls. 'Don't worry, I'm okay. I'll be okay,' I tell him in a hurry. I don't want him to be late for work. 'But I just want you to know that I appreciate what you're doing for me.'

'You'd do the same for me,' he says simply.

Well, yes, I would, but how can he be so sure of that?

'What has happened to you . . . Well, I wouldn't wish that on anyone.' He pats me on my shoulder and then he's gone.

I wait until Carmen is out of the house before I start on the housework. She's working in the gift shop today, she tells me. Javier and Eric are nowhere to be seen, but I don't imagine they'll care much what I get up to. Then of course there's Leo. And there's no way I can predict how he'll react.

I start by lifting the dirty dishes out of the sink and placing them in a pile so perilous that even Carmen would be proud of me. I run hot water and clean out the dirty sink first, then look around for washing-up liquid. There's some in the cupboard under the sink, along with a very old washing-up brush. I decide to buy a new one today, but for now I'll have to make do. There's nowhere to put the clean dishes, so to start with I have to dry up and put away as I go along, but soon I clear a space next to the sink where I can let them drain. It's methodical work and it takes my mind off things. It's the first time I've washed up in weeks, and I find I actually enjoy it. I think of the state our apartment was in when I left it – I could barely drag myself out of bed to get to work, let alone tackle the housework. Matthew did most of it, and so he bloody should. He rendered me incapable of doing any-thing, I think blackly. I wonder if he's at the airport yet and I feel a tiny prickle of guilt when I realise I've really dropped Marty and Bridget in it. They'll have to explain. I feel bad for them, but right now I need to put myself first. Nobody else is.

When the dishes are clean and in the cupboards, I wipe over the counters before tackling the cooker. It's practically sparkling when I've finished and I'm properly pleased with myself. I hope Carmen is, too. Funny that I should care what she thinks, but I'd be lying if I said I didn't. I study the cupboards and realise I could clean them as well, but I decide to save them for another day. I remember the dirty coffee table in the living room. That's what I'll tackle next. And I know the living-room floor could do with a mop. Then, with a frown, I notice the dirty kitchen floor and find myself sighing. Nope, I can't move onto the living room until the kitchen is finished. Where would I find a mop? There isn't one in the kitchen, but this is a big house. I bet there's a laundry room here somewhere. I set off out of the room with determination and walk smack bang into Leo.

'Oh!' I gasp.

I stare up at him. He's never looked more intense. I don't think he's angry, but he sure as hell doesn't look happy to see me. He looks almost ... hurt. But can that be right?

He takes a step backwards.

'Sorry,' I murmur, tearing my eyes away from him. He says nothing, but the immediate awkwardness is broken and he steps around me into the kitchen. He stands there for a moment, surveying the scene.

'Did you do this?'

I take a deep, shaky breath and nod, even though he's not looking at me. I add, 'Yes,' but it comes out sounding croaky so I clear my throat. 'I had nothing else to do.'

He goes to the cupboard next to the fridge and gets out an espresso cup, flicking on the kettle.

'You want one?' he asks without looking at me.

'Sure.'

He gets another cup out of the cupboard and reaches for the instant coffee, muttering under his breath as he spoons it out. He likes it strong. He's wearing his battered blue jeans with a crumpled black T-shirt, which he could have slept in. His hair is messier than normal, partly falling down across his forehead and he has a shadow of stubble across his jaw. He looks dishevelled and hung over, but oh so hot.

'Sugar?'

I come to with a start. 'Please. One. Only in coffee.'

He spoons three into his own cup, and I have to bite my tongue from saying anything. 'Carmen really needs to get a machine,' he mutters more loudly this time. 'I hate this instant shit.'

'There's a good coffee shop down the road,' I say hesitantly. 'Do you want me to go and get you one?'

He glances over his shoulder and looks momentarily amused. 'I think you've done enough work for one morning, don't you? It's only ten o'clock.' He hands over my coffee, his dark eyes flicking up to meet mine.

'Thanks,' I say, taking the cup gratefully. I never did make one for myself after Jorge left. 'What time did you come back last night?' I find myself asking.

'I have no idea,' he says grumpily as he leans back against the counter and slurps from his cup.

I remain standing gawkily in the middle of the room. 'Jorge said you haven't been here much this weekend . . .'

'How would Jorge know that?' he asks calmly. 'He's been in Miami.'

I realise my mistake. 'Sorry, I meant Carmen.'

'Doesn't she have anything better to do than talk about me when I'm not here?' It's a rhetorical question, so he doesn't wait for me to answer. 'Apparently not,' he adds for good measure.

I'm guessing he'd react badly if I told him they were also talking about his mother, so naturally I keep that quiet.

'Did you sleep well?' he asks me, pushing off from the counter and nodding in the direction of the living room. I lead the way through.

'Not too bad, considering.' Considering my husband now has a baby son who isn't mine ... Considering Leo appeared at my doorway in the middle of the night ... I don't say either of these things out loud. 'How about you?'

'Not too bad, *considering* . . .'

I glance back at him. 'Considering what?' I can't help asking.

'Considering the elephant crashing around in my kitchen.' He says it lightly, and I raise one eyebrow at him.

'Are you calling me an elephant?' I ask drily.

'I had no idea someone so small could make so much noise,' he teases as we sit down. 'How on earth my nephew is sleeping through that . . .'

I smile. 'Did you see him last night when you came back?' I'm still curious to know what time that was.

'No.' He shakes his head. 'He was already in bed.'

'How did you know ...' that I was here? I finish the sentence inside my head.

'Jorge left me a note,' he replies, studying his fingernails.

I really want to know what that note said. Does he know what happened at the airport? Curiosity gets the better of me.

127

'What did it say?' I ask cautiously.

He delves into his pocket and pulls out a crumpled piece of paper, handing it over.

Laura is here. In your mother's bedroom. Will explain tomorrow.

So he knows nothing. I look up at him with surprise. 'You don't even know I bumped into him and Javier at the airport?'

He looks surprised. 'Did you?'

'I had just spoken to Matthew. My husband,' I add, although I can see in his eyes that he'd already guessed as much. 'She's had the baby. The girl . . . It's a boy.' Leo looks shocked. He rubs his hand over his mouth. 'I couldn't go home,' I say, shaking my head quickly. I so want him to understand, to support me. But I'm not sure what's going through his head. 'I hope you don't mind me being here. I'll go back to the hotel if it bothers you.'

He looks up sharply. 'Why should it bother me?'

'I don't know. I . . .' I want to say that he doesn't seem very pleased to see me, but that isn't fair. Plus it sounds desperate, and I don't want to come across like that to him. 'Do you mind me staying in your mother's room?' I ask tentatively.

'No.' His reply is short. 'It hasn't been used for years. It's a big house. You can stay as long as you like,' he tells me, repeating Jorge's words from yesterday.

'Thank you,' I say quietly. I finish my coffee and rub at my nose to try to stop it from prickling before looking at the coffee table. I can't bear it. I get up and walk determinedly through to the kitchen, bringing a sponge and some washing-up liquid back through with me. I couldn't see any proper cleaning products in the cupboard under the sink, so I add them to my mental shopping list.

'What are you doing?' Leo asks with a frown when I return.

'Cleaning the coffee table,' I reply as I set to work.

'Laura, you don't have to clean for us,' he mutters.

'I want to,' I say firmly as I rub vigorously at a particularly tough stain and try to ignore the way him saying my name makes my pulse quicken. 'I need something to occupy myself.'

He tuts and sighs, but he realises he can't stop me. I go through to the kitchen and rinse out the sponge, grabbing a tea towel to polish the glass.

'There.' I look at my handiwork. 'Much better.'

He places his coffee cup down on the table.

'No, no,' I chastise. 'Where are your coasters?'

'We haven't got any goddamn coasters, woman!' he snaps, but I *think* it's good-naturedly.

Grinning, I lift up his cup and wipe the coffee ring, then I take the empties back through to the kitchen and wash them up. He comes in after me, snatches the tea towel and dries them. I watch with amusement as he puts them away.

'Happy now?' he asks with a raised eyebrow.

'Happi-*er*,' I correct. 'Do you have a bath towel I could borrow? I promise I'll buy myself one today.'

'We have plenty,' he says, waving me away, then he sets off up the stairs. I follow him. There's a cupboard under the second smaller staircase and he opens it and gets out a towel, passing it to me.

'Thanks.' I turn and walk towards the bathroom. Glancing back, I find him still standing in the same place. 'Where's your bedroom?' I ask in what I hope is a casual voice.

'Upstairs,' he says. I hesitantly halt in my footsteps and face him down the corridor. 'If you plan to do anymore cleaning, I

Paige Toon

would start on ... *your* room.' He puts emphasis on *your*, as though he corrected himself at the last moment.

'Okay,' I say, pausing at the door to the bathroom. 'See you in a bit.'

He nods and turns away, his footsteps pounding the stairs matching the pounding of my heart.

I probably need a cold shower, but the water is blissfully hot. I borrow some shampoo and conditioner and then get dressed into yesterday's clothes. Cleaning Leo's mother's room can wait. At the very least I need to call the airport and buy some new underwear. I head back into my room and pick up my phone from the dresser. I'm nervous as I switch it back on. It's now getting on for eleven o'clock in the morning, which means ... Oh no, it means I should have arrived in London hours ago.

Buzz, buzz, buzz ... The sound of all my messages coming in is deeply distracting. I so want to call the airport first, but I know I won't be able to concentrate until I've dealt with things at home. Just as well I made that decision naturally, because suddenly my phone starts to ring and one look at the caller ID tells me it's Matthew.

'Hi,' I say upon answering.

'Laura? What the hell are you doing?' Matthew screeches down the line with what sounds like barely contained fury. 'I've been trying to get hold of you for hours!' he adds. He really does sound quite pissed off, I muse mildly.

'I've only just switched my phone back on,' I tell him.

'What the hell are you doing?' he repeats his earlier question – clearly this is the thing that's playing most on his mind.

'Did Marty not tell you?'

'Bridget told me more. Who the fuck is Leo?' As he spits out

130

the words in this last sentence, I can tell he's absolutely beside himself. He's probably tearing his own hair out.

'What has Bridget been saying?' I ask carefully.

'Why don't *you* tell me *your* version of events?'

'Well, as you know I'm not coming home.' I don't know how I say this so calmly, but I do.

'Not now? Not ever?' His voice is immeasurably strained.

'Not ... *now*,' I confirm. 'I'm staying with some friends.'

'*Who is Leo?*'

'Leo is just a friend,' I tell him. 'So is Jorge. They're helping me out.'

'Laura, *come home!*' he begs. '*I should be the one helping you!*'

'Oh, you're not helping me, Matthew,' I say quietly. 'You're not helping me at all.'

'Laura, please ... It was a mistake—'

'I don't want to hear you say it again.' My volume turns up a notch. 'Shut up. Shut the hell up. Do you hear me?'

He hesitates; taken aback, I think. 'Yes.'

'I cannot deal with what is happening at home right now. Do you understand, Matthew?' I don't wait for him to reply. 'Do you get it? What you have done is unforgivable—'

'Don't say that,' he interjects.

'I do not know how we can ever get past this,' I say strongly.

'So, what, you're just going to jump in the sack with some other bloke, instead? Or have you already done that?' He sounds so bitter. I actually laugh.

'I'm not you, Matthew. But what I do from here on in is really none of your business.'

Then I hang up on him. And boy does it feel good.

Chapter 16

Something happens to me as I walk down the streets past the beautiful old colonial houses with their intricate gingerbread carvings and gardens full of tropical flowers. My spirits begin to lift. The sun shines down from the light blue sky and I can smell the ocean. I breathe in deeply and feel free, as free as I did underwater that first time I did an Open Water dive. I really do want to go diving again. Nothing is stopping me, here. Okay, so I should try to do work of some sort. And I definitely need to call Becky. I promise myself I'll ring her and my parents as soon as I get back home. *Home?* I snort with laughter. Well, it sort of is, for now.

I buy some underwear, a beach dress and, to hell with it, even a new bikini, a red one this time. I might go to the beach today. Why not, right? I head to a convenience store and stock up on cleaning products and equipment. I also buy some fruit, cereal and a few bits and pieces. I don't want to be a freeloader. As soon as I feel comfortable enough to ask Carmen, I'll offer to cook, too. I think of Eric lazily slumming it on the sofa and feel momentarily sorry for her, going out to work and then coming home to cook for everyone. I wonder if anyone else helps her out. No wonder she doesn't much fancy cleaning.

When I get back to the house, there's no sign of anyone, but the door is open.

I get out my phone with the intention of calling Becky and my parents, but as my battery is getting low, I decide to text them instead. A bit of a cop-out, but I promise them I'll call when I get my charger from my suitcase. I rang the airport earlier and they told me they can deliver my bag tomorrow. Apart from the odd text, I haven't been in touch with my parents in two weeks. They weren't convinced it was a good idea for me to go away with Marty – they've never considered her to be a particularly good influence, even before she didn't come home from Ibiza. She was always my quirky, cool, but slightly dodgy, smoking-behind-the-bike-sheds, dyeing-her-hair-every-colour-of-the-rainbow best friend. Poor Marty. They'll probably blame this on her, too, but I'll explain soon enough.

Putting my phone to one side, I unpack the shopping and get on with the cleaning. I mop the kitchen floor first, tidy away the breakfast things left by Javier and Eric, and then tackle the living room. Apart from the dust, grime and dirt, it's not too bad. At least it's not stacked high with dirty dishes, like the kitchen was. Once that's done, I go upstairs to the bathroom and clean it until the taps shine and the enamel glints, and then I finally make a start on my bedroom. The dust is so thick it becomes ingrained in the sponge, so I have to replace it with a new one after a while. I clean the mirror and the window – and even though it's still pretty dirty on the outside, it makes a big difference; I polish the wooden chests of drawers, dresser and bedhead; I sweep and mop the floor. And then I open the window. The warm air flows in and

I sigh with contentment and lean my elbows on the windowsill. The garden is still a tip, I think, as I look down at it. I wonder how much work it would take to get that tidied up. This would be such a beautiful house if only someone cared enough to put in the effort. I've never been much of a gardener, but I'm sure I can clear the junk and cut the grass. Perhaps I'll tackle it sometime, but not before I head to the beach. I'm in for a bit of a walk, which won't be much fun in the afternoon heat, but it'll be worth it in the end.

I step outside my bedroom door and listen. Nothing. I put away the cleaning products and equipment in the laundry room I have finally managed to locate, then I empty the bins and take the rubbish out to the trash cans on the street. I dust off my hands and turn to go back inside, but my eyes shoot up to the eaves of the house. Leo is leaning out of the window of the loft room, his tanned elbows resting on the sill. I smile and wave up at him. He looks vaguely entertained as he lifts his fingers in a lazy wave back at me.

'You want a coffee? I'm going to pop to the coffee shop,' I say on a whim. I wasn't planning on going there at all, but if it makes him come down and chat to me ... He shrugs and then nods. 'Cool. Back in a bit.'

I smile to myself as I return inside and locate my purse. I'm back within ten minutes and by then Leo has decamped to the sofa in the garden.

'What do you do if it rains?' I ask with a furrowed brow as I kick the gate shut behind me.

'Move them to the porch, if we can be bothered.' He jerks his head to the side. There's a small covered porch, adorned with classic gingerbread. The white paint is flaking after years of neglect, and there's no first-floor balcony, but I imagine with a quirky colour-coordinated paint scheme, it could look lovely.

'Have you ever thought about turning this place into a guest house?' I hand him his paper cup and sit down in one of the armchairs.

He snorts. 'Do you think I look like someone who mingles well with tourists?'

'You mingled well enough with me.'

He regards me through half-closed eyes for a long moment and I will myself not to blush. 'You're different.'

'You worked as a conch train tour guide,' I point out, trying not to stare at his bare leg, now up on a rock that's doubling as a footrest. He's changed into shorts and a shirt, and his hair is still damp from the shower. Concentrate!

'*That* was different,' he tells me, changing tack.

'Why was it different? You could make a lot of money running a guest house here.'

'You're forgetting my sister-in-law.'

I take a sip of my coffee. 'I could never forget her,' I say innocently.

He raises his eyebrows at me.

'Anyway, wouldn't she get in on it? She could cook that *pollo* rice dish as her speciality and make a killing.'

'*Arroz con pollo?*' he asks with amusement. 'Has she been trying to impress you?'

'Me?' I scoff. 'You've got to be kidding. She made it for Javier, of course.'

'Aah.' He blows at the top of his coffee.

'Yeah. She saved you some.'

He nods and sips his drink. I notice he's shaved.

Paige Toon

I swing my legs around and lie sideways on my chair, resting my head on the armrest and staring up at the sky. A few wisps of cloud drift over our heads.

After a while Leo gets up, muttering something about food. I study his departing back as he wanders across the garden and into the house. I hear the ping of a microwave a few minutes later.

'Where's the dog?' I ask curiously when he returns with a bowl of heated-up leftovers.

'Eric's taken him to work.'

'Eric's gone to work?' I ask with surprise. 'What does he do?'

'He's working on some boats in Summerland Key today.' That's the next key up. 'He keeps them clean, that sort of stuff. Javier's helping him.'

'Oh. That's nice.'

I watch as he tucks in. He glances up at me and I realise I'm staring.

'Do they get on well?' I ask hurriedly.

'Pretty well,' he replies between munches.

'Sorry, I should let you eat.'

I follow the clouds with my eyes as they pass overhead and idly kick my legs until my flip-flops begin to feel loose. I kick them off completely.

'Did you speak to your husband?'

Leo's question takes me by surprise. I glance across at him. He's still eating, his eyes on his food.

'Yes.'

He nods but doesn't look at me, so I turn my head back up to the sky. 'He wasn't very happy.'

Nothing, and then, 'Hmm ...'

I look over at him again. 'Serves the wanker right, though, eh?'

136

He takes one more mouthful and then puts his bowl on the ground beside him. 'Hey, do you want to come to the beach with me?' I ask impulsively.

'When?'

'Now?'

'Um . . .'

'Have you got something better to do?' I say quickly, because I can see him wavering.

He shrugs. He does this a lot. 'I guess not.'

'Cool!' I sit up and beam at him.

He scratches his chin. 'Which one are you going to?'

'Higgs Beach?' That seems to be the main one here and I don't know any others.

'Nope.' He shakes his head abruptly. 'Go get your things.' He nods towards the house.

What does that mean? Is he taking me somewhere else? I don't care as long as he's coming with me. Yay!

'Get a couple of beach towels from the cupboard,' Leo calls up the stairs.

'Okay!' I call back down, doing as he says. The cupboard smells of years gone by – slightly musty, but not unpleasant. It's full of linen, but there are beach towels untidily stacked up so I take two before hurrying back to my room to change into my bikini.

Leo is leaning against the wall at the bottom of the stairs.

'Ready?' I ask with a smile. He picks up a set of car keys from the table next to him, before pushing off the wall and languidly walking to the door. His car is parked on the street outside the house. The smell of leather is still present, and there's sand in the footwells. I imagine he's had it for years. He reaches across to the glove box and opens it so it falls onto my knees. Pulling out some black sunglasses he pops them on and shuts the glove box again, his fingers brushing against me as he does so. I'm still tense from his touch even after he's started the ignition and driven away from the curb. The car is a manual and I keep glancing down at his hands and the dark hair on his arms as he changes gears. Luckily I'm wearing sunnies myself so it's easier to spy, but after a while I force myself to stare out of the window before he notices me watching.

Whichever beach we're going to, the approach to it does not make it seem massively appealing. We drive past the docks and Leo points out an enormous – absolutely mahoosive – cruise ship. I can't believe that something so big can come so close to the keys without becoming grounded.

'It'll be in Miami in a couple of days,' he tells me. 'I've seen it go from here to there.'

'When are *you* going back to Miami?' I ask, trying to keep the fear from my voice. What the hell will I do when that happens?

'Not until the end of the season.'

'Which is when?'

'A couple of months,' he replies casually. 'I tend to do a swap with the boat captain in the summer while he goes back to the West Coast to see his mother.'

We park in a medium-sized car park under the shade of tall pine trees. Through the small wood I can see the sandy beach and then the ocean. We walk through the wooded picnic area, my flip-flops slippery on the pine needles beneath my feet, until we come out the other side into the hot sun. The sand is cream-coloured, the water calm and bluey-green. There are a few rocks by the waterline and some sea grass washed up on the shore. It's not picture-postcard perfect, but it's not rammed full of people, either.

We lay out our towels and sit down. Leo loops his arms around his knees. He's wearing a short-sleeved Hawaiian shirt today, unbuttoned at the top. He looks cool, as far from cheesy as you could get. I peel off my beach dress, locate the sunscreen I remembered to pick up at the convenience store earlier, and start to apply it to my arms.

'Want some?' I ask him, offering it.

'Don't need it,' he says, and I take in his deeply tanned forearms.

'Really? Don't you ever burn?'

'Nope.'

'You're lucky.' I start on my stomach.

'You want me to do your back?' he asks with a sideways glance.

'That'd be great.' I turn away from him, glad that he can't see my face. I think about unclasping my bikini strap so he can apply it properly, but I chicken out. His hands are warm as they smooth cream over my back and under my straps, but he's finished all too quickly.

'Thanks.' I lie down and a little sigh escapes me. I watch him furtively from underneath my dark glasses. He stays sitting upright for a moment before unbuttoning his shirt. God, give me strength. He takes off his shirt, giving me a perfect view of his broad, muscled back, and then he lies down. I can see from here that his stomach is taut and toned. It's all I can do not to sit up and congratulate him on his really quite awesome body. I can't relax for the life of me, lying there next to him in the hot sun, both of us barely dressed. I won't last long before I need to take a swim to cool down, that's for sure. In fact, that's a really good idea.

I sit upright, wracked full of tension. 'I think I'm going to go for a swim.'

'Already?' he asks, lifting his head to look at me. 'You've only just got here.'

'I'm not very good with the heat.' I glance at his chest.

He props himself up on his elbows. 'I'll come with you if you wait a bit.'

Well, now, that's an offer . . . I turn around and lie on my front so I can face him. There's no way I can remain here in silence. I'll go crazy.

'Do you come here a lot?' I ask, resting on my forearms.

'Not that much anymore. I used to come when I was a kid.'

'With your parents?'

'Mostly just my mum and brother.'

I frown. 'What happened to your dad?'

'You ask a lot of questions.'

I can't tell if he's annoyed with me. 'I don't mean to pry.'

'It's okay.' He smiles. 'My father died when I was eight. Heart attack.'

My face falls. 'I'm sorry.' He was so young.

He looks up at the sky, contemplatively. 'I didn't see him much. I felt guilty for not missing him more after he was gone.'

'Were your parents divorced?'

'No.' He lets out a little laugh and takes off his sunglasses. 'No, no. They weren't even married.'

'Really?'

'My mother was his mistress,' he tells me and I can't hide my shock. 'He was a cigar manufacturer in Cuba. He had a wife, four children – two boys, two girls.'

'You have half-siblings?' I ask with surprise.

'They don't know that I exist.'

I instinctively put my sunglasses on top of my head. 'Are you sure? How can you be sure?'

'I'm sure.' He meets my eyes for a long moment and my heart starts to flutter. I'll be the one having a heart attack if he keeps this up. My most vital organ has been through quite a rigmarole recently. I shake my head slightly, trying to keep track of the conversation so we don't go off it.

'So ... How did they meet? Your mother and father.'

He breaks eye contact to look out at the ocean. 'He met her at a market, here in Key West. She sold fruit. He used to come here for business. Illegal business,' he reveals cautiously, but I withhold any reaction, so he continues. 'I know that he loved her. I still remember the way she made him smile. But he had a family. It wasn't the done thing. He bought her the house. He would come to visit us when he could. But we were his secret. When he died we didn't go to his funeral.'

I'm aghast. 'But that's awful. You couldn't even say goodbye?'

'I was used to saying goodbye to him. Every time he left to go back to his other family.' He pauses for a moment. 'But I was very close to my mother.'

'How did she die?' I ask gently.

He swallows, and I'm worried I've pushed him too far, but he says a single word. 'Suicide.'

I gasp. I can't help it.

'She suffered with depression,' he reveals in an even voice. 'Sometimes she would shut herself off for months, even a year. It was all I could do to keep her alive.'

141

'Oh Leo, I'm so sorry.' It seems like she tried to take her own life more than once.

'I wasn't there when she did it …'

His mind is far away as he remembers. I realise I'm holding my breath.

'Where were you?' My voice comes out sounding choked.

'Miami. With Alejandro.' He shakes his head. 'He was in a bad place. He left home when he was sixteen – I was twelve – and got in with a bad crowd in Miami. He met Carmen when he was nineteen. She was good for him – two years older. She helped him to get off the drugs … for a while. But she fell pregnant almost immediately. They got married before the baby came.' He smiles sadly. 'I still remember how happy my mother was when she held Javier for the first time.' He sighs. 'They should have moved back to Key West, *then*. My mother begged them to. Maybe if they had, things would have been different … I don't know.'

'You *don't* know,' I agree. I think back over our conversation.

'Anyway,' Leo continues, and I remember we were talking about where he was when his mother died. 'Carmen called me for help – Alejandro hadn't been seen for two days – so I went to get him back.'

'Back from where?'

'His shithouse friends. Drug dealers,' he spits. 'But when I got home, it was too late.'

'You found her?' My voice is scarcely more than a whisper.

He nods slightly.

'Oh Leo,' I say again as I imagine him returning home to that scene, whatever scene it was. 'How did she …' My voice trails off.

'She slit her wrists in the bathtub.' He says it in such a

detached fashion, but his words have an overwhelming effect on me.

'Oh, God!' I try to stifle a sob, but I can't. To my horror, I start to cry. I get up onto my knees and try to control myself.

'Hey,' he chastises gently, sitting upright and leaning over to rub my shoulder. 'Don't cry.'

'I'm sorry!' I gasp, but I can't stop. At least the beach is pretty much deserted.

'Don't cry,' he says softly once more, but his sympathy sets me off in the opposite direction.

'I'm sorry, I'm sorry.' And then, before I even have time to think about what I'm doing, I lean towards him and hug him tightly, pressing my face into his neck. A good few seconds pass before he hugs me back.

'Shh,' he says into my hair as he strokes it soothingly.

I've so wanted to have him hold me. It's an urge I've been trying to control ever since I met him – it's like a drug. I thought I'd forget about everything else, if only I were in his arms. Then all of a sudden I feel ashamed that he's the one comforting *me*. My tears come to an abrupt stop. I pull away and brush them off, too embarrassed to look him in the eye.

'I don't know what came over me,' I mutter. He wraps his arms around his knees and I can feel his eyes on me as I dig around in my bag for a tissue. Always have them handy, thankfully.

'You've been through a lot,' he says evenly.

'Not as much as you.' I blow my nose loudly, not caring how I must look. 'I'll never feel sorry for myself again.'

He shakes his head, then he lightly punches my arm. 'Time for a swim?'

'Sure.' I get to my feet and then impulsively start to run across the sand. 'Race ya!' I call over my shoulder, which is a big mistake because he catches me quickly, and then shocks the life out of me by scooping me up in his arms. I scream as he storms into the ocean and drops me in the water.

'You bastard!' I squeal when I come up for air, my hair absolutely drenched. I splash him and he dives under the barely existent waves. He re-emerges and flicks his head back so his black hair falls off his face. I sink below the water so it comes up to my neck – hell, I need to cool off – while he eyes me with a teasing grin.

I push away from the sand with my feet and swim into deeper water. He follows me, doing a slow front crawl, and then turns so he's lying on his back, floating in the water. I purse my lips and push down on his stomach so he gasps and has to stand up before he sinks. I laugh and duck away from him before he can splash me.

'That was fun,' I say later when we're back in the car. 'Well, I mean—' Obviously not the pouring-out-your-heart-about-your-mother's-suicide bit, but the other stuff.

'It was,' he interrupts, thankfully before I can say the sentence out loud.

We cross over Duval Street, which is already packed full of revellers.

'What's the time?' I ask with a frown.

'Don't know,' he replies with a shrug. No, I don't imagine he's the type to ever wear a watch, and I didn't bring my mobile, so . . .

I sigh. 'I'd better call my mum when we get back.'

He doesn't comment.

When I'm showered and sand-free and dressed again in

Sunday's going-home outfit of jeans and a T-shirt, I turn on my phone to check for urgent messages. I've been keeping it switched off until I get my charger back tomorrow. It buzzes to alert me to one message, then it buzzes again. And again. I sigh and listen to my voicemail. The first one is from my mum.

'You need to call me, right now, darling.' She's using her firmest tone. 'One text message is not going to cut it. Laura? Do you hear me? Ring me.'

Bollocks.

The next one is from Marty. She sounds downbeat ...

'Hey, you, just a quick one to let you know we're back safely. Matthew was pretty messed up when we came through Arrivals without you. I think Bridget might've put her foot in it. Anyway, call me when you get this. I need to hear your voice.'

The next one: Matthew.

'Laura ...' He sounds resigned, flat. 'I don't know what you're doing, but please call me. I need to talk to you.' Pause. '*Please*.' His heavy sigh is cut off when he ends the call.

The next one is Mum again, but I realise if I keep listening to my messages then I'll drain my phone battery, so I decide to call her first. She answers on the third ring.

'Mum, it's me.'

'Laura, thank goodness! Are you okay? Where are you? Are you still in Key West?'

'Mum, I'm fine,' I say calmly. 'Yes, I'm okay – well, as okay as I can be under the circumstances – and yes, I'm still in Key West.'

'But what are you doing there? Darling, I don't understand!'

Gone is the firm, in-control woman from the first voicemail message. Now she's worked herself up into a bit of a state.

'I'm just taking a break—'

'But you've had a break!' she exclaims. 'You've had two weeks away!'

'It's not enough,' I say simply.

'But that girl has had the baby! Laura, you need to come home!'

This is the first time I raise my voice. 'I *know* she's had the baby, Mum, that's why I'm *not* coming home.'

'Oh, Laura.' She sighs with sympathy, but I must be getting slightly immune to it because my eyes don't fill with tears as they have so often in the past.

'Just chill out, okay?' Back to calm again. 'I'm a big girl. I know what I'm doing. I just need some more time away, alright? And I like it here. It's warm and—'

'What's this about a man?' she interrupts again.

'What man?' I ask innocently.

'Leo? Is that his name? Matthew was quite upset about him.'

'When have you been talking to Matthew?' I ask with alarm.

'Well, I've seen him a little bit while you've been away.' Now she sounds guilty, as well she might.

'Mum!' I exclaim with indignation. 'Why are you being nice to him?'

'He's so upset, Laura, he—'

'So he fucking well should be!' I cry.

'*Laura!*' she cries back, but I'm not going to apologise for my language. No way. I'm on a rant.

'*He* did this, Mum. Not me. He deserves everything he gets, so don't you go around feeling sorry for him!' I'm outraged that she's even giving him her shoulder to lean on. She's *my* mum! 'I'm going,' I snap.

'No, darling, don't . . .' She seems contrite.

'No, I have to, Mum. My battery is about to run out and, anyway, I don't want to talk about this anymore.'

'Give me your address.'

'Why?'

'In case something happens to you! I need to know where you are.'

'It's the house next door to the hotel we were staying in. Marty knows where I am. I don't know the address.'

'Well, can you get it?'

'I'll text it to you,' I promise. I sigh. 'Look, I've gotta go.'

'Okay. Be careful!' she blurts out.

My voice softens. 'Mum, really, it's fine. I'm with good people. They're looking after me.'

'Even that Leo?' she asks, slightly snootily, to my annoyance.

'Leo is a friend. *Just* a friend,' I clarify. 'I'll call you when I have my charger back, okay?'

'Okay.' She sniffs.

'Bye.'

'Bye, darling.'

I hang up first and flop back onto the bed, staring up at the ceiling. Suddenly I feel tired, oh so tired. I switch off my phone again and edge up the bed and under the covers. It won't hurt to have a little kip. I'm done with talking for now.

Chapter 17

When I wake up, it's dark outside. I lie there for a moment, listening, and I can just make out the sound of laughter and music coming from the garden outside my window. I get up and go to look out. I smile to myself at the now-familiar scene before me: sofa, chairs, fairy lights, cigar smoke, cans of beer, Leo, Jorge, Carmen, Eric – and now Javier, too. I go into the bathroom and splash some water on my face, then head downstairs to join them. Something smells good in the kitchen as I approach it, and my stomach rumbles. Jorge is grabbing some beers out of the fridge.

'How's it going?' he asks with one of his trademark twinkly smiles. 'How did you sleep?'

'Pretty well,' I reply self-consciously. 'Was I asleep for long?'

'About four hours.'

'Whoa.' *Four hours?*

'Ready to party tonight, eh?'

Dammit. He's right. I'm never going to get to sleep later after that mammoth afternoon nap.

'You want something to eat?' he asks.

'That would be great. It smells amazing.' I look around the

kitchen and see that it's still pretty clean, even though there are a few dishes stacked near the sink. Nothing like the disaster zone of this morning, though.

'Go and sit down. I'll bring some out to you. You want a beer?'

'Um ... Sure.' I'd prefer a glass of wine, but I'm not going to be fussy. He passes me one. 'Want me to take those to the others?'

'Sure. Thanks.'

I feel a bit shy as I walk outside. Max is the first one to spot me and he barks and growls his acknowledgement until Eric shouts at him to shut him up. Well, I've certainly got their attention now.

'Hi,' I say sheepishly.

'Hey,' Leo replies, looking over his shoulder.

'Who wants one of these?' I ask, referring to the beers. Leo lifts his hand up, so I pass him one. Eric reaches forward to take the other.

Carmen and Eric are sharing one of the two armchairs – she's sitting on his lap – and Javier is in the other one. There's room on the sofa next to Leo. He doesn't say anything to me as I sit down. Carmen is teasing Javier about girls he met on his travels. She seems to be in a pretty good mood. I crack open my beer can and take a sip. I'm so not in the mood for beer tonight.

'Make some room.' Jorge is standing next to the sofa, indicating for me to move along so he can sit down. I edge closer to Leo, who doesn't move an inch to accommodate me. Jorge slumps down on the sofa and lands practically on top of me.

'Whoa!' I exclaim, shifting even closer to Leo to make room for Jorge. He laughs and hands me a bowl of steaming-hot food. 'Thanks.' I put my beer down on the rock in front of me and

149

perch on the edge of the sofa so I can eat in a more upright fashion. 'What is it?' I ask Jorge, glancing at Carmen.

'Coconut curry,' Jorge tells me.

Max comes to sit at my feet. You like me now, do you? Now that I've got food?

It's heavenly: fluffy white rice and creamy chicken, fruity with coconut and something else ... bananas? And just the right level of spice. 'That is absolutely amazing,' I enthuse, regarding Carmen with wide eyes. 'Will you show me how to make it?'

'I didn't cook it,' she replies a little defensively. 'Leo did.'

'Did you?' I glance over my left shoulder at him, unable to keep the astonishment from my voice.

'Don't sound so surprised,' he huffs. 'I'm not completely useless.'

I grin at him and he takes a swig from his beer can, rather than return my smile. I eat while the conversation kicks off again. My amazement doesn't leave me, though. I wonder if his mother taught him to cook. This thought fills me with sadness. Finally I put my empty dish down on the rock coffee table and pick up my beer, edging backwards to sit properly on the sofa. This is a two-seater sofa with three of us sitting on it, but I'm still taken aback by how close I am to Leo. His right-hand side is pressing so firmly into my left-hand side that his body heat flows into me. I can barely breathe. He leans forward to pick up a small tin case from the rock. 'You mind?' he asks, opening it up and pulling out a cigar.

'Not at all,' I tell him, willing him to settle back next to me again. He remains upright as he lights it, then he falls backwards and – bliss – his body presses against mine once more. We're so close. Too close, perhaps, because he chooses to put his right arm up on the top of the sofa to make some more room for us. All this does, however, is make me feel like he has his arm around me. It's all I can do not to lean back against his chest. I take a sip of my beer and try not to smirk. He holds the cigar in his left hand and breathes away from me, but the sweet-smelling smoke trails in my direction anyway. I'm fighting such a desperate urge to look at his mouth that I'm completely oblivious to the conversation going on around me. Suddenly I realise Jorge has asked me a question.

I come to with a start. 'Sorry? What?'

'I said, would you like to come on a night dive tomorrow night?' He says it slowly, to make light of my lack of attention.

'A night dive?' I ask in confusion.

'A dive which takes place at night time.' Again, he says this slowly, teasing me.

My brow furrows. 'But how do you see anything?'

'With torches.'

'Isn't that really scary?' I inquire with slight alarm.

'Surely not when you have Leo as a buddy,' he says with a grin, looking past me to Leo. I turn my head to see Leo raising one eyebrow at him.

'Are you going?' I ask Leo.

'Looks like it,' he replies sardonically.

I breathe in quickly and speak before I can change my mind. 'Okay, count me in.' I notice Carmen giving Eric a snidey look.

'Do you dive, Carmen?' I ask this question boldly so she's aware I've caught her out.

'No.' Her reply is blunt.

'Why not?'

'She's too lazy to do the course,' Jorge interjects jovially.

'I have better things to do,' she says with a disdainful look at her brother.

'Did you speak to your mother?' Leo asks me quietly.

'Yeah.' I feel too physically close to him to be able to look him in the eyes for long. I take a mouthful of beer to distract me from this fact and can't help pulling a face.

'You want something else to drink?' he asks, clocking my reaction.

'I might pop to the offie later.'

'The offie?'

'Off-licence,' I explain. 'Liquor store, I think you call them here.'

'I'll go for you if you tell me what you like.'

You, please. Oh, he means alcohol. I swallow. 'Some white wine would be good. Or vodka?' I ask weakly, meeting his eyes for a moment. 'I'll give you some money.'

'Don't worry about it.'

'No,' I say a little too loudly. I turn to see eight pairs of eyes staring at me. 'I want to. In fact,' I address everyone, 'I really need to talk to you all about paying rent while I'm here.'

'How long are you planning on staying?' Carmen's direct question catches me off guard.

'I . . . I . . . I don't know,' I admit.

'You don't have to decide now.' Jorge pats me on my knee. 'Just take your time.'

I smile at him gratefully.

'Actually,' Carmen speaks up, and we all look at her. 'It's not up to you, is it, brother?'

Jorge shifts uncomfortably in his seat.

'No, but it *is* up to me,' Leo says firmly. Carmen looks taken aback. 'In case you've forgotten, this is my house.'

Even I freeze at his tone, and Carmen, for once, is lost for words. Eric is the first to speak.

152

'Anyone for a beer?'

Only Jorge, Javier and I react, and we politely decline. Leo and Carmen say nothing. Eric sets off towards the house and Carmen seems to change her mind because she jumps up and hurries after him. Jorge exhales loudly. Javier is still amongst us, and the silence is deafening. In fact, it's a relief when Carmen and Eric return. They sit back down in their armchair.

'Nice tidy house,' Carmen says, glancing across at me.

'Thanks.' I'm surprised that she's commenting on it, however begrudgingly. 'I needed to do something.'

She shrugs. 'It looks good.' She cracks open her beer can.

Suddenly Leo gets to his feet and we all look up at him in alarm. 'I'll go to the offie,' he says, winking at me so I know he's not pissed off anymore.

'Are you sure?' Cool air hits my left side unpleasantly. I want to ask if I can go with him, but I have a feeling it would be better for my personal relations if I stayed here with the others.

'Yep.'

'I'll get you some money.'

'Later,' he says, setting off across the garden before I can stand up.

'You don't like beer?' Carmen asks me.

'Not really,' I reply, hoping this isn't going to give her another excuse to be mean to me, but she holds her tongue.

'Did you contact the airport today?' Jorge asks me.

'Yeah, they're delivering my suitcase tomorrow.' I smile at him. 'I'll be relieved to have some more clothes. And my mobile phone charger,' I add.

'You can always use the home phone if you need to make calls,' Carmen chips in, and again I'm surprised.

'Okay, thanks,' I reply.

'Eric will give you the internet password, too, if you want it.'

'Oh, um, thanks,' I stutter again. Being nice so doesn't suit her. 'But I don't have my laptop with me.'

A thought strikes me. If I *did* have my laptop, I could actually work from here. I could actually do my job! Not to the best of my abilities, but enough to help out Becky, and enough to earn a wage. My stomach fills with hope and excitement as these thoughts race through my head. I wonder if I could get Matthew to courier it to me. I hate the idea of asking him. There's no way he'll agree easily – he wants me home, not here – so I'll have to beg. Maybe I should just buy a new one . . . I would love a new computer. I've been making do with that one for years. Perhaps I could go to Miami one day and pick up a nice new MacBook? Surely they have an Apple store there?

My mind is still ticking over when Leo returns with a plastic bag. I get up and follow him into the house.

'Is there an Apple store in Miami?' I ask as he gets a wine glass down from the cupboard.

'Yeah,' he replies, wondering why I'm asking this question.

'I was thinking I might go and buy a computer so I can do some work.' He pulls a bottle of chilled white wine from the plastic bag and grabs a bottle opener out of a drawer. 'You're not planning on going to your apartment anytime soon, I don't suppose?'

'Um . . .' He thinks for a moment as he opens the bottle. 'I suppose I could go back one weekend. When are you thinking?'

'I don't know – this weekend?' I pull a face, not expecting him to go for it.

He shrugs and hands me the glass. 'I could do that.'

'Really?' I ask hopefully.

'Yeah. Sure. We can go Saturday, come back Sunday. Or Monday,' he adds, taking a second bottle of wine out of the bag and putting it in the fridge.

'Saturday/Sunday would be perfect!' I say excitedly. 'I'll book a hotel,' I add quickly, feeling my face heat up.

'Don't be crazy.' Damn, he looks sexy when he frowns. 'You can stay at mine.'

'Do you have room?'

'It's a one-bedroomed apartment, but I'll sleep on the couch.'

'No, I'll sleep on the couch!' I exclaim.

He tuts and casts his eyes heavenwards, putting his hand on my lower back to guide me outside. My stomach is full of butterflies when we return to the sofa, or couch, as he calls it.

I feel much happier drinking wine, and I'm instantly more chilled out as we settle back down. Leo puts the opened wine bottle on the ground near his feet and leans back, returning his arm to the space behind my head. I'm full of anticipation about going to Miami with him. The wine goes down easily – he tops up my glass occasionally – and soon we're all relaxed and laughing at Jorge and Javier's silly jokes. I'm surprised when Carmen and Eric stand up and say their goodnights.

'What's the time?' I ask.

Eric digs into his pocket and pulls out his mobile phone. 'Twelve thirty,' he drawls.

'You off to bed, honey?' Carmen asks Javier sweetly in the background.

'Yeah.'

'I should go to bed, too,' Jorge says, heaving himself up from the sofa. 'Early start tomorrow.'

I survey the scene with disappointment. I'm not in the slightest bit tired, thanks to my afternoon nap. Then it occurs to me that Leo hasn't moved an inch.

'Don't stay up too late,' Jorge warns over his shoulder as he starts to walk off. 'You're working tomorrow, remember?' He's talking to Leo.

'Yes, sir,' Leo replies, in an unusually jaunty voice, for him.

'Night,' Carmen calls from the door, calling to Max to bring him inside. He sleeps on the laundry floor.

'Night!' I call back, suddenly aware that there's too much room on this sofa. I shift away from Leo and pull my knees up so I'm leaning against the armrest and facing him. He stretches lazily and reaches for the bottle of wine.

'Thanks,' I say as he tops me up. 'Have I drunk all of that?' I ask with alarm, spying the near-empty bottle.

'Yep,' he replies with a smirk, reaching for his cigar case and lighting up.

I can watch his mouth from here, I realise with a thrill. He swivels so he's facing me, his eyes closing slightly as he puffs on the cigar.

'Do you *smoke* smoke?' I ask, for want of a more interesting conversation.

'No.' He shakes his head, scrutinising the cigar in his fingers. 'Only cigars occasionally.' He hesitates. 'These were my father's.'

'Your father's cigars?' I'm confused.

'I've got boxes of them in my room.'

'No way? You still have a load of his cigars?'

He shrugs. 'Yeah. I smoke only when I'm here,' he says, gazing around him. 'I shouldn't smoke at all. These are illegal, for a start,' he adds with a grin. His father must have imported these Cuban cigars into the United States during the trade embargo.

But he continues before I can comment. 'Besides, my mother hated it.'

'Did she?'

He smiles fondly. 'She beat me the first time she caught me with one of his cigars.' He tilts his head to one side, thoughtfully. 'I wanted to be like him.' He studies his cigar again. 'You know, it was five weeks before we even knew he was dead.'

I breathe in sharply.

'Nobody told us. But my mother knew something was wrong.' He gazes off into the distance. 'He said he'd come back at the end of August, I remember that much. But she was . . .' His voice trails off. 'She knew something was wrong before that.'

'How?'

He rolls his eyes. 'She had her palms read.'

'No way,' I exclaim. 'Not by that guy on Duval Street?'

He nods wryly. 'The very same.'

I shudder. 'What did he say?' I ask nervously.

'He totally freaked her out.' His smile falls. 'And after that she went down to the docks at all hours until she managed to speak to one of his colleagues . . . They confirmed it.' He puffs on his cigar one last time before stubbing it out. 'Colleagues,' he repeats, and I wonder why he says it sarcastically.

'They came looking for his stash after he died,' he reveals.

'The cigars?'

'They didn't find them. My father stored them under the floor-boards in the loft room – it wasn't my room, back then. Alejandro tried to scare them off with a baseball bat.' He laughs darkly as he remembers. 'My mother was furious.'

I'm holding my breath again. I really must stop doing that.

'Am I scaring you?' he asks when I exhale.

'No, not at all,' I reply quickly.

'Are you tired?'

'Not after that nap.' Pause. 'Are you?' Please say no, please say no.

'No. Although I should be, thanks to you making all that noise this morning.'

'This morning? Oh, the cleaning!' Was that only this morning? It feels like days ago.

'I'm going to get another beer,' he tells me, getting to his feet. 'You want me to open the other bottle?'

'Better not. Can I just have a water, please?'

'Water,' he mutters, shaking his head with disgust as he walks off.

'Tell me something funny,' he says on his return.

'There's not much funny about my life at the moment,' I reply sardonically.

'Have *you* had your palms read?' he asks curiously.

I shift on the sofa. 'How did you guess?'

'The way you reacted when I told you about my mother.'

'Oh.' I laugh uneasily. 'Yeah, I did once.'

'Is it all bullshit?'

I shrug and meet his eyes. 'I don't know. What do you think?'

'Who knows? He told her something which freaked her out. My father, Alejandro, my mother . . . They're all dead, so he can't have been very positive.'

I sigh. 'I had my palms read when I was eighteen and on holiday with Marty. The woman – Deadly Diane, we nicknamed her – told me that something bad would happen to me and that it had something to do with a black car.' I shake my head. 'I avoided taking black cabs – taxis,' I explain, 'for years.'

He stares at me directly.

'In the end, it wasn't me I had to be worried about,' I say quietly. He waits for me to continue. 'My boyfriend before Matthew died in a car accident. He was a racing driver. He drove a black car. Well, it was black, white and silver, but . . .' My voice trails off.

'What was his name?'

'Will Trust.'

Leo looks shocked. 'That was you? You were his girlfriend? I read about you in the papers.'

I give him a small shrug and meet his eyes.

'I thought we were supposed to be talking about something funny!' I exclaim, and he smiles at me, accepting my change of subject. 'What time do you have to be at work tomorrow?' I ask.

'Eight.'

'Shit! Eight?' I ask with horror. 'But that's like, only a few hours away!'

He stands up and holds his hand down to me. 'Come on, let's get you to bed.'

He pulls me to my feet and I wobble. He steadies me with his hands and suddenly I'm alive with goosebumps. With you? Can I come to bed with you? I don't say this out loud, but surely one look into my eyes as I stare up at him tells him what I'm thinking. Right now I don't care.

He meets my gaze for a long moment before dropping his hands from my arms and taking a step backwards.

I quickly avert my gaze before he can see my humiliation. I may be drunk, but I can still feel it. I call goodnight over my shoulder as I hurry up the stairs.

Chapter 18

The house is quiet when I wake up the next morning with a pounding headache. Why didn't I choose vodka? The hangovers are much more bearable. The memory of last night comes back to me and my face heats up as I recall Leo stepping away from me. I bury my face in my hands, even though there's no one there to see me. I'm so embarrassed. Maybe I'm overreacting. I try to rationalise the situation. He steadied me with his hands and then let me go. That's not so bad, is it? Who's to say he knew what was going through my mind? I take a deep breath and spend a considerable time trying to convince myself. Finally I climb out of bed and pull on my beach dress before going downstairs. My phone battery has well and truly conked out so I have no idea of the time. The house seems deserted, and when I eventually locate the time on a news channel I see that it's already after eleven. I slump down on the sofa and veg out in front of the telly until I can bring myself to go and grab a bowl of cereal and hunt out some ibuprofen.

My suitcase arrives at around one thirty, and by then my mood has improved. I'm so pleased to have my things back. I charge up my phone and feel strange as I unpack my things into the drawers and wardrobe. For a moment everything seems very surreal – I can't actually believe I'm here, that I *stayed* . . . I wonder what's going on back home. I change into my favourite light-blue sundress, then I switch on my phone. There are three messages from Matthew asking me, in an increasingly resigned voice, to call him, two from Marty, pretty much saying the same thing, one from my mum, and one from Becky, wondering what's going on. I ring her first.

'Laura!' she exclaims. 'Where are you?'

'Still in Key West,' I admit with embarrassment. 'I'm so sorry, I should have called you.'

'What's going on?' she asks with surprise.

'I'm afraid I'm not coming home yet.'

'What do you mean?' She's confused.

'Matthew's . . . The girl, Tessa . . . She's had the baby.'

'Oh.' Silence.

'Yep.' I half laugh.

'That's pretty early, isn't it? Is it okay?'

'It's a he. And yes, they say he'll be fine.'

'Fuck.'

Gotta love Becky. Never afraid to swear in front of her boss.

'How are things there?' I ask.

'Fine, it's all fine,' she replies. 'Everything's pretty much sewn up for the ball next month.'

'Bollocks, I forgot about that.'

'Don't worry, it's under control. We've sold seventy-five per cent of the tickets and the Twitter campaign is bringing in new sales every day.'

'That's fantastic! You were so right about Twitter.'

'Yeah, well, you gave me the go-ahead.'

I smile. She really was a good find.

'But how are you?' she asks kindly. 'When are you coming home?'

'I don't know,' I reply quietly. 'I can't face it yet.'

'I understand.'

'But listen,' I start. 'I'm going to go to Miami and buy a computer at the weekend. I'll be able to do some work from here as of next week.'

'How long are you thinking of staying?' she asks again, this time with more surprise.

'I *really* don't know,' I respond. 'I might stay for the summer.'

'*Really?*'

My answer takes me aback, and I was the one who said it.

'Don't worry,' she says quickly. 'Look, everything's going well here, and if you can work from there – which of course you can – then, wicked. We'll get it sorted out.'

She sounds so in control, so competent. I'm relieved.

'Thanks, Becky,' I say softly.

'You're welcome. Enjoy the sunshine! I'm jealous as hell!'

We both laugh weakly, because no one could be properly jealous of my situation.

'Call me about anything, okay?' I tell her firmly. 'Consider me back at work from Monday.'

'Cool.' I think she's smiling.

'Speak then.'

We say our goodbyes and hang up. I sit there for a moment staring at my phone. Am I really staying here for the summer? It's the end of May now . . . I'm allowed to stay in the USA for ninety days without a visa. Why shouldn't I? Leo will be here . . . My face

162

burns as I remember last night, but I put the memory out of my head and call Mum. She's okay, just a little worried, but she totally freaks out when I repeat my plans to stay.

'Laura, you cannot just up and leave your home for three months!' she cries.

'Why not?' I ask defensively.

'You're a grown woman!'

'Thanks for that, Mum,' I say wryly.

'You need to come home and talk to your husband,' she says firmly.

'No,' I reply, equally firmly.

'Laura!' she snaps.

Now I'm getting cross. 'Mum, you're right, I am an adult, and I'm capable of making my own decision. I'm staying here for the summer. I'm going to do some work – Becky's happy about it, so why shouldn't you be? I need some more time. If I come back now, I may as well file for divorce,' I end dramatically.

She doesn't speak for so long that I wonder if she's still there. 'Mum?'

'Okay,' she sniffs. 'It's up to you. I just hope you're not doing anything silly.'

'What's that supposed to mean?' I ask and immediately wish I hadn't.

'With that man.'

'I told you, he's just a friend.' I say it too loudly. She who denies too much, and all that. But in this case, it really is the truth. If he's even that. 'Look, I'm going to go. I've got a headache and—'

'Why have you got a headache?'

For pity's sake. 'I drank too much last night, okay?'

I can feel her disapproval radiating down the line from thousands of miles away.

'How's Dad?' I try to sound normal. Why shouldn't I change the subject and ask about my father?

'Worried about you,' she replies haughtily.

'Well, tell him not to. Is he there? Can I have a word?'

'No, he's in the grain shed.' Dad's an arable farmer. He's heading for retirement, but he likes to keep his eye on the ball, even if hired hands do most of the work.

'Well, give him my love when he comes in.'

Pause. 'Okay. I will do.'

'Love you, too, Mum.'

'You, too.'

I don't have the energy to ring Marty after that, let alone Matthew. I send them both texts instead, telling them I have my phone back and that I'll call later. My phone rings instantly. It's Marty. So much for that plan.

'Hey,' I say with no enthusiasm.

'What's up?' she asks. 'Has anything happened with Leo?'

'No!' I cry.

By the time I've managed to convince her that nothing is going on, I'm well and truly knackered. And then Matthew calls. I should have left my bloody phone off!

'Look, Matthew, I'm tired, okay? I don't have the energy to talk.' Those are my first words to him.

'Tough, because you're going to have to,' he snaps. 'You can't stay over there forever, Laura.'

'I'm not planning on staying here forever, Matthew,' I reply pedantically flopping backwards on the bed.

'When are you coming home, then?'

'I think I'll stay here for the summer,' I say casually.

'What?'

'Shh.' He's hurting my head.

'What about work?'

'I'm going to get a new computer at the weekend. I can do some stuff from here,' I explain, quite proud of my plan. He doesn't answer for a long while.

'You've got it all worked out, haven't you?' He sounds bitter.

I sit upright on the bed as anger surges through me. 'Don't you dare have a go at me!' I shout into the phone. 'Do you think I *want* this?'

He has the grace to stay silent.

'Have you seen him? The baby?' I ask angrily.

'Yes. Of course,' he replies quietly, but his words feel like a slap around my face. Of course he's seen his son. Of course he has. But I wasn't prepared for the pain of hearing this. I stifle a sob and hang up on him, then I turn my phone off.

I cry so hard it triples the pain in my head, but it's a long time before I can stop. Finally I go downstairs and get myself some more cereal – I don't feel like eating, but I know I need to put something in my stomach. I sit at the dining-room table and spoon in mouthfuls, my whole body aching with despair. Am I being really stupid? Should I just go home and face up to everything?

After, well, let's call it brunch, I take a couple more ibuprofen and melancholically tidy the house and clean the kitchen. The only time I smile during all of this is when I wash the dishes from last night, remembering Leo's coconut curry. But soon I'm back in the depths of desolation. I go and watch daytime television in a daze.

At four thirty, Leo and Jorge come home and my spirits lift, despite last night's embarrassment.

'How's it going?' Jorge asks jovially, coming over and flopping down into a chair. His hair is extra curly from the salt water. Leo appears in the doorway. He's wearing khaki-coloured shorts and a yellow T-shirt.

'Hey,' he says, looking at me directly.

'How was your dive?' I try to act normally.

'I didn't dive today,' he responds.

'That's right, you were driving the boat.'

'It was good,' Jorge interjects, dragging my attention away. '*Fantastic* visibility. It's going to be good tonight!'

'Tonight?' I ask Jorge with confusion, aware that Leo hasn't moved from the doorway.

'The night dive. Have you forgotten?' he asks in an accusing tone.

'Er, yes, I sort of had.'

'You are coming, aren't you?' he asks with annoyance.

'Um—'

'How was your day?' Leo interrupts. His eyes flit over my dress. 'You been shopping?'

'My suitcase arrived.'

'Happy?'

His eyes burn into mine for a long moment, and I find I can't answer him. Then he looks at my lips.

'So what time are we going for this dive tonight, then?' I ask Jorge, trying to still my beating heart.

'Sunset,' he replies, as Leo turns his attention to the television.

Was it my imagination, or did Leo just think about kissing me?

*

I'm still feeling jittery that night when we're on the boat, heading out into open water. The sun has already sunk below the horizon, but it's not quite dark. There are five other divers, along with Jorge, Leo, Tegan and another man, introduced by Jorge as Bernard, who is piloting the boat tonight. Leo sits opposite me at the back of the boat, his elbows resting on his knees. But neither of us says anything as we zoom away from the shore. By the time we reach the reef, my jittery feeling has intensified, but now it's because of the dive. We're already kitted out in our wetsuits – full body ones tonight – but once we moor up, we have to put the rest of our equipment on.

'You okay?' Leo asks me in a low voice as he helps me put on my jacket.

'I'm nervous,' I admit, fastening the straps.

'Don't be,' he says seriously, putting his hands on my arms from behind. He turns me around to face him and we go through the buddy routine without saying much at all. He follows me down to the platform. We're the second couple to enter the water.

'You want me to go first?' Leo asks.

'Please.' I nod.

He takes a large stride into the water and gives me – and Bernard and Tegan – the okay sign.

'Come on,' he encourages, as he bobs in the waves. I take a large step and splash into the dark ocean, having no idea what lurks beneath in the blackness. This is surely the most nuts thing I've ever done.

And then Leo takes my hand in his. 'Okay?'

I nod and turn to give the sign to Tegan and Bernard.

'Follow the rope down.' Leo lifts his BCD inflator button out of the water and presses it to deflate. I do the same, trying not to freak out as my head sinks below the water. There's a light hanging under the boat, and it glows eerily in the dark as we slowly make our way down the length of the rope to the soft sand below. Finally Jorge joins us and we set off as a group, staying close to our buddies. Jorge, Leo and a couple of the others have torches, and the light streams unnaturally through the black water. The others inflate their BCDs to swim over the reef, but Leo taps my arm and indicates that he wants to go left. I watch with slight panic as the larger group swims away, but one look at Leo and I know I'll follow him anywhere.

The reef looks more alien at night, the coral brighter under the light of his torch. He shines his light into crevices, showing me shoals of brightly coloured fish sleepily moving to and fro with the current. He moves on further, keeping close to the sand so we're going around the edge of the reef, highlighting more fish in the darkness. I begin to relax and am filled with wonder. I'm no longer scared. And then suddenly he stops, his hand on my arm. I follow the light of his torch to see a shoal of barracuda hovering about four metres in front of us. My pulse speeds up at the sight of the fearsome razor-toothed fish, and then Leo's torchlight slides slowly upwards, and there, above them, is a large, stationary reef shark. I begin to breathe more heavily as my core fills with fright. Leo takes my hand and squeezes it. I can't tear my eyes away from the view in front of me. I'm scared, so scared. Out of the corner of my eye I can see lights flashing as the others swim across the reef, oblivious. Yet here I am, alone, with Leo. No, not alone. With a dozen man-munching creatures. I could die here, in the dark. Just because I fancy him enough to follow him anywhere. I'm an idiot.

Leo turns and, still holding my hand, leads me back the way we came. My heart is in my mouth as I imagine them snapping at my heels. Then he points towards the reef and inflates slightly. What? Where is he going? Surely we're getting the hell out of here? But, no! He wants me to follow him across the reef. I shake my head and he looks confused. I point upwards. I'm going back to the boat, buster. He shakes his head at me, then points obstinately towards the reef.

Argh! Where's the rope? I can't get back to the boat without it – I wouldn't dare. Would Tegan and Bernard see me in the dark if I popped up anywhere? Leo nods towards the reef and gives me the okay sign. Bollocks. I nod unhappily and inflate a little. A moment later, my hand is in his again. He squeezes hard and I squeeze back, starting to relax once more as he picks up a sea star and offers it to me to touch. We even see a lobster lurking behind some rocks, but I practically jump out of my wetsuit when an eel slithers out from beside it. By the time we reach the rope, where some of the others are already waiting, I'm actually disappointed that the dive is over. This feeling intensifies once we're safely back on the boat, the emphasis on *safe*. I'm alive! And that was amazing!

'How was that?' Leo asks me with a huge grin.

'Incredible,' I breathe.

'Those barracuda!' he exclaims.

'And that shark!' I cry. It didn't kill me! Yay.

'You made me laugh when you jumped at the eel,' he says.

I giggle. 'That was funny.' Less funny at the time.

As he shrugs himself out of his BCD then helps me with mine, and I unclick my weight belt, we continue to excitedly dissect the dive and everything we saw.

'Good dive?' Jorge asks with a smile as he climbs aboard.

169

'Great,' Leo replies. 'We saw a huge shoal of barracuda, with a reef shark hovering a few feet above it.'

'No shit?' Jorge says. 'You always see the best stuff.'

'You mean that was good?' I joke. 'I was terrified.'

Jorge laughs and Leo wraps his arm around my shoulders and squeezes me quickly but affectionately before letting me go. 'You'll never forget it, though.'

No. That's true. I'll never forget that, as long as I live.

Chapter 19

'We're going to Miami . . .'

It's Will Smith again! But this time I'm in high spirits. I start to bop along enthusiastically to the song playing on the radio and then reach over to put the volume up. Leo slaps my hand away.

'Turn this shit off,' he berates, changing the channel.

'You are no fun at all,' I tease as he settles on Kings of Leon. 'Are you always this controlling?'

'You call this controlling?' He flashes me a look.

'You mean you get worse?' I tut at him. 'How do your girlfriends cope?'

This question makes me feel oddly dizzy.

'Girlfriends?' he scoffs.

'Yeah, you know, girls who are friends,' I say drily.

'I don't have any girls who are friends,' he says slightly crossly.

'Carmen's a friend, isn't she?'

'Carmen is my sister-in-law. Ex-sister-in-law,' he corrects. 'And she's a pain in the arse.'

'What about me? I'm a friend, aren't I?'

171

'Hmm.' He grunts, but his reply makes me grin. I haven't stopped smiling since we got in the car almost three hours ago.

'So you don't have a girlfriend, then?' I try to keep my voice sounding level.

'No!' he snaps, huffing. My insides swell with joy. I didn't think he did, but really, what would I know? 'You talk too much,' he adds.

I look out of the window as the roads grow wider and the cars move faster. We pass the first of what I remember to be many McDonald's.

Carmen was taken aback to hear that Leo and I were going up to Miami together. I think even Jorge was a little surprised, although he did a better job of not showing it. I thought he might have chosen to tag along. I'm not sure how I feel about the fact that he didn't. I'm on my own with Leo for a whole weekend and I'm a little bit excited, a whole lot nervous, and slightly concerned that Jorge thinks he might be the third in three's a crowd. I hope he doesn't believe there's more to this than meets the eye. Fantasising about Leo is one thing; actually making that fantasy a reality is a whole different ballgame, I tell myself gravely. And then I imagine his lips on mine and an illicit thrill goes through me.

I never did make it to the Wynwood district on the morning of my almost-departure. Marty chose to go shopping, and I was feeling so down about leaving that I just went along with her, but didn't buy a thing.

The Walls are incredible. Leo takes me for a quick tour before we go to his place, explaining that back in 2009 a renowned community revitaliser called Tony Goldman had a vision to make giant canvases out of Wynwood's large stock of windowless warehouses, bringing together the greatest street art ever seen in one place. Everywhere I look buildings have been painted with striking images: black and white graphics, like a zebra; a literal rat race, with rats chasing each other through a maze; a huge face of a man, coloured red.

'This is amazing!' I exclaim, feeling bad that I didn't make more of an effort to bring Marty here. I think she would have liked it.

After a while, Leo does a U-turn and heads back the way we came. Soon we're pulling up outside his slightly run-down apartment block. Slightly is putting it mildly – it's a total mess from the outside. I know it's the threat of the unknown, because I have never stayed anywhere like this before, but I feel uneasy. Then I remember who I'm with.

'This is home,' Leo says, climbing out of the car.

'It's . . . nice,' I reply weakly, as he gets our bags out of the boot.

'I bet it's a side of Miami you haven't seen before,' he teases.

'You're right. Not that I liked the glitzy side,' I tell him, although I'm not sure he's convinced. I'm not sure *I'm* convinced, actually. In comparison . . .

I follow him up the external staircase to the second floor. There's a small balcony at the front of every apartment; some have old office chairs rotting outside, others have mostly dead plants, and there's some washing hanging out here and there. Leo has a couple of chairs and they're not too shabby. He unlocks the door and pushes it open for me to enter. It's dark inside. The curtains are drawn, so the first thing he does after gathering up the post pile is pull them back to let in the sunshine. I look around and a smile forms on my face. Retro is the only way to describe it, with a couple of battered brown leather sofas, a wooden coffee table and a swirly orange and brown carpet. He has some cool graffiti art hanging on his walls, and the kitchen is small but clean.

'You can sleep in the bedroom,' he says, taking my bag through there. I follow him, but regret it when I see how small the room is: the double bed dominates the space, and I have to take a few awkward steps backwards.

'What do you want to do?' he asks with a raised eyebrow as he follows me slowly into the living room. The back of my knees bump into the sofa, causing me to sit down. I'm in his space, now, his masculine sexy space, and the effect is overpowering.

We head into Miami to pick up what we came to get in the first place: a brand-new, shiny, whizz-bang Apple MacBook for yours truly. I'm excited about heading back to Key West to set it up, but we have a night out in Miami first, and Leo has vowed not to take me anywhere touristy. I have no idea what's in store, so I choose the safest, most dependable outfit I have, in the safest most dependable colour: black. Black skinny jeans and a tight black top, with heavy gunmetal-hued eye make-up and neutral lipstick. I blow-dried my hair this morning in anticipation, so I don't have to do anything with it. I get ready in Leo's bathroom, which has room for a shower, toilet and basin, but nothing else – so I have to hop around in a tiny circle as I pull on my jeans. I have a quick peek in his bathroom cabinet, but find only his shaving equipment, deodorant and some headache tablets – nothing interesting, although the latter might come in useful later. I emerge to find him standing in the middle of the living room wearing a khaki T-shirt and black cargo pants. I flash him a small smile and he looks amused, but doesn't take his eyes away from mine as I walk towards him.

'Drink?' he asks, picking up two glasses from the coffee table and handing one over.

'Thanks. Cheers.' I chink his glass and put mine to my lips. 'What is it?' I ask, before taking a drink.

'Vodka and lemon. I don't have any cranberry.'

I grin at him and take a sip. I switched to vodka and cranberry a couple of nights ago after my horrible wine hangover earlier in the week.

'My friend Drew will be here soon.'

'Drew?'

'He's driving tonight.'

'Oh! Great.' I hadn't thought about that. I'm glad Leo will be drinking with me.

When Drew turns up, I'm already feeling slightly tipsy. He's black with short braids, a grey T-shirt and weathered jeans. He reminds me of a young Lenny Kravitz.

'Drew is a street artist,' Leo tells me, nodding at the pictures on his walls.

'Are you?' I ask, impressed. 'Did you do these?'

He shrugs. 'Yeah.'

'I had to persuade him to work with smaller canvases,' Leo says wryly, and I glance at Drew to see him rolling his eyes.

'He has a way of persuading people to do things they don't really want to do,' he tells me with a grin. 'Watch out for him.' I laugh and Leo punches him on his arm. 'Ow!'

'Laura saw the Walls today,' Leo says, moving away from what was proving to be a greatly intriguing subject.

'What did you think?' Drew asks me.

'One of the coolest things I've ever seen.' He nods, seeming pleased with my reaction.

I move closer to study one of the abstract paintings. I soon realise that what I'm looking at is a swarm of bees, which are small and realistic in the background, becoming brightly coloured and grotesquely comical as they come to the forefront. Something about them appeals to me.

'I really like these,' I say with a smile.

Later we end up in a dingy basement bar with exposed brickwork and a DJ playing on decks in the corner. A few of Leo and Drew's friends join us, and they're an interesting, diverse crowd. Initially I'm worried that I look out of place, but soon the vodka sinks in and I no longer care. Drew has a great sense of humour and I'm in stitches a few times, namely when he's teasing Leo. They're obviously good mates and go way back. Leo is different with Drew than with Jorge. With Jorge he's more laid-back, with Drew more dynamic, more upbeat. As the night wears on, I become vaguely aware that Drew has started flirting with me. He puts his hand on my cheek to hold me close so he can speak into my ear.

'Why do you want to go back to Key West when you can have Miami?' he asks me, his lips brushing against my ear. I like him enough, although not in that way, for it not to be deeply unpleasant.

'I like Key West,' I tell him, pulling away slightly to look him in the eye.

'Yeah, but nothing beats Miami,' he tries to convince me.

I screw up my nose.

'What? You don't like this?' He gestures around him.

'Yeah,' I admit, 'this place is wicked, but . . .' My voice trails off and I look around, suddenly realising Leo is not with us. 'Where's Leo?' I ask with alarm.

Drew shrugs. 'Probably gone to take a leak. So what do you reckon about staying a few more days, checking out Miami? I can put you up.'

I'm too distracted to reply, as I search the room. And then I see him pushing back through the crowd. His eyes meet mine and I feel such a thrill that I can't take in what Drew is saying to me.

'Sorry?' I ask him weakly, not taking my eyes from Leo as Drew pulls me closer to speak into my ear again. Leo's gaze flickers towards Drew and his expression seems to harden – but maybe it's just the alcohol messing with my mind. Out of nowhere, a girl steps in front of Leo and puts her hand on his chest. He looks taken aback. I can't see her face, but she's petite and has shiny, dark-brown, ringletted curls and my imagination convinces me that she's absolutely beautiful. She reaches up to hold his face as she kisses both cheeks. Leo's eyes flit past her to Drew and me, but she doesn't take her hands from his face, bringing his attention back to her. I feel a sharp pang of jealousy.

'Laura!' Drew laughs, snapping me back to my immediate surroundings. 'Man, you're not listening to a word I'm saying.'

'I'm sorry.' I shake my head abruptly, but can't give him my full attention. 'What was that?'

'Oh, never mind. Aah,' he says knowingly, looking over his shoulder and spying Leo.

'What?' I ask quickly. 'Who is she?'

'Ashlee,' Drew enlightens me. 'Leo's ex.'

'She was his girlfriend?' My stomach swirls with dread as I watch Leo try to move past her. She draws him back, but now I can see her side profile and my suspicions were correct. She's stunning, with a pretty turned-up nose and a sprinkling of freckles. She's smiling as she stares up at Leo, but I notice with relief that he still looks annoyed. He says something to her and nods towards Drew and me. Her eyes dart between us and her brow furrows. Leo breaks away and comes over. Drew is leaning up against the bar, his shoulder pressing against mine, but then Leo's hand breaks contact between us as he pushes past Drew to retrieve his beer from the bar. He takes a swig and looks irritated.

'Drew,' Ashlee says, acknowledging him with a nod. She doesn't look too pleased to see him.

'Ashlee,' he replies. The feeling, it seems, is mutual.

She turns to me, cocking her head to one side. 'I'm Ashlee.'

'Hi,' I say, holding out my hand for her to shake. 'Laura.'

'Are you going to buy me a drink, Leonardo?' she asks meaningfully, not taking her eyes from mine.

Leo turns and holds his hand up to the bartender.

'So—' she starts.

'How's it going, Ashlee?' Drew interrupts, not seeming quite as relaxed as he did before.

'Oh, you know, Drew,' she replies casually. 'Same as always. I wasn't expecting to see Leo back this weekend.' She's speaking to him, but regarding me.

'I only got the call yesterday,' Drew tells her.

'At least you got the call,' she says drily. 'Not saying it's not a nice surprise. So . . .' she starts again, and I just know she's dying to find out what my relationship is with Leo.

Before she can ask her question, Leo is shoving a drink into her hand. The bar is packed, so God knows how he got served so quickly. 'Here,' he snaps. It's something crystal clear and sparkling, on ice.

'Thanks, baby.' She takes a sip and then stares at him, incredulous. 'Water? You got me water, Leonardo?'

'If you want something else, you can get it yourself,' he bites back.

The look on her face ... The look on his! Her body language changes to become more aggressive, almost like she's squaring up to him. He stands his ground, staring her down, but the expression on his face is actually quite frightening: dark and dangerous, but still somehow very, very sexy.

'Screw you,' she spits, throwing her glass of water at his chest before spinning on her heels and storming out.

Leo brushes the water off his T-shirt in disgust.

'Bitch,' he mutters angrily, and it's a bit of a shock to hear him speaking about a woman like that, even one who's just drenched him.

'Welcome back to Miami,' Drew says sarcastically.

'And you wonder why I was in no rush to return?' Leo asks him as one of the bartenders shouts out his name.

'You can't hide from her forever,' Drew replies as the bartender throws Leo a black shirt.

'What ... What happened between you?'

Leo looks surprised when I ask this question, almost like he'd forgotten I was there. He glances at Drew and then whips off his wet T-shirt. A group of girls nearby begin to whoop. Leo glares at them with a look that would stop traffic and I quickly shut my mouth as he pulls on the fresh short-sleeved shirt and irately buttons it up. It has the name of the bar stitched in small white letters in the top right-hand corner, but, as uniforms go, he looks hot in it. I wonder if he works here. He wrings out his T-shirt and stuffs it into his pocket.

All this action hasn't hidden the fact that my question has gone unanswered, so I ask it again. Drew replies.

179

'She's crazy, Laura, don't worry about her.' He tries to brush me off.

'What do you mean, crazy?'

'Crazy.' He makes circles with his forefinger at the side of his head.

'Clinically insane?' I ask, unwilling to let it go.

'She's just a bit screwed up,' Drew says. 'Obsessed with Leo. She's uncontrollable on a few drinks.'

'How long were you together?' I ask Leo this question directly.

It's a moment before he replies, and then it's unhappily. 'Not quite a year.' He doesn't want to talk about this.

I suck in my breath. 'That long?'

'Too long,' he says.

Drew explains. 'She wouldn't take no for an answer, wouldn't let him call it off.'

'Looks like she still doesn't want to take no for an answer,' I comment.

Leo slams his beer down on the bar. 'We've got an early start tomorrow,' he says to me.

'You're not going?' Drew exclaims in dismay.

'Sorry, buddy. We'll catch a taxi.'

'No!' he laments. 'Come on! Laura,' he turns to me, pleading, 'there's this really cool bar you have *got* to see. You'll come with me, won't you?'

'Maybe some other time,' Leo interjects, and then my hand is in his and he's pulling me through the crowds and out onto the street before I can even say goodbye. I'm too taken aback to do anything other than follow him, and then he drops my hand, leaving me wanting. He hails a taxi, opening the door for me and climbing in afterwards. My head is spinning. I'm not really sure what just happened to our night, but I have no idea what to say. Leo stares out of the window, not saying anything, either. He still seems furious and I don't really know how to react. It's only when we're back inside the apartment and he's dragging a sleeping bag down from the wardrobe in his bedroom that I find my voice.

'Are you okay?' I ask from the doorway. The room doesn't feel as small as it did earlier – maybe it's the alcohol, humming through my veins.

'I'm fine,' he says shortly, making to move past me. I press my back up against the wall so he can. He pauses when he's right in front of me, the bulk of his body taking up all the space it can without actually touching me. Goosebumps form on my arms. I look up at him and his dark eyes burn into mine, making me hold my breath. 'Get some sleep,' he says suddenly, moving away. It's only when I'm safely inside his room with the door shut that I can breathe again.

Chapter 20

We barely speak on the drive back to Key West. I doze off, thankful that my mind is no longer racing. Just a few short hours ago all my nerve endings were on edge, knowing that Leo was in the next room, wanting him to burst through my door and ravish my body. His sheets smelled of him, his pillows, too. Thoughts of him consumed me all night long and I don't think I have ever felt so turned on. I realise, as I fall in and out of consciousness, that Matthew has barely entered my thoughts all weekend. I feel nothing when I think of him. I'm dulled to him, muted. Right now it's all about Leo.

When we're approximately forty-five minutes away from Key West, Leo pulls off the road. I sit up, sleepily.

'I need a coffee,' he says. 'You hungry?' It's pretty much the most he's said to me this entire journey.

'A little,' I reply, as my stomach grumbles its own reply.

A waitress seats us at a table on the deck. The air is warm and muggy, but it feels good to be outside. I gaze at the small marina filled with medium-sized boats moored up at jetties, and study the mail boxes outside the houses, some of them fashioned in the shape of colourful fish. I'm tempted to buy one to take home with me. Not that I have a house with a mail box. We live in a flat.

Leo stretches back in his seat. He looks very far away. The waitress brings our coffees over and he leans in and cradles his cup in his hands, his tanned forearms resting on the table between us. For the first time I notice the dark circles under his eyes.

'You look tired,' I comment.

'Didn't sleep much last night.'

'Me neither.'

We meet each other's eyes for about three seconds which seem to last much longer. He breaks away to blow at the steaming liquid. I try to think of something to say.

'Drew seemed pretty pissed off we left early last night' is what I settle on.

'Yeah.' Leo tuts and gives me a look.

'What?' I ask him with a grin.

'He wasn't pissed *I* left early; he was pissed *you* did.'

'What?' I scoff. 'What are you going on about?'

'You know what I'm talking about.'

'No, I don't!' Although I sort of do.

He gives me a look that tells me he can see straight through me. I shake my head and try to act nonchalant.

'Well, I wasn't interested, anyway.'

He takes a sip of his drink. 'I did tell him you were married.'

'Did you? When?'

'On the phone before we went to Miami.'

'Oh, right.' I'm desperate to know exactly what Leo said about me. 'What else did you tell him?'

He shrugs. 'Nothing.'

'Nothing?' I frown. 'But you thought the marriage bit was important?'

'Isn't it?' he asks with a direct stare.

I shift in my seat and try to hide behind my cup. 'I doubt I'll be married for much longer.'

He stares out at the marina and I gather the conversation is over, so I'm surprised when he speaks again.

'Do you really think it's over?'

God, the look in his eyes. My head begins to tingle. I swallow, but my voice still comes out sounding like a whisper.

'Yes.'

There is no denying the sexual tension between us this time, and I know he can feel it, too. I have an almost unbearable urge to climb over the table and kiss his lips, but now is not the time or the place.

The car is so charged with electricity on the next leg of our journey that the engine could almost be powered by it. When we climb out of the car, he doesn't meet my eyes. He gets our bags out of the boot and follows me through the yard. The door is shut, which is unusual as the others tend to leave it open when they're in. Leo unlocks it and I don't quite move far enough away, so his arm brushes against mine, sending shivers up and down my body. I can't bear this for much longer.

The house is silent, empty. We're alone. I stare at Leo, willing him to look at me, to give me some sign. But he goes straight to the stairs. On autopilot I follow him up. He obviously expects me to tail off to my room, so, when I don't, he glances back at me with confusion. I give him a look and walk past him to the second set of stairs. I'm halfway up before I glance over my shoulder to see him still standing at the bottom. His expression is torn. I continue up the stairs and push open his door.

There's a double mattress on the floor – no bed base – with dishevelled cream-coloured sheets and two pillows, dented with the outline of his head. His curtains are drawn, so the light is dim, but I can just make out the ever-present dust motes gliding through the air. He has posters on his walls of old Cuba, and a rail for his clothes to hang on. Most are slung over the top of the rail and on a chair, not hanging, just thrown where he's taken them off. It smells of him, dark and musty, woody with cigar smoke. It smells of sex. He hasn't had a woman here since I've been here. But it smells of sex – the sex I absolutely have to have with him. I hear his footsteps on the stairs and then he's standing right behind me. I can hear his breathing and it matches mine, short and sharp and fierce with desire. I crave his touch, his lips on my neck, but nothing happens. I turn around to face him. His features are taut, his chin tilted up and away from me, but his eyes stare down at me, flashing in the low light. I want him so much. I reach up and touch his face.

'No.' His voice sounds harsh, but he doesn't push me away.

Feeling stung, I let my hand drop, but I can't give up. Won't give up. I'm desperate for him to kiss me.

'You have a husband.' His breathing is laboured.

'Not for much longer.'

He shakes his head. 'You'll go home. Things change. How you feel about him . . .'

'I'll never forgive him,' I say fervently as I place my hand on his chest. It's firm under my touch. How I want his T-shirt off . . .

'Laura. Stop.' It's him saying my name that makes me realise I can do anything but. I place my other hand on his chest and slide both of them upwards to his neck, warm under my touch. He resists when I try to bring his face down to mine, but I stand up on tiptoes and look him right in the eyes. I can smell him from here, the warmth of his breath, the citrusy smell of his shower gel. For a moment I think he looks scared, but I hesitate only a second before my lips are on his. He's frozen under my touch, his lips firm and unrelenting. I pull away, but only by a few inches as I gaze up at him.

'Leo, don't tell me to stop.'

His eyes are filled with pain. I bring one hand around and touch it to his clenched jaw, and then I press my lips back to his, willing his to open, to kiss me back. I lightly trace his lips with my tongue and I think that's what breaks him because his sudden sharp inhalation sucks the breath out of my mouth and then his rough hands are in my hair, pulling me to him as his lips crush mine. I gasp for air and kiss him back. My hands are up inside his T-shirt and I pull it over his head before doing the same to my dress. He hikes me up so I have to wrap my legs around his waist and then he presses me up against a wall and kisses my neck. I think I'm in heaven. I want this man so much – and I can feel how much he wants me, too. I push him away and tackle his shorts, desperate to remove all barriers between us. We fall down to the bed.

In the back of my mind I realise I have no condoms and I think I'll cry if he doesn't either, but before I can ask his hand is in a bedside drawer, rummaging around.

'Fuck!' he curses, then breathes a sigh of relief as his fingers find what he's looking for. Moments later he's ready for me, and I've never felt more ready for him, for anyone. He stares deep into my eyes as he sinks into me, and then my back is arched, my neck stretched, my mind delirious.

'Open your eyes,' he says harshly and they shoot open, meeting his stare, dark with desire. He kisses my lips passionately before cupping my face, his thumb stroking my brow, reminding me to look at him. And then we begin to move together, and it's the most intense sex I've ever had, peppered with ardent kisses, but mostly just locking eyes until that final moment when I let go and scratch my fingernails hard down his back. He shouts out in ecstasy laced with pain before collapsing on me, both of us panting heavily.

I squeeze my eyes shut and press my lips to his neck, which is damp with sweat, as I try to get my breath back.

He recovers before I do, meeting my eyes before rolling off me. 'You're going to kill me,' he says in a low, warning voice. I don't know how to respond, but I know I don't want to let him go so I twist towards him and lay my head on his chest. A moment later his arm curls around me and he holds me tightly. We stay like that until we both fall asleep.

I'm still in his arms when I awake, and I lift my head slightly to gaze at him. He's fast asleep, his features softer and more innocent than I've seen them. I trace my forefinger across his eyebrow and he starts suddenly, his eyes opening to look at mine. His intense expression returns instantly, and I regret for a second that I've woken him. I press my lips to his, and he hesitates only a moment before kissing me back. We're still unclothed under the crumpled bed sheets and I manoeuvre my body so I'm lying partially across him. It's blissful feeling his naked body against mine: skin on skin as we kiss. He brings me up so I'm on top on him and once more I can feel his desire. I hope he has a decent stash of condoms, because I have no intention of leaving his room anytime soon.

*

187

It's early evening before we hear the others return from wherever they've been all day. We've dozed in and out of sleep all afternoon, having sex in between. I lift my head and touch my hand to Leo's neck. He regards me with not quite as much of his usual intensity.

'Do you think they'd notice if we never went downstairs again?' I ask.

He smiles at me and quickly kisses my lips. 'I'm hungry.'

He gets out of bed and I watch furtively as he pulls on some boxer shorts, followed by his shorts and T-shirt from earlier. I let out a small sigh of discontent as I say goodbye to his glorious nakedness.

'Your turn.' He holds his hand down to me and I stand up, feeling more self-conscious now that he's dressed.

I pull on my knickers, followed by my bra and then he passes me my dress. I turn and check my appearance in a small mirror on his old-fashioned dresser – not unlike the one downstairs in my room. I notice his cigar case on top, and smile as I wipe a damp finger underneath my eyes to brush away some errant mascara. I turn to face him and he walks forward, pulling me back into his arms. He holds me tightly for a few seconds, his warm breath in my hair as I press my face against his chest. I suddenly have an almost overpowering urge to cry. I quickly swallow the lump in my throat and pull away, but I'm reluctant to leave this room. He takes my hand and leads me to the door, only dropping it to jog down the stairs. I follow him disconsolately.

'You're back!' Jorge exclaims when we appear in the kitchen, his eyes flitting between us, his brow creasing as he processes the fact that we came downstairs together. 'How was it?' he asks, trying to sound casual, but failing. Or maybe it's just my imagination that he's noticed anything wayward in the first place.

'Good,' I respond weakly.

'Got what we went there for,' Leo adds.

'You got your computer?' Jorge asks, turning to attend to the plastic bags full of shopping on the counter.

'Yep,' I reply, going to help him unpack.

'All set up?'

'No, no, no.' I brush him off. 'I'll do it tomorrow.'

'I'm cooking tonight,' he tells me.

'Urgh,' Leo groans.

'You want some help?' I ask.

'Sure. You can chop a couple of onions for me if you like.'

'No problem.'

Leo leans against the counter next to me. I smirk at him as I unpack the shopping. 'Are you going to help, or what?' I ask cheekily.

'Wasn't my coconut curry enough for you?'

'Is it me or is it feeling hot in here?' Jorge says. Leo flicks a tea towel at him. 'Ouch,' Jorge cries, flashing us both a perplexed look.

I bite my lip and we both try to keep straight faces.

During dinner, Carmen also cottons on that something has happened. I see her eyes flit between Leo and me with increasing confusion. I think it's partly to do with Leo's mood – he's more relaxed and happy tonight, a far cry from his often serious self. 'Did something happen in Miami?' she erupts.

'No,' Leo replies with a shrug, helping himself to more rice and beans. She's too taken aback to press him further.

We converge on the chairs outside later, but I avoid alcohol, choosing a large glass of lemonade on ice. Leo goes for beer, as usual. He sits down first, and I take my seat next to him, with

Jorge on my other side, as we were the other night. This time, though, when Leo's arm rests behind my head it feels only natural to edge closer to him, into the crook of his arm. His finger traces circles on my neck, sending shivers up my spine. I glance at him, my gaze falling on his lips before moving up to his eyes. He looks down at me with amusement, reading my mind.

'What am I missing?' Carmen suddenly demands to know. 'What's going on with you two?'

Leo's finger freezes on my neck and he addresses her directly. 'It's none of your business.'

'It *is* my business,' she says irately. 'Have you two—'

'Shut it,' Leo cuts her off, his finger starting its slow, methodical tracing once again.

She stares at both of us in disbelief, and I sense Jorge's discomfort to my right. Eric, as usual, seems unfazed by any of this. I think it's only Javier's presence that makes Carmen think twice about interrogating us. I see the uncertainty in her eyes as she glances at him, and after that she lets it drop, but I know it won't be for long.

I'm too caught up in the present to care, and as the evening wears on, my body feels more and more strung out and on edge. I want to go to bed with him. I need to go to bed with him. I can't bear to wait for much longer. I turn and look up at him, trying to convey my emotions with my eyes. He gives me a brisk nod and removes his arm from around my neck.

'Night.'

'Already?' Carmen asks with surprise. Leo is usually the last one to hit the sack.

'Me, too,' I say, both of us now on our feet. I can't look her in the eye as I follow Leo inside, and a minute later, when his lips are devouring every inch of my body, she's far, far, far from my mind.

Chapter 21

In the early hours of the morning, nature demands that I take a trip to the toilet. I disentangle myself from Leo's firm grip and pull on his T-shirt before heading downstairs. I brush my teeth and splash water on my face before stepping back out onto the landing, and then I nearly jump out of my skin when I see Carmen, in a white, thigh-length nightie, standing at the top of the stairs like a ghostly apparition.

'You scared the life out of me!' I gasp, putting my hand to my chest.

In response she grabs my arm and marches me into my bedroom.

'What the hell are you doing?' I demand to know as she shuts the door behind her.

'What the hell are *you* doing?' she throws back at me. 'You're married!'

I don't really know what to say to that.

'You can't screw around with him like this!' she hisses, not raising her voice enough to wake the house.

'Are you talking about Leo?' I double-check, because it's possible she's referring to my husband.

'Of course I'm talking about Leonardo!' It strikes me out of the blue that she's not actually angry. She seems . . . anxious?

'Look,' I try to reason with her. 'I really like him.' These words feel so odd coming out of my mouth – especially to her. 'I don't intend to hurt him.'

'Are you insane?' she asks me coldly. 'How can you *not* hurt him?'

'Why are you so worried?' I ask through narrowed eyes.

'You might think that just because we argue, we don't like each other, but you're wrong. He's like a brother to me. When Alejandro died, Leo took care of Javier and me. I won't sit back and watch you hurt him.'

'But I don't want to hurt him!' I exclaim.

'What are you going to do?' she asks incredulously. 'You can't stay here. Your visa will run out and you'll have to go back. And you're *married*!'

'I'll get a divorce,' I reply petulantly.

'What, and marry Leo?' She starts to laugh with disbelief. 'He will never marry you. He will never marry anyone. You're crazy,' she adds, rubbing pinch upon pinch of salt into my wounds. Not that I want to marry him, for pity's sake. 'Leo doesn't believe in marriage. He doesn't even believe in love.'

I stare at her. Then I speak. 'If there's no chance of him falling in love with me, then you really have nothing to worry about, do you?'

Her mouth falls open with surprise, but I don't wait for her response. I walk out of the room and go back upstairs.

Leo is awake when I enter his room and shut the door.

'Hi,' I say with a smile.

'Hi,' he replies, without one.

'Are you okay?' I ask, sliding back under the covers and resting my chin on his chest so I can stare up at him. He has a shadow of stubble on his heavenly jaw and his dark eyes are looking up at the ceiling.

'I was going to ask you the same question.'

'I'm fine,' I say, before correcting myself. 'I'm good.'

'Carmen didn't freak you out?'

'Not really.'

He heard us, then. I reach up and touch his cheek, willing him to look at me. He does. I lean in closer and kiss him, but I can sense him holding back.

'What is it?' I ask, feeling nerves begin to swell in my stomach.

'Nothing,' he replies after a pause, kissing me. He tugs at his T-shirt that I'm still wearing, flashing me a cheeky smile.

'You want me to take it off?' I ask meaningfully.

He slides it up my body and over my head in response.

It's only later that the reality of what I've done begins to sink in. Leo has gone to work at the dive centre – Tegan has returned to New Zealand so he's helping out until they find a replacement – which leaves me alone in the house, with only my thoughts to keep me company. And, for the most part, they're not good company. At first they are: I keep touching my fingers to my lips, remembering Leo's kisses and my hours in his bedroom. I have to force myself to spend time setting up my computer, and I think it's this return to real life that finally makes my head spin. I install myself temporarily at the dining-room table and Becky liaises with me by email, bringing me up to date with the upcoming charity ball she's pretty much organised single-handedly. As the day wears on, my feelings of guilt about the extra work she's had to put in develop into a deep and unpleasant sense of foreboding. I've been having sex with another man while I'm still married to Matthew, and I'm feeling quite sick about it.

I think of Matthew now, properly, for perhaps the first time since I left him. I don't want to think of him pleasantly – it's easier to remember the parts where he hurt me and then I feel justified – and yet I can't help but recall our relationship when it was good. Before he messed it all up.

I sit at the dining-room table and stare out of the window at the silver-grey palms in the garden opposite. They look like plastic. There are trees here I've never seen before in my life. It's beginning to feel surreal.

The first time I met Matthew it was over a pub lunch on Farringdon Road in London, near his newspaper office. It was early December and he was interviewing me about the charity I'd set up in Will's name a few months previously. Will died in the summer, but I was already starting to come to terms with his death. It was a shock to see Matthew for the first time. He was so tall, so good-looking – blond with seriously blue eyes. Will had blue eyes, but Matthew's were piercing. Sitting across from him at our table for two was quite unnerving. I hadn't intended to drink, but suddenly I found myself asking for a glass of white wine. He drank Coke, I remember that. And I remember wondering if he had a girlfriend, but not having the guts to ask. He was funny and incredibly intelligent. I turned the interview around on him on several occasions, asking him about himself. He told me he'd studied English at Cambridge. I told him I grew up in a village just south of there and asked him where he used to go out drinking. We discussed our favourite haunts in the city and I wondered why

I'd never met him before, and then he gently berated me for trying to digress from his questions. I told him I wasn't used to being interviewed, that usually it was all about my ex-boyfriend. I recall the look on his face, the way his smile fell. He had been a little flirtatious up until that point, but suddenly he became serious.

'A friend of mine went to school with Will. It was a shock to all of us when he died.'

I nod dejectedly.

'You were there, weren't you?'

A small part of me thought he was asking me for the sake of his interview, and that I would see this in print and feel used, but I felt compelled to tell him how, yes, I was there at the scene when Will's car flipped and hurtled across the track. I was there in the air ambulance with him as he lay unconscious on a stretcher between his parents and me. I held his hand as my body froze with fear. I loved him more then than I had in the whole year previously. I loved him more then than I ever had, come to think about it. Because I was terrified of losing him. It was serious; I could tell how serious it was. When he was pronounced dead I think I went into shock. He had ended our relationship before that weekend – we were no longer together, no longer destined to marry – but no one knew. I had to carry on this charade of the lover he left behind. I wanted to tell the truth, and I did actually tell his parents, but his mother silenced me.

'He loved you,' was all she could say before emotion stole her words away. She didn't want to hear about it. I didn't know what to do other than go along with it.

I considered telling Matthew this, but I held back. He's a journalist. And he's good at his job.

Yes, he was good at his job. When the interview came out, there was nothing in there that I felt uncomfortable about. He mentioned Will, of course he did, but in a way that would only bring right and good attention to the charity. I tried to put Matthew out of my mind after that, but I couldn't. So I sent him an email to say thank you. He replied within a few minutes – I still remember the thrill I felt, seeing his name pop up in my inbox. I thought about asking him out for a drink – a proper drink – but I chickened out. I still didn't have the answer to the girlfriend question, and I couldn't actually believe that anyone as gorgeous as Matthew could be without a girl in his life. So I invited him to our charity Christmas drinks instead.

I was manic that night, running around like a woman possessed, trying to make sure everything ran smoothly and that everyone had a good time. When I saw him walk through the door, I stopped right in my tracks. He saw me, too, and smiled brightly, looking pleased to see me. I still remember him standing right at the front, appearing sweetly captivated as I stood on a platform and gave a speech about the money we had raised to fund new schools in Africa. I encouraged people to buy raffle tickets and make pledges, and I swear he clapped the loudest and most enthusiastically afterwards.

It was hard to stay away from him that night, but I had to work. I did manage to ask that all-important question, though.

'No girlfriend tonight?'

'No.' He smiled at me. 'I don't have a girlfriend.'

'Really?' I sounded surprised.

'I did have one, but we split up a few months ago.'

I couldn't keep the smile from my face. He wore a suit that night and looked gorgeous. He was much taller than Will had been, which helped me to separate them, even though the blond-hair, blue-eyed similarity did freak me out a bit. I was wearing four-inch heels and a slinky black dress, and I remember musing that an outsider might think we looked like a nice couple.

We stayed in touch after that, keeping it friendly at first, touching base in the New Year by email. Through his contacts at work he scored tickets to a film premiere and invited me. Nothing happened that night – but our flirtation stepped up a notch. It was another month before we shared our first kiss. He'd invited me out for some drinks with his colleagues after work – it was a Friday, and quite last minute, but he knew I was in the area for a meeting. I said yes and went along. The pub was packed, and I couldn't see him at first, but when I did, my heart flipped. He was dressed casually in jeans and a black jumper, and I had to push my way through the other drinkers to get to him. He saw me when I was only a few metres away, and I knew then that he wanted me as much as I wanted him. That evening was like a perfect kind of torture. It seemed destined to end with a kiss, but getting to that point ... The tactile touches, the teasing smiles ... We were at the pub until closing time. The others were going to a bar in central London. Matthew asked me what I wanted to do, and I remember him standing close to me, looking down at me with a glint in his eye.

'I'm not sure I fancy a club,' I said, staring back up at him.

'Do you want to go somewhere else?' he asked with a raised eyebrow.

'Where do you suggest?'

'Back to mine?'

Neither of us spoke as we took the elevator up to his place, in a recently refurbished apartment block in King's Cross.

'Are you hungry?' he asked me as we went inside, and I wondered where the requisite coffee question was. Then I realised that I was indeed hungry.

'I am a bit,' I admitted, and he smiled at me, the ice broken as he set about making us cheese toasties. I worried that maybe I'd misread the signs, that maybe he did see me as a friend, or, God forbid, was looking for a story. But I instantly dismissed the last bit. I could trust him. I knew I could.

With a large sigh I'm brought back to the present. So much for being able to trust him.

Becky sent me the artwork for our Christmas cards earlier. I choose five out of ten designs to make the final cut for our merchandising catalogue and email Becky my decision, then push my chair out from the table and go outside. The air is even more humid than usual and I wonder if the weather is going to break soon. Is it time for another storm? I go and sit on the sofa, needing a break from work. Because of the time difference Becky will have gone home now, so she won't email me again before the morning. I promised her I'd put her in touch with some contacts she's been missing so she can invite them to the ball. I could call them myself, but I think she wants to put together the guest list. I can always do a follow-up email if necessary.

This grass really could do with a cut, I think to myself as I survey the garden. There are weeds everywhere, along with bits of rubbish floating around. I head inside and grab a plastic bag, then walk around, stuffing rubbish into it and pulling up weeds as I see them. There's a small shed in the back yard and I go and have a look inside – it's not locked. There is a lawnmower there, and I wheel it outside, but it doesn't start. I realise the petrol tank is empty, and I spot a petrol can on the floor. I pick it up and find that it's full. Can I work out how to do this? It turns out that I can. Half an hour later, the grass has been mowed. It still looks pretty awful – it's no longer green, but that should change with a bit of rain. It looks a damn sight better than it did earlier, in any case.

Tiredness hits me. It's late afternoon and Leo and the others will be home soon. I feel strange about seeing him again – sort of detached. I decide to go upstairs and have a rest, but as I climb into bed and stare out of the window, my thoughts return to Matthew.

'You make a good toastie.' I put my plate down on the kitchen island unit, a feature of his modern and stylish flat.

'It's the one thing I can do,' he replied, standing on the other side.

'I don't believe that,' I told him. 'I bet you're good at everything.'

He laughed and shook his head, then stared at me. I wished the island unit would disappear – it took up too much space in front of us. He moved around the side of it and into the kitchen, where I was. 'You want a coffee now?'

I couldn't help but laugh.

'What?' he asked, confused.

'I'm good for coffee, thanks,' I replied with a smirk. We stood there and stared at each other for a long moment, him looking a little perplexed. And then I think he just suddenly got it, because he stepped towards me and took my hand. I remember breathing in sharply, my smile leaving my face. But I didn't step away. Maybe he was expecting me to – he didn't seem that sure of himself. So he inched closer and I tilted my head up towards him. He paused only a second before meeting me halfway, touching his lips to mine. I melted under his touch. He kissed me slowly, gently, and it was so strange because he was the first person I had kissed since Will's death. His lips felt so different to Will's – much softer, his tongue more tentative. But when our kiss deepened, my whole body began to tingle. After that I couldn't get enough of him . . .

I breathe in shakily, a lump forming in my throat as tears fill my eyes. I think back to the February before last, when we had been a couple for almost a year . . . We'd been out to dinner before going back to my flat in Marylebone.

'I've never known anyone like you . . .' He shook his head at me, a strange sort of reverence in his eyes that I hadn't seen before. 'I love you so much, Laura. I love you so much.' He pulled me to him, pressing his lips to mine, but before I could take the kiss further, he pushed me away, holding me at arm's length. 'I love you.' He said it almost like a warning, like it was hurting him to say it.

'I love you, too,' I replied, slightly baffled by the look in his eyes.

'I want to marry you,' he whispered.

I couldn't say anything.

'I know it's too soon. I know we haven't known each other long. But I love you. So much. And I want to marry you.' His eyes welled up. His beautiful eyes. I stared at him with shock.

'Are you asking me to marry you?' I said slowly, not quite believing this was a proposal. I had been with Will for years with no sign of us tying the knot. Matthew and I had been a couple for only eleven months.

'Yes.' His reply was another whisper, and I realised he was terrified of what I might say. But he needn't have been. I'd never felt more in love, more passionate about anyone, not even Will.

'Yes,' I whispered back.

'Yes?' His eyes lit up. 'You'll marry me?'

'Yes.' I nodded, smiling.

He engulfed me in such a tight hug that all the air was sucked out of my chest, but I still managed to laugh.

I brush away an escaped tear and squeeze my eyes shut. I loved Matthew so much. I wanted to spend the rest of my life with him. He made me so happy. How did it all go wrong? Will it ever be right again?

Chapter 22

I open my eyes with a start, and for a brief moment I'm not sure where I am. Then I see Leo sitting on the edge of my bed, his hand on my arm.

'Hey,' he says, smiling a small smile.

'Hi.'

I stare back at him and feel once more oddly detached, almost like I don't know him at all. His hand moves up to my face, brushing my hair back and resting on my neck, and it's this intimate gesture that softens my heart. He leans down to kiss me, and then my confused mind is overruled as heat flows through my body and I kiss him back.

'I missed you,' he says, to my surprise.

'Did you?'

He kisses me again in response. I try to push the covers back so he can join me, but he stops me.

'No,' he says, his dark eyes flashing as he glances around the room. 'Not here.' He shakes his head abruptly and stands up, offering his hand down to me. I understand. He doesn't want to have sex with me in his mother's bedroom. I climb

202

out of bed and my old friends the butterflies help carry me upstairs.

'So, you felt like doing a bit of gardening?' he asks me wryly as we lie on his mattress afterwards.

'Sorry about the grass,' I reply with a grin. 'Some rain will sort it out.'

'There's a storm coming. Should hit tonight.'

'Is it a bad one?' I know that America is prone to some nasty hurricanes.

'No. But we'd better bring the couch up onto the porch.'

We go downstairs for dinner. I cooked a meal last week – roast chicken with all the trimmings. We've been sort of taking turns. Leo is cooking tonight, and I'm in the kitchen helping him when Javier walks in.

'How was your day?' I ask him. I've been trying to make more of an effort to talk to him, but it's hard to converse in front of his mother.

'Boring,' he replies.

'Oh.' Something to say ... 'Did you help Eric out?'

'Yeah ...'

He sounds pretty sorry for himself. Leo stops rubbing spices into the chicken and turns around to look at him.

'What's up, nephew? You don't like it on the boats?'

'No, it's crap.'

'What would you like to do?' Leo asks, going to wash his hands.

'I dunno.'

'Well, that's not going to help you, much,' Leo tells him with a look.

'Anything would be better than scrubbing the decks,' Javier says.

'What do your friends do for work around here?' I chip in.

'My friends have all fucked off to Miami.'

'Hey.' Leo frowns.

'What? *You* cuss,' Javier replies grumpily, and for the first time I notice a similarity between them. Something in their expression. I try not to smile.

'He looks like you when he's annoyed,' I say to Leo when Javier mopes off.

'When he's annoyed?' Leo asks pertinently.

'Yeah.' I shrug and grin.

'Am I annoyed much?' He comes over to me and puts his hands on my hips, and there's no trace of annoyance to be found anywhere in the vicinity.

'You were pretty scary when I first met you,' I tell him.

He throws his head back and laughs. 'I'm not scary,' he scoffs.

'You're not scary, *now*,' I correct him.

He hooks his forefingers through the belt loops of my shorts and pulls me towards him. A jolt goes through me. But this time when he kisses me, I can't help thinking about Matthew.

The storm hits later that night so we all congregate inside around the telly, me on Leo's lap on the armchair to make room for the others. Javier is in his bedroom, sulking. Leo has his arms entwined around my waist and it feels so comfortable, yet somehow so alien. I still can't stop thinking about Matthew. I have to remind myself that he cheated on me and got another woman pregnant, but so much of the time my thoughts keep taking me back to the good times – of which there were many. How many good thoughts can you cram into two years? Too many, that's the answer to that.

Carmen keeps glancing over at us. I know she's finding the sight of us unsettling, and I don't feel quite as nonchalant about it here and now. I'm thinking I should sleep in my own bed tonight.

'Did something happen at work today?' Carmen interrupts my thoughts with this question to Eric, which sounds a tad accusatory. Max is lying at his feet, fast asleep. He hasn't barked at me today, which is a result.

'Not that I know of.' Eric shrugs, not taking his eyes away from the telly. They're watching some stupid police fly-on-the-wall documentary. I'm not really paying attention to it.

'Then why did Javier go to bed straight after dinner?' she asks.

'He said he was bored,' I offer up, then immediately wonder if I should have kept my mouth shut. She doesn't want to hear from me, especially with regards to her beloved son. Whoops, yes, I was right. She glares at me. I feel Leo shift behind me and her eyes move past me to him. I know he's staring her down, challenging her to just try to be a bitch to me in his presence. I suddenly feel happy to be in his arms and under his protection. I realise, with surprise, that I feel very safe here. As if reading my mind, his grip around my waist tightens and I place my hands on top of his, hugging him to me. I turn back to the telly, but can't concentrate. Out of the blue a thought comes to me.

'Could Javier help out at the dive centre?' I ask Jorge directly. His brow furrows as he thinks. 'Um . . .' Then his eyes widen with surprise. 'I don't know why I haven't already thought of that.'

'Tegan has just left, hasn't she?' I ask with growing excitement.

'Yeah. We could really do with an extra set of hands. I guess he's old enough now,' Jorge replies.

I risk a glance at Carmen, and notice she's sitting more upright. Have I finally got something right?

'Can he dive?' I ask.

'Yeah,' Jorge replies. 'Leo and I taught him when he was eleven.'

'Did you?' I ask over my shoulder.

'Yeah.' His eyes meet mine and my heart flutters. My attraction to him really is quite uncontrollable.

Suddenly the power goes off and everyone groans.

'Power cut,' Jorge mutters.

'Will it last long?' I ask. It's completely dark in here.

'Long enough.' Leo pats my arms, urging me to stand. 'Come on, up to bed.'

Yours or mine, I wonder, as he takes my hand and leads me behind the armchair, calling goodnight to the others. He lets me go when we pass the bathroom, so I can get ready for bed.

I'm still thinking about sleeping in my own bed tonight as I attempt to get ready in the pitch-black darkness, but I somehow find myself feeling my way down the corridor, straight past my bedroom and up his stairs.

The rain is pelting down on the roof directly above us and the sound is deafening. I can see Leo standing at the window, staring out. He doesn't hear me arrive and I stand at the doorway and watch him for a moment, checking out his profile in the darkness. I seriously have never fancied anyone this much before in my entire life. Is it so wrong, what I'm doing? Haven't I been through enough pain to warrant taking some pleasure from someone who is quite possibly the sexiest man alive? I walk up behind him and slide my arms around his waist, making him jolt. I slip my hands underneath his T-shirt and close my eyes as my fingers trace over his toned stomach. He turns around and kisses me as though his life depended on it, and I kiss him right back.

Chapter 23

It's a week before Marty cottons on to what I've been doing, and by then Leo and I have settled into an easy love affair. Well, as easy as a love affair can be when Carmen is around to shoot daggers at us. That is, when she's not eyeing me with suspicion or confusion.

While Leo trains Javier to work at the dive centre, I spend my days in front of my laptop at the dining-room table, writing strategies and trying to come up with new fund-raising initiatives. Our website also needs some attention, so I've rewritten part of it, added some new copy and now I just need to get onto our website designer. I've also taken over managing the social media side of things, like Twitter and Facebook. This was always Becky's bag, but she's so busy organising the ball that it's falling to me to do some of her assistant duties. It's a bit weird for me to be taking a backwards step while she goes out to lunch with managing directors of major companies and builds our relationships with corporate partners to encourage continuous support. At least it's a distraction from thinking about Matthew.

He's tried calling me a couple of times, but I divert his calls and put him off with vague texts about continuing to need time and space. I feel guilty, which is an unwelcome and peculiar emotion, considering the events which brought me here. No one knows about Leo and me. No one back in the UK, anyway. Until Marty calls.

'What's going on?' she asks me. It's Monday lunchtime and I've spent the weekend entirely in Leo's company, mostly in his bed, although we did make it to the beach yesterday.

'Nothing,' I reply quickly. Too quickly.

'Laura,' she says, immediately onto me. Damn her! How does she do that? 'What the hell is going on?'

'Nothing!' I say again.

'Have you slept with him?' she asks with astonishment.

I hesitate just that split second too long.

'Holyshityouhave!'

'Shut up,' I say awkwardly.

'Holy shit!' she cries again. 'You've fucking fucked him!'

'Would you keep it down?' I hiss. I don't know where she is or who she's with – probably in the privacy of her own bedroom with no one in earshot, but *still* . . .

'Oh my God.'

'Yeah, alright,' I reply defensively.

'I can't believe it.'

'Can we move on?' I ask a little shirtily.

No, it appears we cannot.

'Jesus,' she says.

I sigh. Loudly.

'Oh my God.'

'Marty! Enough!' I snap.

'I knew you fancied him, but . . .'

'Yes, I do,' I say, as if that will be explanation enough.

'What about Matthew?' she asks.

I shift in my seat.

'He's kind of still thinking you're coming home to him,' she says sarcastically.

'I am coming home,' I tell her firmly. 'But I don't think I'm coming home to him.'

'Really, Laura?' She actually has the cheek to sound sad. Whose side is she on?

'What do you mean, "Really, Laura"?' Now I'm cross. 'What does he expect? What does anyone *expect* me to do?'

'No one expected you to do *this*, that's for sure.'

I can just imagine the look on her face.

'Don't tell anyone,' I warn her.

'As if I would,' she bites back. 'Your filthy little secret is safe with me.'

I roll my eyes, even though she can't see me.

'So what's he like?' she asks casually. *Too* casually. She's dying for me to dish the dirt.

'You really expect me to kiss and tell?' I ask drily.

'Damn right I do. Is he as good in bed as he looks out of it?'

'Better.' It's out of my mouth before I can stop myself.

'You bitch,' she curses.

'That's *all* I'm saying!' I raise my voice to make my point.

'I'll get the rest out of you another time,' she vows and, knowing Marty, she probably will.

'I told Marty about us today,' I reveal that night when Leo and I are alone. We're sitting on the sofa in the garden – the others haven't made it outside yet.

'Did you?' He looks surprised. 'Aren't you worried it will get back to Matthew?'

'She wouldn't say anything.'

'But you *are* worried?' He regards me from his side of the sofa. I'm facing him, with my knees up.

I look past him at the rope lights winding their way up the palm tree trunk as I ponder his question, but I can't come up with a proper answer. 'I don't know.'

'What would he do if he found out?' he asks casually.

I frown. 'I don't know.' It's true. I don't. What would Matthew do if he found out I've been having an affair? Would he divorce me? Or consider us even? 'It doesn't really matter right now.'

'Of course it matters.' He looks annoyed with me and I instantly feel horrible.

'What's wrong?' I ask him.

He averts his gaze. 'Nothing.'

'Tell me.' I kick him gently with my foot and he grabs it, pulling my leg across him. I stretch my other leg out.

'The grass is looking better,' he comments. It's too dark to see it now, but we've noticed it's been improving daily since the storm last week.

'Talk about a change of subject,' I tease and he smirks. I look over my shoulder at the house. 'I was thinking we should paint the house.' I turn back to look at him.

'Why?' He appears genuinely confused.

'It's so ... run-down. If all of us helped out, we could get it looking good again.' No response. 'The wood will rot if you don't,' I add, remembering something my dad told me. 'The whole thing will fall down one day if someone doesn't take care of it.'

'Perhaps the people living here practically rent-free should do something, then,' he says drily.

'Do you really see Eric doing anything off his own back?'

He purses his lips.

'Come on, don't you want to restore it?' I press. 'It could look so nice. We could paint it pink with purple shutters,' I add with a grin.

'Pink with purple shutters,' he mutters with disgust. I knew full well that would be his reaction.

I laugh. 'What colour, then?'

He muses for a while. 'White or grey. With blue shutters.'

'Blue?'

'I like blue,' he says with a grin. I sit up and crawl over to him, cupping my hand around his face.

'I like brown,' I tell him with a smile before he kisses me.

'Eugh,' Carmen mutters as she joins us.

I innocently pull away and snuggle back into the crook under Leo's arm, making room on the sofa for another.

'When is it going to stop?' she asks as the others emerge, Eric cracking a can of beer open as he walks.

Leo and I ignore her. Jorge throws Leo another can of beer, which he puts down at his feet because he's barely touched his current one.

Jorge sits down next to me and hands me my mobile phone. 'It's been ringing.'

'Oh.' My stomach falls. I take it from him and stare at the missed calls. Matthew's name is up on the screen. Leo shifts beside me and I know that he saw what I saw. 'Sorry about that.' I stuff it into my pocket and try to put Matthew out of my mind.

Javier went on a dive today and he's in an especially good

mood. We listen as he tells his mum about it. My phone starts to go off in my pocket.

'You going to get that?' Jorge asks wryly. We're so squished together on this sofa that he can feel it vibrating. Leo tenses.

'I'll switch it off,' I say, as the others' ears prick up.

'Answer it,' Leo directs, nodding towards the house. He takes his arm away from behind my head. I stare at him uncertainly. He nods again towards the house. Reluctantly I get up and go inside. Of course the phone has stopped ringing by then, so I go upstairs to my bedroom and listen to my voicemail. There's just one, and it's from Matthew.

'I really need to speak to you. Call me as soon as you can.'

What's going on? There was an urgency to his tone. It's the middle of the night. Has something happened to the baby? My phone starts to ring again. This time I press answer.

'What's wrong?' I demand to know.

'Laura!'

'Is everything okay? Has anything happened to . . .' I can't bring myself to say the rest of that sentence out loud.

'No, he's fine. He's home and doing well.'

It unnerves me that Matthew knew exactly what I was thinking.

'I couldn't sleep,' he adds, explaining his reason for calling me in the middle of the night.

'Oh. Has he got a name yet?' I ask dully.

'Yes, of course.' He sounds surprised. 'We called him Evan.'

'We?' I ask with alarm. 'You had a say in it?'

'Yes, Laura,' he says quietly. 'He *is* my son.'

I almost hurl the phone at the bedroom wall. Hot tears form in my eyes and my bottom lip begins to wobble.

'I'm so sorry,' he says quietly, realising how this small revelation must've affected me. 'I didn't mean to hurt you.'

If I speak, I'll cry, so I stay silent.

'I know you don't want to hear this, but I really wish you were here. I wish you could see him.'

Is he really saying this out loud? To *me*? My mouth gapes open.

'I know what you must be thinking,' he continues quickly. 'But I'm only trying to tell you the truth. I miss you. I miss you so much. It's so weird going through all this without having you to share it with.'

I could laugh with outrage at this sentiment, but I can hear in his voice how desperate he is for me to understand. He sounds so sad, like he might be crying, too.

'You've hurt me so much,' I whimper.

'Baby, I know.' His voice breaks, and I know for certain that he's on the verge of sobbing. 'I'm so sorry about all of this. But please, LL. I love you. Please come home to me.'

'I can't,' I whisper.

'Yes, you can,' he pleads with me.

'No, I can't. I'm not ready.'

'You are ready; you're more ready than you know. It's all going to be alright.'

'No, it's not going to be alright!' I cry out. 'How can you say that to me?'

'Laura, please,' he begs. 'Just come home. If you saw him, I just feel ...'

'Saw who? The *baby*?' I ask.

'Yes!' He sounds surprised that I could be so incredulous.

'I ... But ... I ... I don't want to see him!' I stutter.

'But you *will* see him,' he says calmly, a touch perplexed.

213

'Who says?' Now I know I'm sounding like a bratty teenager.

'Laura,' he says sternly. 'Be reasonable.'

'HA!' I erupt.

'Bloody hell,' he mutters, now a little angry. 'This would be so much easier if we could talk face to face.'

'Well, we can't,' I tell him firmly.

'If you would just come home . . .'

'No. I'm not coming home anytime soon. I'm having a nice time here.'

'With who? *Leo?*' he spits.

'Yes, with Leo,' I find myself replying.

Silence.

'Laura?' he asks uncertainly. 'Is anything going on between you and him?'

My heart begins to pound harder and faster in my chest.

My silence tells him everything he needs to know. 'Jesus Christ, Laura, I know I messed up, but *seriously?*'

He takes a deep breath. I pick some fluff off the bedspread and try to ignore my feelings of guilt.

'Does he make you feel better?' he asks me, still sounding deeply affected by my not-quite-revelation.

I think about this question and reply honestly: 'Yes.' My voice sounds small.

'Revenge is sweet, huh?' he asks bitterly.

'It's not like that,' I try to tell him.

I picture him in the living room in our apartment in Battersea. He's pacing the floor, scratching his forehead. He does this when he's stressed. I close my eyes, pain pulsing inside my chest.

'I don't know what you're doing,' he says, his voice breaking again. 'But please don't ... Please don't do this. Please come home,' he says with anguish.

'I can't,' I whisper. 'Not yet.' I take a deep breath as he starts to cry. 'I've got to go,' I tell him, the lump in my throat increasing in size. 'I've got to go.' Stifling a sob, I hang up on him.

I press my hand to my throat, but it alleviates nothing, so I start to cry properly, full body-wracking sobs. After a long time, I wipe my tears away and clean my face. I look out of the window. Jorge is on the sofa, but Leo is absent. I go upstairs to his bedroom, but find it empty. I scan the rest of the house before going back outside.

'Where's Leo?' I ask.

'He's gone out,' Jorge reveals with an apologetic smile.

'Where did he go?' A feeling of dread settles over me.

'Oh, you know Leo. Just out.' He sounds uneasy.

Actually, I think to myself bitterly, I don't know Leo. I don't know him very well at all.

'I wouldn't wait up for him,' Carmen adds, but she's not looking as bitchy as I'd expect after this comment. In fact, she's not looking bitchy at all.

I sleep in my own bed that night. Or rather, I lie there, hardly sleeping. I'm aware when Leo comes home. I hear his heavy drunken footsteps pause outside my door, but he doesn't push the door open, doesn't come in, so I decide it's best to leave well enough alone and speak to him in the morning.

Chapter 24

I wake to the sound of Jorge shouting up the stairs towards Leo's room, 'I'm going!'

No reply.

'I'll take Javier.' I hear him stomp down the corridor and downstairs again. I take it Leo is not going to work this morning.

I feel ill to my very core. I lie there in bed, staring at the ceiling. What am I doing? I've been here over a month now and I still have no idea. If anything, I'm more confused than ever.

Matthew wants me to see the baby. To see Evan. Why? He wants me to be a part of his son's life. Is he absolutely insane?

I angrily brush away the onslaught of fresh tears and climb out of bed. I don't know if it's a good idea or not, but I really need to see Leo.

I climb the stairs tentatively, unsure of what state I'll find him in when I push open the door. He's out cold on the bed.

The room smells of alcohol and cigar smoke, so I open his window, then turn and survey the room. It really is a tip. Tidying up has been the last thing on my mind this past week or so, but now I set about folding up his clothes, making a pile of dirty ones and putting away the others. I don't even notice that he's awake and watching me until I sit down on his now-empty chair.

'Oh!' I say with a start. 'I thought you were asleep.'

He says nothing.

'Are you okay?' I ask him.

He nods slightly. I take a deep breath and stare at him. He stares back, unspeaking.

'Do you have a headache? Do you want me to get you some tablets?'

'Come here.' His voice sounds gruff. He beckons me over, so I go. I kneel on his mattress and he pushes his hand through the hair at the nape of my neck, running his thumb along my jaw. I lean into his touch.

'Are you going?' His voice is barely audible.

I look perplexed. 'Going where?'

'Home.'

'No!' I exclaim. 'What made you think that?'

'I heard you crying,' he says, dropping his hand.

'Why didn't you come in?' I feel sad that he didn't, if he was right outside.

He shakes his head. 'I . . . couldn't.'

'Do you want me to go home?' I feel anxious about his reply. But he doesn't respond. Instead he pulls me down to him, but he doesn't kiss me. He holds my forehead against his, and it's such a tender gesture, it surprises me. I pull away and look deep into his eyes and my heart flips.

It surely must be a crime to fancy anyone this much. It's bordering on obsessive. When will that pass? Will it pass? Or will I go back to England still so damn attracted to this man that I won't be able to stop thinking about him, fantasising about him . . . ever.

217

If I left him now I think it would break me. I sound like a crazy woman. Then, from out of nowhere, Ashlee pops into my mind.

My brow furrows. 'What happened between you and Ashlee?'

He looks taken aback by my question. Well, it sort of did come out of nowhere.

'What do you want to know?'

'Did you break it off with her?' I ask.

'Yes.'

'Why?'

He sighs. 'She's totally out of control when she's drunk. Which is often.'

'Is that all?' I'm confused. It's not like Leo is teetotal. I change tack. 'Where did you go last night?'

'Just a bar.'

'Why didn't you tell me?'

'I don't know, Laura. I thought you needed to be alone. *I* needed to be alone,' he adds.

'Did you?' I try not to sound wounded.

He pushes himself up onto his elbows.

'You know, Jorge has gone to work without you,' I tell him.

'Has he?' He doesn't look very amused.

'Yeah.'

'I'd better get up, then.'

He sits up and the sheet falls down around his waist, revealing his chest. I place my hand on it and he regards me warily. I give him a cheeky look and push him backwards, leaning down to kiss his navel. He gasps as my kisses trail downwards, then he roughly flips me over so I'm beneath him.

'You really are going to kill me, you know,' he mutters, before giving me what I want.

Chapter 25

A week and a half later I'm halfway up a ladder with a paintbrush, earning my keep. That's the way I'm putting it, anyway, even though I have started to pay rent. I have paint in my hair, paint on my T-shirt and probably paint on my nose. Everyone else is at work – and I should be too. It's Thursday and I'm taking a long lunch. Becky is so organised with this charity ball next weekend that I can't help her with much. In a way it's a relief not to be so involved. This ball marks the anniversary of Will's death. It's been three years since he died and we've held an annual ball around the time of the British Grand Prix ever since. The first one was the hardest, but it was also the most important for the charity. It put us on the map. I struggled through every second of it. Matthew didn't go with me. It wouldn't have been right. How could I possibly have met someone else so soon after the so-called love of my life was taken from me?

I had to face the press, which I hated. That first year – especially those first few months – they hounded me. By the time Matthew and I were married, though, they had moved onto the next big thing. Thank goodness for small mercies. I can only imagine what they'd say if they found out our current situation. 'Poor Laura! Doesn't she have all the worst luck?' Yeah, well, I'm no victim. I'm certainly not the innocent party anymore. Not with what's happening with Leo.

I'll be glad not to go to the ball this year. I wonder if anyone will notice. Hopefully not.

I sigh. Sometimes I wonder what I was thinking, setting up a charity in Will's name. It's a remarkable charity, that's true. We have helped countless children around the world. We've funded schools, aided families living in war-torn countries, and even raised money to help support children living in severe poverty in *Britain*. It's very rewarding. It's also hard. The endless reminders about Will don't help. And seeing the things that I've seen . . . It makes me feel terrified at times about bringing children into this world.

Tessa had no such qualms, I think bitterly, momentarily despising her baby and feeling incredibly uncharitable about him.

I hear the gate latch click and glance over my shoulder to see who it is.

Matthew?

I wobble and nearly fall off the ladder.

'Careful!' he shouts, running to my aid.

'Matthew! Oh my God!'

My eyes must be as big as saucers as he takes the brush from me and helps me to navigate the rungs. We stand in front of each other, my head racing. He's here. He's here. I was *not* expecting this.

'Hey,' he says gently, reaching out to take my hand. I pull back in shock.

'What . . . What are you doing here?' I stutter.

Leo! Oh Christ, what is Leo going to say? What's he going to *do*? This is a nightmare!

Matthew looks crushed. 'I had to see you,' he says, searching my face and then glancing up at the paint in my hair. 'You have . . .' He reaches across to touch my hair and I step away and rub my nose, to make sure the smear has well and truly gone.

'Matthew, you can't . . . You can't . . .'

'I can and I did,' he says quietly. 'I'm here. So you're going to have to talk to me.'

'You can't stay here,' I say fervently.

'I'm staying at the hotel next door,' he tells me, and I notice he's empty-handed so he must've checked in.

'It's a nice hotel,' I say, for want of something else.

'It is.' He holds out his hand again and I realise he's desperate to touch me, to make contact. But I don't want that. His hand falls to his side.

'Will you come and have lunch with me?' he asks hesitantly.

'Um . . .' I glance up at the house. It's not going to paint itself.

'Can that wait?' he asks, giving me an odd look.

'I suppose so,' I mutter. 'I'll go and get changed.'

He follows me inside and I tense up, pausing in the kitchen. It feels wrong for him to be here. I don't like it, and I know that Leo would *hate* it.

'Where is . . . Where is everyone?' Matthew asks, looking around.

'They're all at work. Wait here,' I say, hurrying out of the room and up the stairs.

Shitshitshitshitshit.

I quickly get changed into a fresh T-shirt and shorts, and then attempt to wash the paint out of my hair over the basin. I tie it

221

back up again into a messy ponytail and walk out into the corridor, glancing up the stairs towards Leo's room. I feel so nervous. How is he going to react to this?

Matthew has waited in the kitchen, as directed. It's strange seeing him there, standing on the lino. He's wearing beige-coloured chinos and a white shirt, rolled up to his elbows. He's tanned, as he usually is – he just has that sort of skin – and his blond hair is pushed off his face, as usual. I notice for the first time how tired his eyes look.

'Did you get much sleep on the plane?' I usher him outside and lock the door behind me, the smell of fresh paint immediately filling my nostrils. I feel frustrated at having to stop a job midway. Shouldn't I be more pleased to see my husband? I'm still in shock, I tell myself.

'Planes,' he replies. 'I flew in to Key West, via Atlanta.' I assumed he'd done a road trip from Miami like us, but obviously he just wanted to get here. 'And no, I didn't sleep much,' he adds, his eyes wandering around the garden and over to the sofa. I sat there with Leo's arm around me only last night. I love his arms. So strong and all-encompassing. I realise that he won't want to hold me in his arms for the foreseeable future and I'm surprised by how angry that makes me feel towards Matthew.

'You'll need an early night tonight, then.' I try to sound casual.

He doesn't say anything.

The restaurant around the corner is pretty decent, so we go there. We're seated on the terrace near a water feature, under the shade of palm trees and frangipanis in full bloom. The fragrant yellow and white flowers have fallen on the ground at our feet and they scent the air. I pull out a chair and sit down, facing my husband.

'You look well,' he says, continually watching me. It's a confident gesture – this constant attempt at eye contact – but he also seems more unsure of himself than I've ever seen him. It's like he doesn't know me anymore. I know exactly how he feels.

'Thanks,' I murmur. The waitress comes to give us glasses of water. I stare at the water feature, while Matthew stares at me. The waitress leaves us to it, so I pick up the menu, trying to focus. He does the same.

'What's good here?' he asks.

'You'll like the burgers.' My reply is automatic, but I notice him smile at the familiarity. He puts his menu down and reaches over, but I instinctively jerk my hand away. He leaves his hand in the centre of the table. Something makes me think of animal handlers who believe their subject can be coaxed to come to them eventually.

The waitress appears to take our order. I lean back in my chair and look anywhere but at my husband for as long as I can manage. When I finally meet his eyes he's regarding me with sadness.

I feel like such a bitch, but I have to ask: 'How long are you planning on staying?'

He swallows. 'Five days.'

'*Five days?*' I exclaim. That long?

'I couldn't get anymore time off work at such short notice,' he explains, misreading my reaction. 'I'm hoping it will be long enough.'

'Long enough for what?' I ask. He looks uncomfortable. 'Matthew, you know I'm not coming back with you, right?'

'Don't say that now,' he says quickly.

'It's true!' I can't help raising my voice. 'I'm not coming back. I'm not ready.'

223

I have to avert my gaze because I feel so guilty.

'Where's Leo today?' he asks directly.

'He's helping out at the dive centre a few keys up.'

'He's a diver?' He doesn't look very happy about this.

'Yeah. We met him and Jorge – he was our instructor – when we were doing our PADI course.'

'Oh, right. I forgot you did that.' He tries to sound normal. 'How did it go?'

'Good.' I join his act. 'I'm fully qualified.'

'Well done.' Now he looks genuinely impressed. I really wanted to learn to dive on our honeymoon, but we didn't have enough time to get it all organised.

'What have you been up to?' I ask awkwardly. This is so weird, this small talk.

He looks down at the table. 'Just working, and you know . . .'

'Seeing Evan,' I chip in.

'Not that much,' he's keen to tell me.

'I don't blame you,' I say carefully. 'Not for seeing him, anyway.'

He nods unhappily.

'How's Tessa?' I ask, my voice hardening.

'She's . . . fine,' he replies cautiously, then hurriedly adds: 'You know there's nothing between us, right?'

'So you keep saying.'

'There's not, there's really not.'

'I believe you.' I sigh. 'But it doesn't actually change things.'

'How can I change things, then?' he asks me quietly. 'What can I do?'

'I don't know.' I feel a wave of sympathy for him. He looks so helpless. 'I don't think there's anything you can do.'

'But—'

Our burgers arrive, so whatever he was about to say will have to wait. We eat in silence, but the appetite I've regained since moving in with Leo and the others, vanishes into thin air.

I notice Matthew is also struggling. He puts down his burger and picks at his chips. He used to eat so well. He's always been slim and toned, but now he looks ... Well, he looks quite skinny, and it doesn't suit him. His facial features are almost gaunt, I can see that now. I was too distracted before by the dark circles under his eyes to fully take them in.

'You've lost weight,' I comment with concern.

He lets out an uneasy laugh. 'Yeah.'

'Matthew, you have to look after yourself.' I lean towards him with empathy. He doesn't waste this opportunity, scooping up my hand the moment it's within reach. I tense up, but one look at his face ... This time I don't pull away.

He holds my hand tightly in both of his and takes a deep breath. I relax slightly as my body seems to recognise his touch.

'I love you,' he says in a low voice.

'I know.' I offer him a small smile, but it's the best I can do.

After a while, I gently extricate myself and make a sign to the waitress to indicate we want the bill. 'I should get back to the painting.'

He looks put out. 'Really?'

'Yeah, I want to get as much as possible done before ...' My voice trails off. Before Leo gets home. I want to impress him.

'Can't you take a break? Come for a swim at the hotel with me?'

I hesitate. I hate to admit it, but I miss that pool, and it's hotter than usual today.

'Come on,' he presses. 'Come and see my room.'

225

I give him a warning look.

'Not like that,' he scoffs. 'But it's really nice. It's down by the pool and there are hammocks hanging right outside.'

'I know the rooms you mean,' I say with a smile. 'Ours was upstairs with a balcony, facing the street.'

'Nice.'

'It *was* nice.'

He looks confused. 'Why didn't you stay there?'

'It was too expensive.' I brush him off. 'And Jorge, Leo, Carmen and Eric had room.'

'That's a lot of people,' he comments.

'Oh, and Javier, too.'

'Javier?'

'Jorge and Leo's nephew.'

'Jorge and Leo are brothers?'

'No. Carmen is Jorge's sister, and she was married to Leo's older brother before he died. They had Javier together, but now she's with Eric.'

'Sounds complicated.'

'It is a bit.'

'What are the rest of them like?' he asks.

'They're . . . Well, Jorge is really nice. And I like Javier, even though he doesn't say much to me. Carmen's a bit of a cow, and Eric, well, it's hard to have an opinion about Eric because he's just sort of . . . there.'

'And Leo?'

'What about him?'

'What's he like?'

I sigh. 'I don't really want to talk about him.'

The look of anguish on his face nearly makes me break.

'I think I'd better go,' I say apprehensively, standing up.

He shakes his head quickly as though to rid himself of his thoughts and gets to his feet. 'No, don't. Please come for a swim. I've flown all this way to see you ... Please,' he says again. 'I don't think I'll be long out of the sack.'

I hesitate a moment, before conceding. 'Okay. I'll see you by the pool in a bit.'

'Cool.' He grins back at me and for a moment I see the Matthew I used to know, the easy, charming, sweet Matthew.

I head back to the house feeling distinctly unnerved.

Later that afternoon, I say goodbye to Matthew and go home. He knows I don't want him to come to the house tonight, and I think he will respect that. I can tell he's absolutely knackered, anyway, so I'm sure he'll crash out. I hope he doesn't wake up in the middle of the night and spy on us from the sundeck, like I did that time, the freak that I am.

I have a shower and wash my hair, then I take a book upstairs to wait for Leo in his room. I hear him come home. He jogs up the stairs and enters his room, looking surprised yet pleased to see me waiting there.

'Hi!' he exclaims, as I sit up. He bends down and pecks me on my lips and I briefly close my eyes, wondering when he'll do that again and wanting it to be sooner rather than later, but fearing the latter.

'How was your day?' I ask, chickening out of the big revelation as he straightens back up.

'Good.' He pulls his T-shirt over his head. 'I went on a dive. Saw a leatherback turtle.'

'Cool!' I enthuse. 'Was it big?'

227

'About three feet. It was pretty amazing. First time I've seen one.' I watch as he pulls on a fresh white shirt. He must've showered at the dive centre, because his hair isn't as wavy as it sometimes gets after a dive.

'You got started on the painting,' he says, dropping to his knees and facing me. He looks so fresh and carefree. Happy.

'Yeah.' I smile shyly at him, pleased that he's pleased.

'It looks good.'

'Thanks. I'll do some more tomorrow.'

'I can help you at the weekend. Don't wear yourself out.'

'I won't.'

I take a deep breath.

He cocks his head to one side, sensing that something is wrong. 'What is it?'

I take another deep breath and his face falls.

'What?' he asks again.

'Matthew is here.'

Now anything pleasant about his expression is gone. One after the other his expression becomes shocked, horrified, angry, even disgusted.

'He's staying in the hotel.' I feel unsettled. 'He wants me to go home with him.' Leo gets up and starts pacing the room. 'I'm not going, though,' I tell him quickly and he shoots me a dark look.

'How long is he staying?' he asks.

'Five days.'

He shakes his head and stares at the wall.

'I'm sorry.'

'It's not your fault.'

'I'm still sorry.' My nose begins to prickle.

'Come here,' he says gruffly and I stand up and hurl myself into his arms. He holds me tightly, pressing his lips to the top of my head.

That's the last time he touches me.

He barely speaks to me throughout dinner, and afterwards I go straight to bed. It's clear to both of us that we need to keep our distance for the foreseeable future. The next morning I get up early so I can speak to him before he goes to work. My stomach cartwheels when he comes downstairs, and it hurts not to be able to hold him, but I know he doesn't want me to. I see with alarm that he has a bag packed.

'Where are you going?' I ask fearfully.

'Miami,' he replies.

'For how long?' My voice rises and his expression softens.

'Just for a few days.'

I nod quickly, trying to keep my tears at bay.

'I'll see you,' he says, and walks out of the door.

Chapter 26

When Leo leaves, I want nothing more than to go up to my bedroom and cry my heart out. But I pull myself together and put on a brave face, then I head out to see Matthew. We go for a wander around Key West.

'What did ... *Leo* say when you told him I was here?' he asks me, trying to keep his voice sounding even. I've got to give it to him; he's not freaking out like I know I certainly would. Then again, I don't suppose he's given himself much choice, considering.

'Not a lot. He's gone to Miami for a few days,' I tell him.

He gives me a sharp look. 'Has he?'

'Yep.' I avert my gaze, but I'm sure he can see how unhappy I am.

'Well, that's good. Gives us some space.'

Don't I know it? Leo is right, of course. He's right to leave. He's giving us *all* some space. He must need it, too, and Matthew and I sure as hell do. Matthew has, after all, come all this way. I owe it to him, to the vows that we made to each other, to try to sort this out. Even if I don't want to. Whatever happens, whichever way this goes, a resolution *is* necessary. But how I hate to think of Leo in Miami without me. With Ashlee. What if he goes back to her? What if he tries to dull his pain by finding solace in someone else, *anyone* else? The thought makes me want to tear my hair out.

'When you told me about him ...' Matthew starts, his voice turning harder. 'I thought that was it, that it was definitely over between us ...' I hold my breath. 'But then I thought, if I can forgive you, then maybe you can forgive me.'

He glances at me, but I'm still steadily averting my gaze.

A rooster hops out onto the pavement and Matthew jolts away. *'What the ...?'*

'They're free-range around here.' I laugh at his horrified expression. He laughs, too, and for a moment I forget where we are, and we're just two friends, laughing at each other.

Friends ... My throat closes up. He was my friend. My best friend. What is he now? Friends make mistakes. Marty and I have fallen out before, when she decided she preferred Lucy New to me in Year Three, but I forgave her. Isn't that what friends do? Forgive and move on? Will I ever be able to forgive Matthew? Maybe. But I'm not sure I could ever move on. Not with him, surely. It's too big, what he's done. Isn't it?

Matthew wants to go to Ernest Hemingway's house, and as I didn't make it there with Bridget and Marty, I'm happy to join him. Matthew has always wanted to write a book. He's a fantastic writer of features, and I love reading his work for the newspaper – I feel so proud of him. I know that one day he'll achieve his dream of becoming an author. No wonder he wants to wander around Hemingway's house and soak up the inspiration.

Hemingway had a lot of cats, and since he moved away they've sort of taken over the place. Many of them have six toes on each paw. Freaky. But it's a fun day, and it's oddly nice being in Matthew's company again. We head back to his hotel for a swim later in the afternoon, and to anyone else we must appear to be any other couple on holiday. We could be on our honeymoon.

Mike, the guy from reception, walks past at one point and does a double take.

'Hi!' I say shyly.

'Back again?' he asks.

'Sorry, my ...' And then I don't know what to say. My husband? No. 'Matthew,' I point to him, 'is staying with you. Is it okay if I drop by occasionally?'

'Of course!' he exclaims. 'Knock yourself out.'

'I'm happy to pay extra for my room,' Matthew chips in.

'Don't be silly.' He brushes us off. 'Just enjoy. See you back here for happy hour!'

'Thanks.' I smile at him and he wanders off. 'They're lovely here,' I say to Matthew.

'Yeah. I can see why you wanted to stay.'

'Mmm.'

We both fall silent, both of us realising the idiocy of this sentence. The hotel had nothing to do with why I stayed in Key West.

We go out for dinner and it's ... well, nice. We talk about his work and family – his two brothers, one sister and parents – and generally what he's been up to. We don't talk about anything difficult.

He doesn't ask me about Leo, about any of the details, and I'm grateful. Matthew has never been a particularly jealous person. The way he coped with my heartache on the anniversary of Will's death ...

After that first charity ball I went home and fell into a heap, I was so emotionally drained after putting on a brave face all evening, and in all the weeks leading up to the event. But it was hard having that relentless reminder that someone with such a bright future had been ripped so cruelly from this earth. I know Will and I would have gone our separate ways if he'd lived, but we would have stayed in touch, I'm certain of that. He was the one-time love of my life, and we had known each other since we were children, literally romping around in the haystacks as teenagers on my parents' farm. I would always love him. How it pained me to be at that ball, with people constantly coming up to me and telling me how sorry they were for my loss. I felt like he'd died only yesterday. I longed for Matthew to be there, by my side, and I felt so lost without him. He turned up at my flat later, and I loathed myself for being so snively-nosed and red-eyed when I opened the door to him. A lesser man would have run a mile, but Matthew didn't. He took me in his arms while I sobbed – over another man! And he didn't run away. He made me sweet tea and put on *Michael McIntyre's Comedy Roadshow* to cheer me up. Then he took me to bed, but didn't make love to me that night, and I loved him more then than I ever had. He was a good man. He *is* a good man.

He walks me back to the house. He knows well enough when to call things a night. It's been a pleasant day; we've effectively called a truce, and it's a relief. But there's no need to push it. So we say goodnight outside the gate. I know he wants to kiss me – not passionately, just a peck on my cheek – but he hesitates, not sure how I'll react. I lean up and kiss him on his cheek instead, and then I say goodnight and go through the gate.

I feel nervous as I approach the kitchen. There's someone inside. Urgh, it's Carmen.

'Hi,' I say as I enter. I can hear knives and forks clattering in the dining room. They're having a late dinner.

'Hello,' she says without smiling as she grabs a few beers from the fridge. 'We weren't sure if you were going to be back in time.'

'I've eaten,' I tell her.

She nods.

'Do you want a hand with those?'

'No, it's okay. I've got them.' She makes to leave.

'Have you heard from Leo?' I blurt out.

She turns around and stares at me, coldly. 'No.'

I shrink further into myself.

She sighs. 'He'll be back. Don't worry about him.'

'I do worry about him,' I find myself confessing.

'Yeah, well, he'll be worried about you, too.'

It's the nicest thing she's ever said to me. I don't think she meant to say it.

She frowns and stalks out.

I feel rude about going up to bed so I pop my head around the dining-room door and say a quick hi and goodnight. The room falls into uncomfortable silence when I appear, and it makes me feel like shit. Jorge gives me a falsely bright smile.

'How's it all going?' he asks.

'Fine. It's okay, you know . . .' My voice trails off. 'I'm tired so I'll see you in the morning.'

'Okay. Goodnight.'

I don't hear them resume their conversation until I'm halfway up the stairs.

*

234

I'm the first one up and out of the house the next morning. It's Saturday, so no one is at work. I'll be quite happy to avoid being there today – it's just too awkward. Matthew rented a car at the airport so we conserve our energy and drive to Blue Heaven for brunch.

'This place is wicked,' he says, looking around.

It's a sunny morning so we sit outside at a stone table underneath a green umbrella. The sunlight is filtering through the canopy of leaves dotted with pink flowers, and there are a couple of chickens pecking about.

'It's eclectic,' I say with a shrug.

Leo was at that table just over there, on the morning he took me on a mini tour around Key West. I keep looking at the chair he sat in, remembering him lazing there, reading his newspaper and drinking his steaming coffee. A thrill goes through me as I recall how much I wanted him then, how much I still want him. I picture us in bed together and my face starts to burn. What the hell am I doing, thinking these things in Matthew's company? I'm a terrible, terrible person.

I go for the pancakes today, while Matthew chooses bacon and eggs. He eats better than he did that first day I saw him, but he still seems to have lost his appetite for good food.

'I wish you'd eat properly,' I lament, watching him put his knife and fork together on his plate.

'This is the best I've eaten in weeks,' he tells me with a small smile. 'You look better,' he comments sadly.

'I feel better,' I admit.

He nods and looks down. We don't want to dwell on *why* I'm feeling better, or eating better, but I have put on a little weight since I've been with Leo, and I know I look vastly improved for it.

Matthew is staring at the table. 'There's something I need to tell you.'

'What?' An uneasy feeling settles over me.

He looks awkward. 'I knew Tessa's sister when I was at university.'

'What do you mean? You've been with her, too?'

'No!' He looks aghast. 'No, I just met her once!'

'How?' I ask edgily.

'You remember Lukas?'

'Well, I never did meet him, but I remember you telling me about him. He was a college friend, right?'

'Right. Well, he was going out with Alice, and Tessa's older sister, Lizzy, was Alice's best friend. She came to visit once.'

'That's weird,' I say.

'I know. It freaked me out when Tessa introduced us.'

I feel instantly queasy. 'When she introduced you?'

'Yeah.' He shifts uncomfortably.

'That sounds very cosy. A proper family affair,' I say, and he sinks into his seat at the sarcasm in my voice.

'It's not like that,' he says helplessly. 'She was all set to treat me like the proper bastard that I am, so she was shocked to see it was me.'

Something about his tone makes me soften. 'You're not a bastard.' His eyes light up. 'I know you didn't mean to do this.'

'I didn't,' he interjects quickly.

'But you did it,' I say with a small shrug.

I put my own knife and fork down. He stares at my half-full plate with dismay.

'I wish I could make you feel better,' he whispers.

'Let's get the bill,' I say.

*

I'm avoiding the house and everyone in it today, so I've packed my swimming costume in my bag. We go back to the hotel to chill out for a bit. Matthew shows me his room. It's nice, a lot smaller than ours was, but it has room for a small fridge and a coffee machine. He makes me a coffee and I slump down onto his nice double bed and close my eyes.

'Here you go,' he says after a minute, perching on the bed next to me.

'Thanks.' I sit up. 'I'm so tired.'

'Didn't you sleep well?'

'No.' I shake my head and blow on the coffee, my eyes stinging.

'You could have a kip here?' he suggests. 'I'll go and read my book on a hammock,' he says swiftly.

'Really?'

'Of course.' He puts his hand on my shoulder and rubs it tenderly, before quickly letting me go.

He didn't need to. It was a nice gesture.

I suddenly feel sad. I put my coffee on the side table and fall back onto his pillows, watching as he gathers his things together. He's wearing navy-blue shorts and a pale patterned shirt today. I wonder what Tessa thinks when she sees him. I bet she still fancies the pants off him – how could she not? Jealousy surges through my veins and I eye him with irritation as he walks out of the room.

I sigh and close my eyes. This is so confusing.

I turn on my side and allow my thoughts to lead me back to Leo. He's holding me in his arms as I drift off to sleep.

Chapter 27

'How's it all going?' Marty sounds on edge.

'It's okay,' I say hesitantly into the phone.

'Has he convinced you to come home with him?' she asks.

'He's not going to do that.'

She sighs loudly and I run my fingers through my hair, trying to detangle it. I didn't brush it last night. I ended up staying late at Matthew's, watching old movies together on the television in his room. The others were in the garden by the time I returned. It was awkward, and I went straight upstairs. I bet they feel like they have a stranger living with them at the moment. A stranger who has pushed their beloved Leonardo out.

Oh, Leo . . . I wonder what you're doing in Miami.

I fill Marty in on the events of the last couple of days.

'Hmm,' she says. 'Maybe he's letting you go, putting you out of his mind.'

'Marty!' I exclaim, because that's the last thing I want to hear, and she should know that.

'Come on, Laura, where is all this going to lead? You have to stop it now before it goes too far, before Matthew *doesn't* forgive you.'

For a moment I feel utterly helpless. I shake my head, even though she can't see me. 'I ... I can't give him up,' I tell her.

'Can't or won't?'

'Can't ... Won't ... What's the difference?'

'You don't love him, do you?' she asks wryly.

'No,' I reply quickly, although inside I'm not so sure. My emotions are not that clear-cut and I'm not quite sure how to separate love from lust. I guess I don't know him well enough to love him.

'Then what on earth are you doing?' she demands to know.

I sigh heavily and try to explain. 'I just know that I don't want to go home yet. I don't want to say goodbye to Leo yet. I can't let him go.'

'Maybe it will be a good thing if he lets *you* go, then,' she says.

'Would you stop saying that?' I raise my voice.

'Dammit, Laura.' Uh-oh, no-nonsense Marty is here. 'Your holiday visa is going to run out in, what? A month and a half? You're going to have to go home then, so what on earth are you doing screwing up all your chances of making things work with Matthew? I know he messed up big time, but he's sorry. He made a mistake. He still loves you and I know that you love him, so stop screwing him over!'

'So now you're on his side?' I cry.

'I'm not on his side,' she cries back. 'I'm on your side. Both of your sides – the two of you as a couple!'

'But, Marty—'

She interrupts. 'You know, we did sit there, all your friends and family, in that church under the eyes of God, while the vicar

239

asked us to support the two of you and help you through difficult times.'

'Under the eyes of God?' I say with disbelief. 'Since when have you been particularly religious?'

'Watching you get married was the most religious I have ever felt, if you want to know.' Her voice goes up a notch to drive home her point. 'There was something about that service ... something so serious. You had been through so much.' Now she sounds choked.

'Don't cry,' I say sadly.

'It's true!' She is crying now. 'Seeing you standing up at that altar with him, seeing the look in his eyes as he promised to love and honour you, in sickness and in health and all that other stuff ... It brought tears to my eyes. It still does. Matthew loves you, Laura. You're not going to find another man like him. I know you fancy Leo – God knows, I fancied Leo and Bridget sure as hell did – but where's your future with him? You can't base a relationship purely on sex, you know. However good it is!'

'It's not just the sex,' I say firmly.

She laughs at me, a hostile laugh.

'It's not!' I exclaim, trying not to let my temper take over. 'There's more to him than that.'

'Come on, this is short-term and you know it! We're not eighteen anymore! This is not Ibiza!'

'No shit, Sherlock. I'm twenty-nine, not some idiotic teenager.' This snub is meant to irritate her. 'I'm just saying that maybe this is not temporary. Maybe I do have a future with him, here in the keys.'

'You're not a bloody banyan tree!' she practically shouts. 'You can't put your roots down wherever you like.'

240

'Shut up, Marty,' I snap. 'Now you're really pissing me off.' I told her about the banyan trees and now she's using the damn things against me.

'Good.'

'Has he put you up to this?' I ask with sudden clarity. 'Matthew?'

'No.' But she sounds guilty.

'He has, hasn't he? When did you speak to him?'

She doesn't answer for a moment.

'Marty?'

'We've talked a couple of times,' she admits sulkily. 'A few times.'

'A couple of times? A few times? Make up your mind. Has he called you?'

'Yes.' I know there's more to that reply.

'And you've seen each other, too, right?'

'Mmm.'

I sigh heavily. She's supposed to be *my* friend.

'Don't be mad.' Now she's conciliatory. 'I've met him for lunch a couple of times. He really is so sorry. He misses you so much. I miss you,' she adds. 'We all just want you to come home.'

'Did you tell him to come and get me?'

'That was his idea.'

'But you thought it was a pretty good one.'

'Of course. Look, Laura, if he's willing to forgive you for this . . . *thing* you have with Leo, then surely you can forgive him?'

'It is not the same,' I say angrily.

'No, no, no, I know it's not,' she says hurriedly. 'Of course it's not. I just mean, maybe you can move on from this?'

I squeeze my eyes shut.

'Just think about it, okay?' she says gently. 'I'll speak to you later. Call me anytime,' she adds.

We ring off, but it's a while before I can mobilise myself enough to go and see Matthew.

The house smells of fresh paint, I notice, as I step outside. I look back up to see that the others made huge progress yesterday. This side of the house is completely painted and it looks beautiful. I didn't realise that last night when I came home as it was so dark. I feel a swell of pride as I walk across the garden. This beautiful home will be restored to its former glory. I'll make sure of that before I leave, if nothing else.

Matthew is showered and dressed and waiting for me on a hammock when I appear. He looks happy to see me, but I'm still feeling affected by the phone conversation with Marty.

'Are you okay?' he asks with concern, trying to climb down from the hammock, which is not as easy as you might think.

'I'm alright,' I tell him. 'What do you want to do today?'

'Whatever you like. Although, I was wondering about going on a boat ride later. A sunset cruise, maybe.'

I snigger. 'Those things are so touristy.'

'Oh, and you're not a tourist anymore, hey?'

He says this teasingly and for a few seconds I'm full of adoration for him. He could have sounded bitter and nasty. Matthew has rarely sounded bitter or nasty. I've never been scared of him or scared around him.

'Hey,' he says gently, seeing my expression. I feel like I'm about to crumble. He guides me into his room and closes the door.

'What's wrong?'

'Just ... everything,' I say, sitting down on his bed.

'Can I . . .' He holds his arms out to me, asking for permission to hold me. I edge closer to him and he wraps his arms around me and holds me tenderly. He feels so different to Leo. Slighter, not as broad, not quite as tall. I pull away and scan the room for a tissue. He goes to retrieve one for me from the bathroom.

'I spoke to Marty,' I tell him, taking the tissue gratefully.

'Did you?'

'She's thinks I'm mad, staying out here.'

He smiles sadly.

'I bet everyone does.' I shake my head. 'I can only imagine the conversations my mum and dad have been having.'

'They're worried about you,' he reveals.

'Have you talked to them?'

'A few times,' he admits with a nod.

'Bloody hell,' I mutter, but I'm not really cross. 'Did they encourage you to come here, too?'

He has the grace to look awkward. 'Yeah.'

I tut. 'I'm surprised my mum hasn't rocked up. She likes a bit of drama.'

'If you don't come back with me, she probably will.'

'Jesus Christ, you have to stop her.'

He smiles at me sadly. 'Please come home with me.'

I shake my head. 'I can't.'

He stares out of the window with frustration.

'What's he like?' I find myself asking.

'Who?' he replies.

'The baby. Evan.' His name almost sticks in my throat.

'Oh, he's . . .' He hesitates. 'He's just a little lump at the moment. Doesn't really do much.' But the light in his eyes does not go unnoticed.

I clear my throat. 'Do you have any photos?'

He casts me a wary glance.

'It's okay,' I reassure him. 'I want to see him.'

Tentatively he pulls out his mobile phone and searches through his photos, then hands it over. A tiny little baby stares up at the camera, at me. He has very blue eyes and fluffy dark hair. He's very, very cute. Even I have to admit that. I flick right and another photo appears. This time he's in someone's arms – his mother's? I wonder with a prickle of envy. But the picture is a close-up of him asleep, and as I flick through the next few, seeing Evan in the early days after his birth, when he was very tiny and very pink in an incubator, my heart goes out to him. There are no pictures of Tessa. I'm relieved to see that, and also a bit irritated. I'm glad Matthew chose not to take photos of her, but I'm curious to see again what she looks like. I saw her only the once – and that was in her tiny profile pic on Facebook. She changed the picture to a scan of her baby just days later. I checked.

I glance at Matthew's face and see that light in his eyes again. He's leaning close to me, looking over my shoulder at the photos.

'You love him, don't you?' It's more of a comment than a question, but he smiles sadly and nods.

This revelation doesn't hurt me.

'He's cute,' I find myself saying.

'I really want you to see him,' he blurts out.

I switch his phone off and shake my head. 'I'm not ready for that.'

He visibly slumps and takes his phone from me.

'You leave on Tuesday, right?'

'Yeah.'

'Come on, then,' I try to sound bright, 'how do you want to spend your last couple of days?'

We go shopping and wander the streets, checking out the Southernmost Point and arranging to go on a sunset cruise. Many of the people on the boat are middle-aged men and women, but even more are middle-aged obviously gay men. We raise a glass to each other and giggle.

When Matthew walks me home, I'm taken aback to see Leo's car parked outside the gates. I halt in my footsteps and turn swiftly to him.

'I'll see you tomorrow,' I say quickly.

'Okay. Goodnight.' He gives me a wary look.

I peck him on his cheek and hurry through the gate, not looking over my shoulder. The seats are empty. I run inside the house, my pulse racing. I can hear laughter and the murmur of voices coming from the dining room. I burst into the room and everyone starts, seeing me there. Leo is sitting at the table, surrounded by his friends. My friends? Not quite. He stares at me and I'm unable to read his expression.

'You're back,' I say breathlessly.

'It would seem so,' he replies darkly, no trace of a smile on his lips.

Everyone at the table averts their gaze. This is awkward, even for someone as brazen as Carmen.

'Talk to you in a bit.' I back out of the room, feeling sick.

I wait for him upstairs for what feels like a long time, but eventually he knocks at the door.

'Come in,' I say eagerly.

He pushes the door open and stands in the doorway, giving me a hard stare.

'Come in,' I say again, more hesitantly, sitting up on the bed.

He reluctantly steps further into the room and closes the door behind him.

'Are you okay? How was Miami?'

He irritably runs his hands through his hair. I flinch at the look on his face.

'Leo?' I say tentatively. 'I missed you,' I add in a small voice, holding my hand out to him, willing him to come and sit on the bed with me.

'I think it's best if we stay away from each other while your husband is here.'

He practically spits these words out and it hurts so much to hear him say them with such venom.

'Leo!' I gasp, but he glares at me. 'He's leaving on Tuesday,' I say quickly. 'I'm not going with—'

'Just stop,' he warns, and there's a look of disdain on his face as he turns around and walks out.

I'm too stunned to cry.

The next morning Leo is up and out of the house before I have a chance to talk to him. I spent most of the night awake, wondering what the others have told him. What can they say, other than the fact that I've hardly been here at all? They could tell him I've slept here every night, though. Did they tell him that? I have a sick feeling that maybe they didn't think this was entirely necessary.

I'm on another planet all day. I can barely concentrate, too consumed with seeing Leo again that night and trying to put it right. Matthew drives us to the beach, where we lie on the sand and I pretend to be asleep so I don't have to speak. It's his last night and he asks me to go out to dinner with him. I'm reluctant.

I just want to be with Leo, but eventually I agree. I go to the house to get ready first – and to wait for Leo.

Jorge comes home from work and gives me a wary look. I'm sitting on the living-room sofa, staring at the wall. I don't even have the patience to turn on the telly.

'Where's Leo?' I ask him hopefully.

'He's gone out,' he replies edgily, making to leave the room.

'Jorge, please!' I call after him. 'What have you said to him?'

'I haven't said anything,' he responds.

'Then what has Carmen said? He acted last night like he hated me!'

He regards me with sympathy. 'Don't worry about Leo. Carmen hasn't told him anything much, only that we haven't seen you a lot. Which we haven't.'

'I know,' I say helplessly. 'But not because of anything sinister.'

'No, nothing as sinister as the fact that your husband is staying a few hundred metres away,' he says in a gently sarcastic tone. 'Look, Carmen is only worried about Leo.'

'I know.'

'She wants the best for him. She's not sure you're it.'

I cast my eyes downwards. 'I know.'

'What do you think?' he asks me softly and my eyes fly up to look at him.

'I . . . I really care about him,' I say with difficulty.

He regards me for a moment. 'Tell him that.'

I nod. 'I will. When will he be home?'

'I don't know.' He shakes his head. 'I'll try to find him.'

'Okay. I'm going out for dinner with . . .' I cock my head to one side. 'It's his last night. I need to say goodbye.'

'See you later, then.' He turns and walks out.

'Jorge!' He spins around. 'Thanks.'

He smiles and leaves and I breathe a sigh of relief.

'You know it's your charity ball this weekend?' Matthew says over dessert.

'Of course,' I reply. 'Becky has it all under control.'

'I'm sure she does, but . . .'

'What?'

'Don't you think you should be there?' His tone is stern.

'Maybe.' I shrug defensively. 'But I'm not going to be, am I?'

'Shouldn't you be the one giving the speech? Do you really think she can handle it?'

'She'll be fine.' I try to brush him off, but I'm not as confident as I sound. She's competent, but she hasn't done many speeches before, and this ball is the biggie – of all the events in our calendar, this is the one that raises the most money year-on-year in Will's name.

'It's not too late to change your mind,' he continues.

'I'm not coming home.'

'We could go together,' he tries again.

'I'm not coming home.' My response is firm.

'Yet,' he adds with a frown.

'Yet,' I agree reluctantly. 'Look, I'm really tired. Do you mind if we call it a night?'

He looks disappointed. 'I thought you'd come back to mine for a bit?' He checks his watch, the watch I bought him as a wedding present. He's also still wearing his wedding ring. 'It's only nine thirty.'

I think for a moment. Well, I doubt Leo will be home this early, anyway. I guess I could always swing by there to check.

'What are you thinking?' Matthew asks. 'You've been somewhere else all day.'

'I'm sorry,' I reply guiltily.

'Is he back?'

'Who?'

'Leo,' he says with impatience.

'Oh, yes, he returned last night.'

He won't meet my eyes. He looks hurt and I despise myself for being the cause of that.

'Can we have the bill?' he asks the waitress.

We walk back to his hotel in silence.

'Come in for a drink?' he asks quietly.

'Look, I'll see you in the morning,' I say, trying to reassure him, but I can see that I'm failing. I take a deep breath and change my mind. 'Okay, then.'

He smiles slightly as I follow him through the reception area, waving at Mike as we go.

'Let's sit out here,' he suggests, indicating the deserted hammock area.

'Okay.'

He goes inside to prepare our drinks, returning to the hammocks with two glasses of chilled white wine.

'When did you get this?' I ask.

'Picked it up from the offie earlier, just in case I could tempt you back,' he says with a cheeky grin.

'Yeah, well, don't go getting any ideas,' I warn.

'As if I would,' he replies.

I clamber up onto a hammock and wobble every which way until I'm settled enough for him to pass me my glass.

Matthew climbs into his hammock more deftly and gives me a boyish smile as he raises his glass.

'Cheers.'

'Cheers.'

'Here's to us,' he says.

I take a sip, but don't second that sentiment.

'When are you seeing Evan next?' I ask.

'Er, this weekend,' he tells me, nervously.

I feel a pang of pity. 'You don't have to worry about telling me these things,' I say. 'It's okay. He's your son. You're going to see him.'

I think the alcohol is making me more reasonable. It usually has the opposite effect.

'Thanks,' he says quietly.

'So what are you doing?' I ask casually.

'I'm just going over to Tessa's house. She lives with her dad,' he adds.

'Oh, right.' I sound surprised. 'Isn't she, like, twenty-four or something?'

'Yeah. Her mother died a few years ago, so she lives with her dad to take care of him, but I think she'll get her own place soon.'

Unease settles over me. I'm not ready to discuss this person yet. I don't even know her. It kills me that he does, that she's the mother of his child.

'Are you alright?' he asks worriedly.

'Not really,' I admit. He makes to sit up, but I raise my hand. 'Stay there. Please,' I add.

He obliges, but looks awkward.

'Does she still fancy you, do you think?' I ask.

'No.' He frowns and shakes his head quickly, but I don't think he can be so sure. 'And there's no way ... No way.'

'What if you and I get divorced?'

The look on his face: it's like I've slaughtered his childhood kitten. 'Don't say that,' he begs in what is barely more than a whisper.

'What if we did?' I press. 'Would you and she . . .'

'No. Never. It's not like that. It was only that one night,' he says vehemently. 'I didn't know what I was doing. I was off my face—'

'I know,' I interrupt. I've heard it all before.

'I will never, *ever* do that to you again.'

'I should hope not,' I reply irately, my gaze finding its way to the sundeck. I wonder if Leo is back yet. 'Look, I'm going to go home,' I say with a sigh.

'Home?' He tuts, but doesn't say more.

'I'll see you in the morning,' I say firmly.

'I'm checking out at nine,' he tells me.

'I'll come to you at eight thirty,' I promise, climbing down from the hammock. He does the same. I hand over my glass. 'Thanks,' I say.

He throws the remainder of my wine onto some nearby foliage, and I turn to walk away.

'Laura . . .' he calls. I look over my shoulder. 'I love you.'

I smile sadly and walk back through the hotel grounds.

Chapter 28

I can hear Latin music coming out of the stereo and I hug myself as I pass the yard, feeling in my heart that Leo will be there. I hurriedly push through the gate, to the sound of Max barking. He runs over to me and I bend down to pat him, then freeze, because there in the armchair is Leo, and on the sofa is Jorge, sitting between two very gorgeous girls, one of whom, the brunette closest to Leo, is smoking a cigar and grinning as though I've entered in the middle of a joke. I straighten up, but my feet are stuck to the ground.

'Laura!' Jorge calls jovially. Leo regards me through the smoke trailing from the cigar in his fingers, but he doesn't say anything. 'Come and have a drink!' Jorge shouts.

'This is good shit,' the girl next to Leo says with a giggle. 'Where did you get these?'

I shake my head and walk past the sofa, anger filling every part of me.

'What's up with *her*?' I hear the redhead on the other side of Jorge say in quite a bitchy tone. I run up the stairs and go into my bedroom, shutting the door behind me.

'Bastard!' I screech to myself, and if there were a brick any-where in the vicinity I'm quite certain that I would hurl it out of the window at their little gathering.

I can still hear the sound of Latin music coming from the garden. I hear the tinkle of a girl's laugh and I bite my lip. The door flies open and Leo storms in. I turn my fury onto him.

'You arsehole!' I run at him and thump his chest.

Shocked, he grabs my wrists and manhandles me into the room, kicking the door shut with his foot behind him. 'What the hell are you doing?' he demands to know.

'What the hell are *you* doing?' I scream back at him as hot tears spill down my cheeks.

'I'm not doing anything!' he shouts, stunned, holding me at arm's length.

'That girl . . .' I gesticulate at the window.

'What about her?' he asks with astonishment. 'Jorge invited them back. He likes the redhead.'

'And you like the brunette,' I say, still full of white rage.

'I don't like the brunette,' he snaps.

My face falls and I throw myself against him, wrapping my arms around his torso. A moment later his arms encircle me and I tilt my face up to his, pressing my lips to his lips.

'Laura,' he says into my mouth.

'No, no, don't tell me to stop.'

I kiss him fervently, over and over, taking his face in my hands, not letting him tell me no again.

Finally he sucks in a sharp breath and gives in, lifting me off my feet and pressing my back up against the wall. I wrap my legs around his waist and slide my hands inside his T-shirt, wanting it off. Right now.

'Wait,' he says, pulling his shirt back down.

'I have to be with you,' I plead. 'You're the only thing that feels right about anything anymore.'

He regards me intently. 'Okay. But not here.'

I unwrap my legs and stand on my own two feet. He steps away and my knees buckle, so he scoops me into his arms and carries me up the stairs to his bedroom. He lays me gently on his mattress and I pull him down to me. Our kisses that night are more tender than they've ever been, despite the passion of only moments earlier. We make love. That's the God's honest truth. It's not just sex. Without a shadow of a doubt, I'm falling head over heels in love with Leo. And the thought terrifies the living daylights out of me.

'What's your surname?' I ask him afterwards, surprised that I don't already know this small fact about him.

'I have two.' He tucks my hair behind my ears. Our legs are still intertwined. 'Garcia was my father's surname, and Benedict was my mother's.'

'Garcia Benedict? Or Benedict Garcia?'

'Garcia Benedict,' he tells me. 'In Cuba the mother's surname comes last. Of course, my mother was American. When I was growing up, I was known only as Leonardo Benedict.'

'You couldn't take your father's name?'

'No.' He looks thoughtful and I lean down and kiss his forehead. 'What's your surname?' he asks, running his fingers up and down my back.

'I can't believe we haven't already had this discussion,' I say with half a laugh, trying to ignore the glaringly obvious fact that we really do know so very little about each other. 'Smythson,' I tell him, shivering under his touch. 'Well, Perry.' I avert my gaze. 'Perry is Matthew's name.'

Leo's fingers freeze in their tracks. He looks towards the window. 'We shouldn't be doing this,' he says in a gruff voice.

'Don't say that.' I place my hand on his cheek and force him to look at me. 'There's nowhere else in the world I'd rather be right now.'

Somehow, we oversleep. It's hardly surprising considering we've spent most of the night making love, but when I realise the time I leap out of bed and pull on my clothes.

Leo sleepily opens his eyes. 'What's wrong?'

'I promised Matthew I'd go to say goodbye to him at eight thirty.'

He looks confused. 'What time is it now?'

'Five to nine. He's checking out at nine.'

I sweep my hair back off my face, looking around for a hairband I'm sure I left up here last week. I spy it on the dresser and pull my just-shagged hair up into a tight ponytail.

'I'll be back in a bit,' I tell him regretfully.

He nods and tucks his hands behind his head. I run out of his room and jog down the stairs.

Max starts to bark furiously as I push open the kitchen door. Eric hasn't left for work yet, then. He always takes his dog with him. I see Matthew standing in the middle of the garden like a statue as the dog leaps and bounds around his feet.

'Max!' I shout, but he ignores me. 'Max! Come away!'

Matthew is holding up his hands, as though in surrender, but I can tell he's absolutely petrified. He was bitten by a dog when he was a boy and he's never quite got over his fear of them.

'MAX!' I shout again as he gets to his haunches and growls furiously. Then suddenly Max jumps up and nips Matthew on his elbow.

'Argh!' Matthew shouts, clutching his elbow in pain.

The door bursts open and Leo bounds out, followed by Eric. Leo wrenches Max away by his collar and slaps him sharply on his backside. 'Get him the hell out of here,' he yells at Eric as the dog runs towards his owner with his tail between his legs. Eric quickly obeys, dragging Max by his collar out of the gate and no doubt straight into his car. Leo turns. His features tighten as he regards Matthew.

Matthew, as white as a sheet with shock, is still cradling his elbow.

'Come inside,' Leo directs, giving me a hard stare as he storms past me.

I usher Matthew into the kitchen, gathering that Leo has gone to fetch a first-aid kit. My assumption is correct. He returns when I'm applying warm water from a bowl to the wound. He opens a bottle of Dettol and sloshes some into the bowl. I glance up at him nervously, but his eyes meet mine for only a millisecond. He's furious at me for placing him in this position. The last thing he wants is to put a face to the name of my husband. I'd be the same if I were in his shoes.

Actually, that's not true. I want to see again what Tessa looks like, possibly for all the wrong reasons. Maybe I'm looking for another excuse to hate Matthew. If she's as pretty as I remember from her Facebook profile, then that would be reason enough.

The wound is not that bad. Small, but probably quite deep, and certainly painful from the look on Matthew's face.

'I'm so sorry.' I feel awful for him.

Leo abruptly passes me a bandage.

'Thanks,' I murmur, and gingerly wrap it around the wound.

'You might want to wear a long-sleeved shirt going through customs,' Leo suggests, and I glance at him as Matthew studies the bandaging.

'That's a good idea,' I agree. 'No point in drawing attention to yourself.'

Matthew's eyes narrow as he looks at Leo, perhaps taking him in for the first time now that the drama with Max is over.

'We haven't been introduced.' He offers his hand. 'Matthew.'

Leo shakes it firmly, holding his stare for a long moment. 'Leo,' he replies.

Oh, how I wish the ground would open up and swallow me.

'Aah,' Matthew says, taking his hand away, but not moving his eyes. Leo's gaze is also unwavering. Bloody hell, they could bottle this testosterone and sell it for a fortune.

'What time is your flight?' Leo asks.

'Ten thirty,' Matthew replies evenly.

'You'd better get going!' I interject, trying to usher him back outside. He seems reluctant to leave. 'Haven't you got to return the rental car, too?'

'Yeah.' Matthew shrugs. 'It's no big deal. If I miss my flight maybe I'll just stay on a few more days. What's the worst that could happen?' He glances at Leo, who flashes him a dark look.

'You could lose your job,' I say quickly. 'Come on.'

He allows himself to be pushed by me out of the door, but then he stands his ground, turning around to face Leo.

'Does it bother you that she's married to another man?' he asks, his voice thick with resentment.

I gasp in shock at his direct question.

'Matthew, stop it,' I warn.

He glares at Leo and starts to walk off.

'You made the biggest mistake of your life when you hurt her.'

I spin around at the sound of Leo's voice, so calm and controlled under the circumstances.

Matthew's features shift slightly.

'Don't I know it?' he says, giving me a look that chills my bones. 'I'll see you,' he says to me.

I nod and fold my arms across my chest. And then he's gone.

Chapter 29

Leo is too angry with me to make love to me again for several days after that altercation, but finally he concedes, allowing me back into his bed and hopefully into his heart. We return to our easy routine. But it doesn't last long, because less than two weeks later my mother informs me that she's coming for a visit.

'Mum, don't,' I say firmly on the phone, trying not to give away my underlying panic.

'It's too late,' she crows. 'I've booked my ticket. I'm staying in the hotel next door.'

'Did Matthew put you up to this?'

'He thought it was a good idea,' she replies sniffily. 'You're still seeing that Leo?' she asks distastefully.

'There is absolutely no point in you coming to see me,' I re-iterate.

'We'll see about that.'

Bollocks.

She stays true to her word, so I go to the airport in Key West to collect her a few days later. Jorge lets me borrow his car, because it's slightly more presentable than Leo's. Leo is keen to disappear to Miami, but I put a stop to that. I don't want him going anywhere.

'Goodness me, isn't it muggy, here?' Mum comments with distaste as we climb into the car.

'You get used to it,' I tell her.

'I doubt I would.'

'Just as well you're not staying for long, then.' I smile at her sweetly and start up the ignition.

'Long enough to eat some Key Lime Pie and talk some sense into you, I hope.'

'Long enough to eat some Key Lime Pie,' I agree with the former part, but certainly not the latter.

My mother is a slim, tall, elegant-looking woman in her late fifties, with silver-blonde, bobbed hair. She has blue eyes, like me, although hers are a little paler, and she dresses well. Growing up, I read books and saw films like *Babe*, where the farmer's wife was always a round country bumpkin with rosy cheeks and a big smile. My mother is the polar opposite to this stereotype, although she does often smile. But her smiles are slightly wry, occasionally flirtatious.

'Am I going to meet this Leo, then?' she asks as we drive away from the airport.

'If you want to,' I reply casually. 'But you'd better be nice to him.'

'Oh, I will be.'

'I don't like the sound of that.'

'Just be thankful your father isn't here.'

'What's that supposed to mean?' I snap.

'He's not very impressed, that's all I'm going to say.'

'*What?*' I bark. 'He doesn't even know Leo so how can he judge him?'

'Marty has filled us in, and Matthew, too, of course.'

'They don't know Leo, either,' I say crossly. How dare they judge him? I know him. I *love* him. But I won't say that out loud. Not yet, anyway.

We arrive at the hotel and I see her to her room.

'Back again!' Mike chirps.

'You should be paying me commission,' I joke, taking the keys. 'Don't worry, I'll give her the tour.'

I lead Mum around the complex, pointing out the free water and sunscreen, and telling her about happy hour at four p.m., even though she's not much of a drinker.

'The pool looks nice,' she says.

'It is. We won't go for dinner for another couple of hours, so do you want to go for a swim?'

I pop back to the house to get changed. It's looking stunning now; the blue shutters really lift its appearance. We all worked hard on it, and when it was finished, I bought champagne to celebrate. The six of us sat around and drank it together, feeling more relaxed as a group than we have in all the time I've been in Key West. Even Carmen seems to have chilled out around me. Maybe she realises that I'm here to stay. Well, you know, until that pesky visa runs out . . .

I'm still debating what to do about that. My current thinking is that I'll return to the UK for a few weeks to sort out some things – aka my marriage, or, more accurately, my divorce – and then fly back here again. This is a temporary measure. I'll have to look into getting a proper visa soon, I know that. But this method will at least buy me a few more months. Leo will be going back to Miami at the end of the summer, which is only a couple of months away, and I'm not sure how I'll cope being in Miami with him. I still don't like that city. But I'm willing to give it a try, however much the thought fills me with unease. What I'd really love is for us to stay here, in Key West. He could train as a dive instructor and I could work from home ... That's my dream, anyway. I might share it with him one day.

Leo is in the kitchen.

'Hey,' I say warmly, sliding my arms around his waist and pressing my lips to his back.

'Hi.' He turns around and kisses me lightly on my nose. 'Your mom arrive safely?'

'Yep.' I nod, but don't look at him.

'What are you doing for dinner?'

'I'll take her to that Italian around the corner from Duval Street. You know the one I mean?'

'Yeah. Are you sure you don't want to bring her here?'

'I don't think that's a very good idea.' I screw up my nose. 'You really want to meet my mother? You're such a glutton for punishment.'

He cocks his head to one side and turns back to the food he's preparing.

'Your turn to cook?' I ask him, trying to make casual conversation.

'Yeah.'

'What are you making?'

'Coconut curry,' he says with a raised eyebrow.

'Oh, what?' I groan. 'I can't believe you're doing this to me.'

'You're doing it to yourself,' he says drily.

'Will you save me some?'

'I might do.'

I step up on my tiptoes and plant a kiss on his cheek, then run off upstairs to get changed.

I still haven't told him I love him. I'm too terrified about what he might say in response. Or, worse, what he might not say. Carmen's words still ring in my head: 'Leo doesn't do love', or something like that. He doesn't do marriage, either, apparently. There goes my green card. I smirk at my own joke. It's not one I'll be sharing with anyone.

It's a terrible thing to say about my own mother, but I'm glad that she's jet-lagged so I can send her to bed early. The others are in the garden when I return.

'Hello!' I chirp happily. Leo pats the space next to him and Jorge makes room for me.

'How was dinner?' he asks.

'It was alright,' I reply, holding my hand out for his beer. He hands it over and I take a swig.

'You want me to get you something else?' he offers.

'No, I like sharing with you.' I hand it back and rest my head against his chest, feeling happiness wash over me. I try to stifle a yawn, then give up and let it do its thing. I'm so tired. I could really do with an early night, yet here I am.

'So we're thinking about going back to Miami . . .'

My ears prick up as I hear Carmen say this.

'Really?' Jorge asks with surprise. 'What will you do?'

'Well, Eric has been offered a job on a yacht. You know that hotshot club owner who's been down here since April?'

We all say yeah, because Javier told us about him when he helped out after his return from travelling. He sounded like a bit of a bastard, but Eric has faithfully returned to work for him every day since.

'It's good money,' she adds.

'Is that what you want, Eric?' Jorge asks him.

Eric shrugs. 'Yeah, well, it's good money,' he repeats.

'But is it what you want?' Jorge asks again.

'Sure.' He shrugs.

'Where will you live?' Leo asks Carmen directly.

'Our younger sister moved back to Miami recently. Eric and I can stay with her and her family until we get ourselves sorted.' She looks around. 'There's not really much here for us, anymore.' She smiles at Javier. 'Javier is moving on and moving out.'

He told us a week ago that he's going to get a job further up the keys as soon as he's qualified. A mate of his works at a dive centre in Key Largo, and it sounds like a young, fun place to work. They have a lot of new people in from Miami every weekend. It's certainly not as secluded as Key West.

'What will you do about this house?' I ask.

Carmen nods at Leo. 'It's Leonardo's house. It's about time we gave it back.'

He freezes beside me and I shoot him a quick look. I never expected Carmen would say anything so reasonable, and neither, it seems, did he.

'Would you stay here?' I ask him hopefully, seeing my dreams laid out before me.

He frowns. 'What would I do?'

'You could be a dive instructor.'

His eyes flash past me to Jorge and I turn around to see Jorge smirking. I slap him on his arm. 'He could be! What are you looking like that for?'

I glance back at Leo to see him pursing his lips.

'You *could* be a dive instructor,' I say again.

Brrring . . .

Brrring . . .

Brrring . . .

Leo

She doesn't answer. I stare down at my cell phone and fight the impulse to stamp on it before angrily slamming it down on the side table, where it's still attached to its charger. I lost the damn thing a week and a half ago. Wanted to send her a text a couple of days after she left, but couldn't find it anywhere.

I hardly ever use my cell – I've had the same one for years. I would have bought a new one, except that I wouldn't have had her number, so I turned the apartment upside down instead. Finally drove back down to the keys yesterday and turned the house upside down, too, before finding it between the seat cushions of the couch. Luckily I'd moved the couch up onto the porch. They had rain last week – it would have drowned. I nearly punched the wall when I realised it had a dead battery and I didn't have my charger with me. Ended up driving through the night to get back to Miami.

It's been a crappy couple of weeks.

God knows what's going through her mind about me now. She's tried calling me loads of times, left a few messages. She's probably got herself all worked up, thinking that I've run back to

Ashlee. Yeah, right. I've gone back to work at the bar, but at least she hasn't shown up yet.

I've been thinking a lot about Key West. About Laura's crazy idea to turn the place into a guest house. Being back in that house without her ... It still smelled of her, of her perfume. I caught traces of it in my bed, in her bedroom, even on the couch.

Her bedroom. I don't even think of it as my mother's anymore. I couldn't go into that room for years after she died, but now it reminds me of Laura. I lay on her bed for a bit, musing about how she took the darkness away. I would have stayed there for longer just to feel close to her, if it hadn't been for that charger.

But the house would probably have got to me before long, anyway.

I hated going home right up until a couple of years ago, when Jorge dragged me there for the summer. He's always loved going down to the keys – used to spend whole seasons with Carmen, her loser boyfriend and Javier, and would come back to Miami all chilled-out and laid-back. Eventually I caved and went with him. Best thing I ever did.

I caught up with Carmen last week. She dropped by to say hi to Jorge and me. She and Eric are still staying with her sister and brother-in-law, but it's already frying her brain. She asked about Laura, which wasn't a surprise. She'll always have it in for her, doesn't think she's coming back, reminded me how she'd warned me to keep my distance. I told her to fuck off.

Maybe Laura missed the call. Perhaps I should try her again. I pick up my cell, hitting redial. This time it goes straight through to voicemail, a generic British chick telling me to leave a message. I hang up.

I head into my bedroom then pull my T-shirt over my head and unbutton my shorts before climbing into the bed. I'm too wired to sleep, even though I've been up all night.

Why did it go straight through to voicemail the second time? Has she switched off her phone? Didn't she want to speak to me? I feel edgy and I hate it. No girl has made me feel like this for a long time.

Somehow I manage to get a few hours' sleep, waking up to call her again, with no luck. I'm almost happy when the evening rolls around and I have to go to work. At least doing something might take my mind off her for a bit.

Why isn't she answering? Should I be leaving messages? What if she's angry with me for not calling her sooner? I pick up my phone again and press redial. Once more it goes straight through to voicemail. I clear my throat, waiting for the prompt to speak.

'Hey, *it's me. Sorry I haven't called. I lost my phone. Call me back.*'

I hang up. Hopefully that will be enough. I grab my keys and lock up, jogging down the steps to my car. Maybe I should have said more. I hate leaving phone messages – never do. But I know she doesn't like it when I'm too blunt. I'll call her again later. Actually, I can't. I keep forgetting the time difference. She'll be in bed soon, if she's not already.

Nerves hit me. She'd better not be in bed with *him*.

I climb into the car and screech away from the curb, angry with myself for being such a wuss.

Ashlee turns up around ten and I'm in a foul mood. I thought I'd be safe from her on a Sunday night. She tries to get my attention. I nudge Liam and nod in her direction. I don't want to talk to her.

Liam takes care of her and I move to the other end of the bar to take some guy's order.

'Hey! I was first,' the girl beside him complains.

I pull away, annoyed with them both, but the guy shrugs and jabs his thumb towards the girl.

'Two rum and cokes,' she says.

I nod and grab two glasses. The girl leans further over the bar, exposing more of her cleavage. I glare at her as I place her drinks down and grab her money.

She looks momentarily taken aback, but has recovered by the time I return from the register. 'Keep the change,' she purrs, winking at me.

I turn back to the guy without reacting.

A few months ago I might have screwed her. She's pretty hot, after all. But she's not Laura. I miss her way too much, goddammit. I've got to get a grip.

'Leonardo!'

I turn to see Ashlee calling me. She's drunk, I can tell. I consider ignoring her, but I've tried that before and she'll only get nasty.

'What do you want?' I ask her irritably.

'I heard you were back,' she replies with a smile, completely unaffected.

'You heard right.'

'Came to see you last night. Your boss said you didn't turn up for work.'

'I had to drive down to the keys.'

'Is that right? You never did take me there.' She pouts. 'Hey, you want to hook up later?' She raises her eyebrow and I remember that I used to like that flirty look on her, but now I hate it.

'No,' I say firmly.

'I'm just trying to be a friend to you, Leonardo.'

'Don't.'

'Well, if you change your mind—'

'I won't,' I interrupt. 'Gotta get back.'

She sneers. I take another order.

The bar quietens down around eleven, and that's when Drew turns up.

'Hey, buddy.' I reach across and clasp his hand. 'What can I get you?'

'A beer,' he replies.

'On the house,' I say when I come back with it.

'So, how's it hanging? You spoken to the lovely Laura yet?'

'Not yet,' I confess. 'I only got my phone back today,' I remind him unhappily. 'I'll try her again tomorrow.'

I told him all about us. Wanted to put a stop to him being so smug every time I mentioned her. *As if he would have ever scored with her* . . . He's out of his mind.

'Good luck,' he says, glancing over his shoulder.

My heart sinks as I notice Ashlee catch his attention.

'Hey, Ashlee,' he says without any enthusiasm as she walks over to the bar.

'How's it going, Drew?'

'Not bad, not bad.'

I scan the joint, but Liam is wiping down the bar top and there's no one waiting to be served.

'Have you managed to cheer him up, yet?' I hear Ashlee ask Drew in a silky voice which irritates the hell out of me.

'I'm afraid not,' he replies, and I flash him a warning look.

'What happened to that girl?' Ashlee asks me. 'The blonde British one you so obviously wanted to screw?'

'You should quit drinking,' I say menacingly. 'Don't you have to work tomorrow?' As far as I know she's still at that clothes shop on Collins Avenue.

'I always sober up in time,' she brushes me off. 'So come on, then. Where's the girl?'

'If you don't—'

'You talking about Laura?' Drew interrupts, trying to calm me down.

'Yeah, that's the one.' Ashlee's eyes dart towards me. I've spooked her, but I don't care.

'She's gone back to England, hasn't she, buddy?'

'She's coming back soon,' I say through clenched teeth. I'm not sure I'm that convincing.

I wake up early, even though I'm tired as hell. I try calling her again. My nerves have been tense all night and they're even worse now. Voicemail again. I almost throw the phone at the wall, but stop myself just in time, throwing it onto the bed instead. It's not very satisfying, hearing it thud onto the soft mattress.

I should make a note of her number in case I lose my phone again (or break it). I find a pen and paper, then jot her number down and put the paper in my nightstand drawer. A moment later I get the scrap out again and try to commit the number to memory. I give up and try to go back to sleep.

I lie there for a long time, with scenes playing over in my head. I think about that first time she kissed me, the first time I took her to bed, and I get a hard-on, but then lose it again when I remember she's not answering her phone.

I can't believe that I resisted her for so long. I wanted her so much in those early days. She was beautiful with her blonde hair and blue eyes . . . And those legs! I wanted them wrapped around me from the first moment I laid eyes on her.

But then I got to know her, and I couldn't get past the idea that she was married. I didn't want to be like my mother, subject to someone else's control. Now here I am.

What's she thinking? I wish I could read her mind. She's so frickin' far away.

I huff and get out of bed, then take a shower. I think I'll go to the beach today.

A week later she's still not answering. I don't get it. Carmen is furious. She reckons Laura is trying to tell me that she's moved on – even Jorge agrees. But I don't believe it. She doesn't play games, Laura. It doesn't suit her. She'd tell me if she was going back to him, I'm sure she would.

She said she loved me. She said she loved me, and I said nothing. I'm really proud of myself.

I can't face work tonight so I call in sick. I have to get away. I have to feel closer to her somehow, so I'm driving down to Key West.

What if she never calls again?

I'll keep trying her. She'll have to turn her phone on again soon. Maybe she's lost *her* charger . . . Nah, she's got a newer phone than me; she could buy another charger. Still, it would be ironic. Serves me right for being such an idiot.

The house is dark when I pull up, but I know where I'm going and the street lights just about light my way. It still smells of fresh paint, but I can't make out the colour of the shutters.

They're blue, like her eyes. I've been acting like a lovesick fool. If she has gone back to him, I'll repaint them – if I don't raze the house to the ground first.

I unlock the house and go straight upstairs to her bedroom. I push the door open, sniffing the air, but there's no trace of her perfume. I go and grab her pillow, pressing it to my nose like a freak. There. Just there, wafting past my nostrils, like a ghost. I breathe in deeply and then lie on the bed, hugging the pillow. I'm glad I didn't let her wash the sheets before she left. She liked it when I told her not to, that I wanted to be reminded of her. She smiled and said, 'Aah,' and then kissed me.

If Carmen could see me now, she'd commit me to an asylum.

The next day is Saturday and I'm not supposed to be back at work until Monday so I've got a full weekend ahead of me. I don't know what I'm going to do. Probably head out to the Green Parrot tonight, catch up with some locals and sink a few beers, try to cheer myself up.

I go around the house and open all the shutters. It'll be a pain in the ass to shut them again, but I'm not going to live in the dark for a weekend.

The house is so quiet. It's weird walking through it, going into Carmen and Loser's bedroom, Javier's, Jorge's . . . I miss them all, even Eric. Not something I ever thought I'd admit.

I end up in the bathroom, which doesn't have a window. It still gives me the creeps, even all these years later. I stare at the bathtub and shudder, then go out and close the door behind me.

Even if I did put in new bathrooms, I'm never going to like that room.

Why am I even talking about new bathrooms? I'm not turning this place into a guest house, that's an insane idea.

I go outside and drag the couch down from the porch to the yard, or garden as Laura liked to call it. I smile to myself. She's a funny little thing. So cute with her British accent. I liked the way she said 'offie'. Hell, I liked the way she said everything. I slump down and put my feet up on the rock, wishing I had her here now so I could pull her up onto my lap. I loved the way she needed protecting one minute and was so fiercely independent the next. I miss her warmth.

I take a cigar out of its case and light up, but after a few puffs I'm not enjoying it, so I put it out.

Damn, she was angry when she came home that time to find those chicks here. I laugh out loud and then quickly check the street to make sure no one heard me. I shake my head and lean back, remembering with amusement the way she thumped my chest. Woah, that hurt. But what came afterwards . . . I sigh. Then I pull out my phone and try her again. Voicemail. I decide to leave a message:

'Hey, it's me. Don't know why you haven't called me back. I'm in Key West. House reminds me of you. Call me.'

I hang up and feel utterly miserable.

The kitchen *is* a joke. Really. It's been in this state for over three decades. If I replace it – and the bathroom, yes, the bathroom – it doesn't mean I have to open a guest house, does it? Maybe I'll look into that today. How much do kitchens cost?

*

A lot, as it turns out. More than my savings, but ... well, my father's cigar stash must be worth a bit ...

That evening I go to Duval Street and talk to an old pal working in one of the cigar shops. I've known Herman for years – a permanently sunburned old guy who should have retired a decade ago. I head out back with him before I risk getting his opinion.

'Cuban cigars? Real Cuban cigars?'

'Yeah, none of this "made with Cuban tobacco seeds grown in the Dominican". They're the real deal, almost thirty years old.'

'Whoa. I've got a guy in Miami who would love this shit.'

Obviously what I'm doing is illegal, but I've been illegally stashing them for years. Cuban cigars are still embargoed in America.

'Can you get a price from him?'

'You got any samples?'

I pull out my cigar case and hand a couple over. He puts one to his nose and sniffs.

'Man,' he murmurs, inhaling deeply before getting back to business. 'Okay, I can give him a call, put you in touch—'

'No, no,' I quickly interrupt. 'I don't want to meet him, don't want anything to do with him. No disrespect,' I add, 'I know he's your friend. Can you broker the deal?'

He ponders this for mere seconds. 'I'd need a cut.'

'Of course.'

'I'll do it for twenty per cent.'

'Ten.'

'Fifteen.'

'You've got yourself a deal.' He shakes my hand and smiles to himself.

A week later I have more cash in my hands than I've ever had in my lifetime. I could buy a new car, I could go out and get wasted . . . What do I do? I go and buy a kitchen. I'm telling you, she really has got to me.

Jorge and Carmen come down the next weekend. I still haven't heard from Laura and it's like having an itch I can't scratch. I think about her constantly. Without Jorge and Carmen to take my mind off her, I think I'd go mad.

'I cannot believe you sold all your cigars!' Jorge exclaims with amazement.

'They weren't tasting so good anymore, anyway,' I say.

'What do you mean?' Carmen asks.

'I don't know, nothing tastes good right now.'

She gives me a long look.

'What?' I ask with a frown.

'You know, Alejandro's taste buds went funny when he was depressed.'

I stare at her.

'You're not depressed, are you, Leo?' She narrows her eyes at me.

'I've felt better,' I reply offhandedly, 'but I'm not going to kill myself in a bathtub, if that's what you're worried about.'

Funnily enough, my words don't cheer her up.

Jorge turns out to be surprisingly good at DIY. We drink a few beers and tear out the kitchen, while Carmen goes to buy paint for the inside of the house. Eric's in Miami, working. It's good to have her here by herself; she's always more chilled when he's not around. Seeing her busy, helping out, checking up on me – it reminds me of her old self, when she first came into Alejandro's life and sorted him out. Thought she was Wonder

Woman back then. Couldn't save him in the end, though. After his death, she thinks I looked after her, but it was the other way around. Not sure she can save me this time. Only one person can do that.

Ordered the bathrooms yesterday, too. They should arrive this week, so Carmen and Jorge are coming back. We're turning Javier's bedroom into a big shower room, which will leave six bedrooms in total. Carmen and Eric's bedroom downstairs – the biggest room – will have an en-suite. I've quit my job; I'm not going back to Miami anytime soon. I've got too much to do here. The kitchen's almost done and I keep thinking about Laura's face, what she'll say when she sees it. She'll be proud of me. I'm trying not to lose faith in her – there's got to be some explanation.

'There's no denying the facts, bro, it's been two weeks,' Jorge says that night when we're hanging out.

'She'll come back,' I say.

'Two weeks since you called her, a whole *month* since she left,' Carmen adds ruefully.

'You think I don't know the dates?' I don't even have the energy to give her my death stare.

'Wasn't she supposed to be coming back in a couple of weeks?'

I stare straight ahead. 'Yeah.'

'I'm just saying—'

'I get it, alright?' I snap. 'Enough.'

We all fall into an uncomfortable silence.

'I prefer you without Eric around, you know,' I say to Carmen. I don't know why I just said that.

'What? Why?' She sits up straighter.

'You're less annoying.'

'Okay, gee, thanks,' she says sarcastically.

'It's true.' I glance at Jorge. 'Isn't it?'

'I'm not getting involved.' He holds up his hands, but Carmen glares at him.

'Don't give me that shit. Do you agree with him?' She jabs her finger in my direction. Jorge looks uneasy.

'I do a bit,' he admits.

'Really?' She sounds surprised. She's not as pissed off as I thought she'd be.

'You're less of a bitch,' I chip in helpfully.

'Well, thanks, Leo,' she says with a wry look.

'Less irritable. Less *irritating* . . . Can't say I blame you. He irritates the hell out of me, too.'

'Jesus Christ, Leonardo, speak your mind!' she erupts.

I down the last of my beer.

'Still up for that dive tomorrow, buddy?' Jorge asks me.

'Buddy' reminds me of Laura, but I keep my cool. 'Sure, if Timmy's okay with me crashing.' Timmy's the boat captain. He's the one I cover for during the holidays when he goes to visit his mother on the West Coast.

'Great. Well, I'm going to hit the sack,' Jorge tells us.

'I'm going to grab another beer.' I get up. 'You want one?' I ask Carmen.

'Yes, please.'

I pass a can to her on my return and she cracks it open, staring into space. Neither of us says anything for a long time, but it's not awkward. That's the thing with family, and she's practically my sister after all these years. So much for me being an orphan. I couldn't get rid of my freaky little siblings if I tried.

'Do you really think I should break it off with Eric?' she asks me out of the blue.

I lean forward and rest my elbows on my knees, staring at her directly. 'Yeah.'

She sighs. 'Really?'

'Why not?'

'What would I do?' she asks.

'You could move back here, help out with this guest house, if I ever get around to opening it.'

She smiles a sweet smile, before rolling her eyes. 'I don't think Laura would be very happy about that if she does come back.'

'Give her a break,' I say. 'She could do with a friend like you. And *you* could do with a friend like *her*,' I add poignantly. Carmen doesn't have many friends. I'm sure that's half her problem.

'Where am I going to find another man?'

I scoff. 'You don't need a man. You're good. You've got Javier . . . And anyway, you *would* find someone else before long.'

'You think?'

'Of course.'

'I don't look as good as I did back in the day,' she says, immodestly.

'You still look pretty good.'

She smiles at me and bites her fingernail. I lean back in my seat and cross one leg over the other knee. Suddenly I realise she's staring at me with a weird look in her eyes.

'What's got into you?' I ask.

She hesitates before telling me: 'Sometimes I wonder if I chose the wrong brother.'

Fuck, what's she saying?

'Don't say that,' I mutter. She's had too much to drink. She's starting to remind me of Ashlee.

'You're a good person, Leo,' she says seriously.

I take a long gulp of beer, trying to ignore the tension. 'I hope Laura still thinks that.' I want to put a stop to this conversation, whichever way it's going.

Carmen sighs. 'I warned her not to hurt you,' she adds with a trace of bitterness.

'I don't know what's going on with her,' I admit, downing some more of my drink. 'But I'll find out eventually.'

I wake up in the early hours of the morning with an urgent urge to pee. I go downstairs, finding my way along the corridor. There's an eerie, unnatural light coming from the bathroom. Dread fills me, threatens to immobilise me, but I keep moving, down that corridor, towards that bathroom. Something is wrong – deeply wrong. I put out my hand to push open the door, but my hand looks different. Smaller, younger . . . I see her knees in the bath – white, so white, and then the water, coloured red with blood.

'Oh, Mom, what have you done . . .'

I go further into the room and stare with horror at her face. But it's not my mother, it's Laura. Her eyes – half-closed in the light – shine the most brilliant blue, even in death.

My own blood-curdling scream wakes me up from my nightmare. I bolt up in bed and a cold sweat washes over me. I gasp for breath, hearing footsteps on the stairs. Carmen bursts into my bedroom.

'What's wrong?' she cries.

I raise my hand to keep her at bay, to calm her down. 'Just a bad dream,' I manage to spit out, through heaving breaths.

She doesn't move.

'Go back to bed,' I say.

'No. Are you okay? What was it about?'

'Laura. It was about Laura. And my mother.' I'm suddenly hit with an overwhelming need to cry and I don't want Carmen here to see it. 'Go back to bed,' I say again, more firmly.

'Oh, Leo,' she says with a sad sigh. 'She's really messing with your mind.'

'GO BACK TO BED!' I bellow, then stand up, pulling on my clothes. I know that I'm scaring her, but I can't help that now.

'What are you doing?' she asks nervously, her back against the wall to keep out of my way.

'Something I should have done a long time ago.'

I storm down the stairs and into the laundry room, where we've been storing our tools for the renovation. I grab a sledgehammer and run back up the stairs. Carmen is standing in the corridor, but I don't look at her. I go straight to the bathroom and start hammering chunks out of the bath.

'LEO!' she shouts.

'Stay back!' I yell in response.

'What's going on?' I hear Jorge cry from behind me.

Carmen doesn't answer. The answer, after all, is right there in front of him. I'm getting rid of the bath. I don't know why I didn't do it years ago.

It takes me all of ten minutes to disassemble the bathtub and after that I feel much better, if a bit out of breath. Jorge and Carmen are still watching from the corridor.

'Are you done renovating?' she asks with a touch of sarcasm.

'Yep,' I reply. 'A shower will fit in this room better, anyway.'

*

We go downstairs after that – there's no point in trying to get back to sleep. It's about six o'clock in the morning. Carmen makes coffee. Her coffee always tastes like crap, but so does everything at the moment.

She hands over a mug, her eyes wary.

'You feel better?' she asks.

I don't reply.

'Just as well you've already ordered a new bathroom suite,' Jorge comments.

'Just as well you didn't have it in for the toilet,' Carmen adds.

I grin at her and she starts to laugh. Jorge joins in, and pretty soon we're all at it.

Later they go off to get dressed, but I stay sitting on the couch, staring at the TV I'm yet to replace. My thoughts take me back to that dream.

It felt so real, seeing her dead in that bathtub. A cold feeling settles over me. What if something has happened to her?

As this realisation sinks in, I'm chilled to my bones. I need to find out.

I go and rap on Carmen's door.

'What is it?'

I push the door open as she's frantically pulling her dress over her head.

'Leo!' she berates.

'I think something might have happened to Laura,' I tell her, completely oblivious to her nakedness as fear takes over.

'Why do you say that?' she asks, confused. 'Your dream?'

'She wouldn't do this,' I say quickly, before she can write off my suspicion as superstition. 'She would have called me back.'

Jorge comes out of his room. 'What's this?' he asks.

334

I fill him in.

'How can I find out?' I ask him.

'Internet?'

Eric's taken his computer with him.

'Internet café?' Carmen suggests. 'There's got to be one around here somewhere. Although I can't think where . . .' she muses.

'Hotels have the internet,' Jorge suggests. 'Maybe you could ask to use one of their computers for a bit? Say it's urgent?'

I nod. 'What's the time?'

Carmen checks her cell. 'Nine o'clock.' She pauses, thinking. 'But where would you start?'

'With her name. That might even be enough. She runs a children's charity and she used to date a racing driver who died. If something's happened to her, then I should be able to find out.'

Carmen bites her lip. 'You want me to come with you?'

Bridget

'You have to tell him.'

'How can I tell him?' Marty replies bluntly. 'He couldn't even be arsed to call her back after she left.'

'You don't know why that is,' I say. 'You've got to try to get hold of him somehow.'

'I don't even have his number,' she mumbles, still thinking.

'Did they ever find her phone?' I ask.

'Yeah, but it was crushed to bits. Replacing it has been the last thing on anyone's mind.'

I think for a moment. I don't suppose anyone has tried to access her voicemail, either.

'Matthew won't like it,' Marty adds.

'This is not about Matthew, it's about Laura,' I say firmly, knowing I'm right. 'Laura would want you to let him know.'

She frowns, staring into space. 'How can I do that if I don't have his number?'

A brainwave comes to me. 'Ring the hotel. Ring Mike on reception. I bet he'd drop a note around to the house?'

'That's a really good idea,' she says. 'But Laura said Leo and the others locked up and went back to Miami.'

'They'll go back to the house eventually. It's better to have a note waiting, don't you think? At least then you will have done everything you can.'

'Okay. I'll sort it,' she says.

Leo

A guy is coming up the path when I go outside.

'What's up?' I ask, holding the door open for Carmen. He looks familiar.

'Hey! I'm Mike from the hotel next door,' he says. 'I didn't think y'all would be here.'

'Can we help you?' Carmen says, closing the door behind her.

'I have a note for you.' He comes towards us.

'A note?' I jog to meet him, stretching out my hand.

'It's from a girl named Marty. She stayed with us—'

'I know who she is! What does it say?' I snatch it from him.

'She wants you to call her,' he says warily, as I read these words on the paper, along with a number. 'She said it's about Laura.'

I feel sick as a dog as I dial Marty's number. She answers on the fourth ring.

'Hello?'

'Marty?'

'Yes.' Her voice sounds short.

'It's Leo.'

'Leo!' she gasps. 'Sorry, I'm just heading back into my office after a long lunchbreak.'

'I got your note,' I say in a rush, willing her to get to the point.

'That was quick!'

'Tell me what's wrong,' I demand to know. 'Is she okay?'

'Oh.' Her voice instantly shrinks, becomes very small. 'No. I'm afraid she's not.'

I've been pacing the floor, but now I freeze. I'm barely aware of Carmen watching nervously from the corner.

'What's happened?' I can hardly speak.

'She was hit by a car,' she tells me gently. 'She's alive, but she's in a coma.'

Shivers go up and down my spine. 'A black car?' My voice doesn't feel like my own.

'Yes,' she sounds surprised. 'It was, as it happens.'

'The palm reader,' I murmur.

Silence. 'Oh my God, you're right,' she practically whispers. 'I can't believe I didn't think of that.' She starts to cry.

'Marty, stop,' I interrupt, suddenly feeling more in control. 'Where is she?'

'She's in Cambridge, in intensive care at a hospital near her parents.' Pause. 'She kept trying to call you,' she says, almost accusingly.

'I lost my phone. I've been ringing her three times a day ever since I found it.'

'Have you?'

'Of course,' I snap, annoyed at her tone. 'Just tell me, is she going to be okay?'

'I don't know.' She sniffs. 'Nobody knows. They're hoping she'll pull through. She's broken her left arm and some ribs, and fractured her left leg, but it's the coma the doctors are most worried about. Brain trauma. They won't know how bad the damage is until she wakes up. *If* she wakes up,' she adds quietly. 'I'll keep you posted, of course. Now that I have your number.'

'No,' I say. 'I have to be there. I'll come as soon as I can.'

'What, to England?' she blurts out.

'Yeah.' Thank God I sorted out a passport last year when we went diving with Jorge's mate in the Bahamas.

'But, do you think that's such a good—'

'I don't care,' I interrupt. 'I need to see her. I *have* to see her. I'll call when I've got a flight booked so you can tell me where to go.'

'Oh. Okay.' She sounds shell-shocked.

'Speak soon,' I say, and as I hang up I hear her mutter, 'Matthew is going to kill me.'

The other one, Bridget, comes to collect me from the airport. I was planning on catching a train – I had my journey all mapped out – so I'm surprised to see the brunette holding a piece of white cardboard with my name scribbled on it when I come out of Arrivals.

'Leo!' she calls, waving cheerily. Too cheerily.

'Hello,' I say cautiously.

'I'm here to give you a lift,' she chirps. 'Thought you could do with seeing a friendly face.'

I instantly feel bad. 'Oh, thanks.'

'Come on, it's this way,' she says.

It's grey and miserable when we drive out of the car park. 'Welcome to the UK.' She's being sarcastic.

'Is there any news?' I ask her hopefully.

'No change,' she says disconsolately.

We don't speak for a while. We don't speak much at all,

actually, on the drive to Cambridge. I stare out the window at the green, green countryside. Everything looks alien. The roads are so windy, the cars so much smaller.

'Where do you live?' I ask her.

'West London,' she replies. 'Heathrow isn't far from me.'

We've been in the car for an hour and a bit, so she's obviously going right out of her way. 'I really appreciate this,' I force myself to say.

'It's no trouble.' She brushes me off. 'I wanted to visit her, anyway.'

'Have you seen her, yet?' I ask.

'No. Only immediate family at the moment.'

'Will I be able to see her?' I ask with a frown.

'I don't know,' she admits. 'You'll need to speak to Laura's parents. And Matthew,' she adds under her breath.

'How is he?' I ask uneasily.

'Not the best,' she replies.

I wonder how I might go about avoiding him in the near future.

I'm staying in the cheapest hotel I could find, as close to the hospital as I could manage. I can't waste money on a car rental – I don't know how long I'll be here – but I've got my bus route worked out. Mike from the hotel next door let me use their internet to book flights and sort out the finer details. Carmen asked him, and he was happy to oblige. He seems quite fond of Laura.

A lump forms in my throat and I have to look out of the window until it passes. I don't want to lose it in front of Bridget – or anyone, if I can help it.

'Do you want to check in and then I'll give you a lift to the hospital?' Bridget asks.

'That would be great.'

She comes with me, for moral support, I think. She's a nicer person than I remembered. I thought she and Marty seemed a bit silly and vacant in the keys, messing around with those jocks and leaving Laura out in the cold. I still haven't forgiven them for that, but Bridget isn't so bad. I wonder where Marty is. I thought she was Laura's best friend.

The hospital brings back bad memories. Pale blue walls, strip lighting and long corridors . . . Mom never went to hospital; she was dead long before it got to that point. But Alejandro did, and in my head I can still see him clearly, hooked up to machines, needles going into his arm, a ventilator connected to his mouth, low insistent bleeps in the background. Eventually the bleeps became one incessant noise, announcing his death.

As it turns out, I can't even see Laura. I ask to speak to a doctor and I'm directed to a small Visitors' Room with Bridget. We're the only people in there and we're waiting a long, long time.

'She believed in you, you know,' Bridget says miserably, out of the blue.

I look at her, sitting perpendicular to me on a brown couch under the one window. My eyes are stinging, my body feels like it's weighted down. I've barely slept in seventy-two hours and I'm not going to sleep now.

'What do you mean?' I ask, surprised by her statement.

'She loved you. Do you know that?'

I nod, because I can't speak.

'She told us, Marty and me. She thought you loved her, too.'

I look away, then lean forward, resting my elbows on my knees, rubbing my hand over my mouth in agitation and fighting back tears.

The door opens and a middle-aged man walks in. I glance up at him.

'Leo?' he asks.

'Yes.' He's not dressed in green scrubs like all the other medical staff I've seen.

'I'm Barry, Laura's father,' he says gently, his face tired and pale.

I leap to my feet and offer my hand for him to shake. Laura's father! 'Pleased to meet you, sir.'

He shakes my hand, but can't meet my gaze for long. He looks like her, more like her than I thought he would. Something about his nose and the shape of his face. She told me most people say she takes after her mother.

'Sit down.'

He indicates the chair I was sitting in, taking a seat opposite.

'Is there any news?' I ask quickly.

He shakes his head abruptly. 'I'm afraid not.'

'Can I see her?'

He looks uncomfortable. I wait for him to speak.

'I'm not sure, at this point,' he eventually replies. 'You can't see her now because they're doing the afternoon ward round. You might be able to see her tomorrow.'

'Okay.' I exhale loudly. 'Not later? I'm happy to wait.'

'I'm afraid . . .' he starts. 'I'm afraid Matthew hasn't given permission yet for you to visit.'

'*What?*'

'He's Laura's next of kin,' he says, holding up his hands as though to deflect blame. 'It's up to him who sees her.'

'Well, can I speak to him?' I'm trying to control my anger. 'Where is he?'

'He's gone back to London.'

'Why isn't he here?' I ask accusingly. 'If he's her *next of kin* ...' There's venom in my tone, and I can't help it, even if it gets me nowhere.

'Matthew works during the week. He's a journalist.' And? 'He'll be back on Friday.'

'But that's three days away!' I get up and start pacing, which isn't easy in this small space.

'Can't ...'

I look at Bridget, who's trying to say something.

'Can't you call Matthew?' she asks.

Laura's father looks pained.

'He's come all this way,' she implores. 'Will the nurses really object if Laura's father gives permission as to who sees her?'

I stand and stare at my beautiful Laura's father, weakened by him, by Matthew, by the whole situation. He glances up at me and his face softens.

'I suppose not,' he agrees, looking down at his hands.

'Thank you.' Swallowing is difficult. He meets my eyes and nods before checking his watch.

'They'll be finishing their round in an hour and a half. I'll go and speak to the nurses.'

An hour and a half is a long time to wait. I tell Bridget to go home, but she insists on staying. I'm grateful, but I don't speak to her. I cross my arms, close my eyes and think about Key West, willing my girl to come back to me.

Laura's father returns at some point and hands us both cups of tea. It tastes crap – I'd kill for a coffee right now, even one of

Carmen's – but I appreciate the gesture. Finally, they let me go in.

I pause at the door, glancing over my shoulder to check no one is behind me. I don't want to be with anyone other than her right now. I'm alone, so I push open the door and enter.

I've thought about this moment countless times over the last seventy-two hours, but nothing prepares me for the sight of her now. Her body is partially covered with a white sheet. Her left arm and left leg are in casts, the leg elevated. Her hair is limp around her face, and her eyes are closed. There's a ventilator hooked up to her, with a large tube going into her mouth. Her chest rises and falls, but she looks so frail, so vulnerable. Just like Alejandro did before he died, and he was my brother, my big, powerful brother, reduced to nothing.

My feet are glued to the floor, so I stand and stare, aware that the persistent bleeping noises from her attached monitors are the only sounds in the room. I force myself to put one foot in front of the other until I reach her bed. There's a chair waiting, so I sit down and reach for her hand. It's the fact that it's still warm, like she's asleep, that brings me crumbling down. I kiss her hand as my tears run off her fingers.

My father, my mother, Alejandro, and now Laura. *Papi* ... That's what I used to call my father. When did he become 'Father'? A long time after he was dead, I think, when he started to feel like a stranger. Even Mom has become 'Mother' in death, so unfamiliar, so alien, so far from the Mommy of my childhood. How the hell will I go on if Laura is also destined to become a stranger?

I reach up and touch her cheek.

'Wake up,' I whisper.

But she doesn't. And when her father enters the room after I don't know how long, he has to help me walk out of there.

Bridget drives me back to the hotel. I hope she knows I appreciate what she's done, because I can't convey it with words. I go inside, up to my room, and fall into the deepest sleep of my life.

Every waking hour of the next two days I spend at the hospital – by her side when they let me. I've seen Laura's mother, Lottie, a couple of times. I met her in the keys, that time Laura was so upset about her mom visiting the baby. She didn't like me much then, and she doesn't like me much now, so I try to keep out of her way.

Mostly I'm in the Visitors' Room staring at the wall. It's claustrophobic in here – small and stuffy. A fan whirrs left and right to move the air, but the window is always closed, the vertical blinds turned so there's hardly any natural light. A Bible sits on top of some magazines – but that's not going to help me now. It didn't help when Alejandro died. Even the clock batteries have run out, the time permanently set to 10:07 and sixteen seconds. I don't know if it's a.m. or p.m. but I do know that if I have to stay here much longer, I'll go insane. The hardest thing is when there are strangers in the room with me, friends and family of other patients in intensive care. Hearing them talk about their pain, about the chances of their loved one pulling through ... I soak up their despair like a sponge. Perhaps Laura's father can see the effect being in this room is having on me, because on Thursday he appears during the morning ward round and insists I go downstairs for a break. It doesn't take much to persuade me.

I take the elevator one floor down to the food court, where my mood instantly lifts. It's not as depressing; some people are actually laughing, as though they're not here because of a tragedy. I wander through a couple of shops and notice that even the candy looks different here. I also discover I can get decent coffee instead of the crap out of the vending machine upstairs. I'll have to make each cup last as long as I can – I don't want to run out of money. Not that anything tastes good at the moment, anyway, but psychologically I feel a bit better.

On Friday afternoon Laura's father pulls me to one side. 'Matthew is on his way,' he says in a stern, firm voice. I know what he's telling me: it's time for me to make way for the revered husband. The man's been decent to me so I reluctantly agree to wait for his call letting me know when I can next come in.

I don't know what to do with myself. I catch a bus into Cambridge and walk around for a while, peering through archways into grand courtyards and wandering down narrow alleyways crammed with crooked old buildings. The craziest thing of all is King's College Chapel. I've barely travelled outside America and there's sure as hell nothing like this in the USA. I sit in a pew, staring up at the high fan-vaulted ceiling. I wish Laura could have shown me around. It doesn't feel right being here without her.

My ringing cell phone makes me jump. I'm expecting Mr Smythson – Barry, as he's said I can call him – but it's Marty on the other end of the line.

'Hey, Leo,' she says gently.

'Hi.'

'Where are you?'

'In King's College Chapel,' I say in a low voice, aware of the looks I'm getting for talking on my cell.

'Do you want to have dinner with me?'

'Oh. Um . . .'

'I thought you could use the company.'

'Er, yeah, okay,' I say awkwardly. God knows what we'll talk about.

'Are you happy to stay in town?'

'Sure.'

'In that case, I'll meet you in an hour.'

We go to a Mexican restaurant on the river. Marty says she thought I'd need cheering up, so she opted for somewhere lively.

'I need cheering up,' she says as we wait to be seated. 'Have you seen her much this week?' she wants to know.

'As much as I've been allowed,' I reply.

'Matthew is there now, right?'

'Yeah. Laura's dad thought I'd better keep away.'

She doesn't say anything as we're taken to a table, but once we're seated, menus in hand, she turns to me.

'I'm sure Matthew will come round,' she says. 'He's a reasonable guy. Barry just needs a bit of time to talk to him.'

'I'm sorry for him,' I surprise myself by saying. I also surprise Marty, from the look on her face. 'I don't want to hurt him by being here, but I need to be here, too, you know?'

'I know,' she says, giving me a sad smile and then turning to her menu.

Later we find ourselves talking about Key West, and about Laura. I tell Marty about the night dive, about how spooked Laura was when we saw that shark hovering above a shoal of barracuda, and we both start to laugh. The couple of beers I've had have loosened me up.

'She was so funny; you should have seen her face. She wanted to abort the dive, but I wouldn't let her.'

'I can't believe she actually went on a night dive in the first place!' Marty exclaims. 'She used to be scared of the dark as a child.'

'Did she?' I ask.

'Yeah. She had four night lights in her room when she was growing up. I remember them: a fairy, Winnie the Pooh, a butterfly and ... I can't remember the other one. They used to glow in the room and keep me awake if I ever had a sleepover, but she wouldn't switch them off for anyone.'

I smile as I try to imagine a young Laura.

'I'm sorry, Leo,' Marty says suddenly. 'I'm sorry for doubting you. I should have known there was something wrong, some reason why you didn't call. She had faith in you.'

'I hope so,' I say quietly, my mood taking a nosedive. 'I hate the thought of her thinking she meant less to me than she did. Than she does,' I correct myself.

'I think it's clear to everyone now,' she says, looking down at her hands. 'I should have tried to help you more when I knew you were coming here.'

'Don't worry about it,' I brush her off.

'At the very least I should have booked your flights. I feel bad.'

I forgot she was a travel agent. 'Forget it,' I say, before remembering a question I've been meaning to ask. 'Hey, what happened to her cell phone? Didn't anyone ever get my messages?'

'Not that I know of. Her phone was run over by the car that hit her, I think. I doubt anyone has had the time or inclination to sort out a new one. It's a bit weird,' she says thoughtfully, 'because nothing in her bag was damaged.'

I ponder this for a moment. 'Was she talking to someone at the time?' I ask with a frown.

Marty shrugs. 'I don't know. Maybe.'

'What time was she hit?' I ask. I want to know what her last minutes were like.

'She'd just been out for brunch with Matthew,' Marty says, oblivious to the fact that these words cause me pain. The idea of Laura going out with him ... anywhere ... I can't blame her for doing that, of course I can't, but did she still have feelings for him? 'We'd all been to her dad's birthday party the night before,' she explains and I try to concentrate. 'She was hit at around eleven thirty, apparently. She ran straight out into the path of an oncoming car as she tried to hail a cab on the other side of the road.'

'Why didn't Matthew give her a lift home?' I ask, confused.

She also looks perplexed. 'I don't know, actually.'

'It was Sunday, right?' I check, feeling bad for not trying to piece this together before.

'That's right.'

'Sunday morning,' I muse aloud, then I get it. My face must fall because Marty asks me what's wrong. 'Eleven thirty,' I say with increasing panic. 'That's ...' I count out the hours on my fingers as Marty watches me. Miami time is five hours behind, which means eleven thirty in the UK is ... 'six thirty in Miami.'

I pull out my phone and frantically scroll through my recent calls. The blood drains from my face.

'What?' Marty asks again.

'I called her.' My voice comes out in a whisper.

'You called her?' she asks with confusion.

'I called her at that time. It was me.' I feel like I'm going to be sick. 'She took out her phone to answer my call. It must have been me ringing.'

'Oh my God.' Marty puts her hand over her mouth in shock.

'It rang,' I whisper. 'And when I called back it went straight through to voicemail. In that minute, she must've been hit.'

'Oh God,' Marty repeats, and I feel like the room is spinning. 'It's my fault.'

'No one is to blame,' Marty says firmly, jolting out of her shock to reach over and clasp my hand.

I shake my head and take my hand away, feeling strange about any woman – other than Laura – touching me. 'That's not true.'

'Leo!' she says sharply, grabbing my hand again and squeezing it. 'Stop it. No one is to blame,' she reiterates. 'You think we haven't all wondered if there was something we could have done? You think Matthew isn't kicking himself for taking her out for brunch?'

'For making her catch a taxi home?' I say bitterly.

'Stop it. You have to let it all go. It was an accident. She was distracted crossing the road, but that could have happened at any time, to anyone. It's not your fault,' she says again.

I don't think I could live with myself if it was.

Mr Smythson calls me the next morning and says it will be difficult for me to visit that day. I'm angry, and I let him know. I can't help it. He says it's out of his hands, but that I'd be wise not to rock the boat. Matthew can have my visitation rights revoked if he chooses to. After that comment I shut up.

I catch the bus into town, pass hours wandering the streets and sitting by the river watching people stand on the back of long, narrow boats and use poles to push it along. Marty is staying at Laura's parents' house along with Matthew, so I won't be seeing her tonight. I'm so on edge I could tear my hair out. Late that afternoon I go to the hospital. I have to be near her, even if I can't be *with* her. I'm guessing that the others will have gone home during the afternoon ward round, but I'm nervous opening the door to the Visitors' Room. Thankfully it's empty. I'll wait here until the round is finished and then ask if I can see her. Then the door opens and Matthew walks in.

He stops in his tracks. Laura's mother is behind him, looking worried and anxious.

'Matthew,' she says calmly, putting a hand on his arm to pull him away. He doesn't move, and I'm damned if I'm going to break eye contact first.

'Who said you could come here?' he asks coldly.

'No one,' I reply. 'I thought you'd have left.'

'We're leaving now,' he tells me.

'Come on, Matthew,' Laura's mother – Lottie – says gently.

'No,' he says, stepping into the room. 'How dare you?' he asks me, his face white with shock and underlying fury.

I don't want to cause a scene – certainly not here – and I know that he holds the key to Laura's room, if not her heart anymore, so I speak calmly.

'It's not my intention to hurt you. But I had to be here.'

'You don't even love her,' he says, shaking his head. 'You couldn't even tell her that.'

I look away from him. What am I supposed to say?

'I knew it, I knew you didn't.' I can tell he's close to tears and I don't want to watch a grown man cry, especially not him.

'You don't know what you're talking about,' I murmur.

'Come on, love,' Lottie tries again. 'Let's go downstairs to the food court. I still think we should go home.'

She gently pulls him away from the room, from me, and then

I'm left alone feeling jealous and irritable. I know it's stupid, but I want Lottie to care about me the way she cares about him. I'm not the one who got another girl pregnant when I was with her daughter.

There's a new nurse on night duty and she won't let me into the room. I'm not on the list so there's nothing she can do. I spend the night in the Visitors' Room. I've realised that the kitchenette in the corner has cupboards the colour of the shutters back home, the colour of Laura's eyes. There's a small TV and a radio, too, but I can't bring myself to switch them on. I sit upright on the couch because it's too short to lie down on. I'm still there the next morning when Matthew returns.

'Have you been here all night?' he asks, looking a bit shell-shocked to see me. This time Barry is with him.

I nod and put my head back into my hands, where it was before he came in.

They don't stay in the Visitors' Room long, moving to her room as soon as they're allowed. I know I have to be patient but I do believe he'll let me see her.

He joins me in the Visitors' Room while they do the usual morning ward round.

'Can I get you boys a tea or a coffee from the coffee shop downstairs?' Barry asks jovially.

Matthew speaks first. 'Thanks, Barry. A latte would be good.'

I shake my head and politely decline. He gives me a concerned look and leaves us to it. Matthew doesn't say anything for a good few minutes.

'I don't get it.' He shakes his head at me. 'Why would you come if you didn't love her? You must care about her a lot.'

'I do.' I meet his gaze.

He sighs with frustration, trying to figure me out. Good luck with that, pal.

'Marty said you've been renovating.'

What, so now he's going to make small talk?

'That's right,' I reply, leaning back on the couch, before adding: 'It was Laura's idea.'

He looks confused.

'She had some crazy idea to turn the house into a guest house,' I elaborate.

He looks horrified – he stares at me like I've just punched him in the face – and then he gets up and walks out of the room. Maybe I shouldn't have told him that.

Barry reappears and looks around, confused. 'Have they let him go in?'

'No,' I say. 'He walked out.'

'Oh.' He sighs with resignation. 'Are you sure I can't offer you a latte?' He tries to pass Matthew's cup over. 'No point in it going cold.'

'No, thanks,' I say, not wanting to take anything from him, particularly not something that was meant for his son-in-law.

'I don't suppose I blame you.' He settles himself down on a chair near me and puts the spare cup on the table between us.

We fall into a reasonably amiable silence.

'So how's your hotel?' he asks.

More small talk. 'Fine,' I reply.

'Bed can't be that good if you wouldn't even sleep in it last night,' he comments.

I half laugh. 'Damn sight more comfortable than these chairs,' I reply.

'They didn't let you see her?' he asks, looking at me.

'No. I'm not on the list.'

'I'll try to sort that out,' he promises, slurping at his drink.

Jeez, I'm thirsty. Hungry, too.

'Maybe I'll pick up a coffee, after all,' I tell him, getting to my feet. My legs ache – everything does.

He's gone by the time I return, visiting Laura, I guess. I wonder if Matthew is there, too. Eventually I cave and pick up a magazine. I'm flicking through my third when Matthew returns.

'You can see her,' he says in a pained voice.

I'm taken aback, but I don't miss this opportunity.

'Thank you,' I breathe, hurrying past him.

Laura's dad is standing at her bedside. He leans down and kisses her forehead. 'Bye, bye, sweetie,' he says. 'I'll be back tomorrow.'

I feel like an outsider looking in. He turns and sees me, fleetingly startled, but he quickly recovers.

'I'm taking Matthew to the train station,' he says. 'You have as long as you like.'

'Thank you,' I tell him, and I mean it.

I stay in the Visitors' Room again that night, going to see her first thing in the morning. I'm so tired that I rest my head on the mattress next to her hand – her good hand, the one that isn't locked up in a cast.

I must have fallen asleep, because all of a sudden I jolt awake. My hand is in her hand and I felt some movement, I'm sure I did.

'Laura?' I ask uncertainly, hopefully. The familiar bleeping is my only response. I squeeze her hand, willing her to do it again, to show me it wasn't just a dream. 'Laura?' I say again. 'It's me, Leo. I'm here.'

It happens again. I jump out of my seat and press the buzzer to call the nurse, my heart pounding with adrenalin. A young woman in familiar green scrubs comes in.

'She squeezed my hand!'

'Okay, okay,' she says calmly, checking over Laura's monitors.

'But she did!' I've never heard my voice sound this high before.

'It's probably just a reflex,' she tells me. She means to sound kind, but I think she's an idiot.

It wasn't just a reflex. She's coming back to me, I know she is.

My hotel room is almost a complete waste of money after that because I refuse to leave her side. The only time I budge is when the staff kick me out or her parents come in together, because there are only two people allowed at her bedside at any one time. But I don't move from the Visitors' Room, however claustrophobic it is. Matthew also makes a reappearance, driving up from London the evening after the hand-squeezing incident, although he seems less convinced than Laura's parents are that it meant anything. Maybe he just doesn't want to believe it because I'm the one who felt the movement, but he stays for a day, anyway.

'It probably *was* just a reflex,' he says sullenly to Laura's dad, who's waiting in the Visitors' Room with me. Matthew has been in the room with Laura's mother.

'It wasn't,' I mutter under my breath as they go out of the door.

Laura's mother hangs back. 'Will you be okay, Leo?' she asks. 'They say that it can take a long time to wake from a coma.'

'I'm not leaving,' I reply. She gives me a tight smile and goes.

It happens again that night, and I'm almost out of my mind with delight.

'That was *not* just a reflex,' I inform the attending nurse excitedly. 'That was real. She squeezed my hand. I was talking to her about Key West and she *squeezed* my hand.'

'Okay,' she concedes with a false smile.

Nothing else happens for three days.

Matthew decides to work that weekend to make up for lost time, so I don't have to attempt to avoid him. It's a relief. It seems to be a relief for Laura's parents, too; they are always less tense when he's absent. I guess it must be hard for them, balancing us both, not really knowing what is the right thing to do. I wonder how much Laura told them about me before the accident.

I've spoken to Carmen and Jorge a few times. I missed a call from Carmen earlier so I go downstairs to call her back. I stand outside under a metal canopy, looking out at the concrete jungle that makes up this hospital. It's very cold and wet today. It's September, so I guess it's only going to get worse from here on in. I shiver as I dial her number. There's no cell phone reception in the food court, but I'm so cold I won't last long out here. I've never had to buy a winter coat in my life, but I won't have a choice if I'm here for much longer. Maybe a thrift store will have a cheap one.

To my astonishment, Carmen tells me that she and Jorge have finished the bathrooms.

'You what?'

'They're done. I've started painting the inside of the house, too.'

I'm so touched, I can hardly speak. 'I don't know what to say.'

'You never know what to say, Leonardo.'

Her comment makes me smile. 'Wow. Seriously, Carmen, that's great.'

Pause. 'I know.' Another pause, when neither of us speaks. 'Hey, Leo?' She sounds uncomfortable.

'Yeah?'

'I keep meaning to explain . . .' Her voice trails off.

'What is it?' I press.

'You know what I said? About choosing the wrong brother?'

I know exactly what she's talking about. It weirded me out when she said that. 'Yeah?' I ask uneasily.

'I don't mean ... I *didn't* mean ... You and I ... Urgh. I was just trying to say that you're a survivor. So keep doing what you're doing, okay? Keep surviving. Look after yourself.'

'Okay, Carmen,' I say quietly, relieved.

A short pause and then she's back to the Carmen I know, cutting straight through the crap. 'So what now, little bro? When are you coming home? You can't stay there forever, you know.'

'No, I know. I don't know.' I scratch my stubble. It's itchy. I've only managed to shave, at best, every other day since I've been here. My clothes are starting to stink as well. I really need to find a Laundromat before I make myself even more unwelcome than I already am. 'I can't afford the hotel for much longer, but I'm not leaving her. I don't know what I'm going to do.'

I see movement out of the corner of my eye and look around to see Laura's mother standing there.

She instantly looks guilty for eavesdropping. 'Sorry, I was just getting some fresh air.' She turns around and goes straight back inside.

I return inside soon afterwards, noticing for the first time a sign outside the main reception.

It will pass, whatever it is.

Laura used to like the billboards outside churches in America. I remember her telling me about one she saw once. What was it? 'Don't wait for the storm to pass; learn to dance in the rain.'

Something like that. Outside the rain starts to pelt down. I turn and stare out of the window for a while before going back upstairs.

Later that day, Lottie and Barry ask me to stay with them. I can't believe it.

'Laura would want this,' Lottie says when she tries to convince me. And I do take a lot of convincing; I don't want to put them out any more than I already have. I know I've been unwanted since the beginning.

'Come on, son,' Barry says to me and I tense. No one has ever called me 'son' before. 'There's no point in letting the hotel clear you out. You're hardly there, anyway. Plus, we have room.'

'What about Matthew?' I have to ask.

He sighs and leans forward, meeting my eyes. 'Matthew has only just told us some things that we didn't know,' he says in a strained voice. Laura's mother averts her gaze.

'Like what?' I ask with a frown.

'He said . . .' He's clearly finding this difficult. 'He said that on the morning Laura was hit, she told him she forgave him for what he had done.'

I feel like he's punched me in the gut. She was taking him back?

'But,' he continues, 'she added that it was over. She said she wanted a divorce because of how she felt about you.'

I stare at him, unable to speak as my eyes well up with tears. I quickly look away.

'We didn't know,' he adds quietly. 'We thought they would still work things out.'

'Maybe they still will,' Lottie chips in, but Barry puts up his hand to silence her.

'That's enough, love. You've got to respect her enough to know what she wanted. Matthew has accepted it. At long last.'

She looks close to breaking point as she gets up and leaves the room. I feel bad for her.

'She'll be okay,' Barry says. 'This is hard for her.' He pauses. 'And I – *we* – know this is hard for you, too. We can see how much you care about our daughter.'

I nod. My mouth opens to say, 'I do,' but no sound comes out. He knows, though, and I'm grateful.

They take me to the hotel to collect my things and wait for me to check out, then they drive me home. They have a big, dark-green Range Rover, and I sit in the back, looking out of the window as we drive away from the city and into a more rural landscape. The fields are mostly muddy. Tall towers of haystacks stand in some of them, like giant sentries overlooking the land. We pass through villages full of old thatched houses with crooked walls and exposed beams. I stare at them in wonder – some look like they're going to fall over. I've only ever seen stuff like this on TV and in films – it's like I'm in a fairy tale, yet this is Laura's life. This is what she's used to. We drive over tumbling streams and beside village greens, past old country pubs and red telephone boxes, and finally we come to the house where Laura grew up.

An old red-brick wall surrounds the front garden. It's low enough that I could jump over it, but high enough to keep a child in, and I imagine Laura playing in that garden as a little girl, under the shade of the old pine trees soaring overhead. The house itself is a beautiful, quaint English farmhouse, painted cream and with a red-tiled roof. I can see a black-painted wooden barn and other farm buildings further down the driveway, and to the right, up a hill, a small stone church. I'm still looking around with wonder when Laura's dad opens my car door.

'Sorry,' I say with embarrassment, climbing out.

'That's okay,' he says, leading me towards the house.

Inside I can smell woodsmoke and a warm earthiness that fills me with an odd sense of calm. This feeling grows stronger when I go into the old farm kitchen, with its stone floors and a cooker that radiates heat. I stand in front of it to warm myself. Lottie tells me it's an Aga, and she used to hang Laura's socks on the front rail after she ran outside without shoes on.

'She'd do it all the time,' she says good-naturedly with a roll of her eyes. 'Her favourite job each morning was letting the chickens out and collecting their eggs, but she could never be bothered to put on her welly boots, however much I chastised her.'

I wonder what welly boots are.

'Do you want to come for a walk with me?' Barry asks.

'Sure.'

I follow him across the kitchen to a back door, where several pairs of muddy rubber boots are lined up on the stone floor underneath a bunch of bulky coats hanging on hooks. Barry looks over his shoulder at me. 'Do you have a coat?'

'No.' I shake my head.

'Here, you can borrow one.' He rummages through the clothing until he finds one for me and then looks at my sneakers.

'I take it you didn't bring wellies with you?' he asks with a smile, picking up a pair of the rubber boots. So that's what they are.

'No,' I reply with a smile.

'These look to be about your size, but say if not. We have plenty.'

They must have a lot of guests coming and going, because, as far as I know, it's just the two of them. Laura is an only child.

'Thanks.' I'm trying not to feel uneasy about putting her parents out, but I guess I'd better just go with the flow.

When I'm all kitted up and feeling warm, we head off. There's a muddy patch of garden out at the back with a few things growing in it.

'Lottie's veggie patch,' Barry tells me. 'Not much in it anymore.'

We pass through a gate at the end of the garden and then we're in a large, muddy farmyard.

'What do you farm here?' I ask, trying to make polite conversation.

'Wheat, mainly,' he replies. 'We also have some horses. Can you ride?' he asks.

'No. Can Laura?' I ask with interest.

'Oh, yes,' he says offhandedly. 'Ever since she was three.'

'Three?' I exclaim. 'She never told me she could ride.'

He smiles and shrugs. We come to a green field. 'That was her horse over there. Pandora.' He points at a tawny brown horse.

My face breaks into a grin as I watch Pandora eat grass. He leaves me at the gate for a moment and wanders off to pluck a lone apple from a nearby tree. He throws it to me and I catch it easily. He nods at the horse, then clicks his tongue. Pandora wanders over and I hold out the apple. I laugh as she takes it from my outstretched fingers, praying she won't bite me.

He reaches over and strokes her mane. 'Laura loves this horse,' he says sadly. 'She wouldn't let me sell her, even after she grew out of her. She's retired now.'

I tentatively reach forward and stroke her nose, then the wood beneath me cracks and gives way.

'Whoa!' I step off the wooden gate.

'Bloody thing,' Barry mutters. 'I've been meaning to fix it for weeks. Sorry about that,' he apologises.

'I'll help you,' I find myself saying.

'Are you good at DIY?'

'I'm okay,' I say with a shrug. The truth is, I'm probably better at breaking things than I am at fixing them. I think of the bathtub back home.

'That would be great. Maybe we'll tackle it in the morning,' he says.

We walk away from the gate and the field. I nod up the hill towards the church. 'Do you go?'

'We try to,' he replies, setting off in that direction. 'Do you ever go?'

'Not anymore,' I say, staring ahead at the uneven path.

We reach the top of the hill. There's a small village hall here, too, and a view across rolling hills.

'Cambridgeshire on the whole is pretty flat,' Barry tells me. 'But here we have a few small hills.'

'It's pretty,' I say. I glance around at the higgledy-piggledy gravestones and one catches my eye. It's a newish gravestone and a wreath of red flowers lies on top. The name reads: William Henry Trust.

'Will Trust?' I ask Barry with surprise. Laura told me about her former boyfriend, the Formula One racing driver.

He nods slightly, and we wander over to the grave.

'Will's parents live in the house next door.' He indicates down the hill towards the farmhouse and beyond, where I can just make out a large country house through dense trees.

'The funeral was in Cambridge. He was a big personality

and this little church couldn't have held all the guests. But they brought his body back here to be close to them.'

I fall silent, because I really don't know what to say.

'So young. Too young.' His voice sounds choked.

We stand there in silence for a long time until he points at another grave further along the path. I walk ahead and look down at it.

'Bernard Smythson?' I ask Barry with a raised eyebrow.

'My father,' he replies, nodding at the next grave: Mary Smythson. 'And my mother. My grandparents are also buried just along there. We have a family plot,' he adds, giving me an odd look before quickly averting his gaze. I stare at his profile and suddenly I realise what he's saying.

Laura will be buried here if she dies.

I feel ill as I picture her cold and dead in the ground beneath my feet. I can't imagine going home if she dies. I can't imagine going on at all.

'Come on, son,' Barry says gently, putting his hand on my shoulder.

I fight back tears as we walk down the hill to the farmhouse.

Lottie cooks dinner that night – a warm and comforting chicken stew packed with potatoes and carrots. For once, my taste buds seem to be doing the right thing.

'Did you grow up in Key West?' Lottie asks me as she fills up my glass with red wine. I want to say I feel quite relaxed, but it's the wrong word. I have a permanent sense of foreboding, just below the surface, and I know that won't leave until Laura wakes up. But it's the calmest I've felt in a while; that's the truth. And she will wake up. She has to. God, she has to.

'I did,' I reply to her question. 'My mother was American, my father was Cuban.'

'Marty told us that your parents weren't married?' Barry sounds curious, rather than disapproving, so I don't mind his question.

'That's right. My mother was his mistress. Making my brother and me his illegitimate offspring,' I add flippantly.

'Your mother and brother aren't around anymore, though?' Lottie pries. 'Or your father?'

'No, they're not.' I look down at the table.

'I'm sorry. That must be hard.'

I meet her eyes again and see the sympathy in them. I'm not sure I want it. It's hard enough to cope with everything else at the moment. But I can't push her away. She's trying, after all.

'Do you have any other family?' Barry asks gently.

'Jorge and Carmen are like family to me,' I say, deflecting the question, because the answer is no. 'Jorge is Carmen's brother, and she was married to *my* brother. They're good to me.'

They exchange a look and after that we change the subject.

I'm staying in a room at the top of the stairs. The guest room. Laura's bedroom is next door, Lottie tells me.

'Do you mind if I . . .' I can't finish my sentence. I feel too uncomfortable in case she says no or thinks it's weird, but her reply is easy.

'Of course you can have a look.' She leads me further down the corridor and pushes open the door. Laura's perfume instantly fills my senses and I'm shocked.

'I'll leave you,' she says gently, going out of the room.

I stand there for a long time, breathing in the scent of my girl, looking at the bed. Her bookshelves are still full of books, some

365

old, some new, even some from her childhood with battered colourful spines. Then I spot a night light in the shape of a butterfly. I sit on the bed and my whole body heaves as I sob like a baby.

My poor girl. From the outside looking in she had such a perfect life. A perfect home, perfect parents who love her, a perfect husband who turned out to be not so perfect . . . I should feel like an impostor, being here. But I don't. Her life wasn't perfect. And I know that I helped her. I'll be here for her until she wakes up, and if she ever asks me to leave, I'll go. But I don't think she will.

'There, there.'

I jump at the sound of Lottie's voice, at the touch of her hand on my shoulder.

'I'm sorry, I'm sorry,' I choke out, knowing I must look bad.

'There, there, it's okay. Sometimes we need a good cry,' she says softly, rubbing my back. 'She'll be okay. I just know. A mother is usually right about these things.'

I look up at her to see her own eyes are filled with tears.

On Tuesday morning, I'm with Lottie at Laura's bedside.

'When is Matthew coming here again?' I ask her.

'I don't know,' she replies. 'He thought it might be best if he stayed away for a while.'

I'm blown away by this revelation. Am I taking his place? Are they accepting this fact?

'He doesn't have to do that,' I mutter.

'He feels like he does,' she says quietly, then suddenly blurts out: 'She just squeezed my hand! I felt it! She just squeezed my hand!'

I smile at her delighted face and my heart soars. 'It's not just a reflex.' I shake my head determinedly.

'It's not, it's not,' she repeats, breathless with excitement and anticipation. 'Laura? Laura, darling, it's me, Mum.' She presses Laura's hand and continues to talk as I move closer to the bed. I sit on the other side, stroking her hair while the ventilator breathes for her. 'I'm with Leo,' she says. 'He's here with me. He came for you, my darling. Come back to us. Please come back to us.'

'HER EYES FLUTTERED!' I don't mean to shout it so loudly, but I'm so astounded I can't help myself.

'Her eyelids fluttered? Come! Somebody, come!' Lottie leaps up from her seat and leans over her daughter, manically pressing the call button. A doctor arrives within moments, but neither she nor I can tear our eyes away from our girl. He checks over her vital signs.

'It's probably just a reflex,' he says kindly, and Lottie and I make eye contact. Perhaps she doesn't want to deck him as much as I do, but at least we're on the same wavelength.

Barry comes that afternoon, so Lottie and I take turns in the Visitors' Room. Neither of us will leave the hospital. By early evening, though, when nothing else has happened, we're all feeling deflated. The nurse encourages us to go home and get some rest. We'll need it if she wakes up, she says.

When, not if.

But I'm not leaving, so they say their goodnights and leave me to it.

I talk to her that night, more than I ever have. I don't stop talking. I tell her about my childhood, about the time my father took my brother and me snorkelling and we caught fresh lobster for my mother to cook. I tell her I'm going to cook her parents my coconut curry in the next few days and wonder if they'll like it. I tell her that I took a sledgehammer to the bathtub and now Carmen and Jorge have put in a shower. And at the end of all of this, when I can think of nothing else to say, I kiss her hand and get up and kiss her forehead, then I tell her that I love her.

'I love you, Laura. I'm sorry I didn't tell you before. I was crazy not to. But it's true. I love you.'

I suddenly realise someone else is in the room with us, so I quickly wipe away my tears before turning to see a young nurse standing at the door.

'I need to change her catheter,' she says with an apologetic smile.

'Okay.' I stand awkwardly to one side for a moment before saying: 'I'll be back in a minute.'

I turn left out of ICU and go into the men's bathroom by the elevator. I take a leak and then wash my hands before splashing water on my face. I turn around, looking for a paper towel, but there isn't one, so I wipe my face on my T-shirt, catching my reflection in the small mirror. Christ, I look a mess. Red-eyed, unshaven. I push my hair back off my face and wish I had a razor. I don't want her to wake up and see me like this. I'll shave tomorrow, I promise myself. I'll put in a load of washing, too. Lottie won't mind. She's asked me often enough.

I take a deep breath and regard the man staring back at me in the mirror. The man in love. The man in waiting. And then I go back down the corridor and wait for my love to wake up.

Epilogue

'He told me to tell you he loves you,' my mum says with a smile.

I grin goofily and try not to roll my eyes. This is all I ever hear. *All*. I'm not joking; it's become a bit of a catchphrase to my friends and family.

When I finally came out of the coma, it took me a while to recognise people, to understand what had happened, to finally come *to*. They told me all of this afterwards, because I wasn't very present. But apparently Leo told me he loved me a lot in those early days. And when he wasn't by my bedside, he made other people tell me he did. Eventually I grew stronger, more conscious, and started to take it all in. I'm still a little forgetful, though. I probably always will be, they say, with a brain injury. But as long as I have my loved ones around to remind me of the things that are most important, I'll cope. I'm so very lucky to be alive.

'Has the flight landed yet?' I ask Mum as she waits outside the door while I dry myself off. I heard the phone ring while I was in the shower. I know that Leo was right to get rid of the bath upstairs, but I do miss it sometimes. My leg could do with a good soak when it's feeling especially tender. Lovely Mike next door

369

lets me use their hot tub whenever I like, though, so that helps a great deal.

'Not yet, but it won't be long,' she says. 'He asked me to crack on with chopping the onions.'

'Is he doing his curry?' I ask eagerly, popping my head around the door.

'Yes.' She smiles at me. She looks so well; the sunshine suits her. But if you think her tan is good, you should see my dad's.

'Can you help me with this?' I ask, struggling to wrap the towel around my head.

'Of course.' She bustles in and takes the towel from me as I gingerly bend over. She secures it around my wet hair and I straighten up again. It still hurts to do some things, but I'm doing my exercises several times a day, trying to build up the strength in my arm and leg. At least my ribs don't hurt anymore when I laugh.

I laugh a lot.

I didn't think I'd have time for the hot tub today, but then we found out that Marty and Bridget's flight into Key West was two hours' delayed with mechanical issues. Leo and Dad went to pick them up, stopping for a beer on the way. I'm amazed at how well they get on. I still can't believe he lived with them for months while I recuperated in hospital. Apparently Leo helped out with odd jobs around the farm. Dad said he's pretty good at DIY, although Carmen thought this was absolutely hilarious when I relayed it to her. She filled me in on the bathtub incident. She meant to make me laugh, but it made me shudder. I felt so traumatised for Leo, the thought of him having that dream and then finding out about my accident. It still reduces me to tears, thinking about what he – what we *all* – went through. My friends and family – even the nurses – told me about the weeks he spent at my bedside. His devotion takes my breath away.

It's been nine months since my accident, and everyone says I'm doing well. I had a lot of help, a lot of love. I still can't believe how lucky I am.

This weekend, and for the next two weeks, we have a full house. Jorge, Carmen and Javier, Bridget and Marty, and Mum and Dad, who have been with us ever since we returned to Key West two months ago. They wanted to come. They didn't ever want me to leave the UK, of course. But I had to. Was desperate to in the end. Leo, too. I could see it in his eyes, although he never once mentioned it. So as soon as I was well enough, Marty booked our flights. Then my parents asked if they could come, too. They won't stay for much longer. Leo gets on well with them – I think he enjoys having parental figures in his life. But only up to a certain extent – there's only so much time you can spend with your in-laws. I don't mean in-laws in the technical sense, by the way. We're not married, nor are we engaged or planning on getting engaged anytime soon – if ever. But I have some very good immigration lawyers working on my visa, so whatever we do will be by choice and not by necessity. Anyway, Jorge occasionally promises he'll be my back-up option when he wants to wind Leo up.

I am officially divorced. It came through a month ago. I spoke to Matthew a couple of weeks ago, but we don't speak much. He seems pretty good. Evan is a year old now and he sees a lot of him. When we sold our apartment he bought a place in North Finchley so he could be nearby. As far as I know, there's still nothing going on between him and Tessa. But that's only as far as I know, and it's none of my business anymore, anyway.

This weekend we're celebrating the opening of our guest house. I can't believe we've actually pulled it off. The house is fully renovated, and we have our first proper paying guests coming in a few weeks. It won't be a very busy season, but that's okay. We'll ease ourselves in slowly and hopefully I'll be back to full health by the time high season comes around next year. Mike has offered to give any customers our details when he's fully booked. We're not exactly competition at our small size: five guest bed-rooms compared to his twenty-odd.

I never knew this house had a name because Leo took the sign down before he left to live in Miami all those years ago and it just became a number on the street. But now Casa Lorelei – named after his mother by his father – is once more. I think her name is beautiful. We were all touched when the sign went back up.

Mum goes out of the room and leaves me alone to get ready. Leo and I have the main bedroom downstairs now, with a brand-new en-suite, leaving the bathrooms free for visitors. The stairs were too much for me to manage at first. I miss our old bedroom at the top, and I sometimes go up there to take some time to myself, although that doesn't often last for long, because Leo hunts me out. *As if I mind . . .*

My lovely boy. He looks younger these days than he did when I met him. Happier, more carefree, at peace with the world. I love him so much. He's the best thing that ever happened to me. Funnily enough, he says the same about me.

I get dressed and dry my hair, taking things slowly so as not to wear myself out too much, then I go outside to wait for the posse to arrive. We've retired the old seats because they don't really fit in with the new look of the place, but I'm nostalgic for them, and even though my memory might not be at its best right now, I'll never forget those early days sitting out here with Leo, those long looks with his dark eyes, the shivers trailing up and down my spine . . . What am I talking about? I still get shivers up and down my spine every time he gives me one of his come-to-bed stares, which is often. I'm tingling now just thinking about last night . . .

I sit down on a new deckchair and survey the scene, looking forward to seeing the effect of the extra rope lights we have trailing up the new potted palm trees we've dotted around the place. We might get a small pool one day, but that's in the future.

'Hey, girl!' I turn around to see Carmen coming out of the kitchen door. 'You want a drink?'

'No, thanks, I'll wait for the others,' I reply with a smile as she takes a seat beside me.

Leo is right: she's much nicer without Eric around. She's been a rock, actually. She's taken over Leo's lease on his apartment in Miami and has started working as a care worker in a nursing home. She comes down here most weekends to catch up with us and I never thought I'd say this, but I look forward to her visits. Maybe she'll move back here one day, but for now she seems to be enjoying her new free single life . . .

Jorge is also thinking about giving up his apartment in Miami and moving to the keys for good. He and Leo have been talking to Timmy at the dive centre about becoming business partners and buying a share in his boat. He wants to spend more time with his mother on the West Coast, so it could work well for everyone. To Jorge's immense amusement and my immense pride, Leo has decided to train to be a dive instructor. Jorge isn't teaching him, although that was suggested (by me), but Leo said hell would freeze over first. He starts his course next week.

I hear a car pull up outside on the road, followed by a loud: 'Woo-hoo!'

I'm laughing as I get to my feet. Marty has arrived – and Bridget, too. Leo told me what she did for him and I'll never forget that. She's a true friend now, not just a friend of Marty's. I'm so glad the pair of them have come back to help us celebrate the opening.

I go down the path to see my dad, tanned and looking great in shorts and a white shirt, leading Marty and Bridget into the yard. They drop their hand luggage and engulf me in the biggest girlie hug of my life. Dad pats me on my back, then picks up their hand luggage and heads towards the house while we squeal like teenagers checking each other out. Bridget has cut her dark hair into a short, sharp bob and she looks fantastic, Marty has got a new pair of glasses, but is otherwise the same, and they tell me I look amazing. I do look well these days. If you didn't know me, you would never know I almost died.

My mum comes out of the house and cries out hello, so Bridget and Marty break away from me and hurry off to see her.

But I hang back, waiting for him, for my love. He appears a minute later, with a suitcase in each hand. I can tell immediately which one is Bridget's.

'Fuck, that's heavy,' he says, dropping it with a thud.

'I missed you,' I reply with a smile as he takes me in his arms. He kisses my lips gently, but the shivers are there – always. I slide my hands around his neck and he pulls back to look at me, those dark eyes burning into mine.

'When can I get you alone?' he murmurs, his fingers trailing up my arms and making my knees feel like jelly. Not fair, I have a bad enough leg as it is.

'Soon.' I pull him in for another kiss. He holds me to him, supporting my weight as his kiss deepens.

'Stop snogging each other's faces off!' Marty hollers down the path towards us. 'Let's get this party started!'

We break away and grin at each other.

'Two weeks,' I promise, 'then you'll have me all to yourself again.' I take his hand, but he tugs me back.

'Oi,' he says.

'What?'

'I love you.'

'I know,' I reply with a smile.

And I do, I really do.

Acknowledgements

Thank you, always, to my readers, who continue to make me smile, well, I would say every day if I were more organised about going onto Twitter and Facebook, but I promise I'll be better this year! Please keep your messages coming – they really do mean the world to me.

Thank you to my editor Suzanne Baboneau – you're the best! – and to everyone at Simon and Schuster, but in particular Maxine Hitchcock, Emma Capron, Clare Parkinson, Sarah Birdsey, Florence Partridge, Nigel Stoneman, Matt Johnson, Dawn Burnett, Ally Glynn, Sarah Jade-Virtue and Alice Murphy. Thanks also to Knight Hall Agency for handling the theatrical rights to my books.

Enormous gratitude to my old friends Susan and Dean Rains for their recommendations on where to go in Key West and Miami. We loved Blue Heaven, and the Wynwood Walls were indeed very, very cool. Special thanks to Susan for her help with Leo's Americanizations (note the use of the 'z' instead of 's' on this one occasion . . .)

Big thanks to Jo Whiting from St Elizabeth Hospice, Suffolk, for her insights into working with a charity – especially at such short notice. Massively appreciated! And thank you to her fabulous sister and fellow author Ali Harris, for not only suggesting I contact Jo, but for being such a fantastic sounding board for the last year and a half. Long may it continue!

Many thanks to Davina Sycamore for her help with all things hospital related, and thank you to Mike, Lucy and Diane for organising the Birmingham event last year – I hope you enjoyed your little cameos . . .

Thanks to the Bilbao hens, Cheryl McGechie (congrats to you and Mike!), Susan Powell, Natalie Andrew, Amy Wettenhall, Allison Grant, Andrea Southey, Shona Wilson and Sharon Gigli for the hen night inspiration. M&Ms, mmm . . .

My family and I stayed at Eden House in Key West while I was researching this book, and although no one there knew what I was up to, this gorgeous hotel really brought Laura's experience to life, so cheers for that.

Thanks to my parents, Vern and Jen Schuppan, and last but most definitely not least, thank you to my husband Greg, my son Indy and my daughter Idha. I love you all very, very much.

Turn the page for a sneak peek of Paige Toon's
heart-warming new novel

the LAST
piece of
my HEART

Prologue

The problem with giving your heart away to someone is that you never fully get it back. Long after you've fallen out of love with them, they still own a little piece of you. That's why first love is always the strongest: it's the only time you ever love wholeheartedly. And I do mean that literally.

I came up with this theory a few years ago when I was belatedly reflecting on why on earth I had ever broken up with David, my boyfriend at university. He was great, but *something* was missing, so I called it off and started a new search for the complete package. Over a decade later, I'm still looking.

It's not that I haven't been around the houses. I have. And the caravans, apartment blocks and skyscrapers, to boot. At the end of the day, it all comes down to Elliot Green. He's entirely to blame. He was my first love and he took a piece of my heart – and my virginity, while he was at it – and then emigrated to Australia with his parents at the age of sixteen, never to be seen or heard from again, once his initial frenzy of letter writing had died out. I figured he'd found a fit Aussie bird and had forgotten all about me, so I tried to forget about him, too. Many moons later, I'm still trying.

It doesn't help that I'm currently in Sydney, where he moved all those years ago. I've been daydreaming about bumping into him here and melodramatically declaring, 'You've got something that belongs to me,' before demanding that he give me the piece of my heart back.

Never in my wildest dreams did I think I actually *would* see him again, yet there he is, completely oblivious to me gawping as he has a beer with some mates at a harbourside bar.

Despite his changed appearance, I recognised him instantly. His long, lean body has broadened out and his arms are tanned and muscular. His brown hair is the same unruly length, but he now has sexy stubble that's bordering on beardy. From where I'm standing, Elliot Green is hotter than ever. And now he's looking at me.

He's looking at me!

And now he's *not* looking at me.

Before I can register disappointment, he does a comedy double take and his blue eyes widen. His face breaks into a grin and then he's on his feet and my heart is threatening to beat out through my eardrums.

'Bridget?' he asks with disbelief, opening up his arms.

'Hello, Elliot,' I reply warmly, as he crushes me to his hard chest. *Oh, my God, he smells amazing.* What was it that I was supposed to say to him again?

'You've hardly changed at all!' he exclaims, withdrawing and holding me at arm's length as he takes me in.

My figure hasn't altered a lot since he last saw me. I'm tall and fairly slim and my eyes are, obviously, still blue – more of a navy, compared to his lighter swimming-pool shade.

He fingers a lock of my dark hair. 'Even your hair's the same,' he comments.

It comes to the midway point between my chin and shoulders, which is more or less how I wore it as a teenager.

'I've been growing it out, actually,' I say with a shrug. Turns out blunt-cut bobs are high-maintenance. 'Was that an Aussie accent I heard?'

'Maybe,' he replies with a grin.

'It *is*! That's so weird.'

He laughs and shakes his head at me. 'What are you doing here?'

'I'm on my way home.' I nod towards the ferries chugging in and out of Circular Quay.

'You live in Sydney?' he asks with amazement.

'Sort of. I'm here for a year.'

'Seriously?' His eyes dart searchingly between mine. 'Do you have to rush off? Can I buy you a drink?'

'No, I don't have to rush off, and, yes, I'd love a drink.'

He smiles at me and the words pop into my mind from out of nowhere: *You've got something that belongs to me.*

Of course, it's immediately apparent that I'll sound like a right idiot if I say them out loud, so I follow him mutely to his table instead.

Over the next couple of hours, I sit with Elliot and his mates, drinking and laughing and establishing that he is excellently single. When his friends call it a night, Elliot and I stay, and, as the white sails of the nearby Sydney Opera House glint gold in the setting sun, and bats swarm out of the nearby Botanic Gardens, I'm ready.

'So,' I say, swirling the ice around in my glass of vodka tonic, 'I have a theory.'

Elliot cocks one eyebrow and listens with amusement as I enlighten him.

'And that's why I haven't found The One,' I conclude.

He looks confused. 'But you've been in love since we went out, right?'

'Yeah,' I scoff. 'Loads of times.'

'Well, if that's true, you'd better hunt down all of *those* guys and demand that they give you their pieces back, too.' He takes a gulp of his beer and plonks the glass down on the table, looking a little too pleased with himself.

Is he right? Have I whittled my heart down to such a small chunk that I'm never going to be able to fall hook, line and sinker for *anyone*? Damn.

'Your theory is flawed,' he adds annoyingly.

'No, no, no.' I shake my head with renewed determination. 'You were my first love. You've got the biggest piece. The most important piece. And I want it back.'

'What if I don't want to give it back?' he asks.

I force my brow into a frown, while secretly thinking it's adorable that he's indulging this silliness. 'Why would you want to keep it?'

'I don't know.' He shrugs. 'Maybe I like having it around. And anyway, if you want your piece back, then it's only fair that you give me mine back, too.'

'I have a piece of your heart?' I ask with surprise, hoping no one is eavesdropping on our bonkers conversation.

'Of course you do,' he replies, barely refraining from adding, '*Duh!*'

I think about this, the alcohol muddling my brain. 'I suppose we could do a straight swap,' I mutter eventually.

His lips tilt up at the corners as he stares across the table at me with those very blue eyes of his. Momentarily I'm back in the past with him and butterflies are going berserk inside me.

'Shall we continue this discussion over dinner?' He slides his hand towards mine and touches the tips of my fingers with his. A shiver runs down my spine and I can almost feel fresh perforation marks being punched into my body's most vital organ.

'All right, then, if you insist,' I reply with a smile.

If he wants to tear off another piece, I don't think I'll stop him.

Chapter 1

'Hello again!' my literary agent, Sara, exclaims as we air kiss each other's cheeks. Her smile is a hundred watts brighter than the last time I saw her back in February. 'Thank you for coming in.' She directs me to a seat. 'How's it all going? I see you've topped ten thousand followers on Twitter!'

'Yes, last week,' I reply. 'And the comments on the last post were off the scale.'

'That was the Gabriel reunion?'

'That's right.'

'Oh, I loved that one!'

'Good!' I grin. 'It cost me enough to get to Brazil.'

She laughs. 'You sounded like you had a lucky escape with him. What a chauvinistic pig! *How* many children did he have again?'

'Nine.' I grimace. 'I felt so sorry for his poor wife.'

'Whoa, did *she* have her work cut out for her! Were those kids really as badly behaved as they sounded?'

'I'm sure they have their good days,' I say benignly, wondering why I'm here.

It's been three months since our last meeting when I pitched Sara an idea for a book, but it wasn't as well received as I had hoped it would be.

'Forgive me, Bridget,' I remember her saying, as she eyed me shrewdly. 'But, when you asked for a meeting about a book, I assumed you'd be pitching an idea about your experiences of navigating the globe, not your experiences of navigating men.'

It was a fair assumption. I was – *am* – a well-established travel writer.

'I *do* plan to take the reader on a journey,' I said with what I'd hoped was a winning smile, 'and we *will* travel all around the world together, but our voyage will take us, yes, via all of the men I've ever been in love with. Travel writing will feature prominently, but, ultimately, this book will be about love.'

She smirked. 'Are we *really* talking about love, here? You're thirty-four, and you say you've been head over heels in love with twelve different men? Some weren't simply holiday romances or one-night stands?'

I waved her away dismissively. 'Oh, there were *loads* of those, too. But I could probably spin a couple out if I'm stuck for material,' I added with a grin, as she blanched at me.

It was Elliot who gave me the idea, when I bumped into him in Sydney, a year ago last December. That night was the start of something new and beautiful between us, and I'm delighted to announce that we're still together.

At least, we're together as a couple. We're not together literally, because I'm now back in the UK *sans* visa and he's on the other side of the world in Australia. I could move over there if I married him. But that would mean one of us asking.

I'm slightly scared of him asking.

I love Elliot so much, but, when we were sixteen, my feelings for him were all-encompassing. He meant *everything* to me.

The love I feel for him now is not as powerful, and I'm worried that it's because I've become jaded over the years. Have I had too many relationships to believe in happy ever after?

Maybe I've just grown up. Maybe love as an adult can never compare to that of a teenager.

Or maybe something *is* missing. And maybe there's a chance that I can get this *something* back…

That night we met up again, Elliot put forward the tongue-in-cheek notion that perhaps I needed to hunt down all of the men I've ever loved to ask for their pieces of my heart back. Before I left Australia, he brought up the idea again, but this time he was serious. He knows that I'm struggling to commit to him wholeheartedly, but he believes that, if I use this time apart from him to revisit the past, I might be able to make more sense of the here and now. He suggested that I write about all of my encounters, and then he came up with another genius idea: if I could get a book deal, my time and travels would be funded in the form of an advance.

I should point out here that my boyfriend is not the jealous type. This was one of the first questions Sara asked when I put the idea to her back in February.

She also said that I needed to blog about my reunions and raise my profile before she'd consider approaching publishers, so that's what I've been doing for the last three months.

My readers have joined me on voyages to South Africa

(David), Iceland (Olli), Spain (Jorge) and Brazil (Gabriel), and, of course, I've also written about how Elliot and I rekindled our relationship in Australia. I'm yet to meet up with Dillon in Ireland, Freddie in Norway, Seth in Canada and Beau, Felix, Liam and Vince here in the UK.

My contacts in journalism have helped to spread the word about my blog, and, if you just ignore the trolls, I'd say it's all going swimmingly.

Elliot, meanwhile, has been hanging onto his piece of my heart. It's still the biggest piece – the first *and* last piece – and, once I get the other bits back, my path will lead me back to him. A walk down the aisle really would be the happiest of happy endings.

Late yesterday afternoon, Sara's assistant called and asked me to come in for a meeting as soon as possible. Apparently, my agent had some news and she'd explain in person.

I got a little bit excited.

I know that Sara has started talking up my blog to publishers, but while the feedback so far has been good – they like my style, they like my wit – no one has wanted to commit to a relationship-blog-turned-book in the current market. Sara claims that publishers won't be able to argue with the numbers if I keep growing my readership, so I intend to crack on. But has something changed in the last twenty-four hours?

'You must be wondering why you're here,' Sara says to me now, reading my mind.

'I'm pretty curious,' I admit.

'Yesterday, I had lunch with Fay Sanderson.'

The name isn't familiar to me, but Sara explains that she's an editorial director at a top publishing house.

'She's been avidly reading your blog and was raving to me about how well you strike the balance between warm and likable, and feisty, funny and fresh. She *loves* your voice. She *absolutely loves* it,' Sara stresses, and there's something about her tone that has me sitting up straighter in my seat. *Am I about to be offered a book deal?*

'She has a proposal,' she continues. *Yes!* 'Have you heard of Nicole Dupré?'

'Er, that name sounds familiar,' I reply.

Sara swivels on her chair and takes a book down from the shelves behind her. 'Nicole had a runaway bestseller with *The Secret Life of Us*, which was published last autumn. It took us all a little by surprise, to be honest.'

'I remember hearing about it.' I pick up the novel she's placed in front of me. The cover has a photograph of a lone girl standing on a beach in Thailand. I turn over the book and scan the blurb. It's about a travel writer who falls in love with two different men on two different continents.

Where is Sara going with this?

'Nicole passed away shortly after that was published,' Sara explains, her tone growing sombre.

I breathe in sharply and glance up at her. 'Oh, God, that's right, it was in the news. Was she one of your authors?' I ask with surprise.

She nods.

'I'm so sorry. I had no idea you represented her.'

'It's okay. It was very sudden,' she tells me. 'She had a brain aneurysm. She was only thirty-one.'

I shake my head, horrified. That's three years younger than I am now. 'That's so tragic,' I murmur sympathetically.

'Nicole was writing a sequel,' Sara continues, drawing my attention back to her. '*Secret* ended on a cliffhanger. The readers are crying out for more. And, Bridget…?'

I haven't been sure up until this point what any of this has to do with me, but, from her more upbeat tone, I sense I'm about to find out.

'Fay thinks your voice is perfect!' she concludes, triumphantly.

There's a long moment where neither of us says anything.

'To write the sequel.'

She thinks she's clarifying it, but I'm even more confused.

'I don't understand,' I say, shaking my head. 'Fay loves my blog?'

'Loves it!' Sara repeats. 'She thinks your voice is spot on!'

'I thought you were about to tell me that she wants to sign me up.'

Sara clears her throat. 'She does. For the sequel to *The Secret Life of Us.*' She points at the book I'm holding.

What?

'Nicole was about a quarter of the way in,' she explains. 'She left behind a stack of notes. Fay's been trying to find the right person to complete it.'

'She wants me to be a *ghostwriter*?' I splutter. 'But what about *my* book?'

'You'll still write it,' Sara says evenly. 'Think of this as a stopgap, your way in. This is your chance to get your foot through the door of a major publisher. You can write your own book alongside this one while you continue to build your profile, and the advance you'll get will pay for your travels. It's the *perfect* solution.'

'But…' I'm still reeling. 'What makes anyone think I'm up to the job? Surely there are a million other more qualified authors who could do this?'

'Oh, I'm sure there are, too,' she says smoothly. 'But Fay wants you. She's even read the novel you wrote a few years ago. The plot wasn't quite there,' she says hurriedly, quashing any hope of resurrecting my old romantic-fiction dream, 'but the point is, Fay knows you have it in you to pull off fiction. She thinks your style is fabulous.'

'She does?' I allow myself to feel a little flattered, as well as incredibly daunted.

'Have you read *The Secret Life of Us*?' Sara asks.

'No,' I admit, studying the book in my hands.

'Take that copy,' she says. 'You won't be able to put it down. The protagonist is a travel writer just like you, so you should be able to identify with her brilliantly. It is the biggest compliment that Fay believes you can carry Nicole's baton to the finishing line.'

'I just… I'm not sure…' I'm struggling to get my head around all of this. A young woman, dying so abruptly… A bestselling author leaving behind an unfinished sequel… Me – *me!* – being the one to complete her work…

'Read the book,' Sara urges, and I sense she wants to wrap up our meeting. 'And keep in mind, Bridget, this is a *great* opportunity. Give me a call as soon as you've reached the end so we can discuss the finer details. I'm around all day tomorrow.'

She seems very confident that I'm going to go along with this hare-brained scheme.

Her conviction is founded, because I call her back first thing.

Chapter 2

It's a beautiful sunny day in early June when I step off the bus in Padstow, Cornwall. The tide is out and the view stretches right over the Camel Estuary as I climb the hill, revealing a series of long, smooth sandbanks punctuating the clear, bluey-green water. The smell of fish and chips wafts through the air, making my tummy rumble. My appetite will have to wait. It's already three thirty in the afternoon and Nicole's husband, Charlie Laurence, is expecting me.

When Sara explained that Charlie wanted to oversee the writing of his wife's book, I was apprehensive. The job was already going to be challenging enough – would he make it even more difficult?

I come to a stop outside a modest, terraced, redbrick house. A narrow, slate-topped veranda stretches across the front, sheltering a charcoal-grey door and a bay window. Apart from a lavender hedge bordering the wall adjacent to the street, the tiny paved area is devoid of plants.

Movement catches my eye at the window, so I quickly walk up the path and knock on the door. There's not even time to check my reflection in the glass before it opens to reveal who I'm assuming is Charlie.

He looks to be in his early thirties, and is around six foot tall and slim, with green eyes and shaggy dark-blond hair held back from his forehead with a mustard-yellow bandana. He's wearing a faded orange T-shirt and grey shorts, and his face and limbs are sun-kissed the colour of honey, all the way down to his bare feet.

Wow.

'Charlie?' I check hopefully.

'Hello,' he replies with a small, reserved smile, holding back the door. 'Come in.'

I don't know what I was expecting, but it wasn't this.

'Tea?' he offers.

'Thank you, that'd be great.' I jolt as the door closes with a clunk. I'm nervous.

Charlie gestures down the hall, indicating that I should lead the way. The television is on in what I presume is the living room, but I don't look in as I pass, and a moment later we spill out into a galley-style kitchen. It continues onto an extension containing a two-seater sofa backed up against the left wall and a round table at the end.

He fills the kettle and gets out two mugs. 'How was your journey? Did you drive?'

'No. Tube from Wembley to Paddington, train to Bodmin, and bus to here.'

'Sounds harrowing.'

He's polite and well spoken, but he hasn't made eye contact with me once since I stepped over his threshold.

A noise sounds out from the direction of the living room. 'Excuse me,' he says, exiting the kitchen.

I take a deep breath and force myself to exhale slowly while taking in my surroundings.

The internal walls are exposed and the bricks have been painted with thick, white masonry paint. The worktops are fashioned out of old railway sleepers, sanded and varnished to a dull shine. French doors at the end open up onto the back garden. It's neat and tidy in here, but it looks like a right tip out there. My attention drifts to the table and the wooden chairs encircling it.

Two chairs.

And one highchair.

That was another thing Sara neglected to mention at our meeting last week.

When Nicole died, she left behind not only an unfinished manuscript *and* a grief-stricken husband, but a five-week-old baby daughter, as well.

Life can seriously suck.

Charlie is talking in low tones in the living room. Another wave of nerves washes through me.

Babies freak me out. They don't seem to like me, and I don't particularly like them. What if I make them cry? What if I make *this* one cry? If she takes offence at me, Charlie probably will, too, and he may well pull the plug on this idea.

Earlier this week, I met up with Nicole's editor, Fay. She's a lovely, warm woman in her late forties and she revealed that the decision to go ahead with the sequel came down to Charlie. He wasn't at all sure, from what I gather, but he felt a responsibility towards Nicole's readers and in the end, gave the go-ahead, as long as the job was done well by the right person. I'm still not convinced that I'm the right person, but, after reading Nicole's book, I'm as keen as anyone to find out what happened next. Even if I have to write it myself.

The prospect is admittedly terrifying, but I'll cross that bridge when I come to it. If this meeting with Charlie doesn't go well, there won't be a bridge to cross.

The kettle boils, so I distract myself by pouring hot water into the mugs. A moment later, Charlie returns.

'CBeebies only distracts her for so long at her age,' he says, knowing he doesn't need to explain his circumstances because I've already been made well aware of them. 'Milk?'

'Yes, please.' I move away from the worktop to give him some space. 'How old is your daughter?' I ask.

'Eight and a half months. Sugar?' He flicks his eyes up to meet mine.

'No, thanks.'

'My mum was supposed to be here, but she had an emergency at work,' he reveals, stirring two teaspoons into his own cup.

'What does she do?' I ask.

'She and my dad run a campsite. They had a burst water main or something.'

'The campsite on the hill?'

'No, they're about an hour away. A couple of mates of mine run the one on the hill. Do you know it?' Charlie picks up his cup and finally looks at me properly. I thought his eyes were green, but they're getting on for hazel.

'Only because my dad mentioned it. He's stayed there a few times in his campervan,' I explain.

His daughter cries out again.

'We'll go through,' Charlie says quietly, nodding at the door. I wait until he leads the way.

I see her legs first, bare and chubby and kicking back and forth like nobody's business. Then the rest of her comes into view – her pastel-coloured babygrow adorned with bunnies, and fine, slightly curly, light-blond hair. She's strapped into a bouncy chair in front of the television, and Charlie drags the contraption across the wooden floor towards him as he takes a seat on the sofa nearest to the bay window. He pushes on the back of her bouncer to make it move and she giggles.

'This is April,' he says, sticking his tongue out at his daughter before nodding at me. 'That's Bridget,' he says more civilly.

'Hello, April!' I reply, cringing because my voice sounds too loud and overeager.

April looks over her shoulder at me, her expression vacant. Then her mouth breaks into a toothy grin and she says something unintelligible. Charlie pushes on the back of her bouncer again and she happily returns her attention to him.

I'm tense as I sit down on the second sofa, hoping she'll ignore me from here on in.

'Where are you staying?' Charlie asks, back to making courteous small talk. He picks up the remote control and turns the volume down on the TV, not quite muting the ludicrously enthusiastic and eccentrically dressed man doing something bizarre with an egg carton.

'A B&B in Padstow. It's cheap and cheerful. My bus leaves early in the morning.'

'You're only here for one day?' He seems surprised.

'Yes, but… Obviously I can come back if…' He looks at me expectantly, waiting for me to complete my sentence. 'If I get the job,' I finish awkwardly.

'Oh.' He averts his gaze and takes a small sip of his tea. 'Fay said you're a travel writer.'

'That's right.' I smile with relief. This territory I can talk about for hours. 'My mum works on a cruise liner so I grew up seeing the world in my school holidays.'

'Bet that was an interesting childhood.'

'It was. I lived with my dad during the term, but we visited Mum pretty regularly.' He nods, listening. He doesn't ask any more questions, so I carry on pitching myself to him. 'I used to write about the places that I saw, then I built my own website and eventually started to pester magazine and newspaper editors for work. I can pretty much get work writing about anywhere, these days.'

'That would've been Nicki's dream job,' Charlie says with a fond smile. *Nicki, not Nicole,* I note. 'Before she got a book deal,' he adds.

And before her life was cruelly stolen from her.

He breaks the long, awkward silence. 'So you liked her novel?'

'I *loved* it!'

He smiles properly now, a smile full of pride, but its light reaches his eyes only briefly.

How bad do I feel? He shouldn't have had to prompt me – I should've been raving about his lovely wife's book from the moment I got here.

'I *really* loved it.' I'm trying to make up for my gaffe, and for the next few minutes it's all I can talk about.

In Nicole's novel, the heroine, Kit, is a travel writer who falls in love with two men at the same time: Morris, a laidback surfer-turned-entrepreneur from right here in Cornwall, and Timo, a sexy Finnish rock climber who is based in Thailand. At the end of the first book, Kit goes to Thailand to break up with Timo because Morris – her first love – has proposed to her. But, before she can come clean, Timo asks her to marry him, too. And she says yes.

I know! WTF, right?

'I detest cheating with a passion, so I shouldn't have liked this book on principle,' I tell Charlie, arguably too honestly. 'But somehow Nicole made it… I don't know. It's so believable. She wrote in such a heart-wrenching way that I couldn't help but be swept up in the story. I felt like I was inside Kit's mind, feeling every emotion she was feeling and somehow understanding the crazy decisions she was making. It was…' I shake my head, finally, yes, *finally* lost for words.

I think I've said all the right things from the look on his face.

'Do you know what was going to happen in the sequel?' I ask. 'Do you know who Kit was going to end up with?'

He shakes his head. 'I'm not sure even Nicki knew.'

I feel a surge of disappointment. Charlie leans back to put his empty mug down on the windowsill behind him. 'But, if she did, the answer will be in her notes. She made lots of them. Let me show you her office.'

April seems to be content sitting in her bouncer for the moment, so Charlie turns the sound back up on the television and leads me upstairs. He walks straight ahead, pushing open the door to a small room that looks out over the messy back garden. Any view of the estuary would be from the other side of the house. A large desk fills the area under the window, and there are bookshelves and filing cabinets lining the walls. A slick Apple computer takes pride of place in the centre of the desk. The room is tidy, but I can see from here that the computer screen is dusty from underuse.

Charlie pulls open the top left desk drawer to reveal a series of notebooks crammed inside.

'Nicki was always writing in these,' he says.

He closes that drawer and opens the next to expose more notebooks.

'I haven't gone through them.' From the tightening of his voice, I take it he hasn't wanted to. 'But all of her research is in here.' He opens another drawer. 'She also used to keep diaries when she was younger. Her dad moved to Thailand for work and she'd visit when she could. A lot of what she wrote about back then made it into *Secret*. I think you'll find clues as to where she planned to go with the sequel.'

I look up at the crowded bookshelves and notice several Post-it notes sticking out of the tops of some of the books. What pages did she mark? Were they significant?

Nicole did a couple of interviews around the time *Secret* was published last October, so I already knew that her father is a French chef called Alain Dupré, and that she wrote under her maiden name. But, as she died just two weeks after her book was released, before the sales had taken off, her readers and I don't know much more about her – it's very surreal to be standing here in her office.

'Did she leave notes on her computer, too?' My mind boggles. *Where would I start?*

Charlie hesitates almost imperceptibly before reaching

behind the screen and feeling for the ON button. The computer fires up with a loud *dong*.

'I would've thought so,' he says.

His back is to me, his posture tense. I stare at his frame and out of the blue think of Elliot. It's been almost six months since we've seen each other and, on the whole, I'm coping. But suddenly I miss him intensely.

April lets out a cry downstairs, making Charlie start. 'Take a seat and have a look,' he mumbles, leaving me to it.

Is he sure he doesn't mind? Uncertainly, I pull out the chair and sit down. The screen in front of me lights up and then I'm looking at a small photograph of Nicole, under which is a request for her password.

She's laughing and her slim, oval face is basked in warmth from the sunshine. She has dark hair that brushes her shoulders and her eyes are sky-blue. Across her head is a familiar yellow bandana headband that doesn't quite obscure her fringe, and a sprinkling of freckles dusts her nose. She looks happy. I find myself wishing that I had known her. The posed black-and-white publicity shot on the inside cover of her book doesn't do her justice.

'It's *Thailand*.'

I almost jump out of my skin at the sound of Charlie's voice from behind me.

'The password is *Thailand*. Uppercase *T*.'

'Oh!' I type it in. I press ENTER and Nicole's desktop swings into view.

I hear Charlie inhale sharply and know better than to turn around.

An image of him holding a newborn baby has filled the

screen. His hair is shorter and he's gazing with love at the tiny bundle in his arms.

'I've barely been in here since we lost her,' he says softly.

'We don't have to do this now,' I murmur. His wife died just over seven months ago. I'm not at all sure that he's ready for this. I'm not sure that I am.

'It's fine,' he says, leaning in and taking the mouse. I scoot my chair over to the left, watching as the arrow hovers over a blue folder on the dock at the bottom. The name comes up: 'SECRET'. Charlie moves the mouse to the right and clicks on a folder called 'CONFESSIONS'.

'Is that the title of the sequel?' I ask, alight with interest.

'*Confessions of Us*,' Charlie tells me. 'Sara wasn't sure about it.'

Sara was Nicole's agent, too, of course.

'I like it,' I tell him, peering more closely at the contents of the folder: *Characters… Confessions… Research… Synopsis… Timeline…*

'You'll have to check out her *Secrets* folder, as well. I'm not sure she moved everything across.'

'Okay.' I nod.

'If you want the job, that is.' He lets go of the mouse and straightens up.

'Isn't that up to you?' I ask him carefully.

He stares down at me. 'I've read a couple of your blog entries,' he replies instead of giving me an answer. 'Fay was right. Your tone of voice is very similar to Nicki's.' Charlie leans against one of the filing cabinets and folds his arms across his chest. 'But are you sure you have the time to take this on?'

'Absolutely,' I state. 'This will take precedence over all of my other work,' I assure him. 'I can blog in my spare time – I don't have a deadline and there are no other pressures on me.' I take a deep breath before announcing, 'I think I'd do a good job.'

He eyes me thoughtfully as the seconds tick past, and then he finally nods in what I hope is agreement. 'I'll speak to Fay.'

Chapter 3

'I don't *do* camping, Dad!'

'Campervanning is not camping, Bridget. There's a fold-down bed, for Christ's sake! You'd love it. Don't you remember how much you once adored messing around in your little playhouse? It's not so different to that.'

'That was back when I used to make mud cakes.'

'I'm not advocating you make mud cakes in *Hermie*. In fact, I'd rather you didn't.' He pauses before being sure to add, 'I'd *definitely* rather you didn't.'

Hermie is the name he gave to his seventeen-year-old Mercedes Vito campervan. Originally *Herman the German* – chosen by his now ex-girlfriend when he brought it over from Germany a few years ago – the name swiftly morphed into the far cuter variation. And *Hermie is* kind of cute. I just don't want to live in the bastard for two months.

'Charlie *really* liked you,' Sara effused after my recent trip to Cornwall. I suspect this was a bit of an overstatement. 'He definitely wants you on board,' she added.

'Really?'

'Yep! There's just one little thing…' she said.

Apparently, Charlie panicked when Sara asked him if he could box up Nicki's things for a courier to collect. She assumed it could all be delivered to me in London, but Charlie wasn't ready for Nicki's diaries and notebooks to leave the house. The solution? I go to Padstow and work from her office.

It's just as well I don't have much of a life at the moment. I don't even have an apartment. I'm staying with Dad in Wembley because my place in Chalk Farm is still being rented out to the people who took it over when I went to Australia. I say *my* apartment, but it's technically Dad's – he bought it as an investment, although he accepts only enough rent to cover the mortgage. The current tenants pay way more, so, when they asked if they could extend their lease until October, Dad suggested I move in with him to save money. He knows I struggled financially in Australia, but really he just likes my company. We're very close. He raised me practically single-handedly from the age of six.

I love hanging out with him, but there's something a little bit creepy about living at home at my age. So I came around to the idea of Cornwall pretty quickly. After all, who wouldn't want to spend their summer at the seaside? I only really started to stress this morning after calling around and discovering that all the B&Bs and hotels in Padstow are booked out, if not completely, at least for a good part of the summer.

I gave up and came straight to the pub. Not to drown my sorrows, mind. Dad owns the place. It's a medium-sized, definitely-not-a-gastro-pub that's a fifteen-minute walk to Wembley Stadium in one direction and about the same distance to his house in the other. On game and gig days, it gets pretty hectic, but right now it's quiet, save for a couple of regulars.

'Honestly, darling, that campsite on the hill is really lovely,' Dad says, coming back over to me after taking an order for two scampi and chips and a lasagne.

As I say, not a gastro pub.

'I can just see you climbing the hill and having a drink while watching the sunset.' He pauses, cocking his head to one side. He still has a head of thick, bushy hair, but it's dark in colour now, thanks to his regular Just For Men habit. 'You'd be able to hook up some solar-powered fairy lights,' he continues, 'and fill up the fridge with mini-bottles of Prosecco.'

Now he's talking!

'You could even take the attachable tent and portaloo,' he adds.

'Portaloo?'

'So you wouldn't have to walk to the toilet block in the night.'

'You've got to be kidding. I can hardly get my head around sleeping in a car for two months, let alone emptying my own shit.'

He laughs and shakes his head at me.

I'm not the sort of travel writer who relishes slumming it. I didn't mind so much in my early twenties, but these days I write more about top-notch honeymoon destinations and five-star hotels.

It's a hard job, but someone's got to, and all that.

'To be honest, Bridget, I'm jealous,' he says, propping himself up at the bar. 'I'd give anything to be able to jack in this job for the summer and join you at the seaside.'

'Hold your horses, Dad. You know I love you, but your *house* is only just big enough for the two of us. Don't go getting any ideas about squeezing into *Hermie* with me.'

He reaches over and musses up my hair good-naturedly. I bat him away and rest my elbows on the bar top, rapidly taking them off again because it's sticky. I should know better at my age.

'It'll be an adventure,' he says. 'And, if anyone loves an adventure, it's you.'

I'm counting on it.